END GAME

END GAME

Jeffrey Archer is one of the world's bestselling authors, with sales of over 300 million copies in 115 countries and 48 languages.

Famous for his discipline as a writer who works on up to fourteen drafts of each book, Jeffrey also brings a vast amount of insider knowledge to his books. Whether it's his own career in politics, his passionate interest in art, or the wealth of fascinating background detail – inspired by the extraordinary network of friends he has built over a lifetime at the heart of Britain's establishment – his novels provide a fascinating glimpse into a range of closed worlds.

A member of the House of Lords, the author is married to Dame Mary Archer, Chancellor of The University of Buckingham, and they have two sons, two granddaughters and three grandsons. He splits his time between London, Grantchester in Cambridge, and Mallorca, where he writes the first draft of each new novel.

www.jeffreyarcher.com

Also by Jeffrey Archer

THE WILLIAM WARWICK NOVELS
Nothing Ventured
Hidden in Plain Sight
Turn a Blind Eye
Over My Dead Body
Next In Line
Traitors Gate
An Eye for An Eye

THE CLIFTON CHRONICLES
Only Time Will Tell
The Sins of the Father
Best Kept Secret
Be Careful What You Wish For
Mightier than the Sword
Cometh the Hour
This Was a Man

NOVELS
Not a Penny More, Not a Penny Less
Shall We Tell the President?
Kane and Abel
The Prodigal Daughter
First Amongst Equals
A Matter of Honour
As the Crow Flies
Honour Amongst Thieves
The Fourth Estate
The Eleventh Commandment
Sons of Fortune
False Impression
The Gospel According to Judas
(with the assistance of Professor Francis J. Moloney)
A Prisoner of Birth
Paths of Glory
Heads You Win

SHORT STORIES
A Quiver Full of Arrows
A Twist in the Tale
Twelve Red Herrings
The Collected Short Stories
To Cut a Long Story Short
Cat O'Nine Tales
And Thereby Hangs a Tale
Tell Tale
The Short, the Long and the Tall

PLAYS
Beyond Reasonable Doubt
Exclusive
The Accused
Confession
Who Killed the Mayor?

PRISON DIARIES
Volume One – Belmarsh: Hell
Volume Two – Wayland: Purgatory
Volume Three – North Sea Camp: Heaven

SCREENPLAYS
Mallory: Walking Off the Map
False Impression

JEFFREY ARCHER

END GAME

HarperCollins*Publishers*

HarperCollins*Publishers* Ltd
1 London Bridge Street,
London SE1 9GF
www.harpercollins.co.uk

HarperCollins*Publishers*
Macken House,
39/40 Mayor Street Upper,
Dublin 1
D01 C9W8

First published by HarperCollins*Publishers* 2025

25 26 27 28 29 LBC 5 4 3 2 1

Copyright © Jeffrey Archer 2025

Jeffrey Archer asserts the moral right to
be identified as the author of this work

A catalogue record for this book is available from the British Library

ISBN: 978-0-00-864021-7 (HB)
ISBN: 978-0-00-864028-6 (US-only HB)
ISBN: 978-0-00-878520-8 (Special sale-only)
ISBN: 978-0-00-864022-4 (TPB)
ISBN: 978-0-00-864027-9 (IN)

This novel is entirely a work of fiction.
The names, characters and incidents portrayed in it are
the work of the author's imagination. Any resemblance to
actual persons, living or dead, events or localities is
entirely coincidental.

Typeset in New Caledonia LT Std by Palimpsest Book
Production Ltd, Falkirk, Stirlingshire

Printed and bound in the United States of America

All rights reserved. No part of this publication may be
reproduced, stored in a retrieval system, or transmitted,
in any form or by any means, electronic, mechanical,
photocopying, recording or otherwise, without the prior
written permission of the publishers.

Without limiting the exclusive rights of any author, contributor or the publisher of
this publication, any unauthorised use of this publication to train generative
artificial intelligence (AI) technologies is expressly prohibited. HarperCollins also
exercise their rights under Article 4(3) of the Digital Single Market Directive
2019/790
and expressly reserve this publication from the text and data mining exception.

In memory of Susan Watt
1938–2024

The important thing in life is not the victory
but the contest; the essential thing is not
to have won but to have fought well.

Baron de Coubertin, 24 July 1908

AUTHOR'S NOTE

In my novel, *End Game*, you will discover twenty-two incidents that took place during the London Olympics of 2012. Thirteen actually happened, which the public were never made aware of. Two of the incidents – which were prevented by the security forces – would not only have ruined the Olympics, but destroyed Britain's reputation around the world. Nine of the incidents are no more than figments of my imagination. However, I will leave you to decide which are fact and which are fiction.

I am particularly grateful for the advice I was given by Commander Bob Broadhurst OBE QPM (Ret.), who was the officer in charge of Olympic security.

My special thanks also go to:
Lord Coe CH KBE
Sir Keith Mills GBE DL
Jackie Brock-Doyle CBE
Professor Kim Wolff CBE
Chief Superintendent John Sutherland (Ret.)
Detective Sergeant Michelle Roycroft (Ret.)

PROLOGUE

The London Bid

2005

July 2005

'DO YOU THINK WE'RE IN with a chance?' asked William.

'An outside chance,' responded the Hawk. 'But don't hold your breath.'

Commander William Warwick and his superior officer, Jack Hawksby, Assistant Commissioner of the Metropolitan Police, were seated at the back of the packed ballroom in the Raffles Convention Centre in Singapore. For now, they were observers, not participants. Only if London won the bid to host the 2012 Olympics would they become participants.

Five cities had made it to the final round, but only one would be returning home with the gold medal. There were no prizes for second place in this particular race. Although five cities were lined up in the starting blocks, everyone in the room knew that there were only three serious contenders left in the race. Paris were the clear favourite, having lost out to Beijing four years ago, and were now telling anyone who would listen that the 2012 Olympics was theirs by right. Madrid was considered to be their only serious rival, while the bookies had London trailing in third place at ten to one.

During the next hour, four cities would be eliminated, leaving only one team to go home sporting the garland of victory.

The restless buzz in the convention centre was palpable, with several languages competing with each other. Most delegates assumed Moscow would be the first city to be eliminated, as they'd held the Games as recently as 1980 and were being tipped to host the Winter Olympics in Sochi in 2014.

Another rumour William had picked up during the past few days was that if Moscow were eliminated, their votes would be transferred to anyone but London, as Margaret Thatcher had tried to boycott the Moscow Games in 1980, and Putin was someone with a long memory.

The electorate, was made up of one hundred and four delegates, representing countries large and small. This meant Luxembourg's vote was as important as China's, which was one of the reasons no one could be sure of the outcome.

Another reason no one could predict the winner was that almost every one of the delegates would have lied at least four times during the final week, always pledging their vote to the last person they'd spoken to.

A door at the far end of the room opened, and everyone in the room fell silent as Jacques Rogge, the President of the International Olympic Committee, accompanied by the returning officer, entered the cauldron. They walked slowly up onto the stage, and by the time Rogge had taken his seat in the centre chair, there was pin-drop silence, as everyone waited to find out which city would be the first to be eliminated.

A thousand eyes stared up at the President as he opened the envelope and pulled out a card with a single name on it. He tapped the microphone a couple of times before he announced, 'The city of Moscow will not be participating in the second round.'

A few people nervously applauded, while others looked relieved. But a fifth of the audience sat in stony silence, their fate decided. In a few hours' time, they would be boarding a plane back to Moscow. Six years of hard work dismissed in a single sentence.

'Win or lose,' said William to the Hawk, as they made their way out of the hall to enjoy a short walk and catch a breath of fresh air before the loser of the next round was announced, 'Beth and I will be going on holiday.'

'Where?' asked the Hawk, not a man who wasted words.

'On a Viking cruise from Amsterdam to Budapest,' said William. 'No gallery en route will escape our attention.'

'With or without the twins?' enquired the Hawk.

'Without,' said William firmly, as they left the Convention Centre. 'We're the last people on earth they'll want to spend a holiday with. Peter's going to Galway with some friends later in the summer, and Artemisia has a holiday planned with her boyfriend, Robert. But right now, the twins are just as nervous as anyone in that hall: they're waiting to find out their A-level results.'

'And what are their plans afterwards?' asked the Hawk.

'Peter wants to go to my old alma mater, King's College London, and study law, while Artemisia has already been offered a place at Bristol University to read English – where she'll join Robert, who's already there studying politics.'

'I recently read in *The Times*,' said the Hawk, 'that Robert's father has just been appointed chairman of Kestrals Bank,' he paused, 'thanks to you.'

'More thanks to Ross than me,' said William. 'After all, he was the one who finally proved that Robert's father was innocent of all the charges brought against him.'

'And a fat lot of good that did him,' spat out the Hawk.

William nodded grimly. After proving Simon Hartley's innocence, Ross ended up being suspended for a year and demoted for his troubles, while his old adversary Miles Faulkner got away scot-free.

'Frankly, I was surprised that Sergeant Hogan even returned to work after his demotion,' added the Hawk.

'Alice was able to convince him,' replied William. 'With Jojo and little Jack growing up fast, I suppose it was the sensible decision.'

The Hawk nodded. 'If it's the last thing I do,' he said, with considerable feeling, 'I'll put Miles Faulkner behind bars for the rest of his life.'

'With Booth Watson sharing the same cell,' suggested William.

'Amen to that,' said the Hawk. 'But how is Ross holding up?'

'He has never really settled after his run-in with Commander Sinclair,' admitted William. 'They keep giving him jobs where he can't get into any trouble. But let's face it, Ross wasn't born to be a saint.'

'Should we win the bid,' said the Hawk, 'we could do with Sergeant Hogan being back on our team, because we'll have our work cut out. One thing's for certain, while there's several billion swilling around, every crook north of the river will be dipping their noses in the Olympic trough.'

'Along with one or two south of the river,' suggested

William, 'including Miles Faulkner, who won't want to miss out while there's a chance of making a quick buck.'

'There's no doubt about that,' agreed the Assistant Commissioner, as they joined the delegates making their way back to the Convention Centre, each anxious to hear which city would be the next to be eliminated.

• • •

Six thousand miles away, Miles Faulkner and Mr Booth Watson QC got off a bus and began walking towards a pub they'd never frequented before. Not their usual mode of transport, but Faulkner had decided to leave Collins and the Rolls in Cadogan Place, as a chauffeur sitting behind the wheel of a Silver Cloud would attract too much attention in an East End car park full of second-hand cars, some of them stolen.

Collins had already visited the Newham Arms several times during the past month and gathered all the information Miles needed to carry out his planned coup.

'Why did you choose Collins?' Booth Watson had asked.

'Horses for courses,' Miles had replied. 'In any case, he's utterly trustworthy.'

When Miles entered the pub, he spotted two locals sitting one each end of the bar. Neither of them acknowledged him, as had been agreed with Collins. The two newcomers perched on the empty stools between them, and Miles ordered a couple of pints, whilst glancing up at the television to see that the results of the next round of voting would be declared shortly.

Huw Edwards was taking viewers through the voting procedure and explaining why he thought New York would be the next city to be eliminated, leaving Paris, Madrid and London to move on to the crucial round.

The landlord placed two pints of bitter on the counter, his eyes rarely leaving the television.

'You seem interested in who wins,' said Miles innocently.

'My future depends on it,' replied the publican, without looking back at his customer.

'Is that so?' mused Booth Watson, as he reluctantly sipped his beer.

'I'm not sure I understand,' said Miles, who understood only too well that the pub and the adjoining car park would be right in the middle of the proposed Olympic Stadium, should London win.

'You're sitting at the start of the one hundred metres,' said the landlord, 'and the long jump pit would be in my car park, so if London gets the nod, I'll make a fortune.'

'A fortune?' repeated Miles, hoping to find out what the publican considered to be a fortune.

'I've already been offered a quarter of a million by a local developer,' said the landlord. 'But only if we win.'

Miles already knew exactly who the developer was: a local mafia boss called Bernie Longe, but he remained silent, as his lawyer would be delivering the next line.

'And if London doesn't win?' asked Booth Watson, coming in on cue.

'I'll be lucky to get fifty thousand, which is why it's not only their future that's on the line,' said the landlord, pointing up at the television. 'I'll either be seeing out my days in a council house on the local estate or exchanging it for a country cottage in Essex.'

'Let me pose a hypothetical question,' ventured Miles, as he put down his glass. 'As Paris is looking like the odds-on favourite, how much would you settle for if I made you an offer for the site right now?'

The landlord looked surprised and took his time considering the proposal. 'Two hundred thousand,' he finally said, his eyes once more fixed on the television.

The President of the Olympic Committee stood up, opened the envelope, withdrew the card and announced, 'The city of New York will not participate in the next round.'

• • •

'If London is eliminated next, which seems likely,' said the Hawk, 'I've already packed my bags ready to head back home.'

'But if London were to win,' replied William, 'you'll have to unpack them again.'

'Not necessarily,' said the Hawk. 'If London is selected as the host city, the first thing I'll do is return to London and bring my old team back together again.'

William considered this. 'We would have seven years to prepare.'

'And it still wouldn't be long enough.'

'What makes you so sure the whole team will want to come back? After all, Paul has recently been promoted to second in command of the organized crime squad.'

'They will have to learn to live without him,' said the Hawk, 'as I would offer Detective Inspector Adaja the chance to be Silver Commander, putting him in charge of day-to-day operations at the Olympic Stadium.'

'And Rebecca?'

'Detective Sergeant Pankhurst would be my first choice for Bronze, keeping a close eye on the two hundred and fifty thousand spectators who will be visiting the Olympic Park every day.'

'She might not want to leave the drug squad,' suggested William, 'where I hear she's being tipped for further promotion.'

'She won't be given a lot of choice,' said the Hawk.

'And Jackie – will she be given a choice?'

'Detective Sergeant Roycroft has already intimated that, should London win, she'd be happy to leave the arts and antiques squad and join us for the Olympics.'

'Us?' said William.

'Of course. I'll be appointing you as Gold Commander in charge of the national Olympic security operation,' said the Hawk. 'And if the Games are a success, I will finally retire in glory and you will have taken the next step to becoming Commissioner.'

'I don't believe you'll ever retire,' replied William. 'You've been putting it off for years.'

'But I can't for much longer,' said the Hawk.

'And if the Games aren't a success?' asked William, unable to resist a smile.

'You, Constable Warwick, will be back on the beat, while I'll tell everyone I'd always considered Commander Sinclair to be the obvious choice as our next Commissioner. However, if you make a success of the Olympics, you can rely on my support,' said the Hawk with a grin.

'That's a big *if* while so many imponderables remain in the balance,' suggested William, 'not least what's about to take place on stage in a few moments' time.'

The Hawk nodded. 'I think Madrid will be the next city to be eliminated.'

'Let's hope so,' said William, 'because if it's Paris, I'm told they'll vote for Madrid in the final round, as the last thing they want is for London to host the Games.'

The door opened once again, and Rogge walked back up

onto the stage. He looked down at the remaining delegates, but didn't open the envelope until he had complete silence.

Rogge took his time extracting the card and putting his glasses back on, before he announced, 'The city of Madrid will not be participating in the final round.'

The outburst that followed made it almost impossible for William to hear the Hawk say, 'Now the odds are down to fifty-fifty.'

• • •

'The result of the third and final round will be announced in a few minutes' time,' said Huw Edwards, staring down from the television screen at several million expectant faces. 'As Madrid had thirty-one votes,' he continued, 'which the experts are suggesting have already been pledged to the French, I think one can only assume we're not the favourites.'

'So how much would you be willing to take now?' Miles asked the landlord, after he'd ordered another pint for himself, but not for Booth Watson, whose glass was still half full. Miles had told him firmly he couldn't order his usual double gin and tonic.

'One hundred and fifty thousand,' said the publican, no longer sounding quite so confident.

'I'll give you one hundred thousand right now,' said Miles, 'but that's my final offer.'

The landlord stared back up at the screen to see television crews, journalists and photographers now surrounding the French delegation, while one solitary hack remained loyal to the British.

A camera zoomed in on a member of the French team, who was placing a bottle of champagne on the table in front of him, while another produced two glasses.

'It's all over,' said one of the locals, coming in bang on cue as Miles downed his pint and put the empty glass back on the counter.

'No prizes for guessing who will be in second place,' said the local at the other end of the bar, as Miles slipped off his stool and began to walk slowly towards the door.

'All is not lost,' said Huw Edwards – the landlord smiled – 'because London will surely be the favourite for the 2020 Olympics.' The landlord frowned.

'How much would you give me now?' asked the landlord, just as Miles touched the door handle.

'Seventy-five thousand,' said Miles, not looking back.

'One hundred thousand,' said the landlord, as Miles opened the door and stepped outside, with Booth Watson following a pace behind.

'Alright, alright,' shouted the landlord. 'It's yours for seventy-five grand.'

'Good decision,' said one of the locals, as his fellow conspirator nodded sagely.

Booth Watson quickly returned to the bar and placed his Gladstone bag on the counter.

They all looked up to see Rogge entering the arena for the final time.

Booth Watson opened his bag and extracted a well-prepared contract with no loopholes. He turned to the last page, as Miles sat back down at the bar and wrote out a cheque for seventy-five thousand pounds.

The publican hesitated as he stared at the figures. He looked up at the television screen to see the French already on their feet, some linked arm in arm, singing 'La Marseillaise'. Booth Watson removed the top from his pen.

Rogge rose slowly from his place on the centre of the stage

to address the delegates. He began by praising both teams for their dedicated hard work and excellent presentations, then reminded everyone that, in the end, only one city could be selected to host the Thirtieth Olympiad. He took even longer opening the envelope before extracting the card. He tapped the microphone once again before he looked down at the name of the city that would host the 2012 Olympic Games.

All the French delegates in that room were already on their feet waiting in anticipation.

The landlord grabbed the proffered pen and quickly signed on the dotted line.

An eerie silence fell on the gathering both at home and abroad when the President of the International Olympic Committee declared, 'The Games of the Thirtieth Olympiad in 2012 are awarded to,' he paused, 'the city of London.'

The ink had dried.

• • •

'Prepare for the toughest assignment of your career,' the Hawk said to William, as he rose from his place at the back of the hall and joined in the applause. 'And don't even think about relaxing until you hear that man say,' he added, pointing at Rogge, 'I declare the Games of the Thirtieth Olympiad closed.'

'That won't be for another seven years,' William reminded him.

The Hawk turned to him. 'Seven years may sound like a long time to prepare for a single event,' he said, 'but you know as well as I do that it isn't – not when that single event is like no other on earth.'

William nodded. In the past, he had been involved in the security for the Queen Mother's funeral, several state visits, including that of the President of the United States, and countless FA Cup Finals. However, come the summer of 2012, he would be expected to police forty-two world championships in the space of just a few weeks. A few weeks that would define his career.

He watched the British team, led by Sebastian Coe, continue to leap up and down as the realization of triumph began to sink in.

The French sat alone at the other end of the room, desolate, voices silenced, champagne unopened, like a deserted bride waiting for an absent groom to appear.

• • •

The landlord switched the television off, looking not unlike a member of the French team.

Booth Watson hurried after his client, who had already left the pub, along with the two locals. Miles slipped them both a hundred pounds in cash. After all, they'd played their walk-on parts without fluffing a line.

Booth Watson caught up with Miles just as he was climbing into a taxi, and quickly joined him in the back. Once he'd got his breath back, he asked, 'What would you have done if Paris had been awarded the Games?'

'As it's a Wednesday,' Miles reminded him, 'the landlord couldn't have hoped to see the cheque cleared before the weekend and, sadly, by then it would have bounced all the way back to his pub with the words "insufficient funds", making the contract null and void, if I remember the wording correctly.'

'Whereas now, you can call the bank when it opens for business tomorrow morning to make sure the cheque is cleared immediately,' said Booth Watson. 'And if he doesn't cash the cheque, the contract is still valid – the wording makes that perfectly clear.'

'And I won't be in any hurry to part with my new asset,' said Miles, 'because if the government wants to buy my pub and car park, or – should I say – my home straight and long jump pit, it's going to cost them.'

• • •

Less than twenty-four hours later, Commander Warwick was among the first in Singapore to hear the news. He was sitting alone in his hotel room, watching breakfast television. Three bombs had exploded on the London underground and a fourth on a bus, killing fifty-two and injuring over eight hundred innocent victims, most of them on their way to work.

William recalled that Sebastian Coe, during his confidential chats to delegates over the past fortnight, had frequently repeated the fact that twenty-five thousand people a day would be able to travel from Victoria to the Olympic Park on the London underground in half an hour.

As the new head of Public Order and Operational Support for the 2012 Olympic Games, William was preparing to address the British bidding team in the same room where only the day before they had celebrated a famous victory.

The following day, a sombre, but not altogether sober, group arrived back in London, not to the deserved accolades of an exuberant, welcoming crowd, but to be slipped quietly through a private exit so they could avoid the press, who would have only one question on their lips: if the bombing had taken place the day before the final vote, and not the day after, do you think London would have been selected to host the 2012 Olympic Games?

Everyone knew the answer.

BOOK ONE

Countdown

CHAPTER 1

August 2005

FOR SEVERAL REASONS, VLADIVOSTOK was the chosen venue for the meeting between the two heads of state, primarily because of its proximity to the border of both their countries, meaning that the leaders could return to their capitals with very few prying eyes aware that the get-together had ever taken place. The press had not been invited to attend, and if the story had leaked, the meeting would have been cancelled.

The two presidents met in a railway carriage at the far end of a shunting yard, with no tall buildings overlooking them. The carriage had once been part of the *Trans-Siberian Express*, and exuded the kind of gracious opulence of a bygone age that was considered appropriate for such a momentous occasion.

On arrival, only moments apart, both dictators took their places at each end of a long table. They sat in large, high-backed chairs with cushions to make them appear taller. The two remaining seats at the table were occupied by their ambassadors to London. Half a dozen senior mandarins sat around the outside of the carriage, notebooks open, pens in hand.

President Putin was the first to speak. 'May I enquire, comrade,' he began, 'how your preparations are going for the 2008 Beijing Olympics?'

'They are proceeding to plan,' replied Hu Jintao, 'and even the West will have to admit they have never seen a spectacle like it.' He paused, then added quickly, 'It will be comparable only with the 1980 Moscow Olympics.'

Putin waved a dismissive hand. 'Once the Americans failed to turn up and took their quislings with them, we were never given the opportunity to prove our true worth, but with London now set to host the Olympics in 2012, I intend to return the compliment.'

'Does that mean that Russia will be boycotting the London Olympics?' asked Hu Jintao.

'Certainly not,' said Putin. 'We must appear to be magnanimous, while not losing any and every opportunity to compare the London Games unfavourably with Beijing. The Olympics have long been a symbol of power and prestige. Every four years, athletes from across the globe come together to compete, while every country in the world looks on. All eyes will be on the host city.

'The city that is chosen and given the opportunity to host the Olympics reveals what everyone thinks about that country, but the world is behind the times. They still trust the British – and we cannot allow that to continue. It is vital that we demonstrate to every country around the globe that power is shifting and it's no longer the West that holds the cards. If we were able to destroy Britain's reputation, we would at the same time destroy the trust other countries place in them. Once we've achieved that, we become more powerful.' He paused. 'With that in mind, comrade, I will ask my Ambassador to London to brief you on our plans.'

He turned to his right and nodded.

Anatoly Mikailov, the Russian Ambassador to London, had been carefully selected for the job. Mikailov had been educated at Harvard and Oxford, and many people in London and Washington counted him as a respected colleague, while he considered them nothing more than fairweather friends. His new mission was to ensure the London Olympics were perceived as a disastrous failure from which they would never recover, and he'd already begun to put detailed plans in place to achieve that outcome.

'For a start, London's budget will be less than half of Beijing's,' he began. 'However, you can be sure the British will put on a good show,' he added, with an exaggerated posh accent. 'One must remember, theatre is in their DNA, and they will be performing on the largest stage on earth. To that end, I have selected a team who have been working on a dozen different scenarios, which cannot be revealed yet, for obvious reasons, but I can assure you that any one of them will make London wish they had never been selected as the host city, as their reputation will be in tatters.'

Putin gave a faint smile. 'And how about you comrade?' he asked, as he looked towards the other end of the table.

The Chinese leader didn't respond, but turned to his right and nodded at his London Ambassador.

'Although we intend to work closely with you in the build-up to the London Games and during the opening ceremony,' began Wei Ming, without referring to a note, 'it has already been agreed that you will take the lead once the

Games begin, but we will be in sole charge of what takes place at the closing ceremony.'

'If they ever get that far,' said Mikailov, loud enough for his leader to hear.

'Naturally,' the Chinese Ambassador continued as if he hadn't been interrupted, 'the Olympics will have tight security measures in place, so the strategy we have agreed on is simple: distract the police with as many irrelevant, time-consuming inconveniences as possible, thus keeping their eyes away from our ultimate goal: our own particular *closing ceremony*.' He smiled. 'To that end, we have selected a highly trained team led by a woman who's lost count of how many people she's killed. Most of our operatives are more frightened of her than the enemy.'

It was Hu Jintao's turn to smile.

'And may I ask what exactly she has planned?' asked Putin, raising an eyebrow.

'The downfall of what's left of the British Empire in a single evening,' said Wei Ming. 'A disaster that the rest of the world will agree could have been avoided, if only the British had been better prepared to deal with security threats.'

A faint smile crossed Hu Jintao's lips. 'I can assure you, last month's terrorist attack on the London underground will be nothing compared to what we have planned for the closing ceremony.'

CHAPTER 2

11 May 2012 – 77 days to go

'SEVENTY-SEVEN DAYS LEFT until the opening ceremony,' said Assistant Commissioner Hawksby.

'After seven years of preparation,' Commander William Warwick reminded him, 'we're as ready as we can be.'

'But it still won't be ready enough,' said the Hawk. 'Prepare for the unexpected, because that's what you'll be up against.'

They were sitting in William's office, the desk between them piled with reports, files and other paperwork, along with a few scattered family photos. One picture showed William and his wife Beth on their wedding day, two and a half decades ago, while the latest frames displayed graduation photos of the twins.

The Hawk looked down again at the 'for your eyes only' report in front of him. 'I'm glad your latest meeting with Professor Meredith at GCHQ went well – we may need him and his team's expertise during the next few months. Nobody is better at predicting the unpredictable than Meredith, as well as knowing how to counter it when it does arise. But is there anything else you need?'

William hesitated. 'If it's the unpredictable I'm to face, you know what – or who – I need.'

The Hawk sighed. 'Commander Sinclair is still making difficulties about Ross being taken off traffic control, but if I have to overrule him, I will.'

'Frankly, Ross is surplus to requirements in traffic control,' said William.

'And if I were able to rescue him, how would you take advantage of Sergeant Hogan's particular skills?'

'For a start, no one knows the East End mafia better than Ross,' responded William. 'And I just don't have the time to deal with the likes of Bernie Longe and his gang of petty criminals, who will certainly be trying to get their hands on the millions that are swilling around in the Olympic trough. And it's not just the mafia. The Olympic Games are a potential target for everyone from fraudsters to terrorists and, if and when anything goes wrong, I need someone not only with Ross's expertise, but also someone not known to be part of my security team.'

'Then perhaps Sergeant Hogan should go undercover and only report back to you. That way, Sinclair will also be left in the dark. In fact, it might be wise to keep the rest of the team out of the loop as well,' said the Hawk, 'me included.'

'Until something goes wrong,' said William, 'when everyone will find out what Ross has been up to.'

The Hawk sighed. 'If Ross is involved, something is bound to go wrong.'

William laughed as he checked his watch.

'You have a more important appointment, Commander?' suggested the Assistant Commissioner.

'Far more important,' said William.

The Hawk raised an eyebrow.

'It's my birthday,' said William, 'and Beth is taking me out to dinner, so I can't afford to be late.'

'Congratulations, my boy,' said the Hawk, his tone suddenly changing. 'Don't let me keep you any longer.'

'Thank you, sir,' said William, as the Hawk rose from his seat.

Once he had left the room, the Hawk walked quickly across to the lift and pressed the down button. When the doors slid open on the ground floor, he marched across the entrance hall, pushed his way through the swing doors, and jumped into the back of a waiting car.

The Hawk pulled the door closed, leant forward and barked at his driver, 'Just be sure I get there before he does.'

• • •

William placed the thick file in the top drawer of his desk, locked it and left the office. He walked along the corridor and stuck his head around the door of the ops room to let them know he was leaving early. No sign of anyone – and then he remembered they'd all gone across to the Olympic Park to be among the first to have a guided tour.

He jogged down the steps to the ground floor, left the building, and made his way across to the senior officers' car park. William drove his Volvo out of the yard, turned left onto Victoria Street and headed for home. He checked the dashboard clock. With a bit of luck, he should just about make it before Beth could complain.

On the journey back to Fulham, he mulled over the Hawk's

sanguine words, painfully aware that the Olympics would be far more of a challenge than anything he'd tackled during the past seven years as the Commander in Charge of Public Order and Operational Support. Even a royal wedding felt like a village fête when compared with the Olympics.

William had accepted long ago that he didn't have enough trained officers to cover the nine venues that littered the Olympic Park. The support of seventy-thousand volunteers was welcome, but their enthusiasm would not make up for their lack of experience. Last week, the Prime Minister had agreed to assign an additional 3,500 members of the military to Olympic security for the summer, which would be a huge help, but Willliam was still concerned.

He tried to put such problems out of his mind as he backed into a residents-only parking space a few yards from his home. He was looking forward to celebrating his fiftieth birthday with Beth at his favourite restaurant. No persistently ringing phones, exhausted police officers with endless questions, not to mention the Hawk barking orders at everyone in sight. Tonight, the only orders would come when he selected his meal and handed the menu back to the head waiter.

He locked the car, strolled up the path, put his key in the lock and opened the front door.

'I'm home, darling,' he announced, as he closed the door. There was no reply, so he went in search of his wife. He first checked the front room, then the kitchen, and finally her study, but there was no sign of Beth. His chance to tease her about being late for a change.

As he walked back into the corridor, he saw Artemisia coming down the stairs. He could scarcely believe the twins were now twenty-five – partly because it seemed like only yesterday they were crawling around the house, and partly because Peter still lived at home. He was saving every penny while training to be a barrister. Artemisia, who was trying to break into journalism, had recently moved in with her boyfriend, Robert. He missed her.

'What a nice surprise,' said William.

'Just wanted to wish you a happy birthday,' she said, giving him a hug.

'Have you seen Mum?'

Artemisia shook her head. 'No, but Peter said she might be late tonight. Something has come up at the gallery.'

'How unlike her to forget,' said William.

'Forget what?' asked Arte.

'We're meant to be going out for dinner,' said William, only to be interrupted by the dog barking. 'At least Peel hasn't forgotten it's my birthday,' he grumbled, as he headed for the garden.

He opened the back door – and found himself confronted not by the dog but by a large crowd of friendly faces. He barely had time to express his surprise before an untutored choir, conducted by the Hawk, began a raucous rendering of 'Happy Birthday, dear William'.

A drink was thrust into William's hand by Beth. He looked around their pocket handkerchief garden, which was currently packed with fifty guests and a tail-wagging Peel, who had all come to celebrate William's fiftieth birthday. He spotted family and friends amongst the group, along with most of his team from the Yard. The garden was noisy with chatter and laughter, and he had the feeling that the drink had been flowing freely long before he arrived.

'Who organized this deception, dare I ask?' William whispered to Beth.

'Guilty as charged,' she replied.

'And your accomplices?' demanded William, as he took his wife in his arms.

'Artemisia and Peter, assisted by Ross, who specializes in deception,' she added, as his oldest friend strolled across to join them.

'You're a devious man, Sergeant Hogan.'

'What do you have in mind as a reprimand, guv?' asked Ross.

'I'm putting you back on the beat,' said William.

Ross laughed. 'Lambeth, where we both started?'

'No,' replied William. 'Underground, where you belong.' He lowered his voice, stepping back from Beth. 'I'm serious, Ross. The Hawk's going to pull rank and get you out from under Commander Sinclair's watchful eye. Say goodbye to traffic, because we've got more important work for you to do.'

Ross made no attempt to hide his surprise and delight at the news. 'The Olympics?' he ventured.

William would have briefed him, if he hadn't been interrupted by Artemisia, who came weaving through the crowd to join them.

'Happy birthday again, Dad,' she said, with a grin. 'Glad we all had you fooled. But if you don't mind, I need to steal my godfather for a minute.' William nodded.

'I need your advice,' Artemisia explained to Ross, as soon as they were out of earshot.

'And what is it you clearly don't want your father to know about?' enquired Ross.

'I've been offered a job at the *Daily Mail* as a trainee reporter,' said Artemisia.

Ross beamed. 'Congratulations. I know how hard you've been trying to get a job in Fleet Street. But surely your parents must know about the offer?'

'Of course they do,' said Artemisia. 'But what they *don't*

know is how I plan to hold on to the job. You see, it's only temporary, during the Games, but the editor has said he'll consider offering me a full-time position if I can come up with an exclusive. He hinted that I could take advantage of my father's position.'

'Clearly a man who specializes in bribery and corruption,' suggested Ross. 'Although I'm sure a smart kid like you will have no trouble coming up with an exclusive without your father's help.'

'Not much of a kid any more,' said Artemisia, wistfully. 'I have a few ideas but . . . if I'm to land an exclusive, I could do with your particular brand of,' she paused, 'wickedness.'

Ross laughed. 'Fire away, young lady.'

'I need to find a way of getting into the athletes' village, but I don't have a pass.'

'You could ask your father to supply one. After all, he's in charge of security.'

'I don't want him to know what I'm up to,' admitted Artemisia, as she looked over Ross's shoulder. 'Which is why I need you and not my father.'

He grinned. Unlike the commander, Ross had never exactly followed the rulebook to the letter. Even his recent reprieve from traffic couldn't hold him back. He remained silent for a few moments, before he said, 'You'll have to get hold of an official accreditation badge that will allow you access to the athletes' village at any time.'

'How do I get one of those?' asked Artemisia.

Ross lowered his voice and said, 'First, you'll have to find a competitor who . . .'

. . .

Across the other side of the garden, William was chatting to his mother, Mary, while Beth was deep in conversation with Christina and her husband, Wilbur. Beth and Christina's friendship had been long and not always smooth. Christina had lived an unusual life, that included a brief and tumultuous marriage to Miles Faulkner, and there had been a time when Beth was never quite sure if she could trust her – but since marrying Wilbur Hackensack twelve years ago, her friend had been transformed. They had been working together at the Fitzmolean Museum for several years now, with Beth as director and Christina as chair of the board.

'I'd love to know what those two are scheming,' said Beth, as she looked across at her daughter and Ross.

'No good, would be my bet,' suggested Christina, with a grin.

'So dare one ask,' said Wilbur. 'How's the special exhibition coming along?'

'So far so good. All being well, *The Hermitage Comes to the Fitzmolean* will be opening in two months' time,' replied Beth. 'I can't believe it's finally happening. It seems years ago that I first wrote to the director of the Hermitage in Saint Petersburg to suggest an exchange of Dutch paintings for a dual exhibition. Back then, I didn't even receive a reply.'

'But that was before London landed the Olympics,' said Christina.

'That reminds me – the Russian Ambassador has invited me to a gala reception at the embassy next month, and they've asked for a list of people who should be invited.'

'Yes, I know,' said Christina. 'My invitation arrived this morning.'

'A gala reception came as a surprise, considering how

uncommunicative most of our exchanges with the Hermitage have been so far.'

'A goodwill gesture, perhaps,' suggested Christina.

'I don't think you'll find the word goodwill in a Russian dictionary,' chipped in Wilbur. 'And one thing's for certain, they don't make gestures.'

'It's probably nothing,' said Beth, 'but . . .'

'What does William have to say on the subject?' asked Christina.

'I haven't mentioned it to him,' admitted Beth. 'He's got enough problems of his own at the moment. And, to be honest, I don't really know what I'm concerned about. It's just an uneasy feeling that something isn't quite right.'

'Why not have a word with Ross?' said Christina.

'He'd tell me I'm just overreacting,' Beth said, as she looked across at William's mother on the other side of the garden.

• • •

'What's Ross up to these days?' asked Mary.

'Still issuing parking tickets to anyone caught on a double yellow line,' said Alice, 'although I know he'd much prefer to be chasing real criminals.'

'And Jojo?'

'She's about to graduate from the Slade School of Fine Art,' replied Alice, as she glanced across at her stepdaughter. 'But as she's been offered a modelling job by Chanel, all that potential may no longer be quite so promising.'

'But Jojo told me that once she'd graduated, she plans to become an out-of-work artist.'

'And she would have done,' responded Alice, 'if she hadn't

been offered an extortionate sum just to walk up and down a catwalk modelling clothes neither of us could afford.'

'Pity,' said Mary, 'as I think she's got a real talent. In fact, we have one of her paintings hanging in our drawing room.'

'I think she's hoping the income from modelling can support her while she tries to establish herself in the art world,' said Alice.

'Let's hope so. And how's little Jack faring?'

'No longer little,' said Alice. 'He's starting secondary school in September – can you believe it? He's already taller than me.'

Mary followed Alice's eyes to where Jack had joined his step-sister and some of the police officers. 'And is he as bright as his mother?' she teased.

'No, just as stupid as his father,' replied Alice. 'He wants to be a policeman and join that lot over there.'

• • •

Jojo was chatting with Detective Inspector Paul Adaja and Sergeant Jackie Roycroft, while her little brother stared up at them in awe.

'How are the preparations for the Olympics going?' asked Jojo.

'We won't know the answer to that question,' responded Paul, 'until after the curtain comes down on the closing ceremony and the Games have moved on to Rio de Janeiro.'

'It must be great fun,' enthused Jojo, 'being participants in something this huge.'

'It's the most exciting thing *ever*,' added Jack.

Paul smiled down at him. 'That's one way of looking at it.'

'We're not participants,' said Jackie Roycroft. 'We're onlookers whose only job is to try to anticipate any problems that might or might not arise in over thirty different venues in fifty-one different languages.'

'So fun certainly isn't the word that springs to mind,' added Paul.

'Well, *I* will be a participant,' said Jojo, taking them all by surprise.

'Doing what exactly?' asked Jackie.

'It's a secret,' whispered Jack, grinning up at his sister.

'And as you're in charge of security,' said Jojo, smiling at Jackie and Paul, 'I'd rather assumed you'd already know.'

• • •

On the other side of the garden next to the drinks table, Peter was in conversation with Robert, his sister's long-term boyfriend, who'd been around for so long he considered him one of the family. In fact, Peter could only wonder how long it would be before they became engaged.

'And how's work?' Peter asked Robert. 'Still hoping to become a Member of Parliament?'

'No one's asked me yet,' admitted Robert, 'but there's still some time to go before the next general election, so watch this space. With any luck, I'll be a candidate for a safe seat next time round. Of course, that's no guarantee I'll end up in Parliament, as it's looking unlikely we can beat Cameron at the next election, but as Harold Wilson said, "A week is a long time in politics".'

'What does Arte make of all this?' asked Peter, as he glanced across to see his twin sister, head bowed, listening intently to Ross.

'She's incredibly supportive,' Robert said warmly, 'even if she is working for the opposition.'

'The Tories?' said Peter in disbelief.

'No, the *Daily Mail*, who are almost as bad. But what about you?' asked Robert. 'Are there enough criminals to keep you well occupied?'

'They are all innocent,' protested Peter.

'Have you managed to get one off yet?'

'Not yet,' admitted Peter. 'I did manage to get a shoplifter off with a suspended sentence, but only because the prisons are so overcrowded.'

Robert was about to ask about Peter's next case when he was interrupted by the tapping of a spoon on a glass.

They all looked around to see Assistant Commissioner Hawksby standing on a step at the far end of the garden, a champagne glass in hand. Once he'd gained their complete attention, he stopped tapping and began. 'It is my privilege to say a few words on behalf of the accused, but as I haven't been able to come up with anything in mitigation, I shall move on to his prosecution, followed by a lengthy sentence that I feel confident you, the jury, will deliver on behalf of the Crown.'

Laughter followed the Hawk's opening remarks, accompanied by a prolonged round of applause.

'I have, over the years,' continued the Hawk, 'watched William climb effortlessly up the promotion ladder from Constable on the beat in Lambeth to the dizzy heights of Commander in charge of the Olympics,' said the Hawk, 'and only time will tell how many more rungs of that ladder are yet to be scaled. In fact, I'm rather hoping to retire before I have to call him *sir*.'

More laughter broke out, although the Assistant Commissioner hadn't considered that particular line to be a joke.

'Along the way, he has acquired a wife, who is successfully

climbing an equally challenging ladder, a daughter who has already seen the inside of a prison cell, where she met her boyfriend, and a son who is following in his distinguished grandfather's footsteps as a criminal barrister. But, members of the jury, I feel the time has come to let you know the defendant left the Yard this evening before six o'clock, allowing hardened criminals a night off.'

Cries of *Shame!* and *Resign!* greeted this revelation.

'However,' continued the Hawk, 'when Commander Warwick returns to his desk in the morning, the countdown will continue on the most challenging assignment of his career to date, the outcome of which will decide if he continues to climb that ladder and reach even greater heights.'

'Or slithers back down a waiting snake,' piped up Ross, to even louder laughter.

'Whatever the outcome,' came back the Hawk, 'I ask you all to raise your glasses to William on his fiftieth birthday.'

'To William,' went up the cry, followed by, 'Speech, speech,' from the assembled gathering.

William quickly tried to compose his thoughts, aware he was facing a very demanding audience. 'Tonight,' he began, 'I thought I was going out for a quiet dinner with my wife.'

'No such luck,' shouted someone.

'Had I known what Beth and her fellow conspirators had been planning, I would have stayed at work.'

'In which case, we would have happily celebrated without you,' said another, raising his glass.

William waited for the laughter to die down before he continued, 'Let me begin by thanking the Assistant Commissioner for his few kind words,' he paused, 'very few. And my wife, who ditched me in favour of you lot, which means our dinner date may have to be put off for some time, as almost every one of us will be returning to work tomorrow to prepare for the greatest show on earth. I have no doubt that, as Ross has suggested, there will be several snakes awaiting us. It will be a challenge that no one has experienced in this country since 1948, long before any of us were born.' He paused. 'With one or two notable exceptions.'

This time, the cheering was prolonged.

'I was six at the time,' said the Hawk, 'and could name every one of our gold medallists.'

'No mean achievement,' said Sir Julian, William's father, 'as if I recall it was a record haul that year.'

'Seeing so many of my friends here this evening only reminds me how fortunate I've been during those fifty years,' continued William. 'Two wonderful and supportive parents, an amazing and tolerant wife, as well as two children any father could be proud of.'

A round of applause followed, before William ended with the words, 'And how grateful I am to have been allowed to do the job I've always wanted to do, and finally ending up in charge of security for the Olympics, which is a bonus.'

'Perhaps not ending up,' hinted someone.

William smiled, but didn't respond, other than to say, 'I ask you all to raise your glasses to the success of the Thirtieth Olympiad, in the fervent hope I will avoid any perils along the way and will make it to my fifty-first birthday.'

This time the applause lasted for some considerable time.

'If he does,' whispered Julian to his wife, as he raised his glass, 'his chances of being Commissioner won't be harmed.'

'And if he doesn't?'

'I won't be the only person retiring at the end of the year.'

CHAPTER 3

21 May 2012 – 67 days to go

BOOTH WATSON PLACED TWO FILES on the desk in front of him, checked his watch and waited. Miles was always a few minutes late for any appointment, almost as if he needed to make a point. Booth Watson didn't care, as he charged by the hour.

At fourteen minutes past, his client marched into the room without knocking. He took the seat on the other side of the partners' desk, as if it was his by right, and said, 'You asked to see me, BW.'

No *good morning*, no *how are you*, just *you asked to see me*.

'Yes,' responded Booth Watson. 'Two matters have arisen since we last met that I felt you ought to be informed about immediately. One concerns the police, while the other is a private matter. Which would you prefer to start with?'

'The police,' said Faulkner as he lit a cigar, despite there being no sign of an ashtray.

Booth Watson opened the second of his two files. 'I've had a call from the Met, who asked me to set up an interview with you to discuss your involvement in, and I quote,' he glanced back down at the file, '"the unauthorized sale of tickets for the opening ceremony of the Olympic Games," from which they claim you've made a profit of over a million pounds.'

'I haven't made anywhere near that amount,' snapped Faulkner, unable to hide his irritation.

'I don't think it's the sum that will matter in this case,' suggested Booth Watson, 'but the fact that—'

'Whatever the sum,' interrupted Miles, 'they don't have a shred of evidence to show I was involved in any way.'

'Possibly not,' responded Booth Watson. 'But I think you'll find one of your touts may have turned Queen's evidence in exchange for a shorter sentence.'

Faulkner blew out a large circle of smoke. 'Then find him and pay him off. Because I can tell you one thing, BW, I have no intention of going back to prison.'

'And I feel confident, Miles,' said Booth Watson, almost purring, 'that as long as I represent you, you need have no fear of that.'

'So, what's the private matter?' asked Miles, moving on.

Booth Watson sighed. 'Mr Bernie Longe has been in touch.'

'Him again?' snapped Miles. 'A two-bit East End hoodlum who isn't worth the time of day, so you needn't waste any more energy on him.'

'He continues to insist that he had a prior claim to the purchase of the Newham Arms in Stratford, having had a contract in place with Mr Wilson, the former landlord, long before you ever approached him. He is aware of the two million you've already made and says he'd be willing to split the difference.'

'The only thing I'd split,' said Miles, 'is him in half. Don't forget, he's been threatening me for the past seven years – if he had a leg to stand on, you'd have already heard from his lawyer. We needn't concern ourselves with the likes of him.' Miles let out another large grey circle of smoke.

Booth Watson coughed. 'He then went on to ask me if I would represent him in his attempt to bring the case to court.' This time, Miles didn't interrupt. 'I explained to Mr Longe that would not be possible, as I am retained by you at all times. He offered to double my retainer, which, of course, I rejected out of hand, and that was the end of the conversation.'

'You won't be hearing from him again,' said Miles. 'He's all mouth, and I can assure you, he has no real money.'

Booth Watson decided this wasn't the time to remind his client that Mr Longe had twice in the past been charged with a gangland murder and had yet to see the inside of a prison cell. However, that wouldn't stop him from raising the subject of his retainer in the not-too-distant future.

• • •

Sun Anqi and Sergei Petrov were both considered to be the leaders in their chosen field: torture, maiming and elimination were carried out with impunity according to their masters' wishes. Officially, they were both officers in their countries' militias. Unofficially, they were state terrorists holding the rank of captain, although generals feared a visit from them. This was the reason why they'd both been chosen for the most important assignment of their careers: to ensure the 2012 Olympics ended in failure for the host nation, using whatever means they considered appropriate. Both already had clear ideas of what the word appropriate meant.

Natural rivals, they had disliked each other from the moment they had first met. Petrov's background was with the KGB and the GRU. Sun Anqi's was as a political assassin. He was clever, careful and always had a backup plan. She was ruthless, unpredictable and always quick to act. He thought she was a loose cannon. She thought he was weak.

They had been charged by their respective ambassadors and heads of state to work together, and work together they would. But each wanted to stand on the podium alone. Not unlike any Olympic rivals, their chief purpose was to cross the line in first place.

Petrov was responsible for covering everything that would take place up to and including the opening ceremony.

Once the Games had been officially opened by Her Majesty the Queen, Petrov would remain in charge during the Games and Sun Anqi would not walk on to the stage until the closing ceremony when Boris Johnson handed the Olympic flag over to the Mayor of Rio de Janeiro. A ceremony she intended would never take place.

The two operatives agreed to meet regularly while stationed in London, but never at the same time or in the same place. They would discuss their progress, but rarely told the other the whole story. Petrov liked to speak in codes and riddles. Sun Anqi didn't like to speak at all.

They both reported back to their ambassadors in London and told them even less than they told each other.

Sun Anqi and Petrov only met at all because their ambassadors had insisted they should, in the spirit of collaboration between their two great nations. Ambassador Mikailov reminded everyone that Sun Anqi was an invaluable ally, while Ambassador Wei Ming confirmed that Petrov must be kept close, if for no other reason than to please President Putin.

END GAME

That morning, they met at London Bridge station on a bench near the departure boards. Sun Anqi eyed every passing commuter suspiciously until Petrov joined her.

'Ten weeks to go,' murmured Sun Anqi.

'Ten weeks until your services will no longer be required,' Petrov hissed. 'In fact, you'll be able to return home before the starter's pistol is even fired – because it won't be.'

She didn't ask why – she never did – but he still told her.

'If everything goes to plan,' he said quietly, 'the Queen won't be attending the opening ceremony of the Thirtieth Olympiad, but will be escorted back to Buckingham Palace having failed to reach the stadium.'

'Your trivial plans are of little concern to me,' responded Sun Anqi. 'You're nothing more than a distraction, if I recall my leader's words. My closing ceremony will be the main event.'

Sun Anqi knew that her plan mustn't fail. It had, after all, received the blessing of her President. In fact, Hu Jintao had thanked her on behalf of a grateful nation, not least because, in order to carry out such an audacious coup, Sun Anqi would have to sacrifice her own life.

President Hu Jintao had assured her that if she succeeded, she would become part of Chinese folklore.

Reward enough to serve my leader – the only God she believed in.

Her own life was of little importance; she was driven by higher ideals. Petrov, on the other hand, was only interested in promotion and the illusionary bubble of fame, which was one of the many reasons she despised him.

'But if my plan succeeds, we won't be calling on your expertise,' Petrov reminded her.

'Commander Warwick and his team will be up against

us,' Sun Anqi said, keeping her voice low, her eyes fixed on the departure boards. Anybody glancing at the two figures on the bench would not have even noticed they were having a conversation. 'I have been watching him closely for the past four years and he is a worthy adversary. Never underestimate your enemy,' she said pointedly.

Petrov couldn't be certain which enemy she was referring to, but simply said, 'I intend to keep the Commander and his team well occupied, so neither he nor his flatfoots will work out my end game.' He paused, smiled, and got to his feet, glancing down only to add, 'Until it's too late.'

• • •

In another London venue, on the far side of the city, another covert meeting was taking place. Ross and William sat in the corner of a café, talking about Ross's assignment during the next few weeks.

'So, I'm officially on your team once again?'

'Unofficially,' William clarified, 'but the Hawk did get Commander Sinclair's agreement, not that he knows what you'll be up to.'

'And what did Sinclair have to say about that?' was Ross's next question.

'He wasn't exactly pleased,' admitted William. 'But, as we both know, the Hawk is not someone to pick a quarrel with.'

'When do I start?' asked Ross.

William checked his watch: 7.03. 'You started three minutes ago,' he replied.

'And what are my responsibilities?'

'To think of anything we might have missed that could compromise the Games and then make sure it never happens.

Whether it's a terrorist threat or a crook trying to make money on the side. I've had my eye on Bernie Longe for some time. He will have found dodgy land deals and fake ticket scams irresistible, so I want you to be two steps ahead of him. If a problem arises that you can't deal with, you report back to me immediately.'

'Understood.'

'And at all times keep your head below the parapet,' Willian added. 'I don't want the rest of the team to be aware of your presence, at least not yet. In fact, I don't want anyone to know we're working together again. As head of Public Order and Operational Support, I'm conspicuous – anyone planning any kind of disruption knows who I am. But they mustn't even know you exist.'

'They won't,' said Ross, who stood up and left as if the meeting had never taken place.

CHAPTER 4

7 June 2012 – 50 days to go

THE RUSSIAN EMBASSY in Kensington Palace Gardens was busy that afternoon. The final preparations for the evening's gala reception were in full swing, and the rooms were busy with staff hoovering carpets and setting out chairs, while caterers and florists hurried up and down stairs. Every now and then somebody would stop to admire the masterpieces on the walls, with one particular painting that had been moved from the ambassador's office to the drawing room attracting by far the most attention.

Three individuals were meeting in a back room around a small conference table. The door was closed – and locked – and the conversation was carried out in hushed tones. This was a far more conspicuous place than they were used to meeting. The presence of the Russian Ambassador, Anatoly Mikailov, and his security officer, Sergei Petrov, was of course unremarkable, and in the hurried rush of this busy day, it was easy for the diminutive figure of Sun Anqi to come and go unnoticed.

'Why am I here?' Sun Anqi asked the men seated opposite her.

'Because,' explained Mikailov, 'Petrov has made a decision I thought you ought to be made aware of.'

'I did not consider it was necessary to inform you,' said Petrov, his eyes trained on Sun Anqi, 'but I have been advised otherwise.' He cleared his throat. 'I have come to accept that if my plan is to have any chance of success, I will need an Englishman to join the team.'

Sun Anqi remained silent. She stared across the table, focusing on the space between the two men, but didn't offer an opinion.

'What I need,' Petrov continued, 'is someone who can be at ease among the establishment, while at the same time having reliable contacts in the criminal world. Even more importantly, they need to be bright, resourceful and ruthless in equal measure, while also possessing a weakness that we can take advantage of, so we can be certain of their total commitment.'

'Does such a person exist?' demanded Sun Anqi, wanting to make it clear she was against the whole idea of allowing an outsider to join their team.

'I initially wondered that myself,' admitted Petrov. 'I feared it might prove impossible to find someone who could carry out the job and at the same time be willing to betray their country. I had four candidates on my shortlist. However, two of them were quickly eliminated, as their only interest was how much they would be paid,' he paused, 'in advance.'

This was proof enough of a bad idea, as far as Sun Anqi was concerned. She folded her arms and asked, 'And the other two? What were their weaknesses?'

'For one, women,' replied Petrov. 'After a couple of nights with one of our more experienced escorts, he revealed all the details of his most recent assignment, so she didn't need to spend a third night with him.

'However, my fourth candidate comes recommended from a Russian who came across him in jail. He told me even the prison officers were cautious when dealing with him, so I believe I have found someone who is not only well-qualified for the job, but also has one particular weakness, almost an addiction, that I feel confident we can take advantage of.'

'If it isn't sex or money, what's left?' asked Sun Anqi.

'Masterpieces is the simple answer,' replied Petrov. The Ambassador nodded. 'Our target once crossed an ocean to try and get his hands on a Titian and came back empty-handed. He has a passion for art bordering on an obsession. For him, a unique piece of art is like a mistress he has to possess.'

'And what masterpiece do you have to tempt him with?' asked Sun Anqi, still sounding unconvinced.

'The Van Gogh, currently hanging in the drawing room,' Petrov replied.

'But where has this masterpiece come from?' pressed Sun Anqi.

'The painting was originally part of Hermann Göring's private collection,' explained the Russian Ambassador. 'However, I have now acquired it from the Hermitage – after President Putin had a word with the director.'

'The disappearance of such an important work of art wouldn't go unnoticed,' suggested Sun Anqi.

'That shouldn't prove a problem,' said the Ambassador. 'The Hermitage has nine Van Goghs, and I suspect the moment our man sets eyes on the self-portrait, he'll be trapped.'

'But if it's an addiction, when he wakes up in the morning,' said Sun Anqi, still unconvinced, 'perhaps he'll want another fix.'

'I think you will find, Sun Anqi,' said Petrov, 'that I've identified a mistress, not a one-night stand.'

There was a long pause before anyone spoke.

At last, Sun Anqi looked up. Her eyes met Petrov's. 'Be warned. He'll end up a liability.'

'He is a necessity,' Petrov replied sharply.

Sun Anqi raised her voice. Whenever she did so, it sounded like a threat. 'Don't expect me to trust him.'

'We are in need of a traitor; an honest man is of no use to us. However, if we persuade the candidate to join us, it will be entirely in his interests to remain loyal – and he will no doubt be made aware of the consequences if he does not.'

Sun Anqi smiled at the thought that her particular skills might still be required. She wanted him to fail.

'He will have no reason to betray us,' said the Russian Ambassador. 'If he wants to keep the Van Gogh, he will have to do as we say. And once the Games are over – and I mean *over* – he certainly won't want to admit to anyone how he came into possession of such a masterpiece.'

'He also has another weakness that we can take advantage of,' added Petrov. 'He has a long history with the officer in charge of security for the Olympic Games – and they are anything but old friends.'

Mikailov nodded. 'He will not be able to resist the opportunity to get one up on his old enemy, while at the same time adding a masterpiece to his collection.'

'This man will need to see the painting before he can be tempted,' said Sun Anqi, frowning. 'I suppose that's what tonight's gala reception is all about?'

'Precisely,' replied Mikailov. 'Officially, tonight is a celebration of the upcoming Hermitage exhibition, which is being held at the Fitzmolean Museum at the time of the Olympics. However, it's also a trap for our chosen candidate, and the bait will be the Van Gogh.'

'But what I still don't understand,' said Sun Anqi, 'is why we need this man in the first place.'

'He is a fair-haired Anglo-Saxon, who was educated at Harrow and could stroll around the House of Lords or his local pub without anyone giving him a second look,' said the Russian Ambassador, 'which I fear none of us could do.'

'He also has a lawyer who appears to be at his beck and call,' added Petrov, 'who, I'm assured, is every bit as crooked as his master, so in truth we'll be getting two for the price of one.'

'I'd rather hold on to the Van Gogh,' said Sun Anqi, 'than trust an Englishman.'

• • •

Miles arrived fashionably late at the embassy. When he'd first received an invitation from the Russian Ambassador to attend a gala reception, he had assumed it must be a mistake, until he discovered that it was to celebrate *The Hermitage Comes to the Fitzmolean* exhibition, which would be held at the museum as part of the official Olympic programme. Miles had decided to come, if for no other reason than to annoy his ex-wife, currently the chair of the Fitzmolean board.

He was greeted with a long queue of people waiting to be introduced to Ambassador Mikailov. Miles didn't do queues. He decided his time would be better spent enjoying the remarkable collection of paintings that adorned every wall:

Rembrandt, van Ruisdael and Steen – but when his eyes settled on a Van Gogh hanging above the mantelpiece, it quite literally took his breath away.

He continued to stare at the self-portrait until a voice behind him said, 'Being aware of your reputation, Mr Faulkner, I suspect you can put a date on the work.'

'Circa 1889. About a year before he died,' said Miles, 'by which time the only painting the artist had ever sold was to his doctor, Paul Gachet.'

'In exchange for his fee, if I remember correctly,' said the Ambassador.

Miles turned around, gave his host a slight bow and said, 'Good evening, Your Excellency.'

'Anatoly, please,' said the Ambassador, pretending to take an interest in the Van Gogh, 'and you are right, 1889.'

Ambassador Mikailov was standing at Miles's side when Miles turned to see if anyone was taking an interest in them. He spotted a man gazing down from the balcony above. One of the Ambassador's bodyguards, perhaps, thought Miles.

'I last saw this painting in St Petersburg,' said Miles, turning back once more to admire the Van Gogh.

'Right again, Mr Faulkner.' Mikailov paused, then said conspiratorially, 'Some people would give a great deal to own such a masterpiece.'

Miles glanced at him suspiciously. This was clearly no chance meeting. He was beginning to understand why he had been invited tonight. 'Would they indeed?' he replied.

'But surely, Mr Faulkner,' said Mikailov, 'a connoisseur such as yourself must appreciate that. You would no doubt give a great deal, hypothetically, to add such a unique work to your collection.'

'Hypothetically,' responded Miles, 'I might.'

'Would you, for example, kill your own grandmother?' asked the Ambassador.

'No, I wouldn't,' said Miles, 'but only because she died some years ago.'

Both men laughed.

'I think we can do business together, Mr Faulkner,' said Mikailov. 'However, now is neither the time nor the place to continue this conversation. I'll be in touch.' He smiled, before leaving to play host with some of his less important guests.

Miles gazed at the Van Gogh, trying to interpret the Ambassador's words, while Petrov continued to stare down from the gallery above. He was confident that he'd identified the right man to assist his cause and that they wouldn't have to bargain over the payment.

• • •

'I wonder who invited him,' said Beth, looking across the crowded room at Miles. 'I can assure you, Christina, that your ex was not on the list of names I submitted to the embassy as guests.'

Christina looked more closely at her ex-husband. The Russian Ambassador had left him moments before, and he was now standing alone, admiring the Van Gogh. 'Miles, like a bad penny, always turns up when he's least expected,' said Christina, 'but even I can't fault his artistic taste.'

'The Van Gogh self-portrait,' said Beth, 'was acquired by Hermann Göring from a prominent Jewish businessman in 1938, in exchange for three one-way tickets to New York.'

'Then how did the Russians get their hands on it?' enquired Christina.

'Plunder from the spoils of war,' explained Beth. 'When

the Russians entered the outskirts of Berlin in 1945, they reached Göring's private residence just hours before the Americans – otherwise the portrait might have spent the last few decades hanging on the walls of the Met rather than the Hermitage.'

'The way Miles is looking at the work,' said Christina, 'he might well be the next person to try and repatriate it.'

'With the Ambassador's blessing, perhaps,' suggested Beth. 'They looked rather cosy together, don't you think?'

'Possibly,' said Christina, 'but what would the Russian Ambassador expect in return?'

Beth only wished William was among the guests, as he might well have offered an opinion. But with the Games almost upon them, her husband hadn't been able to take a night off. He was practically living between Scotland Yard and the Olympic Stadium, and she barely saw him for more than a snatched half-hour. Not that he had been invited tonight. Another coincidence, or was she overreacting? Her eyes settled on Wilbur, who was currently chatting to the Ambassador's wife. Why had the chairman's husband received an invitation but not the director's? Another coincidence?

Perhaps she was reading too much into it – or perhaps the time had come to have a word with Ross. If there was one person who knew how Miles Faulkner's mind worked as well as William did – and despised him just as much – it was Ross.

• • •

'Will you get a chance to see any of the Olympics?' asked Alice.

'From the opening ceremony to the closing ceremony,' replied Sir Julian, with a smile of satisfaction.

'How come?' demanded Alice.

'The IOC have invited me to chair a panel of judges during the Games.'

'And what do they do?' asked Alice.

'Not a lot,' admitted Julian. 'Unless there's an unresolved dispute between two or more countries, when I become the final arbitrator. It's pro bono, of course, except I get to see any event I wish to attend – in my own box.'

'Some people . . .' began Alice, but was distracted by the tapping of a spoon against a glass.

'Good evening,' said the Ambassador, 'and may I begin by welcoming you . . .'

Miles turned to slip away. Speeches, like queues, were not on his to-do list. He stepped out – unnoticed.

• • •

Once Miles was back in his car, he phoned Booth Watson and asked him to join him for dinner at the Savoy. It would not have crossed Miles's mind that BW might be otherwise engaged.

Once they'd given their orders to the maître d', Miles reported to his lawyer the conversation that had taken place with the Russian Ambassador.

Booth Watson was not slow to offer an opinion. 'Whatever he's willing to offer you, Miles, walk away,' he said firmly. 'We're not talking about a gang of two-bit criminals here. This is the Russian Ambassador, briefing you on behalf of his masters. You are never going to get the upper hand with that lot – it's far too dangerous a game. Try not to forget. You can't hang a Van Gogh in a prison cell – or in a coffin.'

But Booth Watson knew his client wasn't listening.

CHAPTER 5

8 June 2012 – 49 days to go

ROSS HOGAN'S LIFE HAD CHANGED so much in the fifteen years since he first met Alice. Then, he was a widower, trying to balance parenting his young daughter Jojo with a full-on job in Royal Protection. Now, Jojo was grown up, and Ross and Alice's son, Jack, was about to start secondary school. But Ross's career had stalled. A particularly unfortunate encounter with Miles Faulkner twelve years ago had seen him suspended for a year, before eventually returning to the force – not as Chief Inspector Hogan, but as Sergeant Hogan. He had spent his time issuing parking tickets, which had given him more than enough time to nurse a grudge bordering on hatred. And to make matters worse Faulkner had been released after only four years. Ross had been in traffic control for far too long and was once again considering resigning. William's recent lifeline had changed all that overnight and given him a second chance.

But if there was one thing about Ross that hadn't changed over the years, it was his early morning run through Hyde Park and across Kensington Gardens.

He rose at six, left home in his well-worn tracksuit and jogged across to Hyde Park, before setting out on a four-mile run around the Serpentine that took him less than twenty-five minutes. When he arrived back at the Prince Albert Memorial, he stretched for another fifteen minutes, before returning home in time to join Alice, Jojo and Jack for breakfast.

Beth had once joined Ross on the morning outing, and once had proved quite enough. She'd only caught back up with him as he finished his stretching. He then jogged home, while she continued to run, and even then she could only just keep up with him. Never again.

Beth rose early the morning following the Russian gala reception and left the house a few minutes after William had set out for the stadium. She took the tube to South Kensington and walked up Exhibition Road to Hyde Park. She sat on a bench some hundred yards from the entrance, which offered her a clear view of everyone who entered the park. Beth didn't have long to wait before Ross appeared and set off at the same frightening pace towards the lake.

Once he was out of sight, Beth strolled across to join Prince Albert, where Ross would do his stretching. She began to question whether she should share her worst fears with William's oldest friend, when she hadn't raised the subject with her own husband.

She still hadn't made up her mind by the time he came striding down the path, overtaking several runners half his age.

When he spotted Beth standing on the grass by the side of the royal statue, he didn't mask his surprise. He slowed down, came to a halt by her side and, although breathing heavily, managed, 'This has to be important.'

'Or a complete waste of your time,' suggested Beth, as Ross began his warming down routine.

While Ross carried out a series of exercises that made her feel tired just watching, Beth told him what she had witnessed at the reception the previous evening.

Ross's first question was, 'How much would a Van Gogh self-portrait be worth?'

Beth considered the question while Ross completed forty press-ups. 'One hasn't come on the market for several years,' she said, as Ross began to try and touch his toes with his elbows. 'But if I had to put a figure on it, at least fifty million, although Miles Faulkner might put a higher value on it, judging by how he was admiring the painting last night.'

'So, I'm bound to ask, what would the Russians expect in return for fifty million?' Ross said as he whirled his arms like windmills. 'What's William's opinion?'

'I've only mentioned it to him in passing,' admitted Beth. 'He's been so preoccupied preparing for the opening ceremony and I don't want to burden him with my problems.'

'If Faulkner is up to something, then that is his problem,' muttered Ross, 'so I'd better look into it.'

'But it might turn out to be nothing. After all, it's possible Faulkner was doing no more than admiring the self-portrait.'

'With the Russian ambassador standing by his side, I doubt it,' said Ross.

'Which is why I thought I'd ask you, since I know you're not exactly overworked in traffic control . . .'

Ross's faint smile gave nothing away. 'I'll look into it,' he repeated. And then, after one final stretch, he jogged off in the opposite direction.

• • •

The Russian Ambassador called Miles at 9 a.m. Miles could only wonder how he'd got his number. He left Collins and the Rolls behind in Cadogan Place and took a taxi to the Russian Embassy in Kensington Palace Gardens. He'd left his mobile at home, as he'd once been told that if you enter Kensington Palace Gardens with a mobile, at least five embassies, the Russians included, would have stripped every contact on it before you got out of your car. He only had to knock on the embassy door once before it was opened by a uniformed officer.

'Good morning, Mr Faulkner,' he said, although they had never met before.

He showed the guest into the drawing room, where the reception had been held the night before. Three chairs had been placed in a semi-circle around the Van Gogh. Two were occupied by men, who immediately stood to greet him.

'Good morning, Mr Faulkner,' said the Russian Ambassador, as if they were old friends. 'Allow me to introduce Mr Petrov, who is an undersecretary at the embassy.'

It was the man Miles had seen watching him from the balcony last night, and he didn't need to be told that the word 'undersecretary' meant spy. He might as well have had it printed on his passport under job description.

Petrov stepped forward to shake hands with the stranger before the Russian Ambassador ushered his guest towards the centre chair.

'It is good of you to join us, Mr Faulkner,' said Petrov, once coffee had been served. 'I have, of course, been made aware of the conversation you had with His Excellency when you attended the gala reception yesterday evening.' He glanced up at the Van Gogh. 'The Hermitage's loss will be your gain.'

'But what His Excellency didn't tell me,' said Miles, looking directly at Petrov, 'is what you would expect in return.'

'To betray your country,' said Petrov quite simply and without any emotion.

Miles maintained eye contact. 'And what form would this betrayal take?'

'We would require your advice and assistance on several fronts that we have been working on for before, during and after the Olympics,' said Petrov. 'Suffice it to say, we intend to undermine Britain's reputation on the world stage, so they find out the true meaning of a *cold war.*'

Miles became distracted by a young woman who was seated cross legged on the floor in the far corner of the room, who looked more East Asian than Russian in appearance. He hadn't noticed her until then, while her cold grey eyes had never left him, even for a moment.

'And what exactly do you have in mind?' pressed Miles.

'I couldn't consider sharing those details with you, Mr Faulkner,' came back Petrov, 'until I'm convinced you're a fully fledged member of our team and can be relied upon. However, I can explain our overall strategy. We intend to chip away at Britain's façade of confidence and expertise until the cracks are clear for all to see. We have a comprehensive plan of attack to show that the British should never have been awarded the Games in the first place. Over the next few weeks, we will wear the police down, and in particular

Commander Warwick, with incidents he won't have enough officers to deal with. The moment we're convinced they are overstretched and don't know which way to turn, we will strike.'

Miles couldn't help noticing that the woman's cold eyes still hadn't left him, as if he were an animal that might try to escape.

'But why me?' asked Faulkner.

'We need someone who knows how the British think and act when something goes wrong,' said the Ambassador. 'Someone who can go unnoticed in a crowd and, to quote you British, will not stick out like a sore finger.'

Miles smiled at the Ambassador's mistake, which only emphasized his point.

'Some of the *incidents* we have planned,' continued the Ambassador, 'must appear to be the result of the home team's incompetence, while others will look like failures by those in charge of security. But what it must *not* look like, at least to the public, is a well-planned campaign of espionage. If the British were able to lay the blame at our door, we would have achieved the exact opposite of what we are hoping to achieve.'

'And then both of you,' said Miles, glancing between Petrov and Mikailov, 'would be returning to your home country,' he paused, 'and not to a hero's welcome.'

Miles paused to see how they would react, but no response was forthcoming, so he asked the all-important question. 'Why me?'

'It didn't take a lot of research to discover that the man in charge of Olympic security, Commander Warwick, is an old adversary of yours,' said Petrov. 'We are also aware that he has been a thorn in your flesh for some considerable time, and so we were rather hoping we might be able to work together for a common cause. Catherine the Great once said that two men marching in the same direction are a team, three an army.'

'That would depend on what Catherine the Great expects me to do,' said Faulkner, 'and, more importantly, what she has to offer in return.'

Petrov looked up at the Van Gogh painting before turning to face Faulkner. Miles got the message. 'Commander Warwick has clearly surrounded himself with capable officers who are able to think two steps ahead,' said Petrov. 'We require someone who can not only tell us what those two steps are, but can anticipate the third.'

'Warwick is well capable of thinking four steps ahead,' said Miles, 'and you'd be wise not to underestimate him.'

The woman in the corner of the room nodded, her cold piercing eyes moved onto Petrov.

'Which is exactly why we need you to be a fully committed member of our team,' the Ambassador said, matter-of-factly.

'We also thought,' added Petrov, 'that you might consider revenge on Warwick and his team an added bonus.'

Miles stared up at the painting for some time, before he eventually asked, 'If I were to agree to be your agent' – he avoided the word traitor – 'I'll need proof that the Van Gogh will not be shipped back to St Petersburg once the Games are over.'

The two Russians exchanged glances, before the Ambassador offered, 'I'm open to any suggestions.'

Faulkner nodded. 'As you are incapable of paying me my usual ten per cent in advance,' he said, 'I will expect you to make the Van Gogh part of *The Hermitage Comes to the Fitzmolean* exhibition when it opens at the museum next month. I will also require a letter to be sent to my lawyer, Mr Booth Watson, who I feel sure you're well aware of, making it clear that on the day the exhibition closes, he will take possession of the work on my behalf.'

The woman's eyes narrowed slightly. Whoever she was and however she fitted in, it was clear to Faulkner that she did not consider he ought to be demanding terms, just falling in line. She was about to find out he didn't just fall in line – for anyone.

'I feel sure that will be acceptable,' said the Ambassador, his words accompanied by a warm smile.

'I will still need to consider the matter very carefully,' said Miles after another long pause. 'And should you even think of double-crossing me, let me remind you that Mr Booth Watson's chambers are less than a stone's throw from Fleet Street, where they wouldn't have to pay for an exclusive that would end up on the front page of every newspaper, along with photographs of you and your colleagues, thus guaranteeing your involvement would be recorded for the whole world to read about. Not something, I imagine, that would advance either of your glittering careers.'

'You're quite right, Mr Faulkner,' came back Petrov. 'But that's a two-way street. And should you decide to repeat this conversation to anyone outside of this room, I will happily represent the Russian government at your funeral.'

Miles didn't doubt it.

The Russian Ambassador showed no reaction to his colleague's statement. He just touched a buzzer under his chair and the officer reappeared and accompanied his guest to the front door. However, he did notice that Faulkner looked back, not at him, but at the Van Gogh.

• • •

After Faulkner had left the residence, he didn't go home but took a taxi to Middle Temple. During the journey, he changed his mind several times. When the cab eventually pulled up outside a set of chambers in Middle Temple Lane, a secretary ushered him quickly through to Mr Booth Watson's office without being shown into the waiting room. In fact, Miles had no idea where the waiting room was.

'As you rarely come to my office without an appointment,' opined Booth Watson, pushing some papers to one side, 'I can only assume the matter is urgent.'

'Very,' responded Miles, before repeating at great length the conversation that had just taken place at the Russian Embassy.

'So, you didn't take my advice after all,' remonstrated Booth Watson, like a headmaster chastising a wayward child. 'Therefore, I'll repeat my strong recommendation a second time. You must walk away, Miles. In fact, even take advantage of the situation.'

'How do you propose I do that?' asked Miles.

'You can brief Commander Warwick on what the Russians are up to, in exchange for the police dropping any charges against you for the unauthorized sale of Olympic tickets.'

Miles accepted that was unquestionably the sensible course of action to take, until he recalled Petrov's threats and one word in particular: funeral.

'I'm afraid that won't be possible,' said Miles without explanation. 'However, I will take your advice and walk away.'

• • •

Miles returned to the Russian residence the following day, his short speech well-prepared. The same uniformed officer opened the door and once again escorted the guest into the drawing room where the Ambassador awaited him.

The first thing Miles saw as he walked into the room was a portrait by a Dutch artist who had died in poverty, having sold only one picture in his lifetime.

The Ambassador rose from his chair and said, 'So, have you reached a decision, Mr Faulkner?'

'Yes, I have,' replied Miles, his eyes still fixed on Van Gogh's masterpiece.

He changed his mind once again.

CHAPTER 6

21 June 2012 – 36 days to go

SURVEILLANCE SOUNDS FASCINATING to the layman, but for the most part it's endless and boring, not least because you can't risk taking a moment off, in case that is the precise moment something happens. You can go hours without being fed, have to piss into an empty bottle in the car, and only fall asleep when the lights in the target's bedroom finally go off. But you have to be awake and alert once again before they come back on.

William had told Ross that Faulkner was involved in a ticket scam, but what Beth was suggesting was in a different league, so Ross immediately made a change to his daily routine.

Every morning for the past fortnight, he had taken a taxi to Faulkner's home in Cadogan Place and arrived before the milkman. A taxi with a difference, as it was part of the Met's fleet and never picked up a customer – and Ross was in the driving seat.

Sergeant Hogan was quickly reminded that Faulkner was a creature of habit. The lights in his Belgravia town house would be switched on at around six thirty every morning and turned back off soon after eleven at night. The habit of a professional businessman. In Faulkner's case, a professional criminal.

Ross had been regularly tailing Faulkner to the Savoy for lunch, the Middle Temple to visit Mr Booth Watson, and on one occasion to Trumper's on Curzon Street to have his hair cut. Occasionally, he would meet with a legitimate business associate, but more often with someone not quite so legitimate, such as a shady art dealer or even a bookie. Faulkner didn't seem to have any friends.

He rarely shopped, didn't go to the theatre, visit nightclubs or casinos. His only outside interest seemed to be visiting art galleries, which he did at least twice a week. He was invited to all the major openings, which the gossip columns regularly reported. Ross would have liked to join him at some of these galleries, but had to remain behind the wheel.

The routine hardly varied, and Ross was beginning to think that Beth might have overreacted and that Faulkner had been doing no more than chatting to the Russian Ambassador while admiring the Van Gogh masterpiece at the embassy party. Perhaps the time had come for him to turn his attention to more pressing matters, such as Bernie Longe. He'd picked up on the Met's grapevine – deep rooted but not always reliable – that Bernie's drug activities were flourishing. Ross wondered if this could in any way be connected to the Olympics. The Met had been trying to take down Bernie Longe for years, but never came up with enough evidence to charge him.

Once again, Ross followed Faulkner's Rolls to the Savoy. He parked on a cab rank with a perfect sightline to the hotel's front door and waited for Faulkner to reappear.

When he finally did, to Ross's surprise he didn't climb into the back of his Rolls to be driven home, but hailed a taxi that headed towards Trafalgar Square.

Ross kept his distance while he followed, but had to make sure he was never caught at a red light when he could lose his prey.

The taxi continued on its way down Whitehall, past Downing Street and the Houses of Parliament before turning left over Lambeth Bridge and then right along Albert Embankment. They continued on for another mile before coming to a halt outside the Oval, which took Ross by surprise, as he'd never known Faulkner to take any interest in cricket.

He quickly dumped the taxi on another rank, leapt out and headed for Hobbs Gate. He spotted Faulkner about fifty yards ahead of him. He clearly knew where he was going.

When Faulkner disappeared into the Bedser Stand, Ross kept on walking, only stopping when he reached the next entrance. He slipped into an empty seat beside a pillar. He didn't need a pair of binoculars to spot Faulkner, who was sitting at the back of a sparse crowd, next to a man who had clearly never visited a cricket match in his life. He was dressed in a dark suit, white shirt and red silk tie, and couldn't have looked more out of place. He was deep in conversation with Faulkner and rarely looked at what was taking place on the field.

The two men continued chatting for the best part of an hour, and the loss of three wickets during that time didn't seem to interest them. Then the stranger abruptly stood up and, without shaking hands, left the stand and headed for the exit.

Ross immediately made the decision to follow the mystery man, rather than Faulkner, in the hope it would be more revealing. He nipped out of his place back onto the concourse and ran all the way to Hobbs Gate, where he left the ground and jumped back into his cab. He didn't have to wait long before the man reappeared.

Looking around, the man saw Ross and raised an arm. Ross made another instant decision. He pulled down his cloth cap, turned on the engine and headed across the road to pick up his first customer. The man climbed into the back without giving him a second look.

'Where to, guv?' asked Ross, feigning a cockney accent.

'Kensington Palace Gardens.'

Ross didn't need to be told it would be an embassy. But which one?

During the journey, Ross regularly glanced in his rear-view mirror, not to check the traffic behind him but to take a closer look at the customer seated in the back, who was constantly on his phone, speaking in Russian.

After Ross had dropped his fare off at the embassy – no tip – he drove for about a mile before he came to a halt in a side street. He called William.

When Ross recognized the familiar voice on the other end of the line, all he said was, 'I need to see you.'

'Breakfast Monday morning,' said William, 'usual place, usual time.'

The phone went dead.

END GAME

23 June 2012 – 34 days to go

BERNIE LONGE SAT AT HIS DESK, two henchmen perched like bookends on either side of him. He stared at the stack of ten-pound notes in front of him like soldiers on parade. A monthly consultation fee for a man who didn't deal in cheques or credit cards, and only paid tax on his salary as the chairman of the local council's Business Opportunities Committee.

Councillor Dawson had begun life in a council house on the Bevan Estate and ended up as its councillor. After his appointment as chairman, his council house had been exchanged for a penthouse flat in Canary Wharf. His two children were educated not in the borough, but in private schools in the West Country, and his wife preferred to shop in Harvey Nichols rather than M&S. They holidayed in the south of Spain, where they hoped to retire, along with several other past chairmen of Finance, Housing and Business Opportunities.

A knock on the door meant it must be ten o'clock, because Councillor Dawson, like the rent collector, was never late. Their monthly meeting was the only time they ever met. No phone calls, no emails, no letters that might suggest they knew each other.

'Come,' said Longe, which was slightly redundant, as Councillor Dawson had already entered the room.

If you had passed Dawson in the street, you might have mistaken him for a City broker, dressed in his Savile Row suit, Turnbull & Asser shirt and wearing handmade shoes from Loake. However, once he opened his mouth, the illusion was shattered, because you can't purchase a West End accent in Jermyn Street.

Working in partnership, the local mafia boss (or respected businessman, as he preferred to be called) and the bent councillor (re-elected for a fourth term) were about to make a killing by simply being in the right place at the right time. The 2012 London Olympics had landed on their doorstep.

'Good morning, Councillor,' said Longe, who never addressed Dawson by his Christian name. 'Have you earned your commission this month?'

'More than,' responded Dawson, as he sat down, his eyes focused on the stack of notes in front of him. 'In fact, I may have come across our biggest opportunity yet.'

'I'm all ears,' said Longe, as an attractive young woman in a miniskirt appeared carrying a tray with two cups of coffee and a plate of assorted biscuits. She placed the biscuits in the middle of the desk, next to the pile of notes.

Councillor Dawson took a chocolate biscuit before giving her a second look. He'd never seen her before, but then Bernie's 'personal assistants' rarely lasted for more than a month, two at the most.

'Once the Olympics are over, the stadium will be put up for sale,' said Dawson, after placing two lumps of sugar in his coffee.

'But where's the profit in that?' asked Longe. 'Once the Games are over,' he repeated, 'it will be nothing more than a redundant waste of space.'

'Which is why the government has, on this occasion, distanced itself from any involvement,' said Dawson, 'and left the responsibility for selling the stadium to the local council.'

'The upkeep alone,' came back Longe, 'would cost millions, and the occasional pop concert and athletics meeting wouldn't begin to cover the cost.'

END GAME

'But West Ham Football Club might,' said Councillor Dawson, playing his trump card.

Longe put down his coffee and listened more carefully.

'Their chairman has approached the council about renting the stadium for two and a half million a year as their new venue for West Ham United. A good deal for them.'

'But I have to ask,' said Longe, beginning to sound exasperated, 'how does that become a good deal for me?'

'As the council is in need of an injection of cash, my committee has decided to put the stadium up for sale. If you were to bid ten million before I tell anyone about West Ham's interest, a steady income for life could be yours.'

Councillor Dawson began to transfer the piles of ten-pound notes into his Tesco bag, as if they were just another shopping item.

It didn't take Longe more than a few moments to work out that with a guaranteed income of two and a half million a year, he could clear the ten-million-pound outlay in four years, five at the most, and consider trading his home in Hackney for a villa in the south of France.

However, there was one small problem. He didn't have ten million. Something he didn't want Councillor Dawson to find out.

'What deposit would I have to put down?' asked Longe.

'One million as soon as possible,' said Dawson, 'then I'd give you a couple of months to clear the full amount, by which time the council should have sewn up the agreement with West Ham.'

'And what would your cut be, Councillor?'

'Betty and I have spotted a house on the Costa del Sol that would—'

'How much?' said Longe.

'Only half a million, but I would need fifty thousand for the deposit.'

Bernie Longe nodded. He considered the proposition for a few moments before he said, 'You'll get your fifty thousand the day after I sign the contract for the stadium.'

CHAPTER 7

24 June 2012 – 33 days to go

FAULKNER KNEW THAT if the Russians were expected to part with one of their most fabled treasures, it would come at a very high price. He had been left with no choice but to clear his diary for the next few weeks and be on call at a moment's notice, whatever the hour. Meetings of the inner team were always held at a different venue, at short notice, and rarely during office hours.

Despite his reservations, Booth Watson remained on call, well aware he could leave at a moment's notice and take advantage of Bernie Longe's offer to double his retainer. He began his new assignment by trawling the universities for law students who were looking for a holiday job, and after selecting the brightest three on tap, he didn't allow them to meet each other. The first task they were set was to find out if anything had gone wrong during the build-up to the Beijing Olympics which they could duplicate.

One of the three, who thought like a criminal – always useful if you're hoping to be a defence barrister – produced the thickest file. When the torch relay had arrived in Beijing, the runners, he wrote, were continually held up by Tibetan separatists, one of whom tried to put out the Olympic flame with a fire extinguisher. He'd been sentenced to five years in prison.

Faulkner turned up to the next meeting, accompanied by his pliant QC, armed with enough valuable information they could take advantage of. However, they wouldn't be telling Sun Anqi everything they'd discovered.

They gathered in an upstairs room of a quiet London pub. Miles wasn't surprised to find Petrov waiting for him, but the lady with a killer's eyes was sitting on the next table as if they weren't together. She didn't even glance in his direction.

After a ten-pound note had changed hands, the landlord assured his customers that no one would disturb them. Booth Watson shifted in his seat; this was the first meeting he'd attended and he didn't feel at ease.

'You have to understand that security will be tight,' Faulkner warned Petrov, as they discussed the first item on their unwritten agenda: disrupting the Olympic torch relay. 'Even during the night, two police officers never allow the torch out of their sight.'

'Then what chance do we have of carrying out your plan?' asked Petrov.

Faulkner didn't answer the question, but simply replied, 'I've identified a weakness in the system.'

Petrov didn't have to ask the obvious question.

'Eighty thousand volunteers have applied to be among the chosen few to carry the torch,' Booth Watson explained, 'including Angelina Jolie and Brad Pitt, who were both turned down, as the organizing committee were keen to involve only local people on each stage of the torch's journey.'

Petrov made a note.

'I've discovered that a local fireman from Hounslow has been selected to carry the torch on one of the stages between Wembley and Greenwich,' added Faulkner.

'And?' pressed Petrov.

'Unfortunately, the man in question turns out to have a gambling problem and is being pressed by his bookie to pay up. I'm going to solve his problem,' said Faulkner, 'and in return, I intend to take advantage of his particular skills, which will turn the torch relay into a farce and create unwelcome headlines right across the world, without any suggestion that you were in any way involved.'

'Hardly earth shattering,' suggested the lady seated on the next table.

Booth Watson took a closer look at Sun Anqi and after thirty years as a criminal barrister, knew evil when he saw it.

'I have several disruptions planned that should keep Warwick and his lapdogs well occupied during the run-up to the Games,' said Petrov, looking directly at Faulkner. 'The more minor incidents the police have to deal with before the Games, the better, as then they won't be prepared for what I have in store for them.'

'But what do you have in store for them?' asked Sun Anqi, barely able to hide her frustration.

'Operation Blackout,' said Petrov without further explanation. 'And I shouldn't have to remind you, you're simply an observer until the closing ceremony.'

'But, should you fail,' said Sun Anqi, 'which wouldn't come as a surprise, I will then be expected to cover your mistakes.'

Petrov turned back, barely able to control his temper as he faced Faulkner. 'Can I confirm, Mr Faulkner, that you own a Learjet 45?'

Booth Watson was quickly becoming aware just how much intelligence they had on his client and he didn't like it.

Faulkner hesitated, before nodding. 'Housed in a hangar at Biggin Hill and ready to take off at a moment's notice.'

'Good, because at some time in the near future, we will require you to fly to Helsinki, collect a package from our embassy and bring it back to London.'

'Why can't one of your own people cover that?' asked Booth Watson.

'Because, Mr Booth Watson, if we were caught in possession of this particular package, it wouldn't take the Olympic Committee long to work out not only what we have planned, but who was responsible.'

'So what's in the package?' demanded Miles, cutting to the chase.

'That, I'm not willing to reveal,' said Petrov.

'And if my client refuses to go along with your plan?' asked Booth Watson.

'Vincent Van Gogh will be returning to St Petersburg,' said Petrov, staring directly at Booth Watson.

Faulkner nodded.

'Let's move on to item number three. Spiking the urine of two of the world's leading athletes,' said Petrov, without showing any sign of emotion.

'Two athletes who are clearly not Russian or Chinese,' suggested Booth Watson.

'A keen observation,' said Sun Anqi, who never trusted lawyers. In her opinion, they were only too happy to act for either side, as long as their fees were paid.

Petrov took his time explaining the role he expected Mr Faulkner to play.

'Who are the two athletes concerned?' interrupted Booth Watson.

'We'll let you know their names nearer the time,' said Petrov. 'Your job is to make sure their urine can be spiked without anyone becoming suspicious. We assume you have both the facilities and the local contacts, while making sure no prying eyes look our way?'

Faulkner nodded.

'Good, because when the news breaks that traces of performance-enhancing drugs have been found in the urine of the athletes concerned, their medals will be stripped from them.'

'While no doubt your own athletes will sweep the board, despite being drugged up to their eyeballs,' suggested Faulkner.

Petrov graced Faulkner with a smile.

'It's no secret,' said Miles, 'to anyone who reads the back pages of any national newspaper, that eighty per cent of Russian athletes who competed in Beijing were on drugs. And the only reason they weren't caught was because your scientists had come up with a masking drug which, if taken by athletes six weeks before they compete, hides all traces of any previous drug-taking.'

'It's called modern warfare, and if we . . . you carry out your side of the plan, the London Games will only be remembered for one thing.'

'Not unlike the Seoul Olympics,' suggested Booth Watson, 'when Ben Johnson was stripped of his gold medal following the one hundred metres final and Carl Lewis was declared the winner.'

'With a subtle difference on this occasion,' suggested Petrov, 'as the athletes concerned are far better known than Ben Johnson, and one of them is British.'

• • •

Booth Watson was now even more anxious – not merely about the risk his client was taking, but also about his own future. It was true that in the past Miles had often involved him in ventures that could end up with him being disbarred, but never before had he been involved in something that could endanger his life.

When they left the pub, Miles hailed a taxi, and Booth Watson decided the time had come to tell his client, once and for all, to walk away while he still could. If, once again, Miles ignored his advice, he would have to explain to his client why he could no longer represent him – and nothing, he would repeat, nothing, would change his mind.

As they waited for a taxi to pull up, Booth Watson had to admit, if only to himself, that he was heartened by the fact he could always switch his allegiance to Bernie Longe and double his retainer.

'Where to, guv?' asked the cabbie, as they climbed in and Miles pulled the taxi door closed.

'Thirty-Seven Cadogan Place,' said Miles.

'And then on to Middle Temple,' said Booth Watson, as he leant forward and closed the window that divided the driver from his fare. 'There's something we need to discuss, Miles, and it can't wait a moment longer,' he said, unable to look directly at his client.

Miles glanced across to see Booth Watson holding tightly onto the seat, a bead of sweat rolling down his forehead.

'You've been my most important client for more years than I care to remember,' Booth Watson began, 'and I hope you feel I've served you well.'

'None better, and I would suggest that you have become far more than a trusted advocate – a dear and close friend,' said Miles, who'd already worked out why Booth Watson was perspiring.

This silenced Booth Watson for a moment, which Miles took advantage of.

'And as neither of us is getting any younger,' Miles continued, 'I feel the time has come for me to show you just how much I appreciate your friendship and loyalty.' Miles glanced across to see the bead of sweat had reached Booth Watson's nose, while several more had appeared on his forehead, allowing Miles to continue with his well-prepared homily. 'Of course, I'm well aware that my latest enterprise may be stretching that loyalty to breaking point, especially considering I didn't heed the sage advice you gave me earlier.'

Booth Watson turned to face him; his mouth opened but no words came out.

'I suppose it should have occurred to me when I learned that Bernie Longe had offered to double your retainer if you would leave me and represent him. But, typically, you turned the offer down out of hand.'

Booth Watson removed a handkerchief from his top pocket and began to mop his brow.

'So I've decided the least I can do in the circumstances is not only equal Longe's offer, but, aware you are putting your career on the line, add a bonus for your troubles.'

'A bonus?' Booth Watson heard himself repeating.

'Yes,' said Miles. 'Once the Games are over, it is my intention to place a million pounds in a numbered Swiss bank account, so you can enjoy the retirement you so richly deserve, because I can assure you this will be my last venture.' Miles hoped he sounded sincere.

Booth Watson was speechless.

'But I interrupted you,' said Miles, as the cabbie turned into Cadogan Place. 'There was something you wanted to tell me?'

'It can wait until the Games are over,' said Booth Watson, as the cab drew up outside Miles's front door.

Miles smiled as he got out of the taxi and paid the fare.

25 June 2012 – 32 days to go

THE FOLLOWING MORNING over breakfast with William, Ross filled the boss in with everything he'd witnessed when he'd followed Faulkner to the Oval.

'Since then, there's been nothing of interest,' Ross added, 'although he did manage to give me the slip yesterday morning after I got stuck at a traffic light.'

'So, Faulkner has somehow got himself mixed up with the Russian government,' said William thoughtfully.

'So it would seem.'

'What exactly are they up to?'

Ross left the question unanswered, taking a sip of coffee. 'Has Beth told you what she witnessed during the gala reception at the Russian Embassy recently?'

William nodded. 'She mentioned it in passing, but we were interrupted before I got the full story. My phone never stops ringing these days. Something about a Van Gogh?'

'In one,' said Ross. 'Faulkner was taking an unusual amount of interest in a particular Van Gogh self-portrait – a painting Beth has since been told will be part of *The Hermitage Comes to the Fitzmolean* exhibition.'

'So Faulkner may be trying to buy it from the Russians,' mused William.

'Possibly,' said Ross. 'The question is: is he buying it with money, or with something else the Russians need?'

'Good question.' William sighed. 'Look, keep an eye on Faulkner, by all means, but we have bigger issues to worry about right now. With only five weeks to go, all our focus needs to be on the Olympics and any potential threat to the Games – which this isn't.'

'As far as we know,' said Ross.

• • •

Ross decided to carry out William's instructions and concentrate on the Olympics rather than Faulkner, but he still wondered if the two might somehow be connected, so on his day off he was back in his taxi, parked a hundred yards from Faulkner's front door. He was taken by surprise when Faulkner climbed into his Rolls but Collins turned right at the end of the street and not left.

Ross kept his distance as the chauffeur-driven car headed out of central London, passing through the boroughs of Chelsea, Fulham and Brentford, before coming to a halt outside a semi-detached house in Hounslow.

Ross watched as Faulkner got out of the car, strode up a short, weed-infested path, before knocking on a door that was opened almost immediately. He was clearly expected.

Ross drove past the house and carried on for another hundred yards before turning left and disappearing out of sight. He parked the car, got out, and hid behind a tree that afforded him a perfect view of the front door. He waited.

About an hour passed before Faulkner came back out and

climbed into the Rolls, which then headed back towards central London.

Ross made no attempt to follow him. Never follow a target back to their base is a golden rule, as it's the surest way to blow your cover. Ross waited until the car was out of sight before he drove slowly past the house, making a mental note of the number and the name of the road.

It didn't take a great deal of research to discover that the owner was a Mr Dave Timpson, who worked for the local fire brigade, a job he'd been doing for the past twelve years.

It took a little more research for Ross to find out that Mr Timpson was experiencing financial difficulties, which might explain why Faulkner had visited him. But it didn't explain what Faulkner would expect in return for removing those difficulties.

That took considerably more research.

CHAPTER 8

16 July 2012 – 11 days to go

GOLD LOOKED UP FROM HIS PLACE at the top of the table, pleased to see that Silver and two of his Bronzes were already on the podium.

If you had asked William what had taken place during the past few weeks, all he would remember was that he never had enough time to deal with every problem that arose, however trivial or unimportant, while ending each day sleeping for three or four hours on a camp bed in his office.

With only eleven days left before the opening ceremony, there wasn't a minute to waste. In fact, the team meetings had gone from taking place once a month to once a week, and now once a day, in the vain hope of staying ahead of the game.

A knock on the door at five to eight, answered by *come in*, allowed the inner circle to join Gold. Detective Inspector Adaja took his place on the Commander's right, while Sergeant

Pankhurst sat on his left. Sergeant Roycroft occupied the remaining seat at the other end of the table, while William's secretary sat behind him, making notes, and would have the minutes along with a new agenda prepared well in time for tomorrow's meeting.

'As from tomorrow,' said William, 'these meetings will take place at the stadium and will begin at seven o'clock, not eight.'

No one commented, as that was no more than they had all signed up for seven years ago.

'Right,' said William. 'As usual, we have a packed agenda. Don't forget that for the next few weeks, the eyes of the world will be upon us. If anything goes wrong, we'll be on the firing line. So, first on the agenda.' William looked down at the sheet of paper in front of him. 'How can we hope to get approximately one hundred and fifty VIPs to the stadium without causing a traffic jam that will bring London to a halt? Paul,' he said, looking to his right, 'I was glad to receive an email from you at eleven o'clock last night with the words: *Sorted. Will explain at tomorrow's prayer meeting.* Explain.'

'We're going to transport our group of kings, presidents and prime ministers in sixteen luxury coaches, each accompanied by half a dozen outriders and two police cars.'

'I can't see Jacques Delors sitting in the back of a coach chatting amiably to Boris Johnson,' said Rebecca, barely able to mask a grin.

'It will be up to the Foreign Office to handle that particular problem,' said Paul, without missing a beat. 'There will be four royal receptions held in different locations an hour before our VIPs have to leave for the stadium. One at Buckingham Palace hosted by the Queen, a second at St James's Palace with Prince Charles, a third at Lancaster House with Prince Harry and Princess Anne and the fourth, for lesser mortals, will be held at Wellington Barracks.'

'I wouldn't want to be the person who has to decide which head of state goes to which palace,' volunteered Rebecca.

'Again, the Foreign Office will be responsible for that delicate decision,' said Paul, 'as they're well aware who's sleeping with who, which ones are not on speaking terms, and who will be insulted if they don't get invited to Buck House.'

'Who's sleeping with whom,' corrected William. 'So, what's next?' he asked, looking down at item number two on the agenda.

'Disgruntled taxi drivers,' announced Jackie from the other end of the table.

'What's their problem?' asked William.

'They're not being allowed to operate on the official route to and from the Olympic Stadium, which they're not best pleased about.'

'And how do they propose to express their anger?' pressed William.

'Sixty of them intend to circle Hyde Park Corner during rush hour on the evening of the opening ceremony,' said Jackie, 'which will bring London to a standstill in a matter of minutes.'

'How can we stop that from happening?' asked William.

'Lift the restrictions and allow them to ply their trade on the Olympic route,' suggested Rebecca.

'I'll need to have a word with the mayor,' said William.

'He doesn't have the authority to override Transport for London,' Rebecca pointed out.

'Then I'll ask the Hawk to speak to the Home Secretary

and suggest he calls an emergency meeting,' said William, turning round and nodding to his secretary.

Angela continued writing furiously.

'So, what's next?' asked William, looking back down at the agenda.

'Ticket touts,' said Rebecca.

'They're harmless enough,' said William. 'Just lock them up overnight.'

'I wish it was that easy,' said Rebecca, 'but it's not the usual bunch of wide boys who will be out hoping to make a quick buck. These are a far more sophisticated group who are working the major hotels selling expensive hospitality packages that don't even exist.'

'Then arrest them.'

'They're fly,' came back Paul, 'and not that easy to catch.'

'Then how do you know about them?' demanded William.

Paul handed William one of the counterfeit tickets. 'The head porter at the Ritz bought a dozen tickets from one of them, hoping to make a return by selling them on to his guests, but when he checked them against a real ticket, he quickly realized they were forgeries and immediately got in touch with West End Central.'

'And if you want to hear the bad news,' said Rebecca, 'Bronze Crime tells us he thinks it could be Miles Faulkner who's behind the scam. He's got no evidence to prove it, as his only witness is now refusing to talk. However, he's pretty sure it's Faulkner. Apparently, he's charging five thousand pounds just to attend the opening ceremony.'

'Couldn't be better,' said William, taking them all by surprise. He turned to Jackie and asked, 'Do we still have a reserved block on the far side of the stadium that we're holding in case of an emergency?'

'Yes, sir,' came back Jackie. 'We got the idea from the match secretary at Wimbledon. They always keep a small stand empty to handle emergencies such as this.'

'How many seats does our stand hold?'

Jackie checked her notes. 'One hundred and forty,' she said.

'Will they have a good view of what's taking place on the track?'

'They will be on the back straight opposite the finishing line,' said Jackie, looking down at a stadium printout. 'But if we do that, sir, the only winner will be Miles Faulkner.'

'Not if we end up with one hundred and forty contented customers who were rescued at the last minute. And you can be sure that among them will be lawyers and politicians, who always make good witnesses whenever a case comes to court.'

'So this time Faulkner may have caused his own downfall,' said Paul.

'Not to mention having to pay a hefty fine when I let the judge know how much I think Faulkner made out of the scam.' William paused. 'I may be tempted to exaggerate.'

The team began to bang the table with the palms of their hands.

'So what's our next problem?' asked William, looking back down to his list.

'The Olympic torch relay,' said Paul, opening yet another file.

'Why?' demanded William.

'The torch will set out from Land's End first thing on Monday morning before making its way towards the capital.'

'Remind me what happens when the torch arrives in London?' was William's next question.

'The Mother Flame will spend the night in the Tower of

London before starting out on its journey around the capital,' said Jackie, 'ending up at the Olympic Stadium in plenty of time for the opening ceremony.'

'To be greeted by large crowds, no doubt,' said William.

'We are expecting the torch relay team to be met by a vast number of fans as it continues on its journey through the city,' said Paul, 'and we certainly don't have enough police officers to man the entire route should any of them turn out not to be fans.'

'I don't think it will be the crowds who cause the problem,' volunteered Paul.

'Then who?' demanded William.

'The Russians,' announced Paul, which caused William to remain unusually silent.

'The Home Office are reporting that an unusually large number of officials are attached to the Russian Olympic squad,' said Paul, 'and our Ambassador in Moscow has contacted the Foreign Office to inform them that President Putin is planning to make a major speech the day after the opening ceremony, so heaven knows what the Russians have planned for the next eleven days.'

'*Cry "Havoc!", and let slip the dogs of war.* No more than revenge for Margaret Thatcher trying to boycott the Moscow Games, so we must assume the worst and prepare accordingly.'

18 July 2012 – 9 days to go

ROSS COULDN'T BELIEVE HIS EYES as he watched Faulkner's Rolls come to a halt about a hundred yards from Tower Bridge. Not one of his usual destinations. Collins got out of the car, opened the boot and took out a folding bicycle.

END GAME

Then came the next surprise. Faulkner, dressed in a smart blue tracksuit, mounted the bicycle and began to pedal towards the bridge, where he joined a large group of younger cyclists.

Ross abandoned his taxi on a double yellow line, ran across to a row of Boris bikes, and unlocked one before making his way towards the back of the group as quickly as he could. He listened carefully to several conversations going on around him, and quickly discovered the group met fairly often at different points in the city, from where they would set off with a single purpose: to temporarily bring London's traffic to a halt, so the Mayor of London would have to take seriously their demands for more cycle lanes. In fact, one of the cyclists insisted that she wouldn't give up until London was one long cycle lane.

What Ross couldn't work out was why Faulkner had joined the group. After all, he wasn't an obvious candidate to support bicycle lanes. However, whatever Faulkner was up to, it was bound to mean trouble, so Ross was determined to keep him under close surveillance.

Just after six o'clock, their leader addressed his disciples. 'The chosen route this week,' he announced, 'will take us over Tower Bridge, past the Tower of London and then along the Embankment towards Westminster. When we reach the House of Commons, we will circle Parliament Square several times before returning along the other side of the Embankment, when we'll make our way back to Tower Bridge. Remember, we are not in a hurry, and you should slow down at every zebra crossing and occupy the whole road whenever you stop at a traffic light.' Without another word, he mounted his bike and pedalled slowly off, leading his band of warriors across Tower Bridge.

Ross remained tucked in at the back of the group, well out of sight of Faulkner, who was pedalling furiously just to keep up with the group leader. Ross would have liked to overhear their conversation.

It seemed to be an exchange of views that didn't take too long, because by the time the group reached the Embankment, Faulkner had fallen back, and when they came to a halt at the traffic lights opposite the Savoy, he took the slip road on the right, crossed the road, got off his bike and climbed back into the waiting Rolls. Ross waited, watching as Collins folded up the bike and placed it back in the boot.

What exactly was Faulkner up to? Ross couldn't understand why someone like him would be interested in building cycle lanes. He could only wonder what his real purpose was.

He hung back until the Rolls was out of sight, then began to pedal faster and faster, and by the time the group had reached Parliament Square, he'd caught up with their leader. Although Ross was out of breath, he began a stilted conversation.

'I saw you chatting to my friend,' was Ross's opening ploy.

'Your friend?' queried the group leader.

'The older guy on the folding bike, in the smart blue tracksuit.'

'Ah, yes,' said the leader. 'Told me he wouldn't be able to come next Friday, because he has seats for the opening ceremony of the Olympics, and in any case, he assumed we'd be banned from carrying out our usual Friday protest.'

'And will you?' asked Ross.

'Not a chance, I told him,' replied the leader. 'Not now the Law Lords have ruled that cyclists are not protesters, but a public procession.'

Having worked in traffic control for the past few years,

END GAME

Ross was well aware of the Law Lords' decision, and the hold-ups this group had caused over the past two years without the police being able to do anything about it.

'However,' the leader continued, 'your friend made a pretty interesting suggestion which, if we're able to pull it off, would make everyone aware of our cause.'

'What was his suggestion?' asked Ross.

The leader glanced across at Ross, a look of suspicion on his face. 'If he's your friend, why don't you ask him yourself?' He pedalled off.

Ross fell back and tried to work out what Faulkner could possibly have suggested, and, perhaps more importantly, *why* he had suggested anything to this group. He must have some ulterior motive. However, even though he pedalled slowly and kept his ears open, Ross was none the wiser by the time they got back to Tower Bridge.

When the group came to a halt on the far side of the bridge, the leader declared, 'Job done.' He then got off his bike and addressed his followers once again. 'I look forward to seeing you all next week. In fact, a week on Friday, I'm hoping for a record turnout, as the Olympics will give us a chance to bring our cause to the attention of a far wider public. Details of the different starting points will be emailed to each member of the group during the week.' He paused, and as he did so, his eyes ran over the crowd. 'Remember, not a word about this to anyone, as it could harm our cause.'

Ross didn't like the words 'different starting points', nor the emphasis on secrecy. The cyclists were planning something big, and whatever it was, Faulkner had planted the seed in their leader's mind. The real question was: *where and why?*

When Ross arrived home later that evening, he didn't discuss the problem with Alice. However, during supper, his mind kept returning to Faulkner and what idea he could have suggested to the team leader.

He was no nearer to finding an answer by the time Alice turned off the bedroom light. Ross didn't toss and turn, because he hardly slept.

He rose early, skipped his morning run and drove his taxi back to Tower Bridge before first light.

When Ross reached the far side of the bridge, he spotted a large arrow with the words 'Olympic Stadium' printed on it. He swung right and not left. His first thought was: are they going to try to disrupt the traffic heading towards the stadium, causing thousands of spectators to be late for the opening ceremony, possibly even holding it up?

He'd only driven another couple of miles before he worked out exactly what Faulkner must have suggested. He pulled into a petrol station, parked to one side, and made a telephone call.

When a familiar voice came on the line, all he said was, 'I need to see you urgently, and I mean urgently.'

'Where are you?' asked William.

'Parked in the large BP garage about a mile from the stadium.'

'I'll come to you,' said William. 'Stay put and I should be with you in about ten minutes, fifteen at the most.'

It was another twenty minutes before William turned up. His driver, Danny, pulled into the petrol station and parked the car behind the taxi.

Ross jumped out and joined William in the back seat. He didn't waste any time before reporting the details of his unscheduled bicycle ride and the conclusion he had come to.

'But what I want to know,' said William, 'is what does Faulkner stand to gain from all this?'

'I think Beth was right all along: a rare Van Gogh masterpiece.'

William still wasn't convinced. 'Let us assume for a moment that Faulkner is working with the Russians,' he said. 'They will expect far more in exchange for a priceless Van Gogh than simply stopping a few spectators from being on time for the opening ceremony.'

'To embarrass Britain? Make us look like a bunch of amateurs?'

William was still frowning. 'There has to be more to it than that,' he said. 'There's something bigger going on that we have to find out about, and prevent.'

'Now we know what the innocent cyclists have in mind, we'll have to stop them in their tracks.'

William nodded. 'All right. Cyclists will have to be the first item on tomorrow's agenda,' he agreed, 'and you may as well join us, as everyone in the team has already worked out why you're no longer attached to traffic control. But before then,' he added, 'will I see you at the exhibition opening tonight?'

'Wouldn't miss it for the world,' replied Ross. 'And not only because I will be following Miles Faulkner all the way there.'

CHAPTER 9

19 July 2012 – 8 days to go

THERE WAS JUST ONE HOUR to go until the opening of *The Hermitage Comes to the Fitzmolean* exhibition, and Christina was staring at the packed rails of her three wardrobes.

'I don't know what to wear,' she said.

'That's because you're spoilt for choice,' suggested Wilbur, as she turned around and straightened his bow tie.

'Do you think Miles will turn up?' she asked. 'Beth and I rather suspect that he has designs on a particular Van Gogh painting that the Hermitage have lent us.'

'Well, I'm sure he won't be able to resist making an appearance,' replied Wilbur, as she pulled a dress out of the second wardrobe.

Christina held it up for Wilbur to consider. 'I think I'll settle on this one.'

'Why not?' said Wilbur. 'It's the one you selected half an hour ago.'

'Men are so lucky. After all, a dinner jacket's a dinner jacket.' Christina removed a stray white hair from her husband's velvet collar.

'Are you speaking tonight?' he asked.

'No, it's Beth's turn.' Christina sighed. 'Strange to think there won't be many more nights like this. Well, at least not while I'm chairman.'

'Are the board any nearer to selecting your successor?' asked Wilbur, as he walked towards the door.

'There are three candidates on the shortlist,' said Christina, 'but I took your advice and have not offered an opinion.'

'It will be important for Beth to remain in place while a new chairman settles in,' said Wilbur. 'Any large organization requires continuity and stability. But for now, we can't afford to be late. Remember, it will be you who's expected to introduce the guests to the Russian Ambassador.'

'What do I say if Miles is standing in line waiting to be introduced?'

'You've told me several times that Miles never stands in lines,' said Wilbur.

'But if he breaks the habit of a lifetime?'

'Your Excellency, may I introduce my ex-husband? He's a charlatan and a thief, whose only virtue is that he loves art, so if anything goes missing, call me, because I'll be able to tell you where to find it.'

'I do adore you, Mr Hackensack the Third,' said Christina, as they left the house.

• • •

'Let me begin,' said Beth, as she looked down at the packed audience, 'by welcoming you all to the opening of *The*

Hermitage Comes to the Fitzmolean, an exhibition of one hundred and twenty-seven Dutch paintings, watercolours and drawings that have been generously loaned to the Fitzmolean by the Hermitage, one of the most prestigious galleries on earth.'

The applause that followed suggested the guests agreed with the director's assessment. The room was packed with eager art-lovers, sponsors, diplomats and staff who had come to view the unique collection.

'My particular thanks go to Elena Petrovski, the museum's distinguished director,' continued Beth, 'and her two colleagues, who have honoured the Fitzmolean by joining us in London this evening.'

Miles Faulkner, with Booth Watson close at hand, was standing near the back of the crowded room, listening intently. Miles looked around the assembled gathering, stopping only when his eyes settled on two Russians on the far side of the gallery, one of whom he recognized immediately, although he didn't acknowledge him. As far as most people in the room were concerned, he had never laid eyes on Sergei Petrov before. The other had a shy, academic air, and Miles suspected she must be part of the official Hermitage team.

'I do hope you will all enjoy this remarkable exhibition,' continued Beth. 'However, on this occasion, I shall not be ending my speech with the words, "please spread the word, as there are still a few tickets available", because on this, the opening day of the exhibition, I'm able to announce that the show is already sold out for its entire Olympic run. To quote the art critic at *The Times*, it's a "gold medal performance".'

Beth was greeted by even louder applause as she stepped down from the stage to join her family and friends.

'I'm so proud of you,' said Christina, 'and as chair of the

Fitz, I think I can safely say this is the finest exhibition the museum has ever put on.'

'But if I remember correctly,' teased Beth, 'those were the exact words you said about our last exhibition.'

The little group surrounding the director burst out laughing. They all knew that, with Beth as director of the museum, her feet firmly on the ground, and Christina as chair, full of ideas and endless enthusiasm, the Fitzmolean was in safe hands. They had proved to be a formidable partnership. Wilbur, too, more than played his part by constantly supporting his wife.

William looked on proudly, although Beth could tell his mind was elsewhere. She knew it had been difficult for him to attend tonight. He had been working all hours of the day, and recently the night, as he prepared for the opening ceremony.

'I couldn't help noticing,' remarked Sir Julian, 'that Miles Faulkner and his lapdog are in attendance this evening.'

Beth turned to her father-in-law. 'To be fair,' she said, 'however much I detest the man, no one can question Miles Faulkner's genuine passion for art, and particularly the Dutch school. If he were willing to loan us his fabled collection for our next exhibition, Christina would be able to repeat her words with the same conviction.'

'I can't see Miles agreeing to that,' said Christina, as she glanced across the room at her ex-husband. 'And take a look, Beth,' she added under her breath, 'he's still staring at the Van Gogh self-portrait, as if it were the only picture in the room.'

· · ·

'I have a feeling they're talking about you,' said Booth Watson, offering Commander Warwick a false smile.

'In the words of Oscar Wilde,' said Miles, 'it's better than not being talked about.'

'And look where that got him,' said Booth Watson. He immediately regretted his words, but fortunately Miles seemed more interested in the Van Gogh.

'It's quite magnificent,' admitted Booth Watson, before taking a quick photograph of the masterpiece for his records.

'When you next see it,' said Miles, keeping his voice low, 'it will be hanging above the fireplace in my drawing room.'

'That's assuming the Russians keep their word,' said Booth Watson. 'Not something they're renowned for.'

'They have no choice,' replied Miles, 'unless they want the whole world to know what they have planned.'

'And what *do* they have planned?' asked Booth Watson, who once again felt he'd been left in the dark.

Miles hesitated. 'Petrov has finally revealed some details of Operation Blackout,' he said quietly. 'Commander Warwick will be praying, long before the opening ceremony is over: "let there be light".'

'"And there was light",' said Booth Watson, delivering the next line from Genesis.

'I had Exodus in mind,' replied Miles.

• • •

'What are you looking at,' asked Alice, 'because it's certainly not the pictures?'

Jack had been left at home with a babysitter, while Alice, Ross and Jojo had come to support Beth. Jojo had just graduated from the Slade and was moving slowly from painting to painting, wondering if one day she could earn her living as . . .

Meanwhile, Ross was taking an interest in the two Russians standing at the back of the crowd. They didn't chat, but then they had nothing in common. The woman was clearly an art expert, one of the Hermitage's team. As for her colleague – Ross immediately recognized him as the man who'd gone to his first cricket match at the Oval and was now probably attending his first art exhibition. The GRU didn't bother with mood music.

'I was admiring the Van Gogh,' claimed Ross, turning his attention back to the self-portrait, while giving his wife a warm smile.

'Then you were facing in the wrong direction, Sergeant Hogan,' said Alice, 'so I won't bother asking you a second time.'

Ross smiled as he continued to keep an eye on first Faulkner and then the Russian. They never once spoke to each other.

• • •

'I have to leave you, I'm afraid,' said William, as he bent down to kiss his wife. 'Only eight days to go to my opening, though I could do with another month. But congratulations, my darling. It couldn't have gone better.'

'Just as your opening will,' said Beth. 'In fact, it's certain to be even more of a triumph.'

But William barely heard her words, as he'd already turned to leave.

'I can't wait for the closing ceremony,' Beth admitted to Christina and Julian, 'after which I'm hoping to finally be reunited with my husband. This year has been interminable. But once the Olympics are over, William's handing over the responsibility for the Paralympics to Detective Inspector Adaja, when we'll be going on holiday.'

'To some far-off exotic land, I hope?' said Christina.

'Amsterdam to Budapest, via Vienna,' replied Beth.

'How lovely,' said Sir Julian, before adding, 'Have you noticed that Faulkner's showing a great deal of interest in one particular painting?'

'Oh, we've all noticed,' replied Beth. 'The Van Gogh self-portrait that was surprisingly added to our list of exhibits at the last moment.'

'Was it indeed?' mused Sir Julian. 'I've seen the picture somewhere before, but I can't remember where.'

'Above the fireplace in the Russian Embassy, perhaps?'

'Of course,' said Sir Julian, staring at his old adversary, 'So, I'm bound to ask, why did Booth Watson take a photograph of that particular painting?'

'You're as bad as William,' said Beth.

'No, my dear,' said Sir Julian, 'I think you'll find William is as bad as me.'

'Faulkner and Booth Watson are leaving,' whispered Christina, not taking her eyes off them.

Just after they had left the room, a voice behind them said, 'Congratulations. A true triumph.'

Beth swung round to see the former chairman of the Fitzmolean, who bowed respectfully.

'Praise indeed,' said Beth, smiling at her old boss.

'No more than you deserve,' said Sir Nigel. 'And to think we tried to host the Hermitage's collection years ago, and it's only your persistence and hard work that has brought it to reality.'

'With some help from the Olympic Games,' remarked Beth. She only hoped there was no other reason she didn't know about.

CHAPTER 10

Friday 20 July 2012 – 7 days to go

WHEN THE TEAM GATHERED for their morning briefing, no one seemed surprised to see Ross sitting in his old place at the far end of the table. They were all well aware that it could only be a matter of time before he officially returned to the fold.

'I'll let Sergeant Hogan address the first item on the agenda,' said William.

Ross took his time taking them through what he'd witnessed when he joined the mass of protesting cyclists on their slow journey from Tower Bridge to Westminster.

'It's not difficult to work out what their chosen route will be next Friday,' suggested William, 'which just happens to be the evening of the opening ceremony.'

'When they could hold up as many as half the spectators on their way to the stadium,' said Paul, 'who won't arrive in time to see the Queen take her place in the Royal Box.'

'You're halfway there,' said Ross.

'So what's the other half?' asked Rebecca.

'The Queen won't even make it to the Royal Box.'

'Hold on,' said Jackie. 'What are we talking about here – an inconvenient hold-up or a royal assassination attempt?'

Rebecca was shaking her head. 'That would never happen. The cyclists may be a nuisance, but they're not terrorists.'

'Let's hope you're right,' said Ross, 'but while Faulkner's involved, I'm assuming the worst and only hope I'm proved wrong.'

'Has MI5 been fully briefed?' asked Jackie.

William nodded. 'As has GCHQ. They understand our fears, but reminded us how sketchy our evidence is at the moment. They're keeping a close eye on developments, but if anything were to go wrong during the Games, it would be our responsibility. At present,' he added, 'we are not anxious about Her Majesty's safety. What does concern us is the possible disruption to the opening ceremony – and why any disruption would be welcomed by the Russians. We have no idea what else they might be planning on the back of it, but if we have to deal with the unexpected on the night, we need to know what they have planned next, so we're not on the back foot.'

After a moment's silence, Jackie said, 'But the Queen is always accompanied by a group of highly trained outriders, who make sure everyone moves aside so the royal party can carry on without ever having to stop.'

'Perhaps a well organized bunch of determined cyclists won't be moving aside,' suggested Ross.

'There are five routes Her Majesty can take on her journey from the palace to the stadium,' said Paul, looking down at the map spread out on the centre of the table.

'That all end up in the same tunnel,' added William, which stopped any more interruptions.

'The cyclists would not only slow the traffic down,' continued Ross, 'but if they can reach the tunnel before the Queen, they could then abandon their bikes and leave them in the middle of the road. It would take us hours to remove them, while HM would be stuck waving in the back of her car and not sitting in the front of the Royal Box.'

'While we,' added William, 'become fully occupied and they – and by they, I mean the Russians – move on to the second part of their plan, whatever that might be.'

'Turning the opening ceremony into the closing ceremony would be my bet,' said Paul.

No one laughed.

'Then we'll just have to ban any protests planned on the day of the opening ceremony,' said William.

'You will recall, sir,' said Rebecca, 'that the Law Lords ruled cyclists are not protesters, but a public procession.'

'Then we'll have to arrest every one of them before they become a public procession.'

'I don't think you have the authority to do that, sir,' said Jackie.

'Then I'll serve them with a Section Twelve notice,' said William, becoming more irritated.

'But Section Twelve is only used in case of riots,' Rebecca reminded him.

'Or serious disruption to the life of the community,' William countered.

'If we start arresting innocent members of the public,' Paul said firmly, 'they'll certainly take us to court, and win.'

'Which, I would suggest,' said William, 'is preferable to having a half-empty stadium with the Queen stuck in an underpass – or worse.'

No further objection was voiced before they moved on to the next item on the agenda: the upcoming arrival of the Olympic torch in London.

21 July 2012 – 6 days to go

WHEN THE TORCH-BEARER ENTERED Greater London for the first time, Ross was more than ready to take over from his country colleagues. He was relieved that the torch relay had so far gone without a major incident, despite large crowds lining the routes right across the country. Still, he wouldn't relax until the torch had finally reached the stadium.

Ross had kept up his running schedule of four miles a day, as well as spending an hour at his local gym pumping weights. This would be his Olympic final.

During the last few sections of the relay, the members of the dedicated Torch Relay team had remained at a discreet distance surrounding each torch-bearer, looking for the slightest suggestion of trouble or anything suspicious. If such a situation arose, Ross knew he would have to make an instant decision, as there would be no time to consult anyone.

A thousand carefully selected torch-bearers would wind their way through three hundred miles of the sprawling metropolis until they handed the 'Mother Flame' over to seven young athletes chosen by seven former gold medallists. The next generation would then light the two hundred and four petals, representing two hundred and four competing nations, that would continue to burn until the Games ended and the torch was passed on to the Mayor of Rio de Janeiro.

It might look like a lot of pomp and circumstance on the surface, but Ross understood the real significance of such ceremonies. The torch was the symbol of the Olympics, and the Olympics were an occasion when the world came together in peace and friendly competition, not in war and conflict. This simple flickering flame represented a great deal to so many people in troubled times.

Ross waited impatiently until he could hear cheering, just a distant rumble to begin with, then a roar that grew louder and louder long before the torch-bearer came into sight. A local traffic warden was greeted with as many jeers as cheers as he lit the torch of a waiting NHS nurse, who was welcomed with thunderous applause as the flame was passed over and she set off on the next lap.

The atmosphere was intense, and Ross was reminded once again of the weight William and his team had carried on their shoulders for the past seven years. This excited, eager crowd of onlookers were the people who would feel let down if anything were to go wrong.

Ross, accompanied by the Torch Relay team, eyes darting in every direction, remained a few yards behind, just in case anyone decided to join the relay uninvited. Few of the crowd would have noticed the minders, as their eyes were fixed on the torch and its latest bearer. Ross continually scanned the crowd on both sides of the road, looking for the one person he didn't doubt had plans to disrupt the progress of the torch.

Six police motorcyclists and an ambulance hovered a further hundred yards behind Ross and his team of runners, along with an armed car containing the 'Mother Flame', protected by four armed officers, bringing up the rear.

When the nurse came to the end of her leg, she lit the flame of a torch carried by an elderly gentleman who had taken part in the 1948 Olympics. The crowd cheered the octogenarian every step of the way, Ross jogging a few yards behind. The old man managed about a quarter of a mile before he passed the flame over to a local postman, suitably dressed for the occasion, an empty postbag over one shoulder and the torch in his hand. Ross could tell that the torch-bearers were enjoying every moment of the experience, and expected that each torch would remain a family heirloom to be passed down from generation to generation.

Ross had to lengthen his stride, as the next recipient was captain of his local Hare and Hounds cross-country club, every bit as fit as Ross – and ten years younger. He might have got away if he hadn't had to hold the torch aloft for all to see, which slowed him down.

Ross increased his pace when he saw the next runner coming into sight, a local fireman suitably dressed for the occasion, holding a large red bucket in one hand and his unlit torch in the other. Ross recognized him immediately.

When Ross saw that the bucket was full of water, he quickly cut down the distance between himself and the fireman.

The waiting runner placed his bucket on the ground, causing a few drops of water to spill out onto the road. As the captain of the cross-country club approached the fireman, he held up his torch so that the flame could be passed from one carrier to the next without delay.

Once it was lit, the fireman held his torch aloft, for all to see – and that was when Ross knew for certain what was about to happen.

As the fireman began to lower his torch slowly towards the bucket of water, Ross charged across the road and aimed a sharp kick at the bucket, sending it flying, water spilling out onto the pavement, just moments before the eternal flame would have been extinguished. He grabbed the fireman and thrust an arm behind his back.

The crowd around them gasped, and the excitement of

moments before fell to an eerie silence, broken only by the fireman's cries of, 'Let go of me!'

Ross ignored him, handing the still-lit torch over to the captain of the cross-country club, who was jogging on the spot, looking as bemused as the crowd around them. 'Go and don't stop running until you reach the next torch-bearer. Go!' he repeated loudly.

The man obeyed the order just as two of the young police runners joined Ross. Together, they bundled the fireman into the back of a police van before he had any chance of escaping into the crowd.

Ross could only imagine the headlines that would have hit the world's newspapers in the morning had the fireman succeeded in putting out the eternal flame. But Ross had a feeling this was only a taster before the main event . . .

• • •

'I know my rights,' said the fireman.

'I feel sure you do,' said Ross, as the car came to a halt outside Greenwich police station. The two young officers hauled Timpson out of the back seat and escorted him into the nick.

'I have the right to call my lawyer,' the prisoner reminded them, sounding as if he'd been well briefed.

'All in good time,' said Ross, as he showed the desk sergeant his warrant card.

'I'm not saying nothin' until I've spoken to my lawyer,' said Timpson, a little more loudly.

The desk sergeant nodded and pointed to a telephone booth on the far wall.

Timpson walked quickly across to the phone, picked up

the receiver and dialled the number he'd been given. As it began to ring, he looked around to check no one could overhear him. The policeman who'd nearly broken his arm was talking to the desk sergeant.

'What have you arrested him for?' asked the desk sergeant, as he started tapping on his computer.

'I haven't got anything that would stand up in court,' admitted Ross. 'Only wish I could hear the conversation that's taking place behind me.' He didn't look back.

'Can't help you with that one,' said the desk sergeant, 'as you well know.'

'But you *are* able to trace the number he's calling,' Ross reminded him.

'Yes. The supervisor will give you the number, but nothing more,' said the desk sergeant, as Timpson put down the phone. 'So what do you want me to do with him?'

'Put him in an interview room with an officer present. Let him cool his heels for about an hour and then release him with a caution, but don't charge him.'

'Understood,' said the desk sergeant. He placed the charge sheet back under the counter, then nodded to one of the constables, who led the prisoner away.

Ross waited until Timpson had disappeared down the stairs before he walked across to the phone and asked to be put through to the supervisor. A few moments later, another voice came on the line. He told her his name, rank and number.

She asked him to hold on.

It was some time before she came back on the line, but then Ross accepted that she would be double-checking. At last, she enquired, 'How can I help you, Sergeant Hogan?'

'I need to know the last number that was dialled from this phone,' said Ross.

Another shorter wait before the supervisor revealed the number.

'Thank you,' said Ross, before replacing the phone. He picked it back up again and began to dial.

A few moments later, a voice said, 'Mr Booth Watson's chambers. How can I help you?'

Ross put down the phone.

• • •

'Bring me up to speed,' said the Hawk, as he looked across the table at William and Ross.

'We know Faulkner was involved in the torch relay incident,' said Ross, 'and we also know he's encouraged a group of well-organized cyclists to disrupt the opening ceremony to highlight their cause.'

'However, what we suspect but can't prove,' added William, 'is that he's not working alone.' He paused. 'We fear he could be carrying out direct orders from the Russian secret service.'

'Evidence?' snapped the Hawk.

Ross spelled out in detail what he'd witnessed at the Oval cricket ground only a few weeks before.

'But why the Russians?' asked the Hawk.

'After Margaret Thatcher tried to ban our athletes from attending the Games in Moscow in 1980, it might quite simply be revenge,' said William. 'However, I've no doubt there will be other forces at work. Don't forget, the Olympics will be on every back page for the next month – perhaps they'd like to move it to the front page, for all the wrong reasons. Nothing would please them more than to see the British humiliated on the world stage.'

'And there are no prizes for guessing on whose shoulders the blame would be placed, which wouldn't please just the Russians, but Faulkner as well,' added Ross.

'So it will be our job to "prevent and protect", without the public ever finding out what they're up to,' suggested the Hawk. 'A police officer's worst nightmare.'

'Do you want me to go on tailing Faulkner, or should I try to track down the Russian I saw him sitting next to at the Oval?' asked Ross.

'Faulkner,' said William without hesitation. 'The Russian won't raise his head above the parapet while his collaborator can take the blame. But at the same time, we'll stay in touch with MI5, who keep constant surveillance on the Russian Embassy. I'll also contact Professor Meredith at GCHQ to see if he can shed any light on what they might have planned.'

'But what's in it for Faulkner?' asked the Hawk. 'Because he certainly doesn't need the money.'

'A Van Gogh,' suggested William, 'that even his money can't buy.'

CHAPTER 11

25 July 2012 – 2 days to go

'WHAT A PLEASANT SURPRISE,' said Beth, as William strolled into the kitchen. 'To what do we owe this honour, Commander, dare I ask?'

'To a very brief gap in my schedule,' said William, as he took a seat opposite the twins. 'Robert not with you?' he asked Artemisia.

'Visiting the constituency,' she replied, 'so I thought I'd keep mum company.'

'Strange really,' said Beth, turning from the oven, 'that you technically live here and Artemisia doesn't, and yet I see a lot more of my daughter nowadays than my husband.'

William couldn't come up with a suitable reply.

'How long do we have you for?' asked Beth.

'Not long,' admitted William. 'The dress rehearsal for the opening ceremony won't begin until midnight, but I'll be expected back long before the curtain rises.'

'Why midnight?' asked Peter, as his mother placed a chicken salad on the centre of the table, hoping there was enough spare to also feed the unexpected visitor.

'It's our best hope of keeping the big surprise under wraps,' said William, 'while making sure the details don't leak before the first editions come out in the morning.'

Artemisia turned towards her father and gave him a warm smile. 'I don't suppose you'd be willing to tell me what that big surprise is?'

'Not a hope while you're working for the *Daily Mail*.'

'I'm just a cub reporter,' said Artemisia, 'and only while the Games are taking place. However, the editor *has* hinted that if I were to come up with an exclusive, this cub just might be invited to join the pack.'

'I can't help you there,' William repeated, as he helped himself to some salad.

'I'm taking Arte, Jojo, Robert and Grandpops to the opening ceremony on Friday,' said Peter. 'Although I'm not going to tell you how I got hold of five tickets.'

'No mean feat,' admitted William. 'At least ten people have applied for every available seat, and they're now trading on the black market for over five thousand pounds apiece.'

'While you, no doubt, will be sitting in the Royal Box living it up,' said Beth.

'If only,' said William. 'No, I'll be stuck in the Gold Suite below ground with only the television screens to keep me company. All of them zooming in on the spectators, not the participants, in case there's any trouble.'

Artemisia looked up and tried a second time. 'What kind of trouble are you expecting?'

'If I knew the answer to that,' said William, avoiding the question, 'there wouldn't be any trouble.'

'Can I visit you in the Gold Suite?' asked Artemisia, giving her father an even bigger smile.

'Good try,' said William, 'but the answer is still no.' William took a bite of chicken before he added, 'So what have you been up to, Peter?' hoping to silence his persistent daughter.

'I can't go into any detail,' said Peter solemnly. 'Not while there's a member of press present.'

William and Beth burst out laughing.

'Peter's off to Woolwich Crown Court in the morning,' said Artemisia. 'He's appearing in a case for the Crown, as a junior – very junior.'

'What's the case?' asked William.

'Trying to make sure that some two-bit ticket tout isn't granted bail,' said Artemisia. 'A story that wouldn't usually make page fourteen below the fold on a slow day.'

'So that's how you got the tickets?' queried William.

'I can't break client privilege,' said Peter, with a smirk.

William gave up, and turning to his daughter asked, 'How's Robert doing?'

'Working as hard as ever,' Artemisia replied. 'Doing his best to climb the greasy pole.'

'A journalist, a lawyer and a politician in the family. What have I done to deserve that?' asked William, who was eyeing a chicken leg. He turned to Beth. 'So how's the Hermitage exhibition going?'

'Not a spare ticket available,' Beth replied. 'In fact, the demand has been so high we've had to add some extra evening sessions, which won't harm our bank balance. However, I do have something to report that might just be of interest to an astute detective.'

William put down his knife and fork.

Peter grabbed the chicken leg.

'Christina spotted her ex-husband having tea in the museum's café with a member of the Hermitage team.'

'A man or a woman?' asked William, although he was fairly certain he knew the answer.

'A man,' replied Beth.

William nodded, but didn't comment, while his daughter's ears pricked up.

'After Faulkner's continued interest in the Van Gogh self-portrait, I find that rather interesting,' said Beth. 'I don't suppose you're in a position to tell me what this is all about?'

'Not yet,' William replied.

Artemisia had been listening carefully to every word of the exchange and was about to ask her father another question, when he stood up and said, 'Sorry to leave you, but I can't afford to be late for the opening number.'

Artemisia would have liked to know what the opening number was, but didn't bother to ask.

Beth checked her watch. 'But it's still another three hours before the curtain goes up.'

'And no prizes for guessing who has to be standing in the wings long before the stagehands wheel on the props,' said William.

'And what props would those be?' asked Artemisia, still not giving up.

William didn't bother to respond.

'What time can we expect you home tonight?' asked Beth.

'I won't be coming home tonight,' replied William, 'or any night for the next fortnight. I've already set up a camp bed in the Gold Suite, but don't worry, there's a coffee machine in the next room.'

'If you were to come home,' said Beth, 'you could at least have one decent meal a day.'

'Not a chance,' said William. 'I just can't risk being away from the stadium for more than a couple of hours at a time. If there was a major emergency, you could be sure I'd be stuck in a traffic jam halfway between Fulham and the Olympic Park.'

'In that case, Commander,' said Beth, 'don't forget to introduce yourself when we next meet.'

William took his wife in his arms and kissed her gently.

'You two are just soppy,' said Artemisia, turning away.

'If you and Robert are as soppy as your mother and me after twenty-five years,' said William, as he hugged his daughter, 'you can count yourself lucky.'

THE OPENING CEREMONY

Let there be Light

CHAPTER 12

Friday, 27 July 2012

ON THE EVENING OF THE OPENING CEREMONY, William had ten thousand trained police and the same number of military personnel to assist with security at all the Olympic venues around the country. With the help of seventy thousand enthusiastic volunteers, he felt he was well prepared and ready for the arrival of ten thousand athletes from around the world, until the Hawk reminded him, 'You can't prepare for the unexpected.'

Nor could he push the thought of Miles Faulkner from his mind. Whatever he and the Russians were up to, it could only mean trouble. If the cyclists were a distraction, the obvious question was: from what? He would have to be on his guard until midnight – and then every waking moment of the next two weeks.

The Gold Suite, his home for the next fortnight, was a large, windowless dungeon directly beneath the stadium. One wall held a bank of CCTV screens. Below them was William's desk with three phones, a computer, two radios, and several in-trays – everything he needed to coordinate his small empire.

William glanced up at the CCTV screens to see uniformed officers, several with search dogs, carefully checking the stadium. Only when they had scoured every inch would he give the all-clear and allow the public to enter the arena.

William's mobile phone began to ring. 'Paul?' he said, as he picked it up.

'We had a call from a phone box in Dublin this morning,' said Paul, 'a tip-off about a potential IRA threat. We were told to look out for a black van coming off the 13.45 ferry at Holyhead, but the caller hung up before telling us who they were or what they might have planned. And before you ask, I've already spoken to the local police. They've identified a black van that came off that ferry, with two people in front, and heaven knows how many in the back, and it's heading south.'

'Could be a ten-pence terrorist who made the call,' said William, 'or a genuine tip-off. Either way, we can't take the risk. Get someone to pull the van over if it enters the Greater London area and check it out.'

He put down one phone just as another rang.

'Security have given me the all-clear, Commander,' said the stadium manager. 'Can I open the gates and let the public in?'

'Yes,' said William. He switched his attention from one CCTV screen to another to watch a steady stream of early spectators making their way through the turnstiles, before going in search of their seats.

Two phones rang at once. He picked them both up.

'Some good news, sir,' said Jackie. 'The taxi drivers have called off their protest and traffic is almost back to normal.'

Before William could feel relieved, the voice on the other line added, 'Not completely back to normal. I've got a rogue cabbie who's blocking the south side of Tower Bridge and holding up a line of vehicles as far as the eye can see, and he's refusing to budge.'

'Then deal with it, Sergeant,' said William, as yet another phone began to ring.

William had a feeling it was going to be a very long night. Still, if rogue cabbies were the worst he had to deal with, he'd count himself lucky – but then he thought about Miles Faulkner, and looked back up at the screens.

• • •

The sergeant switched off his radio and approached the taxi driver, hoping he could defuse the situation. 'Your mates have called off the protest and gone back to work,' he said calmly.

The cabbie ignored him.

'You're blocking one of the main routes to the stadium, mate, and causing an almighty traffic jam, so I'll have to ask you once again, will you please move your vehicle.'

The cabbie gave him a warm smile, removed the keys from his cab, and with an exaggerated sweep of an arm, tossed them into the Thames. 'Why don't you move it yourself, mate?' he said.

The young sergeant took a pace forward, intending to arrest the man, but the cab driver dodged to one side, jumped up onto the railing of the bridge and stared down into the flowing river below him.

'I don't think that would be wise, sir,' said the sergeant, trying to remain calm.

'Possibly not,' said the cabbie, 'but it will be you who's left to explain to your superiors why the stadium's half empty, not me.'

The sergeant advanced another pace, and the cabbie gave him an even bigger smile before he jumped into the river.

The policeman ran to the edge of the railing, leant over and watched as the cabbie disappeared below the water. A Marine Policing Unit boat reached him just as he came up for the third time.

'That was lucky,' said a gawper who was hanging over the bridge. The sergeant didn't bother to tell him that the river police had been out in full force patrolling the Thames since dawn, checking for any security threats and possible holdups to the opening ceremony.

Another voice came over the radio. 'What shall I do with him, Sarge?' a young constable asked, as he clung onto a soaking, shivering man.

'Take him to the nearest hospital and tell them exactly what happened,' replied the sergeant. 'I'm not altogether convinced the poor devil jumped because of a cabbie protest, so let's be thankful he's still alive.'

He turned around to face his officers and made a decision. With the keys at the bottom of the Thames, they'd simply have to push the cab up onto the pavement and leave it there.

• • •

Miles Faulkner and Booth Watson made their way to an executive box that normally held four – but then sharing, particularly with strangers, was another of Miles's no-nos. Looking around, they could see the stadium filling: thousands of people making their way to their seats. The noise of excited chatter growing by the minute.

Miles's mobile rang.

'The cyclists are ready for the off,' said Collins. 'Far more have turned up than last week. When the leader told them what he had in mind, some left, but those who remained look even more determined.'

'How many?' said Miles.

'At least thirty at this location,' replied Collins, 'possibly more.'

'More than enough,' was all Miles had to say, before he ended the conversation and turned his attention to Booth Watson. 'It's a shame I won't be able to join Warwick in the Gold Suite to see the smile wiped off his face.'

Booth Watson shifted uncomfortably in his seat, 'I wonder how many people you sold fake tickets to are now protesting to the police?' he said.

Miles shrugged. 'Who gives a damn? Warwick will start the evening unpopular with a small group of people who didn't get to see the ceremony, and by the end of the evening he'll be unpopular with all those who did.'

'Regarding those tickets, the CPS have been in touch again,' said Booth Watson. 'Another witness has come forward and named you as the mastermind behind the operation. I'm going to have to prepare your defence carefully if you're not to be locked up again.'

'I've never met this witness, whoever they are,' said Miles confidently, 'so there isn't going to be a trial.'

'I can't see the CPS backing down quite so easily this time,' said Booth Watson.

'They won't have any choice,' said Miles, 'as I will have left the country long before Commander Warwick tries to arrest me. After all, once tonight is over, he'll be far too busy explaining how he could possibly have allowed such a disaster to happen.'

'But when you come back . . .' began Booth Watson.

'I won't be coming back, BW. This is my last job. Once the Games are over, I'll be retiring to my home in Southampton – and not the Southampton in England.'

'But what about the Van Gogh?'

'If I recall your agreement with Mikailov,' said Faulkner, 'the painting will be collected by you so your last job will be to deliver it to me in the states, and when you get back home, you'll find a million waiting for you in a Swiss bank account.'

• • •

Following a lavish reception at Buckingham Palace, all the ambassadors to the Court of St James, including Anatoly Mikailov and Wei Ming, were escorted to luxury coaches which would take them directly to the opening ceremony.

'Let there be light,' whispered Wei Ming, as the coach finally pulled up outside the Olympic Stadium.

'But only until ten past nine,' replied the Russian Ambassador.

'I'm confident it will be your "finest hour", to quote Churchill,' responded the Chinese Ambassador, 'and you will return to Moscow in triumph, before taking up your new appointment as your country's Ambassador to Washington.'

'But only if Operation Blackout is a total success,' said Mikailov.

'Look on the bright side,' said Wei Ming.

'Let's hope not,' replied Mikailov.

• • •

'Great seats, Peter,' said Artemisia, as she and Robert took their places in the lower stand on the home straight. 'Are you finally going to admit how you got hold of them, now that Dad's not here?'

'*I* can reveal,' said her grandfather. 'It was from a ticket tout he was defending at Bromley Crown Court.'

'In exchange for waiving my fee,' sighed Peter, 'but at least I got him off.'

'I'm not altogether sure about the ethics of that transaction,' said Julian.

'Even my Member of Parliament couldn't get a ticket,' said Robert.

Julian gave in. 'So why don't we sit back and soak in the atmosphere, because the curtain won't be going up for some time, and I doubt if you'll see another Olympic Games in London in your lifetime.'

'Speak for yourself, Grandpops,' said Peter.

Sir Julian was about to tick him off when he remembered they were no longer in chambers.

They all looked down on the largest stage in the world. For now, it remained in darkness, waiting to reveal its myriad surprises to the world. The crowd was growing by the minute, every seat and box busy with chatter and excitement.

As Julian looked around, he became aware that several young men, and some not so young, were taking more than a passing interest in Jojo. She feigned not to notice.

'I think I'll just go and get something to drink,' Jojo announced, as she rose from her place and made her way slowly along the packed row before walking up the steps to the nearest exit.

• • •

When two phones started ringing at once, William picked up both at the same time. 'Which one of you has the more urgent problem?' he asked.

'Me,' said Paul. 'We've lost the van. A local officer followed what they thought was the vehicle, but when they pulled it over, there was only one occupant, and it was full of groceries. Meaning the vehicle the call was really about may still be on its way to London. They must have swapped number plates before coming off the motorway.'

William cursed. 'And the latest your end, Ross?'

'We've located five different groups of cyclists all waiting to set out for the tunnel, seemingly with a single purpose.'

'I thought you told me you had it under control,' said William.

'I did,' replied Ross. 'We identified four meeting points on the other side of the river and have already detained over a hundred of the riders, and confiscated their bikes before they could cross the Thames.'

'What about the fifth group?' asked William, all the while keeping his eyes on the CCTV screens in front of him. If the cyclists were a distraction, then above all, he must not allow himself to be distracted. There was so much at stake tonight, and he couldn't afford to miss a single thing. He would have given nearly anything at that moment to be able to find out what was going on in Miles Faulkner's head.

'The fifth group managed to cross the river by cycling across Waterloo Bridge on the wrong side of the road, fooling the inspector on duty – a recently promoted graduate entrant,' Ross couldn't resist adding.

'That's all I need,' said William. 'So how many cyclists are now on the loose and heading for the tunnel?'

'Thirty, possibly forty,' admitted Ross.

'Which means,' said William, 'if the Queen still hopes to arrive at the stadium before Mr Bond makes his appearance, you'll have to intercept every one of them long before they reach the tunnel.'

'Perhaps you could ask the royal chauffeur to put his foot down,' suggested Ross.

'Not a hope. No member of the royal family would consider breaking the speed limit unless security considers their life is in danger,' said William. 'Stay on the line while I speak to Paul.'

He looked up at another screen and watched a Bentley as it left the palace and proceeded slowly down the Mall, accompanied by four outriders in front, two unmarked black Jaguars behind, and a blue van with a doctor on board following behind them, with four more outriders bringing up the rear. William accepted that if HM wasn't willing to break the speed limit, it was going to be a close-run thing. He had no fingers left to cross.

William transferred his attention back to Paul.

'I've just received an update, sir,' said Paul. 'A black van with two occupants has been spotted heading in the direction of the tunnel. It's the same make and model as the one that came off the ferry.'

'If it gets within a mile of the tunnel, pull them over for speeding,' said William.

'But it hasn't broken the speed limit once, sir.'

'Which only makes me even more suspicious,' said William. 'Detain both occupants and, even if it is a false alarm, don't release them until the opening ceremony is over.'

He put the receiver down and once again looked up at a CCTV screen to see Her Majesty's entourage making slow but steady progress along the Embankment. His eyes moved from screen to screen, checking for anything that didn't look right. Most of the cameras within the Olympic Stadium showed him nothing more than excited spectators waiting for the off. He turned his attention back to the phone and said, 'Latest?'

'They're down to twenty-nine cyclists,' said Ross, 'but they're now only a couple of miles away from the tunnel. I also have a helicopter hovering above them: India 9-9, who are keeping us informed of their latest positions. But I still can't be sure who will reach the tunnel first: the black van, the remaining cyclists or the Queen.'

'Could it be possible,' said William, 'that the van driver knows exactly what the cyclists are up to, and is only there to make sure they reach the tunnel before the Queen?' He switched his attention to a different screen, to see Faulkner talking on his mobile. A conversation William would have liked to have overheard, and if they'd been in Russia, would have done. 'Move every available officer to within a mile of the stadium. Give them orders to stop the van and arrest any cyclist still heading in the direction of the tunnel.'

'*Any* cyclist?' repeated Ross.

'You heard me correctly the first time, Sergeant,' said William. 'I can't afford to discriminate between someone out on an innocent evening ride and someone whose sole intention is to reach the tunnel ahead of the Queen. Remember, we have no idea what these people in the van have planned. Whoever it is may be a great deal more dangerous than a group of protesting cyclists. And even if all they are is a distraction to gain more publicity, we still can't afford to risk it. If Her Majesty doesn't reach the tunnel in time, I'll have to send her back to Buckingham Palace, because she won't be jumping out of a car, let alone a helicopter, with or without James Bond.'

William stared back up at the screen, aware that his reputation – and the success of the Olympics – was in the hands of the unknown driver of a black van and twenty-nine determined fanatics. If the Queen didn't get to the stadium on time, she wouldn't be the only person who would be going home early.

• • •

William focused his binoculars on the Russian and Chinese ambassadors, who had just arrived and taken their seats in a diplomatic box.

'What do those two know that I don't?' said William.

'It can't be a terrorist attack,' said Paul, 'or they wouldn't be sitting in a box enjoying a glass of champagne.'

'Unless their presence is proof they couldn't have been involved.'

'You'd have been a match for Rasputin,' said Rebecca.

'And don't forget that he was a Russian,' said William.

• • •

'So, what happens next?' asked Booth Watson.

Miles checked his watch. 'A van and at least thirty cyclists will be on their way by now,' replied Faulkner, 'and they should all reach the tunnel well ahead of the Queen.'

'How will we know if your plan has worked?'

'Her Majesty may well jump out of the helicopter on time, but when the lights come back on, she won't be sitting in the Royal Box.'

'Embarrassing,' admitted Booth Watson, 'but I don't think it will stop the ceremony from going ahead.'

'You could be right,' said Miles, 'but it will give them' – he once again looked across in the direction of the two ambassadors – 'and their undersecretaries all the time they need to carry out Operation Blackout.'

• • •

'So, tell me young lady,' said Julian. 'Are you any nearer to getting your exclusive?'

'A little nearer,' admitted Artemisia, as she gazed down at the unlit stage below. 'I still somehow need to get into the athletes' village without anyone realizing I'm a journalist.'

'You're about the right age to pass for an athlete,' said Julian, 'but it still won't be easy to fool security without some form of accreditation.'

'Easier than you think,' said Artemisia conspiratorially. 'You can purchase an official British team tracksuit from any gift shop in the Olympic Park.'

'But that doesn't solve the accreditation problem,' Robert reminded her, as Jojo returned, carrying five bottles of water, enjoying the attention she pretended to ignore.

'Ross has already shown me how to get hold of a pass,' said Artemisia.

'You're worse than Peter and his ticket tout,' said Julian.

'Don't forget, we're twins,' said Artemisia.

'Just let's hope your father never finds out.'

'If Dad even began to suspect what I have in mind,' said Artemisia, 'he'd lock me up in my old bedroom until the Games are over.'

• • •

'It's going to be a close-run thing,' said Ross when the Queen's Bentley was about a mile away from the tunnel. 'One cyclist is already ahead of her, with another half a dozen not far behind, all of them breaking the speed limit.'

'And the black van?' demanded William, as he watched a lone cyclist approach the tunnel, followed by four police motorcyclists and a Bentley. His eyes flicked back for a moment to the CCTV screen where Miles Faulkner sat in his box, checking his watch again.

'Stopped and questioned half a mile from the tunnel,' said Ross.

'Did the occupants have anything to say for themselves?' asked William.

'No, but there turned out to be six people in the back' said Ross, 'and no sooner had we stopped them than they put up a fight, which kept a dozen of my officers well occupied for some considerable time, while several cyclists sailed past them.'

'All part of a well-prepared plan,' suggested William. 'So, where are they now?' he asked.

'They've been taken off to the nearest nick,' said Ross, 'having played their part.'

William's eyes returned to the screen to see the royal procession approaching the tunnel. When they reached the entrance, the four motorcyclists bringing up the rear of the royal party detached themselves, just as five of the cyclists were about to enter the tunnel ahead of them.

William spent the longest four minutes of his life wondering who would be the first to emerge from the other side, while his eyes kept moving from screen to screen as he waited, and waited, and waited.

The final result: one Bentley and one cyclist. William decided not to ask what had happened to the other four.

The protection officer seated in the front of the Bentley reported back to the welcoming party, who were waiting for them outside the VIP entrance. 'Anticipated ETA in around seven minutes,' he said, as if nothing had happened.

'And the final cyclist?' asked William.

The protection officer glanced in his rear-view mirror to see one of the back-up cars swerve slightly, and smiled as the last remaining cyclist ended up in someone's front garden, sitting in a bed of roses.

'He's been diverted, Commander,' he replied.

CHAPTER 13

'HM HAS JUST ARRIVED,' said Paul, his voice crackling down the line. 'She's being accompanied to the Royal Box by Lord Coe and Boris Johnson, the Mayor of London.'

William smiled for the first time that evening. He had dealt with disgruntled taxi drivers trying to bring London to a standstill, a possible IRA attack, not to mention a group of obsessed cyclists attempting to prevent the Queen from reaching the stadium. Whatever came next – whatever Faulkner had in mind – William felt he was ready.

He barely had time to enjoy the thought before two of the CCTV screens in front of him began to flicker. A few seconds later, all of the CCTV screens in the Gold Suite were showing blank screens.

William froze for a moment, before adrenaline took over.

'Panic slowly,' he told himself, before he picked up his radio hoping someone would tell him what the hell was going on. One of the phones on his desk began to ring. At least the phone lines weren't down.

He grabbed the phone.

'Commander Warwick, it's David Bailsford, Communications Director at the National Grid. I need to warn you we are experiencing a concerted cyberattack on the grid, and from what I can see it's being orchestrated from China, although the British aren't exactly helping. We have it under control at the present time, but you should be aware that the situation could change without warning.'

'What do you mean the British aren't exactly helping?' asked William.

'As I speak,' said Bailsford, looking up at his screen, 'I estimate there are eighteen million households with their televisions on, ten million kettles on the boil, and lights blazing in at least three rooms in every home in the land. It's like having the Cup Final, the Grand National and a royal wedding all happening at the same time.'

'Understood,' said William, only too aware of the consequences if the National Grid were to go down. 'I'll instruct our maintenance team to double-check our back-up generators just in case we lose power. By the way, my CCTV screens went blank for about a minute. Could that be related to a cyberattack?'

'Unlikely,' said Bailsford, 'as they haven't managed to infiltrate our systems yet, but you should check out why you lost power. It may have been nothing more than a blown fuse.'

William put down the phone and grabbed his radio. 'Rebecca, we lost power on the CCTV screens in the Gold Suite a few minutes ago. All the screens are back up now, apart from the one outside the generator room. I've also just received a call that the National Grid is experiencing an unusually high volume of possible cyberattacks. As you know, I don't believe in coincidences, so grab an engineer and try to find out what caused my screens to go blank and why the camera outside the generator room still isn't working.'

'Will do,' said Rebecca, already on the move.

William looked back up at the CCTV screens, his eyes moving slowly along the VIP boxes until they once again settled on Faulkner, who was giving someone a thumbs-up. William's eyes continued to scan the remaining VIP boxes, where he spotted the Russian Ambassador returning the compliment with a nod of recognition.

Had Ross been right all along? Was Faulkner's outing with the cyclists nothing more than a distraction before the main event? If so, what should he expect next? Were the CCTV screens meant to stay off for longer than a minute, or were they blank for just long enough for someone to add another piece to the jigsaw?

Rebecca was back on the radio. 'Sir, I'm with the chief engineer. A fuse had blown, but the back-up battery kicked in, so problem solved. Jim's going to look at the security camera in the corridor in just a minute, but he just wants to double-check the equipment in the generator room first. He'll report back to you directly once he's finished,' she continued.

William wasn't convinced it was going to be quite that simple, his gaze still fixed on the CCTV screens, where he saw the engineer enter the generator room and give him a thumbs-up on the security camera. William pondered why Faulkner had given the Russian Ambassador a thumbs-up sign. Was it connected to the screens going blank? He was still watching the engineer when the door to the generator room suddenly opened and two more maintenance personnel, wearing the same uniform as the engineer, entered the room. One slammed the door and they'd both pulled on balaclavas before William could see their faces.

The engineer turned round, a look of horror on his face as one of them headed towards him.

Willliam grabbed his radio and called an all-stations alert as the larger of the two men knocked the engineer to the ground with a single blow, gagged him and tied him up. His associate produced a spray can, and ran towards the security camera, clearly surprised to find it was working again. Two eyes peered up at William and a spray later they had disappeared from the screen. William knew that time wasn't on his side, and he tried not to think just how many things could go wrong in the next few minutes.

He left his finger jammed on the emergency button of his radio, and didn't remove it until three voices checked in.

'All three of you head for the generator room *now*,' William said. 'There are two intruders. Arrest them and then report back to me immediately.'

'On our way,' said Ross, who was already running towards the generator room.

While William continued to look at the blank screen, he recalled that the generator provided emergency power not just for the internal security cameras but for the stadium's lighting, as well as the media centre which transmitted radio and television broadcasts to hundreds of countries around the world. Now he knew why someone had needed the CCTV screens out of action for a minute, and why Faulkner had given the Russian Ambassador a thumbs-up sign. If only Rebecca had stayed put. It was now obvious the intruders were in no hurry and would have waited for her to leave. But would the home team get there in time to stop the generator being put out of action? If that were to coincide with a successful cyberattack on the National Grid, affecting power both inside and outside the stadium, and the stadium's emergency generator wasn't working, there would be no opening ceremony. He glanced back at the Russian Ambassador's box to see a smug smile on Mikailov's face, as if he knew exactly what was going to happen next.

• • •

Ross and Paul were within yards of the generator room when the two masked men came running out of the room. When they saw the two police officers, they charged off in opposite directions, with Ross and Paul following closely behind.

Paul tackled the first one, quickly turned him over and handcuffed him, while Ross continued running after the faster man. When Ross was only a yard away, he hurled himself at him and managed to pull off his balaclava, only to feel the full force of an elbow being slammed into his jaw, sending him toppling back onto the ground.

Ross was immediately back on his feet and began sprinting after the man, but it quickly became clear he knew exactly where he was going. And just as Ross began to gain on him, he was, without warning, tackled from behind by someone who was clearly part of a well-organized back-up team. Although Ross recovered in moments, by the time he jumped back up, both men had disappeared.

Ross swore out loud. Only one good thing had come out of the failed pursuit. He'd recognized the man he'd been chasing. The man from the Oval, the man who got into his taxi, the man he'd driven to Kensington Palace Gardens. Now Ross knew exactly who they were up against. He turned around and hurried back to the generator room.

Rebecca was the first to reach the generator room and rang William on her radio. She left the channel open so William could hear her conversation with the engineer. Once she'd removed the engineer's gag and untied him, Rebecca asked, 'How bad is it?' And she wasn't referring to his state of health.

'They knew exactly what they were doing,' said the engineer between breaths. 'One of them, who was clearly in charge, tied me up while the other one smashed the distribution box attached to the back-up generator. But that's only half the problem. When I first got here, I found a couple of circuit breakers connected to the power supplies for the stadium lights and media centre that shouldn't be there. Not only that, they can be remotely controlled, so someone, anyone, out there could trigger them at a moment's notice. And to make matters worse, because of the way they've been fitted, it will take some time to remove them. And as the emergency generator is now beyond repair . . .'

'Can you fix the generator?' asked Ross, as he ran into the room, only wanting to hear one response.

'No one can fix it,' replied the engineer. 'It's too badly damaged. We'll somehow have to get hold of a replacement distribution box within the next thirty minutes.'

'Why thirty minutes?' asked Ross.

'Because,' said William, who'd been listening to every word, 'that's when the opening ceremony begins and the floodlights are due to come on, and when the whole world will be watching. Twenty-nine minutes to be exact.'

'This must have been planned for weeks,' said Ross.

'Possibly months,' said William. 'So, if someone triggers the circuit breakers and we have no working back-up generator, the stadium could be left in darkness and there won't be a single TV station in the world showing the opening ceremony.' William thought for a moment. 'Hold on a second while I make a phone call.'

He quickly looked up a number and dialled it. He prayed it wasn't engaged, or worse, just went on ringing, remembering the one man he needed was sitting somewhere out there in the stadium and, like everyone else, was waiting for the curtain to go up on the greatest show on earth.

It was some time before a voice came on the line. 'This had better be good, Commander,' said General Norton, 'because my wife and I are looking forward to the start of the opening ceremony.'

'Without your help, General, there won't be an opening ceremony to look forward to,' said William, and hurriedly explained what had just happened.

'I'll get in touch with Woolwich barracks immediately and speak to their Commanding Officer,' said the General. 'His outfit are the only ones who'll have a spare distribution box available at this time of night. You'd better hold on, Commander, while I make the call.'

'What happens if we can't get a replacement in time and the circuit breakers are triggered?' asked Ross.

'If that happens,' replied Willliam, 'the only people smiling will be the countless journalists and broadcasters from around the world who will all be claiming an exclusive on their front pages in the morning, and what's more they will have enough copy to last them for the next month, by which time the Games will have ground to a halt.

'On top of that,' William continued, trying to sound calm, 'if the cyberattacks are successful and the National Grid goes down, even if we did manage to evacuate the stadium safely, there would be no power for tubes, trains or even streetlights.

It doesn't bear thinking about. But what about those responsible? Did you manage to catch either of them?'

'Paul arrested one of them, but he didn't open his mouth except to swear at us, I think in Russian. I'll question him later, but I suspect he won't say a word.'

'Where is he now?' demanded William.

'Paul took him off to the Olympic police cell – the one no one's meant to know about – where he will no doubt claim diplomatic immunity.'

'And the one you went after?' asked William.

'He got clean away, but not before I pulled off his mask,' Ross admitted, rubbing his jaw. 'I recognized him. He was the man who joined Faulkner at the Oval and who I later drove to the Russian Embassy. It turns out there were three of them, the two in the generator room and a third who came out of nowhere and felled me. I wouldn't be surprised if it was the third one who caused our CCTV screens to go blank so the others could get into the generator room without being spotted. I expect the two who got away are now safely holed up in the Russian Embassy.'

'So at least we know who we're up against,' said William, as the General came back on the line.

'I've managed to locate a spare distribution box,' he announced, 'along with a couple of technicians to install it. I won't repeat their sentiments when they were dragged away from their televisions at a moment's notice, but be assured they are already on their way. The good news,' added the General, 'is that the streets are almost empty. It would seem that over half the nation is tuned in waiting for the opening ceremony to begin.'

'And they'll go on waiting if we don't get the new distribution box in place and quickly,' William responded.

'With the help of your police escort, the new kit should be with you in about twenty minutes,' said the General. 'I'll head for the generator room to meet them.'

'Do you know how long it will take to install it?' asked William.

'I haven't a clue,' replied the General.

William looked at the ticking clock. 'Either way, I've only got another nineteen minutes. In your view, General, what's the worst-case scenario?'

'If there is a power failure and you have no back up generator, the stadium will be left in total darkness, and the least of your problems will be cancelling the opening ceremony. You'll have eighty thousand panicking spectators inside the stadium who won't know whether they're experiencing a technical malfunction or a terrorist attack. Not to mention countless heads of state, ambassadors and other VIPs who will assume the worst.

'Her Majesty will be left stranded in the Royal Box like a sitting duck, while one hundred and twenty-one VIPs, including several heads of state, will begin to panic and, once the news spreads, they will all be joined by eighty thousand spectators asking questions in one hundred and forty-seven different languages.'

'And the best-case scenario?' asked William.

'The cyberattack will fail, the rogue circuit breakers will be removed and the generator will be fixed in time for you to get through the next two hours without any loss of power, in which case no one will be any the wiser.'

'Given the circumstances, General, what would you recommend I should do?'

'I'm a soldier and trained to always assume the worst-case scenario, Commander, so I don't envy you your choice.'

'Thank you,' said William, suddenly aware where the buck stopped. He put the phone down and switched back to the radio. 'Ross, stay put in the generator room with the engineer, while I prepare for the worst-case scenario.'

• • •

The Chinese Ambassador looked at his watch. 'Sixteen minutes left before the lights go out.'

'And by now my team should have eliminated any possibility of the power being restored,' said Mikailov.

'What do you plan to do when we are finally cast in darkness?' asked Wei Ming, as he poured himself another glass of champagne.

'Sit still and enjoy every moment,' replied his Russian counterpart, 'while watching panic set in all around me. I've even brought along a torch for the occasion, so a boy scout couldn't accuse me of being unprepared.'

They both smiled.

'Should I assume your press release has already been written?'

'Yes, but embargoed until midnight,' said Mikailov. 'However, President Putin plans to address the nation first thing in the morning. He will open by offering his sincere condolences for the unfortunate disaster.' He paused. 'I spent some time considering the words *calamity*, *failure* and *disaster*, but finally settled on *disaster*, as it's a word that's easy to translate into any language.'

Wei Ming gave his colleague a slight bow, before he said, 'My President will also be sending his heartfelt condolences, before going on to remind the world's press that our own Beijing Games went without a hitch and our opening ceremony was hailed as one of the most *memorable* in Olympic history. Another carefully chosen word,' said Wei Ming, 'as I feel sure the same will be said about the London opening, with *memorable* having a completely different meaning.' Wei Ming paused before he said, 'How long before . . .?'

'Twelve minutes,' said the Russian Ambassador, as he checked his watch and uncorked a second bottle of champagne.

• • •

A message came through on William's radio. 'The police escort is pulling up outside the main entrance, along with two army technicians and a distribution box,' confirmed Rebecca. 'I'll escort them to the generator room,' she said. 'We should be there shortly.'

'How long do you think it will take them to get the generator back up and running?' asked William.

'Ten minutes at the most, sir,' said a voice William didn't recognize.

He watched the CCTV screen in front of him as two men transported the distribution box as quickly as they could towards the generator room at what seemed like a snail's pace to William.

William checked his watch once again. 'I'm down to seven minutes,' he said, but they didn't need to be reminded.

• • •

A billion eyes looked up into the sky as a single beam of light tracked a helicopter that was heading towards the stadium. On the vast screens, they all saw the door of the helicopter open. The Queen appeared, with Daniel Craig

END GAME

standing by her side. The crowd gasped when James Bond stood back to allow the Queen to jump out of the helicopter.

When her parachute opened moments later, most of the crowd clapped and cheered, while three spectators fainted. The cheering grew even louder as the parachute continued to make its way slowly down towards the centre of the stadium.

William had been among the few people who had known about the secret for weeks. He now nursed another secret the public weren't aware of. But for how much longer?

Five minutes left.

A lightbulb in the Gold suite blew, and William's heart missed a beat, but when he looked back at the screen, the stage remained bathed in light.

He could see the audience looking on in admiration as the performance began to unfold. William could only wonder if the exuberant crowd would ever see the eternal flame lit to officially declare the opening of the Thirtieth Olympiad.

Four minutes left.

As a precaution, he began to set in motion preparations for a worst-case scenario. He first radioed the protection team in the Royal Box.

'Be ready to get HM out at a moment's notice. Have her car up front, engine running. Understood?'

'Understood, Commander,' said a voice, not asking why.

Three minutes left.

William's gaze rarely left the screen. He assumed that at any moment the stadium would be cast into darkness. His heart was pounding as he tried to decide what would be the best course of action. The Queen would have to be moved first, then the Prime Minister, followed by Michelle Obama and Francois Hollande, and the presidents of Germany and Italy, and finally the Mayor of London.

Two minutes left.

'The distribution box is installed,' said the General, 'and all that's left to do is attach the cables, which Sergeant Johnston tells me should only take a minute, possibly two.'

William wanted to say there's a big difference between one minute and two, but simply held his breath.

Moments later, his heartrate doubled when Ross and the Sergeant disappeared from the screen and the stadium was thrown into total darkness for a second time.

His worst fears realized.

• • •

The Chinese Ambassador switched on his torch, refilled the two champagne glasses and raised his hand in a mock salute. 'To the British Empire, on whom the sun never sets.'

'God Save the Queen,' said the Russian Ambassador, as their two glasses touched.

Around them, the audience sat quietly, patiently waiting, assuming the blackout was all part of the build-up before the main event.

'How long before panic sets in,' mused Wei Ling.

'Not too long,' suggested Mikailov. 'In fact . . .' but before he could finish his sentence, the lights came back on. The cheers that followed were deafening. The crowd clearly thought the temporary blackout was all part of the spectacle that was about to unfold.

• • •

'Thank you,' said William, but the General had already turned off his phone and left to rejoin his wife in the stand to enjoy the opening ceremony.

'Such a clever idea to turn all the lights off and leave us in suspense,' she said, as her husband sat back down beside her.

'Very clever,' agreed the General.

'You nearly missed it.'

'The queue for the lavatory was very long.'

• • •

In the hours that followed, over a billion people enjoyed Danny Boyle's memorable production. The crowds, both in the stadium and at home, delighted to see Mr Bean accompanying the London Symphony Orchestra on the keyboard, laughed and cried at the heartfelt tribute to the NHS, and raised the roof when the eternal flame was lit by a group of seven young athletes.

When the curtain finally came down, and the Queen had departed, unaware of any problems, the dignitaries were escorted back to their coaches, while the boisterous, exuberant crowd made their way out of the stadium, some singing, others dancing all the way back home.

• • •

Once again, the two ambassadors sat next to each other on the coach as it made its way back into central London. The noisy chatter all around them rather suggested that the opening ceremony had been awarded a gold medal. It was some time before either of them spoke.

'What do you think went wrong, Anatoly?' the Chinese Ambassador eventually managed.

'I have no idea,' admitted Mikailov, 'but I will have sent a report to my President long before he wakes in the morning. I will leave Mr Putin in no doubt that the failed Chinese cyberattack was to blame, while we carried out our part of the plan to the letter.'

'I'm not sure he'll be convinced about that, after Hu Jintao has read my report,' said Wei Ming, annoyed by his colleague trying to pass on the blame.

'Possibly not,' admitted Mikailov. 'However, I will also remind my President we still have a foolproof plan to switch the urine samples and ensure the Games will only be remembered for one thing.'

'And should that fail, comrade,' said Wei Ming disdainfully, 'be assured when our pocket Exocet takes over, she will be more than a match for Warwick, or Faulkner for that matter.'

• • •

When no one was left in the stands and the lights in the stadium were finally switched off, William's phone rang once again. He picked it up to hear General Norton on the other end of the line.

'Well done, Commander. But if I may be allowed to offer you one piece of advice?'

'Please do, sir,' said William.

'Don't tell anyone in authority what actually happened tonight.'

BOOK TWO

The Games

CHAPTER 14

Saturday, 28 July – day 2 of the Games

WILLIAM WAS SO EXHAUSTED that he couldn't sleep. He toppled out of his camp bed just after five, took a cold shower and got dressed. He left the stadium before the sun had risen and began to walk slowly around a deserted Olympic Park. He would, like Ross, have run, but he found he couldn't fully concentrate while jogging.

He began by trying to get his thoughts in some order. How close had they come to total disaster? Far too close. And if this had been engineered from high up in the Russian government, as he feared, then what was coming next? He would need to gather all the salient facts from his inner team before he could brief the Hawk.

Last night, Ross had attempted to interview the engineer they'd arrested, but with little success; so far, the man wouldn't talk. Ross would try again this morning, but William held little hope of any real information being forthcoming. In the meantime, there was someone else he needed to speak to: Professor Meredith, his contact at GCHQ. If there was anyone who might be able to throw some light on what they could expect, it was Meredith, a man who spent his life thinking outside the box and continually preparing for the unexpected. They had met several times in the run-up to the Olympics, and William knew he could rely on his discretion. But at what hour could he wake him?

William circled the swimming arena and began to make his way slowly back towards the stadium – a stadium that would remain quiet for another week before the starter's pistol was fired for the first track and field event. In the meantime, the opening week of the Games would be colonized by a myriad of different sports ranging from swimming to gymnastics, boxing to weightlifting, cycling to equestrian events, fencing to . . . The list was endless. Forty-three world championships held in a single week in an area the size of a village: the Olympic Village. Most of the competitors had waited four years for their moment on the world stage, and for some, it would be no more than a curtain lowered, while their rivals progressed to the next round, fewer still reaching the semi-finals and only a handful the finals, leaving just three to mount the podium and be awarded a gold, silver or bronze medal. Those lucky few would bask in glory for a lifetime, while one, perhaps two, would lay claim to immortality and add their names to the scroll of Olympic history.

William checked his watch once again as he approached the stadium: 5.43. He returned to his dungeon in the basement to prepare for the morning team meeting. So many items on the agenda fell into the category of 'contingency planning'.

William switched on the light in the Gold Suite, relieved to see the bulb obey his order. He looked up at the bank of CCTV screens. The army engineers had continued working through the night so that the public – and, more importantly, the press – would never find out there had been a problem. The generator room had been fitted with new Banham locks, while two guards were posted outside and another two inside, as well as half a dozen over-qualified electricians carrying out four-hour shifts, so it wouldn't be necessary to once again call on General Norton's services.

At six minutes past six, William decided he couldn't wait any longer. He checked the name on his priority list before slowly dialling the number. Only one ring and the call was answered by a man who sounded wide awake.

'Good morning, Professor Meredith,' said William. 'I hope I didn't wake you.'

'No, you didn't,' said a voice that didn't sound surprised to find the Commander on the other end of the line. 'I've been waiting for your call. Forty-eight seconds was a little too long for a blackout to have been a scripted part of the show. So, what happened?'

After William had recounted last night's near-disaster in detail, he asked, 'Can you draw any conclusions, Professor, that might assist us in the future?'

'Only one of any importance,' responded Meredith. 'There's someone out there whose sole purpose is to ensure that the London Games will not be remembered for their sporting prowess.' He paused. 'If you are able to identify who that person is, you'll be halfway to stopping them in their tracks, if you'll forgive the pun. You said the three men involved are all Russian, so it seems plausible to assume their government may be involved in something on such a grand scale. But somebody has to be in charge of the operation, so that's the person you need to identify.'

'We caught one of them red-handed,' said William, 'and he spent the rest of the night in the stadium's prison cell, but, I confess, the other two got clean away.'

'The one you caught was no doubt nothing more than a foot soldier,' said Professor Meredith. 'Has he been questioned yet?'

'He wouldn't answer a single question last night. But my team will be trying again this morning.'

'I suspect he's no more than a small cog in a very large wheel that is being operated out of Moscow. I doubt he'd know anything of significance anyway.'

Meredith's tone of voice left William in no doubt of the size and potential danger of the threat.

'What do you consider should be my next move, Professor?' he asked.

'I'm not altogether sure, Commander,' admitted Meredith, 'but then, you have to remember that all of us at GCHQ are trained to play the long game. Your particular nemeses have only a two-week window of opportunity available to them, and they will be well aware that another opportunity such as this may not present itself again for several years, if ever – which means they may have to take an occasional risk they would not normally consider. Surprisingly enough, Commander, that could turn out to your advantage.'

William didn't interrupt.

'However,' continued the professor, 'you have an added problem, as I'm not convinced that it's only the Russians who are involved. This could even be a three-headed hydra and, therefore, cutting off one of the heads might not solve your problem.'

'And the other two heads?'

The professor didn't answer the question directly, but said quietly, 'You mentioned that you fear a known criminal may be working for the Russians?'

'Miles Faulkner,' said William, 'a white-collar criminal who has crossed my path several times over the years, and has done time – twice – and after this might well spend the rest of his life in jail.'

'Could Faulkner be strapped for cash?' was Meredith's next enquiry.

'Far from it,' said William. 'Croesus is his brother.'

'Croesus the Great, 620 to 546 BC, didn't have a brother,' said Meredith, 'but I take your point. However, one is bound to ask what's in it for Faulkner if he doesn't need the money, because if he were caught, he could be charged with treason.'

'But if he succeeds,' said William, 'I could lose my job, and he'd like nothing more. And there's something else – Miles Faulkner has been spotted taking a great deal of interest in a Van Gogh self-portrait that is part of the Russian Hermitage collection currently on display at the Fitzmolean.'

'Ah,' said Professor Meredith. 'I begin to see things more clearly. I'll have a team tracking the Russian Ambassador night and day to see if that particular magnet will attract any filings. But for now, I'll let you get on with the day job – and, William, don't hesitate to call if you think I can help.'

'Thank you, sir,' said William, before putting the phone down. *A third party*, he repeated to himself, and then he remembered who else was seated in the Russian Ambassador's box.

• • •

Across the other side of the park beneath the Olympic Stadium, Ross and Jackie were sitting in a police interview room. Opposite them sat the man they had arrested the previous night. He had been down there for nearly twelve hours, having slept in the cell next door.

The three of them had been in the interview room for the past half-hour and, so far, the suspect had barely opened his mouth, other than to drink the occasional glass of water. Whenever he did speak, he gave short, monosyllabic answers in Russian. The only words he spoke that Jackie and Ross understood were: 'No English', although Ross was fairly sure the man understood every word they were saying. They had requested a translator, but while they were waiting, Ross tried again.

'What was the purpose of last night's break-in?'

'No speak English.'

'Under whose orders were you acting?'

'No speak English.'

'Who was the man with you?'

'No speak English.'

'What is your name?'

The man smiled very slightly. 'No speak English,' he repeated. He'd been told that, unlike his compatriots back home, the British didn't go in for torturing suspects.

There was a knock on the door, and when Jackie opened it, one of the constables ushered in the translator. After being cautioned concerning the secrecy of what she was about to hear, the translator was brought up to speed, and was soon conversing with the arrested man in Russian. After five minutes, she turned to Ross and Jackie with a frown.

'This is all a huge mistake,' the translator said. 'This man is not a criminal – he's on holiday in London to see the

Olympics. He's an electrical engineer by trade, and last night he was threatened at gunpoint by a man he did not know and forced to accompany him and tamper with some machinery. He knows nothing about what happened last night.'

'Word perfect,' said Ross, knowing when he was beaten.

'He has asked me to contact the Russian Embassy on his behalf,' the translator went on. 'Might I use your phone?'

'Of course.'

'Well?' Ross said to Jackie, as they closed the cell door behind them.

'I don't believe a word of it,' Jackie replied.

But within half an hour, an undersecretary from the Russian embassy was on his way to the Olympic Stadium to rescue his fellow countryman, and there was little they could do about it.

• • •

'How long were the lights out for?' asked the Assistant Commissioner, once William had brought him up to speed.

'Forty-eight seconds, sir,' replied William.

'How many people know the reason why?' was the Hawk's next question.

'Only General Norton, Professor Meredith and my inner team.'

'Then let's keep it that way,' said the Hawk. 'You arrested one of them?'

'We did.' William sighed. 'It's done us little good, though – he doesn't speak a word of English, seems to know nothing, and is claiming to have been forced at gunpoint to sabotage the generator. An undersecretary from the embassy has interviewed him, and he'll probably make bail. Unfortunately, we only caught the engineer, and not the one Ross saw recently with Miles Faulkner at the Oval, who regrettably escaped.'

'The fact that one of their agents has been caught isn't going to stop them,' said the Hawk. 'So, we'll have to try and anticipate what their next move might be.'

'Not that easy, sir,' said William, 'while my team is occupied night and day with security at over thirty different venues across the country.'

'Once again, take advantage of Ross's particular skills,' said the Hawk. 'Make sure he doesn't let Faulkner out of his sight, as he could still turn out to be the weak link in the chain.'

'Agreed,' responded William. 'And something else I thought it best to mention – President Putin postponed his address to the nation this morning.'

There was a moment's pause, before the Hawk said, 'I don't care for the word postponed.'

• • •

Artemisia rose early that morning, though not as early as her father. She was exhausted but exhilarated after watching the opening ceremony, which had been an amazing experience, but she was also excited to start her new job as a cub reporter with the *Daily Mail*. She wasn't planning on mentioning the word 'cub' when anyone asked her what she did.

After a breakfast of steaming black coffee and a couple of slices of burnt toast, she left for the Olympic Park before Robert had finished shaving. On arrival at the stadium, she went straight to the press centre, presented her credentials, filled in a long form and had her photograph taken. She was then given a pass with the letter *C* printed in one corner, along with a press kit. She quickly discovered there wasn't a category D. The press office knew a cub reporter when they saw one.

Artemisia sat down at a table in the corner of the room and studied the small print: category C did not allow her to attend any finals or evening sessions of the track and field events being held in the main stadium. The athletes' village was strictly off limits, and if she wanted a meal, the C café was self-service with no menu. She was beginning to think her chances of getting an exclusive didn't look too promising.

Then again, Artemisia was good at thinking two steps ahead, and her godfather, Ross, had given her an idea for the third.

She turned her attention to the official British Olympic handbook that listed all the competitors and their disciplines. She turned to the women's section.

As Ross had suggested, she checked each page carefully while searching for a likely candidate. She had almost given up by the time she reached page sixty-one, but then her finger suddenly stopped, and she took a closer look at the image of an épée fencer called Annie Charnock. Annie was twenty-six, one year older than Artemisia and, at five foot nine, one inch taller. But the grainy photograph made Artemisia feel she was in with a chance, even though she knew nothing about fencing.

She read on. Annie had been the All-England Schools' Champion before going on to represent her country at the Commonwealth Games. At the Olympic trials earlier in the year, Annie had reached the final and booked herself a place on the Olympic squad.

Artemisia next turned to the events timetable to discover that Annie would be up against the German épée champion,

Helga Braun. On paper, it looked like a David and Goliath contest, but on this occasion, it didn't seem as if David would fell her opponent with a single blow. Artemisia wanted every Brit to win, but in this case . . .

The bout, Artemisia could see from the timetable, would take place in the Exhibition Centre at twelve thirty that day, in just a couple of hours' time. As it was the opening round, even a category C reporter was entitled to sit in the press box.

Artemisia left the press centre and made her way across to the nearest bus stop, surprised by just how many visitors were strolling around the park simply enjoying the Olympic experience.

On arrival at ExCel, she presented her pass to the ticket collector, who pointed her in the direction of a half-empty press box, where she had a perfect view of the bouts taking place on the floor below.

She had to wait for over an hour before Annie Charnock made her appearance but, after only a glance, she realized they could pass as sisters.

When Annie's name was announced over the loudspeaker, the locals cheered, while the few Germans present politely applauded their opponent.

However, it soon became clear that for Helga, fencing was a blood sport, and twenty-seven minutes later, she had won the best of five bouts, three–nil. The defeated Brit left the floor to polite applause that ceased the moment she disappeared into the changing room.

As the crowd drifted out of the centre, Artemisia remained alone in the press box, her eye fixed on the competitors' exit. Forty minutes later, a forlorn figure appeared, carrying an Olympic fencer's bag over her shoulder.

Artemisia left the press box and walked slowly towards

her. 'Hi,' she said. 'I'm a reporter with the *Daily Mail* and would like to write a profile about you.'

Annie's look of astonishment rather implied that Artemisia must have got the wrong competitor. Annie reminded her she had just been beaten by the German champion three–nil in the opening round, and her Olympic dream had only lasted twenty-seven minutes.

'But as Baron de Coubertin told us,' said Artemisia, 'the most important thing in the Olympic Games is not winning, but taking part.'

'In Coubertin's day, possibly,' said Annie, 'but not in 2012. All that matters now is De Coubertin's other maxim, "Faster, Higher, Stronger", and I was, to put it mildly, "slower, lower and weaker".'

'Why don't I buy you a coffee,' said Artemisia sympathetically, 'and I'll tell you what I have in mind.'

The cub reporter spent the next hour taking notes about a girl from Wakefield who'd been raised by her single-parent mother, who remained convinced that her daughter would win a medal and return to the north in triumph. 'Whereas now when I go home,' said Annie, 'the town band won't be waiting to greet me on the platform at our local station.'

'Don't worry,' said Artemisia, 'when the locals read my article, they'll think Helga was lucky to beat you.'

Annie laughed for the first time, revealing an infectious smile. 'Let's hope so,' she said, 'because the *Daily Mail* is my mother's favourite paper.'

'I'll need a photograph,' said Artemisia, taking a digital camera from her bag.

Annie stood up and gave her the same infectious smile.

'Perhaps you could take your pass off?' suggested Artemisia, not missing a beat.

'Why not?' said Annie. 'I've no use for it any longer.' She slipped off her pass and left the cellophane holder on the table, before posing for several more photos.

'And possibly one of you with the Olympic rings behind you?' said Artemisia, guiding her quarry back onto the floor. 'Yes, that's perfect. Oh, look at the time – I'll have to rush if I'm going to get my copy in.' Artemisia began to head towards the exit.

'Will it be in tomorrow's paper?' Annie asked as she chased after her.

'Let's hope so,' said Artemisia, 'but in the end, it will be my editor who makes that decision.'

Artemisia watched as a more cheerful girl disappeared in the direction of the station.

Once Annie was out of sight, Artemisia rushed back to the ExCel centre. 'Sorry, sorry,' she said as she showed the ticket collector her press pass. 'I left some important notes in the press box. I'll only be a minute.'

He opened the door to allow her in. She ran all the way back to the floor, grabbed Annie's pass and tucked it into her bag before leaving the centre a second time.

Artemisia took the tube to High Street Kensington and had completed her article by the time she reached the *Daily Mail*'s offices. She emailed it to the Features desk, along with all the photos she had taken of Annie.

As she looked down at Annie's pass, she felt a little guilty about the subterfuge, but she hoped Annie and her mother would enjoy the article. Now she just needed to make sure she looked the part.

CHAPTER 15

Saturday, 28 July – day 2 of the Games

BETH DIALLED WILLIAM'S MOBILE for the seventh time that day, and finally a familiar voice came on the line.

'Did you manage to get a good night's sleep, my darling?' she asked.

'Slept like a baby,' said William. Beth waited for the gag every copper makes when asked that question, 'Woke every two hours screaming.'

'Wasn't the opening ceremony magnificent?' enthused Beth.

'I wouldn't know,' responded William. 'I never saw it.'

'Not even Mr Bean playing the keyboard with the London Symphony Orchestra?' asked Beth. 'He brought the house down.'

He wasn't the only one who nearly brought the house down, thought William, but he satisfied himself with, 'No. We had one or two problems this end.'

'You would never have known, watching the ceremony on television,' said Beth. 'Over breakfast, Peter was raving about James Bond and the Queen jumping out of a helicopter.'

'What's breakfast?' asked William innocently.

'A time when families get together over a meal and tell each other what they will be doing that day.'

'So, what *are* you all doing today?' asked William, feeling even more guilty. He kept his eyes on the CCTV screens in front of him as he listened, just in case.

'Artemisia phoned to say she's found a way of sneaking into the athletes' village. Says it's her only hope of getting an exclusive.'

I could have given her an exclusive last night, thought William, but he simply said, 'Did she tell you how she proposes to do that?'

'Are you asking as a father or as a policeman?'

'Both,' admitted William.

'Well, she did ask if she could borrow some money to buy a pair of the latest Adidas trainers, but she wouldn't tell me why.'

'They're part of the British Olympic team's official kit,' said William, who by now had a good idea of exactly what his daughter must be up to. 'But why doesn't she put them on her expenses? After all, the *Daily Mail*'s pockets are far deeper than ours.'

'She wants to prove herself first. Anyway, she's promised to pay me back once her "exclusive" hits the front page.'

'Can you remember a time,' said William, 'when Arte paid us back for anything? Our only hope is that she'll end up marrying a rich man.'

'As Artemisia is far too independent to take a penny of Robert's money, and Robert is far too proud to rely on his family's money, I expect we'll have to go on paying her "little expenses" for some years to come.'

'Do you think Robert and Arte will tie the knot at some point?' asked William.

'Who knows with her generation,' offered Beth, 'but I remain hopeful.'

'Fathers are usually convinced no one's good enough for their daughters, but in Robert's case, it's the other way round.'

'You don't fool me,' said Beth. 'You adore Arte.'

'Guilty as charged, but that isn't what I said.' William glanced up again at the CCTV screens, trying to do two things at once. 'So, how's your sell-out exhibition going, dare I ask?'

'Almost as well as yours,' replied Beth. 'Tickets are selling at double the price on the black market, and we've even got touts trading on the pavement outside the gallery. And one other rather interesting thing has happened today that I thought you might like to know about, bearing in mind that you don't believe in coincidences.'

'Why don't you add to my problems?' teased William.

'This morning, I received a letter from the Russian Embassy to let me know that when our exhibition closes, we should hold onto Van Gogh's self-portrait and not return it to the Hermitage along with their other pictures, as it will be collected at a later date by a third party.'

'Did they name the third party?' asked William.

'They did,' said Beth, 'a certain Mr Booth Watson QC, and there are no prizes for guessing who he represents. What I don't know, though I suspect you do, is whether he's purchasing the painting with money or with something else.'

William was just about to make a noncommittal reply when another phone began to ring. 'Sorry, my darling,' he said. 'I've got to go.'

'Inspector Stuart, sir,' said a voice William didn't recognize, when he picked up the other phone. 'We've got a problem in Glasgow.'

'What kind of problem, Inspector?'

'I'm the security officer at Hampden Park, where the North Korean women's football team is playing Colombia in their opening fixture. I didn't imagine there would be any problems with a first-round match, especially as the stadium is almost empty, but . . .'

'But . . .' repeated William.

'Unfortunately, just before kick-off, a video was played which showed the players of the North Korean team standing in front of a South Korean flag.'

William tried to keep a straight face while he continued to listen.

'The North Korean team have marched off the pitch and are refusing to return until someone in authority makes an official apology on behalf of the British Olympic Association and, frankly, Commander, I don't know anyone in authority except you.'

The smile returned to William's face.

'The North Korean coach, not an easy woman,' continued Inspector Stuart, 'is saying to anyone who will listen, including the local rag, that we have insulted the People's Republic of North Korea and caused a diplomatic incident.'

'But if I remember the rules of the competition,' said William, 'should a team fail to turn up, they automatically forfeit the game and the three points are awarded to the opposing side.'

'But that's the problem, sir. They did turn up, even shook hands with the referee and the Colombian players moments before the wrong national anthem was played.'

'Why don't you put the coach on,' said William. He tried to think while he waited.

'Who is this?' demanded the next voice to come on to the line.

'Commander Warwick,' said William, hoping he sounded suitably pompous. 'I'm the senior officer in charge of policing the Games,' he added, just as Rebecca walked into the Gold Suite. 'Please allow me to apologize on behalf of the British Olympic Association for the unforgivable mistake someone has made and assure you that I will personally track down the culprit and punish them.'

Across the room, Rebecca looked suitably impressed.

A long silence followed, which William took advantage of. 'However, I have to point out that under Law Seventeen of the Olympic code, if a team holds up the start of a game for more than fifteen minutes, that side automatically forfeits the match, and the three points will be awarded to the opposing team.'

Another silence followed before Inspector Stuart came back on the line. 'That seems to have done the trick, sir, because the North Korean coach is ushering her players back onto the pitch and the two captains are once again shaking hands. I'm only sorry to have bothered you.'

'Not a problem, Inspector. Enjoy the game.' William put down the phone.

'Forgive me for asking, sir,' said Rebecca, 'but is there a Law Seventeen?'

'As the head of the policing operation,' said William with conviction, 'I make the laws.'

'I only ask, sir,' added Rebecca, 'because North Korea are unlikely to beat Columbia, let alone win a medal.'

William managed a smile.

But the smile slipped from his face as a new thought occurred to him: what if the switching of the national flags hadn't been a mistake? After last night, there was no doubt the Russians, in league with Miles Faulkner, were attempting to sabotage the 2012 Olympics. On the one hand, the incorrect national flag might be a trivial mistake. On the other hand, nothing that could give the North Koreans cause to complain was ever trivial – and it was possible that this, like the cyclists the previous evening, was just another distraction.

The fireman who tried to put out the eternal flame. Olympic tickets that didn't exist. Were they all part of a bigger picture, and was Van Gogh the artist? They had always been one step ahead of him, but that was before William knew about the triangle of the Russians, the Chinese and Miles Faulkner. But how could he break that triangle?

• • •

Detective Inspector Paul Adaja was walking around what he expected would be his regular beat of the Olympic Stadium when his mobile rang.

'Good afternoon, Inspector Adaja. It's Commander Sinclair calling.'

'Good afternoon, sir,' said Paul, who was taken by surprise, as Sinclair was the last person he'd expected to hear on the other end of the line.

'You may or may not have heard, Inspector, that the Commissioner has just appointed me to head up the murder squad.'

'I hadn't heard,' admitted Paul. 'My congratulations, sir.'

'Thank you, Paul. The reason I'm calling is to offer you

the chance to be my second in command, with the rank of Chief Inspector.' He emphasized the word *Chief*.

'I'm presently working with Commander Warwick in Public Order and Operational Support for the Olympics,' responded Paul, 'as I feel sure you know, sir.'

'As you have been for the past seven years, Paul, but as the Olympics will be over in a few weeks' time, I thought you might be interested in an even bigger challenge.'

'It's very generous of you to consider me, sir,' replied Paul, 'but I enjoy working with Commander Warwick, who I feel sure will be offered an important new role once the Games are over.'

'I can only hope you don't live to regret your decision, Inspector,' said Sinclair, as he put his phone down.

'I can't imagine why I would,' replied Paul, if only to himself.

He continued his circuit of the stadium, checking in with a few of the constables on duty, before making his way back to the Gold Suite about half an hour later. He found the Commander absent – no doubt attending to an urgent matter somewhere else in the Olympic Park – while Jackie was manning the phones and keeping a close eye on the CCTV screens.

Ross was sitting on the other side of the room trawling through last night's CCTV footage for any clue as to where the two Russians had gone after he lost them, but came up with nothing. They clearly knew they what they were doing.

Rebecca was tucked in another corner, talking into her mobile, and Paul arrived just in time to hear the tail end of her conversation.

'Thank you, sir,' she was saying, 'but I'm proud to be a Detective Sergeant in Commander Warwick's team, so I think I'll stay put for the time being.'

Paul picked up a faint annoyed retort from the speaker, and then Rebecca tucked her phone back in her pocket, muttering, 'I'd rather be a Constable in admin than work for that man.'

'Let me guess,' said Paul. 'You've just had a job offer from Commander Sinclair?'

Rebecca laughed. 'I suppose that means I was his second choice?'

'Luckily, neither of us are going anywhere.'

'Should I be offended that I haven't had an offer?' asked Jackie, glancing around from the CCTV screens.

Just then, her mobile phone began to ring.

'Probably him now,' said Rebecca, laughing as Jackie took her phone from her pocket.

Ross smiled, turned from his desk and said, 'If it's any consolation for being the last resort, Jackie, you can be absolutely sure of one thing: Commander Sinclair won't be calling me.'

Jackie laughed as she answered her phone.

'Good evening, Sergeant Roycroft,' said a voice Jackie immediately recognized.

'Good evening, Commander Sinclair,' she responded, to suppressed laughs from the rest of her team. 'How can I help you?'

'By becoming a member of my team, Jackie,' said Sinclair. 'When I was invited to head up the murder squad, the first name to cross my mind was yours.'

And yours would have been the last to cross mine, thought Jackie, but somehow managed, 'How kind of you to even consider me sir, but I currently work for one of the finest officers in the Met, and I wouldn't consider leaving him for someone else, whatever position or rank you offered me.'

END GAME

Jackie only just stopped herself saying, *for a sleazebag like you*.

She put down the phone before Sinclair could respond, and the team all cheered.

• • •

Artemisia was at the tiny desk she'd been assigned in the corner of the *Daily Mail* offices, working on her plan to somehow get into the athletes' village, when the editor's secretary hurried over to her. 'The editor would like to see you immediately.' She repeated the word *immediately*.

'Can I ask . . .?' Artemisia began, but the secretary was already heading back to the editor's office.

Artemisia left her desk and took the lift to the top floor, her mind whirring. In the few minutes it took her to reach the editor's office, she came up with a dozen reasons why he would want to see her. Perhaps he had loved her article? Was he discussing with his inner team which page it should go on?

By the time she arrived outside his office door, she was on the front page, and the cub reporter had become a lioness.

The first thing Artemisia noticed as she entered the editor's office was a printout of her article, along with several of the photographs, spread out on his desk. When he looked up, she gave him her warmest smile.

'What in hell's name do you think this load of crap is?' were the editor's opening words, as he held up her article between a finger and thumb, as if it was contagious.

'A human-interest story,' stammered Artemisia, 'about a girl from Wakefield whose dreams were shattered on the opening day of the Games.'

'The *Daily Mail* doesn't do shattered dreams,' snapped the editor, 'not least because shattered dreams don't sell papers. Our two million readers want stories about winners, not losers, preferably gold medallists in a sport they are interested in, and I can assure you épée fencing isn't amongst them. In future, I expect you to come up with stories no other paper has, not ones no other paper wants, with the possible exception of the *Wakefield Evening News*, and I suspect even they would spike it.'

Artemisia could feel her legs wobbling and was beginning to wish she'd taken up the offer to be a graduate trainee with Peter Jones.

'The word *exclusive*, just in case you didn't know,' said the editor, 'means no other paper has it, not *no other paper wants it*. Do I make myself clear?' His outstretched arm moved slowly across the desk, his eyes never leaving her for a moment, as he dropped the article and photographs into his wastepaper basket.

Artemisia was about to burst into tears, when the editor's secretary touched her elbow and quickly led her out of the room.

Once the door had mercifully closed, the secretary tried to console Arte with the words, 'Be thankful he wasn't in a foul mood, or he might have told you what he really thought.'

CHAPTER 16

Sunday, 29 July – day 3 of the Games

ONCE ARTEMISIA HAD BOARDED the tube bound for the Olympic Park, she would remove the pass and tuck it in a pocket, because while she was on the train, she needed to look like a spectator, not a competitor: that would come later.

One more glance in the mirror before she joined the lions in the arena.

'You certainly look the part,' said Robert, 'but will you fool an alert security guard?'

'I think I just might,' said Artemisia, without taking her eyes off the mirror.

Artemisia took one final look in the mirror before she kissed Robert goodbye and left their flat to begin her new life as Annie Charnock. She was now even more determined to get an exclusive that would make the front page, not to mention the ultimate test for any journalist: every other newspaper would have to follow up her story the following day.

On the tube journey to the Olympic Park, she continued to read her book on épée fencing, in case anyone should ask her a question. The épée was the heaviest of the three weapons used in competition, the other two being the foil and the sabre. While the bout was taking place, you had to remain within a restricted area; if you stepped out, you automatically lost the bout. If you were the first to make five direct hits, you won the bout; three bouts and you won the match.

She'd reached the lunge by the time the train pulled into Stratford station. She jumped off the tube and quickly made her way to the Olympic Park and, with the help of her map, went in search of the athletes' village. It was hard to miss, with its high protective wire fence surrounding the entire enclave, beyond which a large crowd of fans was hanging around hoping to catch a glimpse of their heroes and even get a selfie.

Artemisia slowly circled the eight-foot-high fence to discover there was only one way in. She stood a few yards back from the entrance and watched carefully as several competitors strolled in and out, but only after their passes had been checked. She got close enough to learn that Jim was the name of the NCO on duty. When a couple of the more recognizable faces appeared, he didn't even bother to check their passes.

Artemisia waited patiently and chose her moment carefully. She didn't make her move until she spotted a group of young women from the British team heading for the compound, who were clearly friends. Once she'd established they weren't fencers, Artemisia quickly joined them, and when she showed her pass said, 'Thank you, Jim.'

The NCO smiled and said, 'Good luck, Annie.'

She was in.

• • •

END GAME

Ross was sitting in his taxi at the corner of Cadogan Square, waiting for Miles Faulkner to appear. All other priorities had been dropped now, and he would remain constantly on Faulkner's tail. The events of the last few days had proved beyond question that the Russians were attempting to sabotage the Games and Faulkner was working alongside them. Beth had been right to be suspicious from the outset.

William had already briefed Ross about the letter Beth had received from the Russian Embassy, and they both agreed that the Van Gogh must be the hold they had over Faulkner. Only an unobtainable masterpiece could make a man like Faulkner become involved in something that could end up with a life sentence for treason. Nothing would give Ross greater pleasure than to be the arresting officer.

Ross watched carefully when the familiar Rolls-Royce drew up outside Faulkner's home with Collins behind the wheel. Faulkner appeared a few minutes later, climbed into the back of the car, and no sooner had the door closed than Collins drove off.

But when the Rolls reached the end of the road, Collins didn't turn left as usual, but right. The sudden break in Faulkner's routine took Ross by surprise, but only for a moment. Suddenly, he was wide awake, giving clear orders to his fleet of taxis, none of them driven by cabbies. Ross kept his distance while his team followed their target south out of London, not stopping until they reached Biggin Hill private airfield in Middlesex.

Ross focused his binoculars on the runway just as Faulkner climbed aboard his Learjet only moments before it took off.

Ross was puzzled by the fact that the only passenger didn't seem to have any luggage, so he assumed it had to be a round trip – but to where? An airport official informed him, after he checked his warrant card, that the private jet was bound for Finland – information Ross passed on to William, who immediately briefed Professor Meredith at GCHQ, who in turn spoke to his man in Helsinki.

• • •

The third secretary at the British Embassy set off for Vantaa airport long before Faulkner's plane would seek permission to land. From a corner table in the rooftop restaurant, he watched as the jet landed and taxied to its allocated apron. The man then abandoned his fourth coffee.

Once the third secretary had seen the plane take back off, he returned to his desk at the British Embassy and reported to the professor the unlikely sequence of events he'd just witnessed. 'Once the plane's engines had been turned off,' he said, 'a Volvo with local plates drove onto the runway and headed towards the aircraft. The driver stepped out of the car carrying what looked like a shoebox. He then climbed the aircraft steps, at which point the passenger door opened and a pair of arms appeared. The driver handed over the package, which disappeared inside, and moments later the passenger door was closed.'

Professor Meredith didn't stop making notes.

'Once the plane had been refuelled, the engines were turned back on before it began to taxi back towards the runway. The aircraft took off forty minutes after it had landed.'

Professor Meredith called William the moment he'd put the phone down and reported verbatim what his man in Helsinki had told him, before adding, 'And now you'll have to make a decision I don't envy.'

'Namely?' said William.

'Do you arrest Faulkner as he gets off his plane and discover what's in the box, or do you follow the box to find out who it's being delivered to?'

'If I'm to confirm who Faulkner's working for,' said William, 'I need to know where the box is going.'

'I agree,' said Meredith. 'Call me the moment you know the answer, because you can be sure we'll already have a thick file on whoever receives it.'

William's next call was to Ross, with clear instructions not to arrest Faulkner but to follow the box.

• • •

By the time Faulkner's plane landed back at Biggin Hill, Ross's fleet of taxis was in place all along the route back into London. One of them watched the passenger from a distance as he walked down the steps off his plane, firmly clinging on to what did look like a shoebox. He didn't let go of the box when he stepped into the back of the Rolls, despite Collins offering to take it.

The taxi relay went into action as Collins headed for central London.

'We're being followed,' said Collins, as he glanced in his wing mirror.

Faulkner sighed. 'So it seems Warwick and his team are well aware I've been to Helsinki.'

'I wonder why they didn't check what's inside the box when you went through customs?'

'Because I imagine they're more interested in who the box is being delivered to than what's inside it. Never underestimate Warwick,' said Faulkner. 'We'll have to switch to plan B.' He sent a text message to an unnamed number.

Collins took the next turning off the motorway and smiled when he saw the taxi was still following him.

• • •

When Ross saw the Rolls-Royce leaving the motorway, he swore. He'd been spotted. He would have to switch cars as soon as possible if he was to find out where the box was destined for.

He radioed the nearest member of his fleet of taxis and told them to get into position for a quick changeover, before adding, 'I'll drive, but you stay in the car – if Faulkner gets out and we need to follow him on foot, it had better be an officer he won't recognize.'

• • •

'A different taxi is now following us,' said Collins, as he looked in his rear-view mirror, 'but I think it's the same driver. None other than our old friend Sergeant Ross. Do I stick to plan B?'

'Yes,' said Faulkner, not bothering to look back, while Collins kept to the planned route.

• • •

Ross drew his new taxi to a stop outside Fulham Broadway station, fifty yards behind the Rolls-Royce.

'He's getting out of the car,' said the young detective at his side.

'And still clinging onto the box,' added Ross. 'Get out and tail him. I'll follow the Rolls if it leaves, just in case.'

The young detective leapt out and ran into the tube station, slowing down when he spotted Faulkner going through the ticket barrier. Faulkner stepped onto the escalator, tucking in behind a tall man. The detective remained several steps behind and watched as Faulkner headed for the platform, not looking back as the train pulled in. The detective slipped into an adjoining carriage and took a seat between two passengers, only his eyes moving.

Faulkner travelled for four stops before he got off the tube.

The detective was among the last to leave the train, but he never let Faulkner out of his sight, as the mark headed for the Exit sign.

He was halfway up the escalator before he realized that Faulkner was no longer carrying the box.

Ross had been following Collins in the Rolls-Royce for fifteen minutes when the car came to a halt outside another station. Ross parked on the other side of the road, just in time to see an empty-handed Faulkner strolling out of the station without once looking back. He climbed into the back of the Rolls, and the young detective emerged a second later, looking both embarrassed and ashamed.

Petrov travelled for another four stops before he got off at Westminster. He stood on the escalator, eyes moving in every direction, while keeping the box tucked under his bulky raincoat and sticking to the blind spots of any CCTV cameras wherever possible.

When he left the underground, he hailed a taxi. No one followed him.

Thirty minutes later, the Rolls came to a halt in Cadogan Square. Miles got out and gave Ross a wave before he entered number 37.

• • •

'So we still don't know what he was carrying?' William said, after Ross had phoned to brief him.

Ross sighed. 'Faulkner was at least two steps ahead of us. Again. He even spotted me.'

William frowned. Should he have told customs to check what was in the box when Faulkner's plane landed at Biggin Hill? He had placed his bet on seeing who the package was delivered to, and lost.

'Did you get any photographs of the package?' Ross asked.

'Several, but I don't know how much they can tell us. It looks like a normal shoebox. Blue, probably cardboard. But anything could be inside.'

Before he could pursue that thought any further, Ross added, 'I'll get in touch with TfL and see if the CCTV can tell us anything, but I'm not hopeful. The train Faulkner got on was probably an older one, unlikely to have any cameras installed, and there's no way of knowing where the person he left the package with got off. It could take days to trawl through the footage of every station on the District line.' He paused. 'Do you think this is just another distraction?'

'No, I don't,' said William. 'They wouldn't have tried so hard to lose you if this had just been about wasting your time. Whatever is in that package, it's something they don't want us to know about. I'll call Professor Meredith and see if he can come up with any suggestions.'

'No doubt he will come up with something even worse than the stadium lights going out,' said Ross.

'That's his job,' said William, with a sigh.

One of his other phones began to ring.

CHAPTER 17

Sunday, 29 July – day 3 of the Games

ARTEMISIA HAD SPENT A FEW HOURS roaming around the Olympic Village, making herself more familiar with her surroundings, and by the early afternoon she'd decided it was time to take the plunge – and plunge turned out to be the appropriate word.

Artemisia joined the queue for lunch and selected a salad, a slice of chocolate cake and a Diet Coke, then began looking around the room in search of a table. She spotted a girl wearing a British tracksuit sitting alone in the corner. She strolled across to join her.

When she looked up and smiled, Artemisia said, 'Hi, I'm Annie, and don't ask.'

'I'm Kelly,' she said, offering her hand. 'And don't ask what?'

'How long I lasted,' said Artemisia, as she placed her tray on the table and sat down opposite Kelly. 'Because I was knocked out in the first round of the épée competition yesterday. I only managed to survive for twenty-seven minutes.'

'Then you did far better than me,' said Kelly. 'I lasted for two minutes and nine seconds. I came fifth in my heat of the one hundred metres butterfly and only the first four went through to the second round.'

'But you decided, like me,' said Artemisia, as she took a sip of her Diet Coke, 'not to go home.'

'Certainly not,' said Kelly. 'It might have been my final race before I retire, but that doesn't mean I'm not going to enjoy the next two weeks, because this will certainly be my last Olympics.'

'So is this your second Olympics?' asked Artemisia.

'My third,' said Kelly, 'and before you ask, I came seventh in the mixed relay in Beijing, which was the highlight of my career. And you?'

'I didn't make the squad for Beijing,' said Artemisia, 'so this will be my first and last Olympics, but like you I intend to hang about and enjoy every minute while it lasts. I love the atmosphere.'

'Not to mention the fittest men on earth,' said Kelly, as she glanced across at a table full of Australians, one or two of them glancing in their direction. 'So many of them to pick and choose from,' she added with a sigh, 'and it gets better as the week goes on.'

'How come?' asked Artemisia.

'As more and more competitors get knocked out, you end up with a larger selection.'

Artemisia burst out laughing.

'And you?' Kelly asked.

'Oh, I've got a boyfriend.'

'That shouldn't stop you enjoying yourself for the next two

weeks. No need to tell him.' Kelly's eyes remained fixed on the next table.

'But we're pretty serious,' said Artemisia. 'We've been an item since we were teenagers, and now we live together.'

'All the more reason to have a fling while you still can,' said Kelly, 'because you'll never get another chance like this.' Her expression suddenly turned to anger as she banged a fist on the table.

'What's the problem?' said Artemisia, looking around.

'That's the Russian who stopped me getting into the second round,' said Kelly. 'I beat her in Beijing, but when she turned up this time, she was a completely different shape and size. I hardly recognized her.'

'Drugs?' asked Artemisia, giving the Russian girl a second look.

'Up to her eyeballs,' said Kelly, 'like most of the Russian team.'

'How do they get away with it?' asked Artemisia, the journalist taking over.

'Masking drugs. They all take them for the last six weeks before any major competition, so by the time they step up onto the podium to receive their medal, there's no trace, meaning they get away with it. But not for much longer, I'm told.'

'How come?' asked Artemisia, still probing.

'The good cops have finally worked out what the bad cops are up to, so it can't be too long before they nail every one of them, even after they've taken masking drugs. But it still won't stop *her* and not me being in the semi-final,' said Kelly, still venting her anger.

'But does that mean—?' Artemisia was beginning to say, when she was interrupted by an Australian from the next table who had sauntered across to join them.

'Hi, my name's Blake,' he announced, without sitting down.

'Kelly,' said her new friend, giving him a warm smile, 'and this is my friend Annie. What event are you competing in, Blake?'

'The javelin,' he replied.

'Of course you are,' said Kelly. 'I'm a swimmer.'

'You girls care to join us?'

'Sure,' said Kelly.

'What about your friend?' asked Blake, glancing towards Artemisia.

'Not a hope,' said Kelly. 'That's a no-go area. She's already accounted for.'

'Sorry to hear that,' said Blake, still looking at Artemisia. 'But . . . if you change your mind?'

Artemisia shook her head, so Blake switched his attention back to Kelly.

'He'll have to be satisfied with silver,' whispered Kelly as she stood up.

'Shall we meet up later?' asked Artemisia.

'*Much* later,' said Kelly, as she left her to join the Australians.

Artemisia sat alone, nibbling her lunch while she wrote some notes. But long before she'd taken a bite of her chocolate cake, she became painfully aware she'd only got half a story – and as her editor would surely point out, not the better half.

Artemisia looked forward to seeing Kelly again. She liked her and she had a feeling Kelly might be able to help her. She put down her biro and glanced across at the Australian table. Kelly was nowhere to be seen, and neither was the javelin thrower.

• • •

Shortly after six o'clock on what had been a very long day, William's phone once again began to ring. He picked it up, expecting to hear of some new problem that needed to be solved or a minor disaster only just averted, but instead he found Artemisia's boyfriend on the phone.

'No, Robert,' said William. 'I haven't got any tickets for the one hundred metres final.'

'I was calling about something far more important, sir.'

'Fire away,' said William.

'I'm sorry to bother you when you're so busy,' said Robert, before hesitating for a moment, 'but as I may not be seeing you for some time, I'll cut to the chase. I'm planning on proposing to Artemisia and I wanted to ask for your permission . . .'

For a moment, William was stunned into silence, despite a broad grin appearing on his face, a piece of good news that wiped away any thought of bad news, if only for a moment. 'How wonderfully old-fashioned of you to ask,' he said. 'But then, why should I be surprised when your family can be traced back to William the Conqueror?'

'Ethelred the Unready,' said Robert, 'but to be fair, that's on my mother's side.'

Both men laughed.

'Well, I suppose if you want to marry my daughter, young man,' said William, hoping he sounded suitably authoritative, 'it's nothing less than my duty to ask you about your prospects.'

'Not that promising, sir,' admitted Robert. 'Special advisers don't earn a great deal, but I'm hopeful that I'll work my way up the greasy pole and end up in Parliament, given time. Even then, I wouldn't be paid a great deal more.'

'Well, at least you'll be following in the footsteps of your distinguished grandfather.'

'But not my father,' Robert reminded him, 'because after university, Dad drove straight past Westminster and didn't stop until he reached the City.'

'Where he now chairs one of our leading merchant banks, and if the newspapers are to be believed, has restored the family fortune.' William smiled to himself. 'Unfortunately,' he continued, 'I think Artemisia's prospects are not unlike yours. There are almost as many unemployed journalists as former Members of Parliament.'

Robert laughed. 'I have more faith in her future than mine. She's a natural scribbler and has a sense of justice that you'd be proud of, which is one of the many reasons I adore her,' he paused, 'and want to spend the rest of my life with her.'

'Well,' said William, 'I appreciate you calling, and I'm delighted you want to marry my daughter, but I think we both know that my permission isn't what's needed, which begs the more important question, Robert. Do you think she'll say yes?'

'I'll let you know,' was all Robert had to say.

A few minutes later, William returned to his other world as the next call was from Professor Meredith.

'You have to understand, Commander, that what I'm about to suggest cannot be described as proof, however compelling you might find it.'

William waited for the professor to get to the point.

'A man turned up at the Russian Embassy half an hour ago carrying what looked like the shoebox.'

'Size?' said William.

'About fourteen inches by eight.'

'Colour? Branding?'

'Blue, no visible branding.'

That seemed like a big coincidence, and William didn't

believe in coincidences. 'Were you able to identify the man?' he asked.

'He's been known to our people for some time,' Meredith replied. 'His name is Sergei Petrov. He has the grand title of "undersecretary", but you only have to read his file to know what his real job is. I'll send you full details.'

'But were you able to discover what was in the box?'

'I thought you might ask me that question,' said Meredith, 'but unfortunately that's something even the most sophisticated camera can't tell us. However, if Faulkner went all the way to Helsinki to pick it up, I imagine it's something rather more dangerous than a pair of shoes.'

'Why don't you just expel Petrov as a spy?'

'I wish it were that easy,' said Meredith, 'but sadly that process can take days, sometimes weeks, and always results in what we call "tit-for-tat" expulsions, with one of our boys being sent back from Moscow. No, we're in a far stronger position now we know not only that the Russians were behind the opening ceremony blackout, but the person we've identified is clearly in charge of their operation.'

'Any idea what his next move might be?'

After he and Meredith had discussed a dozen possible scenarios, covering everything from drugs to a terrorist attack, William put the phone down with a sigh. Shortly afterwards, a full profile of Petrov, along with photos, appeared on his screen. He immediately sent copies to the whole team.

His phone rang moments later.

'It's him,' said Ross. 'The man I saw with Faulkner at the Oval. The man who I later drove back to the Russian Embassy.'

William sighed. He was beginning to think it had been a mistake not to check the contents of the box when Faulkner returned to Biggin Hill. Was he about to find out just how grave a mistake?

• • •

If one thing could be relied on, it was Councillor Dawson being on time for his monthly payment. Today was no exception.

Dawson confirmed that the one million deposit had been received, before he asked, 'Can I assume the other nine million will be paid before the August deadline?'

'Long before,' said Bernie Longe, hoping he sounded convincing.

Longe had become painfully aware during the past month that no bank or serious financial institution was willing to do business with him – especially as he couldn't reveal the potential return he expected from the stadium deal, which for obvious reasons had to be kept under wraps for the foreseeable future.

Raising a million hadn't proved too difficult. He'd mortgaged his house, called in a few favours and twisted several arms, but nine million was in a different league. He wanted his rivals to believe he was in that league, but he wasn't.

Longe was beginning to believe there was only one person who could come up with the full amount in time to close the deal. There were, however, two major drawbacks: one, he didn't trust the man, and two, it would mean having to sacrifice half the profits. Not a pleasing prospect, but he hadn't been left with a lot of choice. Something Miles Faulkner would be well aware of.

There were just twenty-seven days left before the contract had to be settled. Otherwise, Bernie would lose his deposit as well as the deal, and there were no prizes for guessing who would happily take his place and end up with one hundred per cent of the profits.

He stared at his phone and had to admit he had run out of options. He dialled a number and waited.

'Mr Booth Watson's chambers. How may I help you?'

• • •

'So, did you manage to get into the athletes' village?' Robert asked, when Artemisia returned home that evening.

'Sure did,' she responded, sounding rather pleased with herself.

'No one suspected that you weren't even a reserve for your school second eleven hockey team?'

'No way,' said Artemisia, as she came into the kitchen, where Robert was filling a saucepan with water before putting it on the stove. 'If you look the part, no one gives you a second thought,' continued Arte. 'However, I'm still no nearer to getting that exclusive, though I do have a few leads.'

Robert couldn't help laughing when Arte went on to tell him about her meeting with Kelly. 'Whatever you do, don't lose her,' said Robert, as Arte began to lay the table for supper. 'Kelly sounds like a rare gem and she might just supply you with that elusive exclusive.'

'Which is why I'll be going back to the village tomorrow morning to try and catch up with her.'

'There's no need to rush,' said Robert, as he continued slicing a tomato. 'Be patient and you might end up with an even bigger story.'

'Patience and deadlines don't make good bedfellows,' said Artemisia, tucking her arms around his waist. 'What sort of day did you have?'

'The House of Commons is in recess, so most members have returned to their constituencies or are taking a short break,' he replied. 'Still, there's always plenty of work for a special adviser.' A little bell buzzed, and Robert switched off the stove and began to drain the spaghetti.

'One day,' said Artemisia, as she grated some parmesan, 'it will be you taking a short break during recess, as the Member of Parliament for . . .'

'. . . whoever will have me,' said Robert.

'And when you do become a Member of Parliament,' Artemisia teased, as she sat down at the table and twisted a fork of spaghetti, 'best not tell the voters how we first met.'

Robert sat down beside her. 'And *where* might be their next question.'

'In prison, I shall tell them.' Artemisia smirked. 'After all, my father taught me to always tell the truth.'

'Then you'd better take your Olympic pass off,' said Robert, 'or someone might think you're Annie Charnock.'

CHAPTER 18

Monday, 30 July – day 4 of the Games

FAULKNER TURNED UP LATE as usual for their agreed meeting in Booth Watson's chambers, but his QC feigned not to notice.

'You mentioned over the phone,' began Faulkner, after he had settled in a seat on the other side of the partners' desk, 'that Bernie Longe has been in touch with an interesting proposition.'

'It *might* be of interest,' Booth Watson stressed, 'but it's hard to say. It seems that Longe has been given the opportunity to acquire the Olympic Stadium for ten million, but because the banks won't deal with him, he can't raise the full amount. He has managed to raise the deposit of one million pounds to secure the deal, but he wonders if you might be interested in going into business with him.'

'By supplying him with the other nine million, in other words,' said Miles.

'The question is, where's the profit?' asked Booth Watson. 'It's common knowledge they'll never be able to fill the stadium once the Olympics are over.'

'The time has clearly come, BW, for you to start reading the back pages of your daily paper, as well as the front,' suggested Miles, 'because if you did, you'd have picked up the rumour that West Ham are considering renting the Olympic Stadium as their permanent home for two and a half million per annum, possibly more.'

'Then how can Longe get his hands on the stadium for just ten million?' asked Booth Watson, still sceptical.

'Because five of the local councillors and two of their officials are on his payroll, as *Private Eye* never stops reminding its readers. My bet is that he wants me to cover the nine million shortfall in return for splitting the profits fifty-fifty?'

'That doesn't come as a surprise,' replied Booth Watson.

'However, it's not the percentage I have in mind,' said Miles, 'which is why I'll need you to draft a contract that will leave him wishing he had offered you more than double to leave me.'

'I'll have the terms drawn up by the weekend,' promised Booth Watson. 'I also wonder whether we might use this new partnership to our advantage, making use of Bernie Longe's particular expertise in another field.'

Miles waited for Booth Watson to continue.

'Don't forget, our Russian friends are expecting us to organize the urine spiking of two prominent athletes in order to get them disqualified. Longe has in the past been arrested, charged, but never convicted, for supplying "enhancing" drugs to young upcoming footballers.'

'And never been convicted,' repeated Miles.

'Shall I arrange a meeting?'

'Why not?' said Miles. 'What have I got to lose?'

'Everything,' replied Booth Watson, 'because if Longe had to ditch you in order to save his own skin, he wouldn't give it a first thought, let alone a second.'

'As long as he needs my money to close the stadium deal, I've got him by the balls.'

'But once he's got your money,' said Booth Watson, 'it will then be in his best interest to see you back behind bars where you won't be able to cause him any trouble.'

'What a good idea.' A smile appeared on Miles's face. 'If *he* was behind bars, you could tear up the contract and there wouldn't be a lot he could do about it.'

'That's a two-way street.'

Faulkner shrugged. 'Then you'll have to insert a clause that makes his a dead end.'

• • •

Artemisia arrived at the athletes' village just after ten, and Jim waved her through without even looking at her pass. She immediately went in search of Kelly, but there was no sign of her. She passed the rest of the morning wandering around the village, listening in to conversations and trying to get hold of something that could lead her to an exclusive – but aside from learning more than she had ever needed to know about the losers of various Olympic events, it was a wasted two hours.

She joined the queue for lunch and took a seat at the table where she'd previously met Kelly. She looked up every few moments, but there was still no sign of her. She was beginning to wonder if Kelly would open any doors, other than bedroom doors, when a familiar figure took the seat opposite her.

Artemisia didn't enquire which countries she'd visited since they'd last seen each other and Kelly didn't enlighten her. They spent a few minutes chatting about who had been eliminated or won medals the day before, although Kelly's eyes didn't stop looking over Artemisia's shoulder, she assumed in search of foreign fields.

'You see those two sitting at the next table?' whispered Kelly.

Artemisia glanced across to see two athletes holding hands under the table. 'Yes?'

'They first met at the Berlin World Championships three years ago,' said Kelly. 'They're both high jumpers. It's so sad.'

'Why?' pressed Artemisia, who smelled the scent of a story.

'I don't know the full details,' admitted Kelly, 'but there's no doubt how they feel about each other and, despite the fact she's now wearing an engagement ring, they always look so unhappy.'

'What's their problem?' asked Artemisia, wishing she could write down every word. She glanced to her left, while trying not to make it too obvious that she was looking at them. 'They look ideal for each other.'

'Except she's Russian and he's French,' said Kelly, 'so there has to be something we don't know about.'

Artemisia took a second look at the couple and wondered if her exclusive was sitting at the next table, holding hands.

Tuesday 31 July – day 5 of the Games

A FEW MINUTES AFTER ELEVEN O'CLOCK the following morning, a Silver Cloud (last year's model) drove into Middle Temple and parked next to Faulkner's Rolls-Royce.

'Longe's on his way up,' said Booth Watson, as he glanced

out of the window. 'He's accompanied by a couple of East End hoodlums who could have come out of central casting.'

'Why am I not surprised?' said Miles.

A few moments later, the door burst open and in marched a man who was dressed in an open-necked red shirt, a light blue suit and a pair of over-priced trainers. Without being asked, Longe sat down in the only comfortable chair in the room, while the two thugs hovered a pace behind him.

'I presume you asked to see me,' began Longe, without introducing himself, 'to discuss terms for my stadium deal.'

'I have given the matter some thought,' admitted Faulkner, 'and I believe we may be able to come to an agreement, and if we do Mr Booth Watson will start drafting a contract. However, as part of that agreement, I need to seek your advice on a subject you're considered to be an expert on.'

'There's a lot of those, Mr Faulkner,' said Longe, 'so which one do you have in mind?'

'Drugs.'

'Whatever it is you or your friends need,' said Longe, 'be assured I can supply it at the right price. And, not unlike your silk,' he added, glancing in Booth Watson's direction, 'I charge for my advice by the minute.'

Miles waited for Longe to stop laughing at his own joke, before he said, 'I feel sure the possibility of a nine-million-pound investment in your stadium project, with one million paid in advance, should prove quite sufficient.'

Longe shrugged his shoulders. 'So, what d'you need?'

Miles paused, before asking, 'If I wanted to spike an athlete's urine sample, just after they'd competed in a race, would you be able to supply an illegal substance that would guarantee he or she would be disqualified?'

Longe realized he was now in the driving seat.

'Difficult, but not impossible,' was his immediate response. 'But I have to ask myself, Mr Faulkner, could this possibly be somehow connected to the Olympics? Or would that be too much of a coincidence?'

Although Miles didn't answer the question, he was fast coming to realize Longe was a man he couldn't afford to underestimate. 'But you still haven't answered my question,' he said.

'Patience, Mr Faulkner,' said Longe, as he extracted a gold cigar case from an inside pocket, took out a Havana and clipped off the end, letting it fall onto the carpet. He then leant back and allowed one of his henchmen to light it. He inhaled deeply, before blowing out a cloud of smoke in the direction of Booth Watson, who started coughing.

'Turinabol,' Longe eventually advised, as if he were recommending a prescription for a headache. 'And I would be only too happy to supply you with the exact amount you'll need. However, I have to warn you, it's a fine balance. You must drop just enough of the drug into the sample bottle to convince the testers it gave the athlete concerned an undoubted advantage, but not so much that the authorities become suspicious.'

'That certainly wasn't worth a million,' said Miles. 'Any street dealer worth his salt could have told me that.'

'Patience, Mr Faulkner,' said Longe, 'and you'll find out what else I'm about to tell you, which is worth every penny of a million.'

Faulkner waited impatiently.

'First, you have to understand that when it comes to drug testing, the Brits are a bunch of amateurs. Especially when they are up against the Russians, who are professionals and have been flouting the system for several years.'

Faulkner had to acknowledge he was dealing with a pro.

'However,' Longe continued, 'I must admit that the Americans are fast catching on to what they are up to, and it won't be too long before the Russians are caught red-handed – a pun I feel sure you'll appreciate, Mr Faulkner.'

Faulkner frowned, painfully aware that Longe now held all the aces.

'So when I read in the *Sun* which athlete has been disqualified, I'm rather assuming he or she won't be unknown.'

Neither Miles nor Booth Watson offered an opinion.

'The process itself is simple enough. After a race is over, all the competitors who advance to the next round have to give either a blood or urine sample, and should they fail, they are automatically disqualified – as happened in Seoul in 1988 when Ben Johnson failed his drug test and Carl Lewis was awarded the gold medal in his place. These days, the tests are far more sophisticated, and all the samples have to be witnessed by a qualified Samples Collection Officer, who cannot come from the same country as the person being tested.'

'So what are the new rules?' asked Booth Watson, still making notes.

'Any athlete who makes it to the next round has to urinate into a receptacle supplied by the authorities, witnessed by the SCO. The urine is then transferred into two small bottles for testing: A and B. If bottle A fails the test, they then test bottle B, and if both show an illegal substance has been taken, the athlete concerned is automatically disqualified.'

Booth Watson continued to take notes.

'Once the sample bottles have been sealed and labelled,' Longe continued, 'they are sent to a drug-testing centre in Harlow, where tests are carried out by a team of scientists led by a Professor Cowan, a man who cannot be bribed.'

'But you said there was a weakness in the system,' Booth Watson reminded him.

Longe nodded. 'As I said, the laws state that a Sample Collection Officer has to witness the athlete concerned urinating, and to avoid the possibility of substitution, they are not allowed to pee behind closed doors. So, instead of swapping the sample, you will have to swap the Collection Officer.'

'But even if we found a way to replace them with our own man,' said Booth Watson, 'and he was able to drop the correct amount of Turinabol into the sample bottles, wouldn't the athlete concerned become suspicious?'

'Not a chance,' said Longe. 'Once they've urinated into the bottle, they hand it over to the Collection Officer and leave. Don't forget,' he continued, 'the Collection Officers are there to see the competitor doesn't get away with anything, not the other way around.'

'And how do we ensure our own Sample Collection Officers are in place before the two potential gold medallists are tested?' asked Faulkner.

Longe smiled. 'You can leave that to me, Mr Faulkner, and I feel sure you'll agree when I've pulled it off I will have earned the first million. Don't tell me, Mr Faulkner, you're not playing for the home team.'

Miles turned to his lawyer and nodded. Booth Watson unlocked the top drawer of his desk, took out a chequebook, filled in a seven-figure sum and passed it across for Miles to sign. Once Miles had penned his signature, Booth Watson handed Longe a cheque for one million pounds.

'That's a down payment on the stadium deal as long as you supply the correct amount of Turinabol to ensure the athletes we select are disqualified,' Faulkner reminded him.

END GAME

Without another word, Longe rose from his place, walked across to Booth Watson's desk and stubbed his cigar out on the blotting pad. 'I must remember to bring an ashtray next time,' he said, giving senior counsel a warm smile.

Booth Watson didn't rise or shake hands when Longe turned to leave, one thug walking in front of him, the other behind.

Booth Watson returned to the window behind his desk and didn't move until he'd seen Longe climb back into his Silver Cloud and disappear out of the front gate.

'It wouldn't have surprised me if he'd driven off in your Rolls,' said Booth Watson.

CHAPTER 19

Wednesday, 1 August – day 6 of the Games

COMMANDER WILLIAM WARWICK and his inner team sat in the dungeon of the Gold Suite, reviewing the last few days of the Games.

'Any update from Professor Meredith on what might have been in the shoebox?' asked Paul, when they had all given their reports.

'A dozen scenarios, and I'd only need an extra hundred trained officers just to follow them up. However, whatever they're planning, Professor Meredith thinks our biggest problem is likely to be the closing ceremony, as that will have the most press attention. But there's no saying what they have planned in the meantime.'

He turned to Ross. 'Any news of Faulkner?'

'We still have him under constant surveillance. But since his Helsinki trip at the weekend, he stayed underground until yesterday.'

END GAME

'Details,' demanded William.

'Faulkner drove to Booth Watson's chambers, where he was joined half an hour later by Bernie Longe.'

'They only have one thing in common,' suggested Jackie.

'Agreed,' said William, 'but that doesn't get us any nearer to finding out what they are up to.'

'No good,' said Rebecca, summing up all their feelings.

• • •

By the time Artemisia returned to the Olympic Park on Wednesday morning, she knew everything there was to know about Natasha and Alain – well, everything except why a recently engaged couple looked so distressed.

Artemisia had spent most of the night trying to work out how she could possibly enter their closed worlds, and was none the wiser by the time her alarm went off.

On the journey back to the Olympic Village, Artemisia had worked out where she might find them if they weren't in the village, which was at least a start. When she arrived at the training track an hour later, she spotted them both stretching in the warm-up area. Ballet dancers would have been impressed.

After forty minutes of well-honed exercises, they moved across to the high jump pit and carefully measured out their run-up to the bar, so that their front foot always landed on the same spot – they had placed two coins on the ground as markers – before take-off. They did not tire themselves moving the bar up inch by inch, as they had been doing that daily for the past four years, but instead satisfied themselves with perfecting their run-ups. If they didn't hit the exact spot every time, they would have no hope of clearing the bar when it reached a personal best.

Eventually, they put their tracksuits back on and left the warm-up area together, once again holding hands.

Artemisia left her place in the stand and followed them, keeping her distance. They stopped on the way back to the village, took a seat on a bench and shared a bottle of orange juice.

They were happily chatting away when Artemisia decided to move in and interrupt their thoughts. She would have to blow her cover, which was a big risk – but one worth taking.

She walked slowly across to join them. 'Hi,' she said, giving them a warm smile. 'My name is Artemisia Warwick, and I'm a journalist with the *Daily Mail*. I wondered if you would allow me to ask you a few questions?'

It was as if the devil had appeared by their sides, because they immediately jumped up and quite literally fled, no longer holding hands.

Artemisia sat down on the bench and tapped Robert's number into her mobile.

'If they want to talk, they'll talk,' he said, after she'd told him what had just happened, 'and if they don't, they're entitled to their privacy.'

Artemisia frowned. 'Of course you're right,' she replied. 'I now know they are my exclusive, but what I don't know is how to get them to reveal it.'

Thursday, 2 August – day 7 of the Games

A WALK IN THE PARK meant only one thing to Booth Watson. Miles had something he needed to discuss urgently and not in chambers.

They always met at ten o'clock outside the Churchill War Rooms in Whitehall. Booth Watson wondered who Miles was going to declare war on today. Churchill was one of his client's biggest heroes, although Mrs Thatcher wasn't far behind. They would then walk around the lake past Buckingham Palace, the home of his biggest hero. Booth Watson could only wonder how his client felt about being involved in disrupting her journey to the opening ceremony.

Booth Watson was wearing his trademark dark blue double-breasted suit – his Savile Row tailor making a gallant effort to disguise his weight problem – cream shirt, Middle Temple tie, and carrying a rolled umbrella, despite the fact the sun was shining. Miles came strolling down Birdcage Walk a few minutes late, not surprised to find BW waiting for him. After all, a thousand pounds a day retainer had the tendency to ensure you were on time.

After a brief handshake, neither of them spoke before they crossed the road and entered the park. They then followed a route that never varied and took about forty minutes, although Miles accepted that he would be billed for an hour.

'How is the contract for my deal with Bernie Longe coming along?' was Miles's first question as they took their usual path beside the lake.

'Almost completed,' said Booth Watson, as a squirrel joined them. 'I should have the final draft ready for you by tomorrow.'

'Perfect timing,' said Miles, as they continued walking. 'I thought you'd be interested to know I received a letter from the Fitzmolean yesterday.'

'Saying what?'

'When the Hermitage exhibition closes, the director has been instructed to hand the Van Gogh self-portrait over to you. They asked if I could let them know when it would be convenient to collect it.'

'So the Russians have kept their word,' said Booth Watson, unable to hide the surprise in his voice.

'For now, yes,' said Miles, 'but they could still change their mind after the closing ceremony. I will, therefore, need you to draft a reply to Mrs Warwick informing her that if the board felt able to accept my terms,' he paused for a moment, 'I would be willing to rewrite my Will and leave my entire collection, including the Van Gogh, to the Fitzmolean.'

'And what might those terms be?' asked an incredulous Booth Watson.

A duck waddled onto the grass, looked up and quacked, but quickly moved on when he discovered they had nothing to offer.

'An invitation for me to join the board of the Fitz,' said Miles.

'That's never going to happen,' said Booth Watson as they reached the bridge and crossed the lake. 'And you know it.'

'Why not?' asked Miles. 'They will be well aware that my collection is worth over a hundred million, which will surely leave the board with no choice but to take my offer seriously.'

'You seem to forget,' said Booth Watson, 'that your ex-wife is the current chairman of the museum and that Commander Warwick's wife is its director, and they'd both resign before letting you anywhere near the boardroom.'

'Exactly what I had in mind,' admitted Miles, as he carried on walking. 'However, should I succeed, and both of them do resign, I will need you to rewrite my Will at a later date.'

Booth Watson didn't comment. After all, it would be the third time in as many years that Miles had rewritten his Will, and on every occasion it had been done to assist him with closing a deal he was involved in at that time, and would welch on later.

'Was there anything else you wanted to discuss?' Booth Watson asked, as they came to the end of their walk.

'Unfortunately, yes,' Miles replied. 'The CPS have been in touch again requesting a date to discuss the sale of counterfeit Olympic tickets. I told them to get in touch with you.'

'They already have,' said Booth Watson. 'It appears yet another witness has come forward. I've fixed a date for them to interview you a couple of weeks after the Games are over. It seems Commander Warwick and his wife are going on holiday following the closing ceremony.'

'But what they don't know,' Miles reminded him, 'is that once the Games are over I will also be taking a holiday. A permanent holiday, as I have no intention of going back to prison.'

'But I thought you wanted to join the board of the Fitzmolean.'

'I do, but only temporarily, although I'm confident that once I am elected, my ex-wife and Dr Warwick will resign, which is the sole purpose of the exercise.'

'And then what?' asked Booth Watson, unable to keep up with him.

'Then, sadly, as I'll be living abroad and unable to attend any further board meetings, I will feel it nothing less than my duty to also resign. That's when you can once again rewrite my Will.'

'But what makes you so confident the board will go along with your plan?'

'One member of the board who sees herself as the next chairman has already written offering her support, and is confident she can muster up four other votes. So I will only need one more to be elected,' said Miles, as they walked back across the road to Whitehall. 'You can't imagine how much pleasure it will give me to see Dr Warwick have to leave while her husband is left with no choice but to resign at the same time, after the Olympics end in disaster.'

Miles shook hands with his lawyer and gave him a warm smile before he climbed into his waiting Rolls, leaving a bemused BW on the pavement. It began to rain.

• • •

Artemisia was beginning to think she could write a dozen articles about Kelly that could be serialized in the *Sun*. Her new friend continued to introduce her to young men who'd be returning home in a few days' time, but it only reminded Artemisia how much she cared for Robert.

That didn't stop Kelly trying to tempt her with more and more forbidden fruit. She should have been christened Eve, thought Artemesia.

'Did you know,' said Kelly, when she met up with Artemisia later that afternoon in the village park, 'that the Olympic Committee have supplied the athletes living in the village with one hundred thousand condoms?'

Artemisia burst out laughing.

'And I consider it no more than my duty to use up my allocation,' she paused, 'as well as yours!'

'Who's next on your list?' asked Artemisia, innocently.

'The French freestyle relay team have, surprisingly, been knocked out in the semi-final, and I intend to offer sympathy and succour.'

Artemisia laughed.

'Anyway, have to rush. See you tomorrow,' Kelly said, as she slipped something into Artemisia's hand.

• • •

'It's a bus ticket,' Robert said when Artemisia got home and showed him what Kelly had given her.

'But not just any old bus ticket,' replied Artemisia. 'If you look carefully, you'll see it's got a time and date on it.'

'Four o'clock on August the fourth. This Saturday,' said Robert, handing it back to her.

'I checked it out before leaving the stadium,' said Artemisia. 'It's for one of those red double-deckers that takes you on the grand tour of the Olympic Park, on the hour, every hour. It's so popular you have to book days in advance.'

'And somebody obviously has,' said Robert.

'I think it's just possible,' said Arte, 'that my Frenchman and his Russian girlfriend have booked tickets on the same bus.'

'Then it's possible,' said Robert, 'they've decided to talk.'

'And it also suggests that Kelly knows exactly what I've been up to, but then I suspect I didn't fool her in the first place.'

'Perhaps she hopes you'll be the one person who could expose the Russians, and that would be an exclusive.'

'But do I tell my editor what I'm on to?' asked Artemisia.

Robert considered the question for some time before he offered an opinion. 'If I were you, I'd get the story sewn up before you tell anyone.'

'And your reason, O wise one?'

'If he thinks the story is big enough, he might hand it over to an old hack,' said Robert. 'And if you discover there just isn't a story, as you did with Annie, then it would be best to remain shtum.'

'Good thinking,' said Artemisia, still clinging onto the ticket. In fact, she didn't let it out of her sight until they went to bed and Robert had turned out the light. She lay awake wondering: exclusive, or just another Annie?

CHAPTER 20

Friday, 3 Aug – day 8 of the Games

'Who'd get the gold medal for causing the most trouble at these Games?' asked Paul, as he put down the phone.

'It would be a close-run thing between the Chinese and the Russians,' said Jackie, as she selected a stale ham sandwich.

'Well, I think you'll find that the Russians have just taken the lead.'

'What are they claiming this time?' asked Jackie, after taking a bite.

'That someone took a shot at their coach when they were driving towards the stadium, but as I'm likely to lose my temper with them,' said Paul, 'it might be wise for you to come along and hold my hand.'

'When you say coach,' said Jackie, abandoning her half-eaten sandwich, 'do you mean a human or a vehicle?'

'Both,' said Paul, 'but I can't make up my mind if I should brief the Commander.'

'I think he's got enough on his plate at the moment,' Jackie said.

'Agreed,' said Paul, as he quickly left the Gold Suite, with Jackie in his wake.

Paul had worked out in the first week that if you hung around waiting for the lift, it took at least another twenty-four seconds of precious time, and even longer on the way down. Six times a day on average meant five minutes wasted every day, and over the two weeks of the Games, that would add up. Paul didn't have one and a half hours to waste.

They jogged up the steps and out of the building onto Olympic Way, where they couldn't miss a coach that was parked a few hundred yards away in the middle of the road with no driver behind the wheel. An irate-looking man, arms folded, was perched on the front bumper.

'I don't hear the sound of an ambulance,' said Jackie, cupping a hand to her ear.

'Because, fortunately, no one was injured,' said Paul, as they walked slowly towards the waiting man.

'Or a siren to suggest a police car is on its way to apprehend the villain who carried out such an audacious crime in broad daylight,' said Jackie. 'Or any independent witnesses to back up their story.'

'They must have got away scot-free,' said Paul, as he approached the man, who resembled a heavyweight boxer waiting for the referee to ring the bell for the opening round so he could land the first punch. He stepped forward when they were just a few paces away.

'Don't say a word,' said Paul. 'Leave the talking to me.'

'Understood,' said Jackie.

'Good morning, sir,' said Paul, as he came to a halt in

front of the man, who towered above him and looked as if he'd already gone three rounds. 'What seems to be the problem?'

'Who are you?' demanded the man, placing his hands on his hips as he glared at Paul.

'Commander Paul Adaja. Head of Olympic Security.'

'Then all I can say, Commander, is you're not doing a very convincing job.'

'And may I ask who you are, sir?' said Paul.

'Captain Sokolov, coach to the Russian volleyball team.'

'And how can I be of assistance, Captain Sokolov?'

'My team,' he said, pointing at the group of people who were sitting in the coach, 'are competing in today's opening rounds of the competition. We were on our way to Earl's Court when someone took a shot at us. You can clearly see where the bullet went through a side window. It's a miracle no one was killed.'

Paul inspected the damaged window, while Jackie climbed onto the coach.

'So what are you going to do about it?' demanded Sokolov, as Jackie got back off the coach and handed Paul the murder weapon.

'Not a lot, Captain,' said Paul, as he bent down to take a closer look at the small stones and pebbles on the ground.

'Well, I'll tell you what I'm going to do, Commander. I'm going to call a press conference and let the world know that someone fired a shot at us and the police did nothing about it.'

'That's your prerogative, sir,' said Paul calmly, 'but you might find the first question the press will ask is: where is the spent bullet that you say entered the coach, and where was the shot fired from?'

'The gunman must have taken the bullet away with him.'

'So you're telling me that after your team got off the coach, the gunman climbed on board and retrieved the bullet,' said Paul. 'That must have taken a lot of nerve. However, if that is the case, we'll need to take witness statements from your team which I'm sorry to say will once again hold you up.'

Jackie somehow kept a straight face while she wrote down every word.

Sokolov remained silent, his hands falling to his side as he waited for the knock-out blow.

'And the second question the press might ask,' continued Paul, 'is: was anyone on the coach injured, and if they were, why didn't you call for an ambulance?'

The captain seemed lost for words.

'And their final question could possibly be,' suggested Paul, as he held up a small stone so the dozen faces staring through the window could see it, 'could this, found on the bus just now by Detective Chief Inspector Roycroft, be the cause of the unfortunate damage?'

Sokolov clenched his fist.

'I think on balance, Captain,' said Paul, 'It might be wise to take your team on to Earl's Court, that's if you're still hoping to be in time for the opening match.'

'You haven't heard the last of this,' said Sokolov, as he climbed back on the coach.

'I thought I was a lowly sergeant,' said Jackie, as the bus moved off, 'not a Detective Chief Inspector.'

'I don't think Captain Sokolov would have been willing to deal with a mere sergeant,' said Paul, 'but be assured, Jackie, your promotion was only temporary.'

When Paul reported the incident to the Gold Commander,

William mused, 'Is this another part of a bigger plan that's simply meant to distract us?'

• • •

There was a quiet tap on the door.

'Come,' said the Russian Ambassador, barely raising his head.

The door opened to allow Sergei Petrov to enter his private domain. The undersecretary walked across the room and came to a halt in front of him. His Excellency didn't suggest he could be seated in the comfortable chair on the other side of his desk. He remained standing.

'You saw our British accomplice earlier this week, I understand?'

Petrov nodded.

'And is everything in place to ensure the two athletes are both disqualified?' Mikailov asked, without mentioning either of them by name.

'Yes, Your Excellency,' Petrov replied, without further explanation.

The Ambassador gave one sharp nod. 'And Sun Anqi?'

'She assures me that everything is in place for the closing ceremony.'

'She has the package from Helsinki?'

Petrov shook his head. 'The handover will take place on Sunday – early in the morning to escape detection.' He hesitated, before saying, 'I'm not convinced Sun Anqi can deliver,' he said, 'and perhaps you ought to distance yourself, Ambassador.'

'That's no concern of yours,' replied the Ambassador sharply. 'The Chinese have their own plan. My only interest is to make sure nothing goes wrong with our plan. What other problems do we have?'

Petrov inclined his head. 'Miles Faulkner is being tailed by the Metropolitan Police and, following the opening ceremony, it seems probable that I have been recognized, but they have yet to discover Sun Anqi's association with us, as she has managed to stay undercover.'

'Good,' said Mikailov. 'Just make sure it stays that way.' He looked up. 'Anything else?'

'Yes,' replied Petrov. 'An agent working for me in the Olympic Park has raised a problem I thought I should brief you on concerning one of our competitors named Natasha Korova.'

Saturday, 4 August – day 9 of the Games

ARTEMISIA WAS STANDING at the front of the queue long before the tour was due to begin. She kept looking back as more and more passengers joined the line, but it was almost four o'clock by the time Alain arrived and took his place at the back. He didn't acknowledge her, which made her wonder if he was alone and she'd only get his side of the story. Better than nothing, she decided. But would her editor describe it as half a story and once again drop it in the wastepaper basket?

Just as the doors of the bus opened, a tall willowy figure appeared and tried to pretend she wasn't there. Not that easy when you're six foot two and as thin as the proverbial rake.

Artemisia was the first on board and knew exactly where she intended to sit. Most of the passengers who followed her onto the bus shot up the staircase and quickly grabbed window seats that would allow them a panoramic view of the unfolding scene below. Artemisia didn't join them, as she had no interest in the view.

She walked slowly to the back of the bus and commandeered the centre seat. She placed her bag and jacket on one side of her, as she waited for Alain and Natasha to climb aboard.

When Alain got on the bus, she raised a hand. He quickly joined her, handed back her jacket and slipped into the corner seat.

A few moments later, Natasha slipped into the place between them, slouched down but didn't speak, as they were joined at the back by a father, mother and their little daughter, who took up the three remaining seats. They began chatting away in a tongue she didn't recognize, while looking out of the far window.

No sooner had the bus moved off than a guide, microphone in hand, welcomed them aboard. She began by telling them what they could expect to see during the next hour.

Artemisia was only interested in what she was to hear during the next hour. She took a small tape recorder out of her bag and switched it on. She didn't want to be seen taking notes.

'Let me begin by asking you,' she said, not needing to refer to the long list of questions she knew off by heart, 'when and where you met.'

'I first noticed Alain,' said Natasha, 'when he was sitting in the stands at the World Student Games in Budapest, pretending not to stare at me. I missed my next jump, but it didn't stop him applauding.'

Alain smiled, clearly recalling the occasion.

'If you look out on the right-hand side,' said the tour guide, 'you'll see the velodrome, which holds six thousand spectators. This is where the cycling competitions are being held, and where Chris Hoy is hoping to add another gold medal to his collection, for Britain.'

END GAME

'For Scotland,' declared a voice with an unmistakable broad accent, which brought laughter and applause in equal measure.

'After I was knocked out of the competition – his fault,' said Natasha, pointing at her fiancé, 'Alain left his seat and came down to the edge of the track. I couldn't speak French and he didn't know a word of Russian, so it wasn't a promising start. We struggled on in pidgin English accompanied by sign language, and finally agreed to meet in the training stadium the following morning.'

'We both ended up at the wrong stadium,' said Alain, as he took her hand, 'but I eventually found her.'

'I did everything in my power to avoid falling in love with Alain,' said Natasha, a sadness creeping into her voice, 'as I felt sure it wouldn't end happily.'

'But why?' asked Artemisia, 'when you're both so obviously . . .'

'We come from different countries,' said Natasha, 'speak different languages, and have been brought up in different cultures, so how could it possibly work?'

'Love has got a lot to answer for,' said Alain, 'because I knew within days of meeting Natasha that I wanted to spend the rest of my life with her, whatever the consequences.'

'But the only time we could see each other was at international meets,' said Natasha, 'and even then, we often ended up only snatching a few precious moments together. But when Alain visited Moscow with the French team last year, he took me to the Bolshoi ballet and proposed during the interval.' She held up her left hand to show Artemisia her engagement ring.

'We never got to see the Black Swan,' said Alain, with an infectious grin.

'On your left,' the guide was saying, 'is the basketball arena, which holds twelve thousand spectators and, surprise, surprise, the Americans won gold yet again.'

A few raucous jeers and cheers greeted this information.

'We both began to train even harder,' said Alain, 'to make sure we continued to be selected for our national teams. But I'm afraid that can't go on for much longer. I'm twenty-eight and coming to the end of my career, and in Natasha's case, it's a totally different problem, as she's having to deal with—'

'State-sponsored drugs,' said Natasha, completing Alain's sentence.

Alain took Natasha's hand once again, but it was still some time before she spoke again. 'About a year ago, I was approached by a man called Grigory Rodchenkov, the director of the anti-doping laboratory, a misnomer only our government could believe would fool anyone. Rodchenkov told me that over half the national team are now on drugs, and if I hoped to be selected for the Olympic squad, I would have to sign up for his programme.'

'And did you?' asked Artemisia quietly.

'No, I did not,' said Natasha firmly. 'My father is a doctor and my mother was a nurse, and they had both warned me from an early age about the long-term consequences should I decide to travel down that particular road.'

'But you still made it onto the Russian team,' Artemisia reminded her.

'Only by a centimetre,' said Natasha. 'During the past couple of years, both of my main rivals, who I used to beat regularly, were suddenly producing personal bests, while I only just managed to squeeze third place in the Olympic trials. So this will be my last Games, and any hope of winning a medal has long gone.' She hesitated, squeezing Alain's hand tightly. 'I've decided that the time has come to speak out, not least because I promised my father I would do so if the opportunity arose.'

'And frankly,' said Alain, 'we thought you might give us the chance to expose what the Russians are getting away with behind everyone's back, and allow athletes like Natasha to fulfil their dream and end their careers on the podium being awarded a medal, not in the changing room, packing their bags.'

'You'll have to help me,' said Artemisia. 'I'm a layman in these matters, so I can't begin to understand how it works.'

Natasha remained silent while the tour guide described the ExCel centre, where the judo, wrestling, boxing and weightlifting had been taking place.

'Not to mention the fencing,' said Artemisia, touching Annie's pass, which still hung around her neck.

Natasha smiled, but only briefly. 'In Moscow, there is a state-funded programme that administers drugs to over a thousand athletes in every Olympic sport, from weightlifting to synchronized swimming. However, the largest number of athletes involved are in the track and field team.'

'But I thought there were checks in place after each event?' said Artemisia. 'So why aren't they caught?'

'Because Grigory Rodchenkov has invented a steroid cocktail, known as a Duchess, that if taken six weeks before any major competition, can mask any drug-taking.'

'And he's the director of the *anti*-doping laboratory?' said Artemisia, trying not to sound incredulous.

'Yes, and he sits in the stand watching the Games every day, and is the first on his feet applauding every time a Russian wins a medal.'

'So how does this Duchess cocktail work?' asked Artemisia.

'You dissolve steroids in alcohol,' said Natasha. 'Whisky for men, vermouth for women. You swill it around in your mouth and then spit it out. You don't even have to swallow it. Then by the time you compete, you're in the clear.'

'That simple?' said Artemisia.

'That simple,' repeated Natasha.

'And in front of you,' said the tour guide, 'you can see the London Aquatics Centre. This is where Michael Phelps won six Olympic medals to add to his tally of sixteen, making him the most decorated Olympian in history.'

Artemisia thought long and hard before she asked her next question, 'But if I were to expose Rodchenkov,' she said, 'wouldn't your life be in danger?'

'Only if I go back to Russia,' said Natasha, barely audible.

Artemisia looked at them both. 'So you'll join Alain in France when the Games are over?'

'Before the Games are over,' whispered Alain.

'It's not going to be easy,' said Natasha. 'What you have to remember is that half the Russian team double up as spies, so if I were to make an unexpected move, it would have to be done while everyone else's eyes were looking in the opposite direction.'

'And when will that be?' asked Artemisia.

'During the opening heats of the one hundred metres on Tuesday,' said Alain, 'while I'll be competing in the qualifying round of the high jump.'

'And you, Natasha?'

'I'll be sitting in the competitors' stand, watching Alain,' she replied, 'which won't come as a surprise to anyone.'

'There are eight heats in the first round of the hundred metres,' explained Alain, 'spread over a forty-minute period.

END GAME

Once I'm knocked out, I'll leave the competition area and watch from the stands.'

'But you might get through to the final,' said Artemisia.

'No chance,' said Alain. 'Those days have long gone and, frankly, no one will be surprised if I'm among the first to be eliminated.'

'And then what?'

'We will wait for the start of the fourth heat of the one hundred metres,' said Natasha, 'when Usain Bolt will be on the starting line. When the gun goes off, the crowd will stand, their eyes never leaving the track for the next ten seconds, which is when we'll both slip out unnoticed – separately – and make our way straight to Stratford underground.'

'I did a dry run yesterday evening,' said Alain. 'It takes about fifteen minutes to get to the station, and my bet is that while Bolt is running, we'll be the only people leaving the stand and the tube should be fairly empty.'

'We'll arrive at Victoria separately,' said Natasha, taking over the baton, 'which will take another thirty minutes, and then we'll join the Gatwick Express. We'll be at the airport thirty minutes later.'

'By the time we board our flight to Lyon,' said Alain, 'the crowd should be engrossed in the final of the ten thousand metres, not least because a Brit is the favourite to win the gold.'

'You seem to have everything planned down to the last minute,' said Artemisia. 'So how can I help?'

'Tickets,' said Alain.

'Tickets?' repeated Artemisia.

'I can't risk trying to book a flight for Lyon while I'm being watched so closely Whereas you . . .' Natasha paused. 'I know it's a big ask – my government are unforgiving – but it's me they are concerned about, not you.'

215

'Consider it done,' said Artemisia, who was eager to play her part. 'Will you be safe in France?'

Artemisia could see the fear in Natasha's eyes. 'I can only hope so,' she said, so quietly and sadly that Artemisia wished she hadn't asked.

She turned the conversation back to practical matters. 'So where do we meet?'

'On the Gatwick Express from Victoria,' said Alain, now back in control. 'Platform thirteen.'

'Here we are back at the stadium,' said the tour guide, as the bus came to a halt. 'I do hope you all enjoyed the tour.'

A warm round of applause followed, which allowed Natasha to slip her passport into Artemisia's bag, along with enough money for her ticket.

The door of the bus opened and the chattering passengers began to disembark.

Artemisia was among the first to leave the coach, and she didn't look back.

• • •

When she shared her news with Robert over dinner that evening, the first thing he said was, 'We have our own booking office at the Commons, so you can leave that particular problem to me. I'll need Natasha's passport.'

Artemisia dug the little red document and the money out of her bag and handed them over to Robert.

'After dinner, I'm going to write a first draft of my article,' said Artemisia, 'while it's still fresh in my mind. I can't wait to show it to the editor.'

'You'll need photographs, so make sure you take a good camera.'

Artemisia made another note to herself.

'This is beginning to look like it might just be your big exclusive,' said Robert.

'Let's hope so, but I won't believe it until I've seen their plane take off for Lyon. I just hope everything works out for them.' She grimaced when she thought about the risk the two lovers were taking, and how tightly they'd held each other's hands on the bus. She couldn't begin to imagine how she'd feel if her government tried to keep her and Robert apart.

CHAPTER 21

Sunday, 5 August – day 10 of the Games

WILLIAM HAD JUST FALLEN ASLEEP for the third time that night when the alarm went off. He came out of his dream and placed the palm of his hand on the alarm button, but the insistent sound didn't cease. He blinked, opened his eyes, and looked across to find it wasn't the alarm but the phone that was ringing.

He grabbed the handset as he checked his clock. It flicked from 6.13 to 6.14 a.m.

'Petrov has just left the Russian Embassy,' said a voice he immediately recognized, 'and I wouldn't have woken you if he hadn't been carrying a shoebox.'

William was suddenly wide awake.

'One of my men is already on his tail,' said Professor Meredith, 'but it won't be too long before he's spotted, so you'll have to move quickly.'

William pressed the emergency button on his phone, and

within moments three new voices said, 'Good morning, sir,' in different degrees of alertness.

'Which of you is closest to Kensington Palace Gardens?' William asked, without explanation.

'I'm in Hyde Park on my morning run, so could be there in a few minutes,' said Ross, as he changed direction and turned his jog into a flat-out run.

'I'm on a bus heading for Scotland Yard, sir,' said Jackie. 'If I get off at the next stop and grab a taxi, I should be there in about ten minutes, fifteen at the most.'

'Call me the moment you're in the taxi,' said William. 'And you, Paul?'

'I'm in bed, sir,' said Paul 'I've just come off the night shift.'

'Then you're just in time to start the day shift,' said William. 'Call me the moment you're dressed and are leaving. You'll need your motorbike.'

'And a good morning to you too, sir,' said Paul, as he almost fell out of bed.

'Where is Petrov now?' asked William, switching back to the Professor.

'He's heading east along the Bayswater Road,' said Meredith, 'and it looks as if he's about to enter Hyde Park. At this time of the morning, the park is fairly quiet, so it will be much easier to spot someone following him. At most, my man has only got a few more minutes before he's blown.'

'I have the eye,' said an out-of-breath Ross. 'He's about a quarter of a mile away heading directly for me. I'm going to have to run straight past him and hope he doesn't recognize me.'

'Is he still carrying the shoebox?' asked William.

'Yes, he's got it under his arm,' said Ross. 'Do I arrest him this time?'

'No,' said William.

'Petrov's next move will be to cross a road,' came in Meredith. 'A simple way to check if anyone is following him.'

'Bang on cue,' said Ross, as he watched Petrov nip in and out of the early morning traffic before reaching the pavement on the other side of the road.

'Where are you, Jackie?' asked William.

'I'm in a taxi, just entering the north end of the park.'

'Look out for a man heading in your direction, holding a shoebox.'

'Got him,' replied Jackie.

'Dump your taxi before he sees you and keep an eye out for who he might be meeting. It's vital we find out who he gives the shoebox to. Take as many photographs as possible, in case we lose them.'

Jackie stopped the taxi, paid the fare and leapt out. She took a seat on a nearby park bench and pretended to read her magazine, while keeping her phone ready so she could take photographs of whoever Petrov might be meeting.

• • •

Petrov slowed down, took out his phone and touched a button on his speed dial. He had not only spotted Meredith's man, as well as the track-suited officer who'd chased after him in the Olympic Stadium, but he couldn't miss the woman who'd just jumped out of a taxi in the middle of the road, then sat on the nearest park bench and pretended to be reading a magazine. Did they take him for a fool? They must be here to intercept the handover, or at least find out who he was handing the box to. If they succeeded, Sun Anqi's identity would be discovered, along with any plans she had for the closing ceremony.

END GAME

'I've been blown,' said Petrov when Sun Anqi came on the line. 'I was followed by a couple of men and now there's a woman in the park keeping a close eye on me.'

'I told you not to underestimate Warwick,' said Sun Anqi, making no attempt to hide her contempt. 'Description?'

'Female. Fortyish. Five foot four to five, blonde hair, slim build. She's carrying a white handbag and is sitting on a bench by the road pretending to read a magazine.'

'Change of plan,' said Sun Anqi, as she turned back and joined a bus queue. 'Call Miles Faulkner and tell him I still need the package, but don't warn him you've been spotted.'

'But—' began Petrov.

'No buts,' said Sun Anqi. 'If anyone else is going to be caught, let it be the Englishman, because I can't afford to show up on their radar.' She rang off.

• • •

Jackie watched Petrov as he ended one call and began another, while still holding firmly onto the shoebox. She was still expecting him to meet up with someone, when the exchange would surely take place.

Jackie looked the other way as he continued walking towards her and saw a small woman, possibly Asian, who was on the phone while joining the end of a bus queue. The woman's conversation ended only moments before Petrov came off the phone. Coincidence?

What wasn't a coincidence was that when the bus pulled up, the woman didn't get on, leaving her standing all alone. Jackie took a photo of her just in case.

• • •

Petrov was back on the phone. Sun Anqi thought about not answering it, but couldn't take the risk.

'She spotted you,' said Petrov, almost triumphantly. 'She even took your photograph.'

Sun Anqi turned away as a Rolls-Royce entered the park.

• • •

Jackie ignored the woman in the bus queue, who had turned her back on her. She concentrated instead on the Rolls-Royce, but when it passed her, she couldn't see who was seated in the back, as the windows were heavily tinted. However, the number plate MF1 told her all she needed to know.

She was not surprised when the car slowed down and Petrov passed the box through an open window to the car's occupant, hardly breaking his stride.

Jackie was immediately on the phone to William to let him know what she'd just witnessed. 'Do I grab a taxi and follow him?'

'No,' said William, 'stay put until they are both out of sight. But tell me what you can about the woman.'

'She was standing alone in a bus queue and was on her phone at the same time as Petrov. But when the bus arrived, she didn't get on it. I took a photo just in case.'

'Description?'

'Barely five foot, Asian would be my guess, mid-thirties.'

'It's a long shot,' said William, 'but go back to Scotland Yard and see if you can find anything in records that matches up with her photograph. Let me know immediately if you find something.'

• • •

END GAME

Sun Anqi got on the next bus, not part of the original plan. She sat upstairs as it drove past the park and looked down at the woman. She was no longer reading her magazine, but had her eyes fixed on Petrov, who was now leaving the park, without the shoebox.

Sun Anqi got off at the next stop and waited.

• • •

'Ross?' said William. 'Where are you?'

'Still in the park, but I think he spotted me, so I ran straight past him and didn't look back.'

'Paul?'

'I can see the Rolls-Royce coming into view,' Paul replied.

'Don't lose it. This time, arrest Faulkner when he gets out of the car and, more importantly, find out what's in that box and let me know immediately.'

'Will do, sir,' said Paul, who swung his bike around and began to follow the Rolls.

'And don't forget that Collins is as sharp as a tack,' said William, 'and he'll spot a motorbike following him within moments. Petrov has played his part, Ross is blown and Jackie's on her way back to Scotland Yard, so, Paul, make a name for yourself.'

William got out of bed and headed for a shower that had been on cold for the past month.

• • •

Faulkner's car phone began to ring. He grabbed it.

'Plan B,' said a voice he immediately recognized.

Faulkner put the phone down.

'We're being followed,' said Collins. 'A motorbike about

fifty yards back. He's been with us for the last couple of miles.'

Faulkner looked down at the box on his lap. He could hear Booth Watson saying, *Get out while you still can.* But it was too late now, and one thing was certain, he couldn't afford to be caught with the box. He carried out the second part of plan B.

'Head for the North Greenwich cable car,' said Faulkner.

Collins made a u-turn and headed for the Thames, followed by the motorbike. He only slowed down when they reached the cable car.

Faulkner leapt out of the Rolls carrying a shoebox. He went straight to the front of a long queue, handed the ticket collector a twenty-pound note and jumped into the first available cabin, while ignoring the murmurs of protest coming from behind him. When the cable car moved off, Faulkner sat back and watched his pursuer dump his motorbike and also run to the front of the queue. He showed the ticket collector his warrant card – a dead giveaway – then jumped into the first available cabin. Faulkner double-checked: his pursuer was five cars behind, but had no way of joining him.

Faulkner thought for a moment, before phoning Bernie Longe. This was Longe's backyard, after all, and it was time to call in a favour if Longe wanted the rest of the ten million.

Longe told him exactly what he should do the moment he got off the cable car.

Paul called William and brought him up to date. After William had put the phone down, he rang the senior officer at Greenwich police station.

During the fifteen-minute aerial journey above the city, most of the passengers enjoyed identifying landmarks – the London Eye, St Paul's Cathedral, the Thames Barrier and the Olympic Park – as they continued on their journey ninety metres above the Thames.

END GAME

Paul sat back and avoided looking in the direction of his quarry, as Faulkner had nowhere else to go.

By the time they came to a halt on the other side of the river, Paul was sitting on the edge of his seat, preparing to leap off the moment he could. When Faulkner reached the terminal and his door was opened, he jumped out of his cabin, but didn't head straight for the exit. He ran to the signal box at the other end of the platform, to find the controller was waiting for him.

The cable car suddenly came to a halt, leaving Paul stranded in mid-air. He would have jumped the last few feet, but his cabin door remained resolutely closed.

Faulkner emerged from the signal box a few moments later, his wallet two hundred pounds lighter. The controller had given him more than enough time to make good his escape.

To add insult to injury, the controller made a public announcement over the loudspeaker apologizing to customers for the short delay. Technical problems, he explained.

• • •

'I've lost him,' Paul said over the line. 'Bloody cable car – someone must have bribed the controller.'

'Not to worry,' said William. 'He's not going anywhere, so catch up with him as quickly as you can.'

Paul didn't need to be told what William had been up to while he was stranded above the Thames.

• • •

Faulkner strolled out onto Western Gateway, shoebox under one arm, wondering how long it would be before . . .

A squad car pulled up beside him. Three officers leapt out and surrounded him.

'How can I help you?' said Faulkner, while offering his most innocent smile.

'We'll take the box for a start, sir,' said the senior officer.

Faulkner handed it over, just as an out-of-breath Paul appeared by their side. He produced his warrant card, and the box once again changed hands.

• • •

'Where are you, Jackie?' asked William, switching phones.

'Just entering the tube station, sir. I'll call you the moment I reach the Yard and report back if the photo reveals anything.'

She stepped onto the escalator as her phone went dead.

• • •

William turned his attention back to Paul and waited impatiently as he climbed into the back of the squad car.

'Get on with it,' said William.

Paul stared at the box for some time before he slowly removed the lid. He gasped.

'So what's inside?' demanded William.

Paul stared down into an empty box.

• • •

Collins drove for some time, taking slip roads and doubling back, but didn't head for the plan B rendezvous until he was convinced no one was following him.

He finally came to a halt outside a Chinese restaurant in Soho, where the head waiter didn't take a booking, just a shoebox, which he delivered to one of his regulars who was seated in an alcove.

'And what would you like for your main course, Ambassador?' asked the head waiter.

• • •

Jackie stepped off the escalator and headed for the District Line. Five stops to St James's, followed by a short walk across to Scotland Yard. As soon as she was back, she would search the photographs stored on the system, and if the woman she'd spotted turned out to be part of the relay team, her description would be circulated to everyone working in Olympic security within the hour.

She didn't notice the tiny woman a few steps behind her on the escalator, hidden behind a large man hugging his girlfriend.

When she reached the platform, Jackie only had to wait a couple of minutes before she heard the rumble of an approaching train in the distance. She looked to her left and took a pace forward as the train emerged from the tunnel.

The woman slipped in behind her, and, with a well-practised movement that would have impressed a seasoned pickpocket, deftly removed the mobile phone from Jackie's bag.

But when she felt a hand touch the small of her back, Jackie swung around, just in time to recognize the woman from the bus queue, before one almighty shove propelled her forward. Jackie couldn't stop herself from falling onto the track.

The driver immediately slammed on his brakes, and although the train came screeching to a halt, it was already too late. Screams and gasps followed from the passengers waiting on the platform as Jackie was hit by the train.

CHAPTER 22

Monday, 6 August – day 11 of the Games

NATASHA SELECTED A SEAT at the back of the athletes' stand that gave her a clear view of the high jump pit. Alain was warming up, and although he knew she was there, he didn't once look in her direction.

Artemisia was sitting at home following the track and field events on television. For a moment, when the camera panned across to the athletes' stand, she caught a fleeting glimpse of Natasha seated in the back row. She could only imagine how nervous she must be. Not unlike being in an Olympic final.

Alain cleared the opening height of one metre sixty-two quite easily, and the bar was raised two more times before he failed to clear it. With a supreme effort, he cleared the height on his third attempt, which raised a cheer from his fellow countrymen in the crowd. Natasha knew he would be eliminated when the bar was raised again.

Artemisia had almost finished her article; all she needed

now was the denouement that would have to wait until she'd seen their plane take off for Lyon, plus whatever photographs she managed to take while they were at the airport. She dropped Natasha's passport into her bag, along with a single boarding pass, business class, in the name of Ms Natasha Korova.

She watched as Alain failed on his third attempt at the next height, but as it was only a couple of centimetres below his personal best, the crowd gave him a warm reception.

He sat down on the grass verge and took his time removing his spikes before pulling on his tracksuit, while the sprinters lined up for the first heat of the one hundred metres. Each of the competitors had their names announced to the crowd, and the British entry got the loudest cheer, even though it was thought unlikely he'd progress to the next round.

The gun went off and, as Alain had predicted, the crowd rose as one, which gave him the chance to look up and nod at Natasha.

When the runners for the second heat walked out onto the track, Alain stood up, strolled across the back straight, hopped over the barrier and joined his fellow athletes in the lower stand. He didn't once look back at Natasha. He pretended to still be engrossed in what was happening in the high jump, which was down to the last four competitors.

Natasha carried out the same routine during the third heat. She stood, she cheered, she sat back down, although her mind was elsewhere. She forgot to applaud when a Russian had come third and made it to the semi-finals. Someone noticed.

The starter called the runners for the fourth heat to their marks, and the crowd fell silent. When the gun sounded and eight athletes shot out of their blocks, the crowd once again rose in unison and followed the sprinters' progress, their eyes never leaving one athlete in particular as he headed towards the finishing line, leaving the rest of the field in his wake.

During the race, Alain slipped out of his seat and climbed the steps that led out of the block, confident that Natasha would only be a few strides behind.

When the cheers reached a fortissimo, they must have been the only two people in the stadium who hadn't witnessed Usain Bolt crossing the line. But they weren't.

Someone else was sitting at the back of the athletes' stand, who wasn't an athlete; he was surprised that Alain hadn't joined Natasha after he'd been eliminated from the high jump, as he was well aware of their relationship. He was even more surprised when Alain left the stadium during the fourth heat, because there would be a Frenchman lining up in the fifth heat, who had a good chance of making it through to the semi-final. Perhaps he was going to the toilet and would be back in time to watch his fellow countryman.

Natasha left a few moments after the gun had gone off and the crowd was once again on its feet. The man at the back of the stand didn't watch the race.

He remained seated, quickly dialled a number on his mobile and reported what he had witnessed to Sergei Petrov at the Russian Embassy. Petrov reluctantly phoned her.

• • •

Once Artemisia had seen Bolt crossing the finishing line to the acclamation of eighty thousand spectators, along with millions around the world, she switched off the television, grabbed her bag and quickly left the flat. Once she was out on the street, she hailed a taxi and told the cabbie, 'Victoria station,' before climbing into the back.

She once again checked that Natasha's passport and boarding pass were safely in her bag. They were. She went over her article one more time, making the occasional emendation. Whenever she looked up, the lights always seemed to be red, but perhaps you only noticed when in a hurry.

• • •

Alain boarded the tube for Victoria – eleven stops, one change at Oxford Circus, twenty-eight minutes. Running on time. Natasha, who didn't join Alain, spent those twenty-eight minutes anxiously looking around, fearing she might recognize someone – or, worse, that someone might recognize her.

• • •

Artemisia was dropped outside Victoria station sixteen minutes later, and after one look at the departure board headed for Platform Thirteen. She sat down on a bench a few yards from the ticket barrier and waited.

She became more anxious by the minute. Was she too late or too early? And then Alain appeared and gave her no more than a cursory glance before he climbed aboard the Gatwick Express. Natasha followed a few moments later, but got into a separate carriage at the far end of the train.

When the station clock ticked over, indicating two minutes to departure, Artemisia got up, showed her ticket to the collector at the barrier, climbed aboard and took a seat in the corner of a packed carriage, halfway between them.

The train departed on time, and a message moved across a thin screen at the far end of the carriage, informing passengers that the journey to Gatwick airport would take thirty minutes.

She waited for another ten minutes before she got up, leaving Alain behind her. Three carriages further along, she spotted Natasha sitting alone in first class. All part of the plan.

As she passed Natasha, she bent down and left her passport and boarding pass on the seat beside her, before carrying on. She found a vacant place in the next carriage, where a Chinese woman in a wheelchair was having a rug placed over her legs by an attentive carer.

When the train arrived at Gatwick airport, Alain was among the first to step out onto the platform, while Artemisia hung back and joined the crowd heading for Departures.

She didn't look to check if Natasha was following. She just assumed she was.

Alain didn't slow down, but headed straight for security. After showing his boarding pass, Alain looked back, not searching for Natasha but for Artemisia. He smiled and mouthed the words, 'thank you', before disappearing from sight.

Artemisia only had to wait for a few more moments before Natasha walked past and followed Alain towards security.

Once Natasha was out of sight, Artemisia took a lift to the observation tower on the seventh floor, bought a coffee and found a seat by the window.

She checked the departures board. The Air France flight to Lyon was due to take off in forty minutes. She used the time to finish her article, describing how the two lovers had escaped the clutches of the Russians right in front of their eyes.

At security, Natasha took off her watch and shoes and placed them with her passport and boarding pass in the tray. She picked them up on the other side. On the move once again, she only broke her stride to check the gate number on the departures board. Lyon. Gate 42. Now boarding. She began to follow the directions for Gates 40 to 50, not even glancing in any of the tempting shop windows as she hurried by.

When she reached the departure gate, Natasha was greeted with a long queue waiting to board the aircraft. She looked anxiously around in search of Alain, who she couldn't see standing in the queue. Then she spotted him seated in the far corner of the waiting room, reading a copy of *Le Figaro*.

When he looked up, she pointed to the toilet. He nodded and tapped his watch. She quickly disappeared inside and found a vacant cubicle.

Moments later, a man pushing a lady in a wheelchair followed her in. An observant person might have wondered why they hadn't taken advantage of the disabled toilet next door. However, the only other people in the washroom were two women washing their hands, who appeared to be in a hurry.

Natasha flushed the toilet, opened her cubicle door and was about to step out when a wheelchair came hurtling towards her, knocking her back onto the seat, while the man remained outside and pulled the door closed. As he did so, the woman leapt out of her wheelchair, grabbed a startled Natasha by the throat and, with her other hand, thrust a heavily scented cloth over her nose and mouth. Natasha tried to put up a struggle, but within moments, she fell back unconscious.

Sun Anqi lifted up the limp body and dumped it unceremoniously in the wheelchair, before placing her woollen hat on Natasha's head and the blanket over her legs. She then tentatively opened the cubicle door, to find Petrov standing there. She pushed the wheelchair out, locked herself back in, sat on the toilet seat and waited.

Petrov wheeled Natasha slowly out of the washroom into the corridor and headed off in the opposite direction.

Alain glanced across to see a man pushing a wheelchair, but he didn't give him a second look, as he'd seen them entering the washroom a few minutes before.

He was becoming more and more anxious by the minute as the queue to board the aircraft was getting shorter and shorter. His eyes switched every few seconds between the dwindling queue and the entrance to the ladies' toilet. He phoned Natasha on her mobile, but she didn't pick up.

He became even more anxious when an announcement came over the tannoy: 'Last call for Flight 043 to Lyon. Please board immediately as the plane is about to depart.'

Alain ran across to the toilet, stopped at the entrance and desperately called out, 'Natasha, Natasha' – but there was no reply. When another lady came out, he asked her if she'd seen a tall, thin woman in her mid-twenties, only to be told there was no one who fitted that description in the washroom.

He ran inside and began to check each of the cubicles one by one, but couldn't find her. And then the only occupied cubicle door opened, and out stepped a small Asian woman, who he could have sworn he'd seen somewhere before.

Alain quickly left the washroom, only to see that the departure gate had closed. He ran across to the check-in desk.

'I'm so sorry,' said the attendant, 'but we couldn't wait any longer. Would you like me to book you onto our next flight in two hours' time?'

• • •

END GAME

Petrov pushed the wheelchair towards Gate 21, arriving just as the plane bound for Lyon began to taxi out onto the runway.

He handed over two passports to the clerk behind the counter. She checked them both before looking down at the young woman in the wheelchair. 'I think my daughter must have fallen asleep,' he said. 'She's had a long day.'

The attendant smiled, looked sympathetic and said, 'I'll make sure you're among the first to board.'

He thanked her.

• • •

Artemisia sat at a table by the window and completed her article, which she would file the moment she saw the plane take off.

She glanced out of the window to see the aircraft bound for Lyon had reached the front of the queue and was waiting to be cleared for take-off. She took several photographs, then read her article one more time, making only a couple of small changes before she called the news desk.

'I'll be filing my copy in a few minutes' time,' she said.

'It's been a slow day,' said the news editor, 'so I hope it's good.'

Artemisia didn't comment.

• • •

Another woman was also looking down from the observation deck, not at an Air France plane that was about to take off, but at an Aeroflot flight that had just begun boarding. She watched as her colleague carried a young woman in his arms up the steps of the aircraft. She was still wearing the woollen hat. An attendant followed close behind with her wheelchair. They disappeared inside.

Sun Anqi dialled a private number on her mobile. When it was answered, all she said was, 'The high jumper's cleared the bar.'

'I'll let Moscow know immediately,' said the Russian Ambassador, 'and we'll make sure someone is on standby at Sheremetyevo to meet her when she lands.'

• • •

Artemisia watched as the Air France plane gathered speed as it set off down the runway. She took one more photograph before it took off and rose steeply into the air. Seconds later, the plane disappeared into a bank of clouds, and she couldn't resist letting out a small cheer.

• • •

The editor only had to read the first couple of paragraphs of Artemisia's article to realize it was Olympic gold dust.

'Get Artemisia Warwick on the line,' he screamed at his secretary, 'and find the news editor. Now!' He went on reading the article until the news editor appeared moments later. 'We've got our front-page exclusive,' he said.

The phone on the editor's desk began to ring. He handed over Artemisia's copy and the four photographs he'd selected. 'I've marked the one I think should be on the front page. The rest will make a centre page spread.' He picked up the phone.

'You wanted to speak to me,' said a voice.

'Where are you, Warwick?' demanded the editor.

'At Gatwick station, waiting to catch the next train back to Victoria.'

'Has their plane taken off?'

'A few minutes ago,' said Artemisia.

'You should have been on it,' barked the editor, 'so make sure you're on the next one.'

Why? Artemisia wanted to ask, but before she could open her mouth to speak, she was told, 'I need a follow-up piece with pictures of the happy couple standing outside the church where they'll be married. Quotes from his mother and father about how delighted they are that she was able to join them, and lots more photos. Report back to me the moment you land in Lyon.'

I suppose that's about the nearest I'm going to get to a compliment, thought Artemisia, as she began running back towards the airport. When she reached the terminal, she headed straight for the Air France desk to purchase a ticket for the next available flight, but she was still yards away when she spotted a forlorn figure leaning on the counter. She felt sick.

'What happened?' she cried, as she ran across to join Alain and placed an arm around his shoulder.

She tried to comfort him as he explained exactly what had happened.

'It was only later I realized,' said Alain, 'that the woman in the wheelchair who went into the toilet was far bigger than the woman who came out.'

'This is an announcement for all passengers travelling on Aeroflot Flight 247 to Moscow. Please make your way to the check-in desk, as the gate is about to close.'

Alain and Artemisia looked at each other. Neither of them

needed to be told where Natasha was. They both took off with the same thought in mind and didn't stop running until they reached security.

The duty officer politely pointed out that neither of them had a boarding pass. She produced her press pass, but he wasn't moved. She pleaded, but it fell on deaf ears.

'But someone is being abducted against her will,' said Artemisia, her voice rising with every word.

'Then you should inform the airport police,' the official told her.

'By then it will be too late,' she shouted.

He shrugged his shoulders. Artemisia looked up and saw that Flight 247 had disappeared from the departure board.

• • •

Artemisia and Alain walked slowly towards the exit. She didn't know what to say to reassure him, and could only hope that Natasha was safe and their only purpose had been to get her back to Russia.

'I'll have to return to the Olympic Village,' said Alain, 'and try to find out if there's any way of contacting her. When I tried her mobile, a male voice answered.'

Artemisia watched as the dejected figure made his way slowly out of the airport and back into the real world. She tried to remain detached and not become involved – first rule for any journalist – but it just wasn't possible. She dialled the editor's number on her mobile, knowing he'd still be at his desk, only to be greeted with the words, 'Why aren't you on that plane?'

'Natasha never caught her flight,' said Artemisia. 'In fact, she's been abducted and is now on her way back to Moscow.'

'Couldn't be better,' said the editor, taking Artemisia by surprise. 'Knock me up a couple of hundred words on what took place while you were at the airport.'

'But I'm not exactly sure what did take place,' said Artemisia.

'Use your imagination, Warwick, and make sure you don't lose the boyfriend. I'll need an exclusive interview with him for tomorrow's edition, plus photos,' he paused, 'looking broken.'

The phone went dead. Artemisia thought about Alain, the undisguised misery on his face, and of Natasha, on her way to Moscow, alone and afraid. She only hoped her two hundred words might make a difference.

• • •

'Get our Moscow correspondent on the line now,' shouted the editor, as he slammed down the phone. 'And I need a black coffee and the news editor.'

A contented man, happily dreaming, was woken by the phone ringing on his bedside table. He picked it up to hear a familiar voice, who never seemed to be aware if it was night or day. 'Bob,' barked the editor, 'get yourself down to Sheremetyevo airport with a photographer sharpish. An Olympic high jumper named Natasha Korova will be on the flight from Gatwick airport, accompanied by a GRU officer, and there will probably be a couple more thugs waiting for her at the bottom of the steps.'

The news editor rushed in and waited by the desk until the editor had finished the call.

'I also want a statement from the Minister of Sport on how it could be possible for an Olympic athlete to be abducted while visiting Britain and then dragged back to Moscow against her will.'

'He'll be in bed,' said Bob, as he pulled back the sheet.

'Then wake him,' said the editor. He slammed down the phone and looked up at the news editor standing in front of him.

'Stick with the escape story for the first two editions, but be prepared to clear the front page, because I've got an even bigger exclusive. I should have words for you in the next few minutes.'

'Can I block a headline?' asked the news editor.

'"Abducted in Broad Daylight",' said the editor, who paused only for a moment before he said, 'No, change that to "Olympic Kidnap".'

• • •

Artemisia reached the platform moments before the Gatwick Express was due to leave for Victoria. She climbed aboard and found Alain sitting alone in a corner, head bowed, tears streaming down his cheeks. She placed an arm around his shoulder, but didn't interrupt his thoughts.

It was when they got off the train at Victoria that Artemisia saw her: a small Asian woman was walking quickly towards the ticket barrier. She tried to recall where she had last seen her, and then she remembered. In a wheelchair.

She took a photograph of her as she disappeared underground.

CHAPTER 23

Tuesday, 7 August – day 12 of the Games

COMMANDER SINCLAIR'S preliminary report on Sergeant Roycroft's tragic death landed on the Assistant Commissioner's desk less than forty-eight hours later.

The Hawk took a moment trying to gather his thoughts. He'd not only lost an outstanding colleague, but a friend of many years' standing.

Everyone knew the risks any officer took on a daily basis, but you never thought it would happen to someone you knew. But he also knew what Jackie would expect him to do and it wasn't mourn.

The Assistant Commissioner picked up Sinclair's report and turned to the first page.

He had to admit it was a thoroughly professional piece of work, even if it was laced with prejudice.

He went over Sinclair's recommendations once again.

1. Commander Warwick should be suspended for not having the shoebox examined by customs officials when Faulkner returned from Helsinki.
2. Sergeant Hogan should be summarily dismissed, having failed to apprehend Petrov and secure the box while they were both in the park, and before the box was handed over to Faulkner. Had he done so, Sinclair concluded, Sergeant Roycroft might still be alive.
3. Inspector Adaja and Sergeant Pankhurst had, in his opinion, performed their duties in an exemplary manner, and once the Games were over should be allowed an extended leave of absence with no loss of pay.

Sinclair summed up with the words: *given the unusual circumstances, Assistant Commissioner Hawksby should take over the responsibility of Gold Commander with immediate effect, with Inspector Adaja as his second in command, until after the closing ceremony, while being aware just how far the perpetrators of this crime might still be willing to go to achieve their final purpose, whatever that purpose might be.*

He closed the file and asked his secretary to summon the team immediately, having decided exactly what course of action he would take.

A few minutes later there was a knock on the door, and 'come' was followed by Commander Warwick, Ross, Paul and Rebecca entering the room and taking their places around the Assistant Commissioner's table.

'You will have all read Commander Sinclair's report,' said the Hawk, 'and no doubt formed your own opinions,' he continued, looking directly at William.

'Let's consider the obvious to start with,' said William. 'Jackie's death clearly wasn't an accident, and it certainly wasn't suicide.'

No one suggested otherwise.

'We also know,' he continued, looking down at a copy of Sinclair's report, 'that an Asian lady was seen standing behind Jackie only moments before she was pushed onto the track in front of the incoming train, giving her no hope of survival. In fact, the woman in question then disappeared, leaving everyone else on the platform in a state of shock.'

'That's all in Sinclair's report,' interrupted the Hawk, 'along with the fact that at the time you had Petrov under surveillance, and once again failed to apprehend him and take possession of the box before he handed it over to Faulkner. And to make matters worse—'

'You don't have to remind me,' said Paul.

'When Paul finally did get his hands on the box,' said the Hawk, ignoring the comment, 'it was empty. A fact that Sinclair highlighted in capital letters, just in case I missed it, so I'm bound to ask if there's any good news – preferably something Sinclair doesn't know about?'

'Yes,' said William. 'Something I picked up at breakfast this morning.'

All eyes were now on William.

'Anyone who reads the *Daily Mail* will know that my daughter was at Gatwick airport yesterday when Natasha Korova was abducted and forcibly taken back to Moscow. However, what they don't know is that while Arte was on the Gatwick Express on her way to the airport, she saw an Asian woman in a wheelchair with her carer. She wouldn't have given it a second thought if she hadn't seen the same woman when she returned to Victoria station later that afternoon, walking quickly towards the ticket barrier, no wheelchair, no carer.'

The rest of the team remained silent.

'However, Arte did manage to get a photo of her before she disappeared underground.'

William handed around a photo of a woman; although she had her back to the photographer, you couldn't miss the tattoo of a scorpion on her neck.

'Like father, like daughter,' commented the Hawk.

'And it gets better,' said William. 'When I showed Artemisia a photograph of Sergei Petrov, she immediately identified him as the "carer" she'd seen on the train with the woman in the wheelchair.'

'So now we know who accompanied Natasha Korova back to Moscow,' said the Hawk.

'But what we don't know,' said William, 'is if he's staying put, or whether he's likely to return to the UK under another name.'

Ross was the first to offer an opinion. 'He'll have been on the first flight back.'

'On balance,' said the Hawk, 'I think it might be wise not to burden Commander Sinclair with all this information until after the closing ceremony, in the hope it will give us enough time to redeem the situation.'

'And if we don't?' asked Rebecca.

'You'll all end up in the Tower with Sinclair as Governor of the Keys.'

'That's incentive enough,' said William.

'With that in mind,' said the Hawk, 'it's my intention to accept Sinclair's recommendation that I should take on overall command of Public Order and Operational Support for the remainder of the Games. However, Commander Warwick will still be Gold Commander on the ground, with Chief Inspector Adaja his second in command. Sergeant Pankhurst will be made up to Inspector and continue with her present duties. Sergeant Hogan,' he paused, before giving Ross a half-smile, 'will be promoted to Inspector and will work undercover in the hope of apprehending the criminal responsible for Jackie's death and bringing her to justice. His promotion will not be gazetted.'

The Assistant Commissioner paused and looked slowly around the table, before he said, 'This is undoubtedly the best way we can serve our fallen colleague. We will now stand for a minute's silence in memory of our dear friend and then do what Jackie would have expected of us: get on with the job.'

They all stood together in silence, heads bowed. Rebecca tried desperately to hold back the tears, and she might have succeeded if she hadn't turned to see that the Assistant Commissioner was weeping.

BOOK THREE

CHAPTER 24

Tuesday, 7 August – day 11 of the Games

WHEN PETROV ARRIVED at Heathrow airport less than twenty-four hours after he'd left the country, he presented a different passport to customs. Mr Petrov was driven straight to the embassy, where the Ambassador and Faulkner were waiting for him.

'Moscow are not pleased about the decision Sun Anqi took on Sunday without consulting us. They were under the impression we were working as a team.'

'That woman is a loner, not a team player,' said Mikailov, as he looked down at the morning papers that were spread out on his desk.

Petrov tried to read the headlines upside down.

'They don't make good reading,' said the Ambassador. 'First Roycroft, then the Natasha Korova story. The *Daily Mail* are speculating that Roycroft's death is part of a bigger plot to undermine the Olympics, and they're already hinting as to who the perpetrators might be. So far, we're not in the frame, but the Chinese aren't going to be pleased.'

'Sun Anqi is claiming,' said Petrov, 'that if she hadn't eliminated Roycroft, she would have had to abort her entire plan for the closing ceremony, as no one could take her place, and it would have meant years of preparation down the drain.'

'You worked closely with her on the Natasha Korova kidnap,' said Mikailov, 'so did she tell you what she has planned?'

'No,' admitted Petrov. 'Other than to warn me that it would be unwise for you or any members of your family to attend the closing ceremony.'

'Then I will have to catch a diplomatic cold,' said the Ambassador, 'while you never returned from Moscow.'

'Any news regarding the spiking while I've been away?' Petrov asked.

'An Italian Sample Collection Officer had been selected to test the winner of the ten thousand metres,' said Faulkner, speaking for the first time. 'However, when he found an envelope in his locker containing ten thousand pounds, he suddenly suffered from a stomach upset and on his doctor's advice was confined to his bed for the rest of the day. Luckily, a Russian official was on hand to take his place at short notice,' Faulkner assured them. 'An hour later,' he continued, 'the Brazilian Sample Collection Officer failed to turn up, after meeting a Chinese masseuse who believed in happy endings. A Chinese observer kindly volunteered his services when they needed a last-minute replacement.'

• • •

END GAME

The results of the day's drug testing reached the chairman of the London Games Committee shortly before midnight. Lord Coe insisted that further tests should be carried out, and after hearing the results, he insisted on a third test, something the professor had never done before. When they revealed the same results, Lord Coe called Sir Julian, just after three o'clock in the morning, to seek learned counsel's advice.

Sir Julian listened carefully to what the Games chairman had to say, while making copious notes on the pad by his bedside table. He then summoned Lord Coe to his chambers in Lincon's Inn Fields and told him who else he considered should be present for the meeting.

Four people were woken during the next twenty minutes. All four of them accepted that it was an emergency and confirmed they would get to Lincoln's Inn Fields as quickly as possible. One was driven in an official Games car, another hailed a taxi, the third drove himself, while the fourth pedalled furiously all the way from Fulham.

After Sir Julian had put the phone down, he took a cold shower and dressed as if he was attending a morning conference, which is exactly what he would be doing. It just happened to be four o'clock in the morning. He walked the short distance from his apartment in Lincoln's Inn Fields to his chambers on the other side of the square.

After picking up five notepads and half a dozen felt-tip pens from his office, he unlocked the consultation room. It usually had to be booked in advance with the chamber's clerk, but not in the middle of the night. He took his place at the top of the table and began going over his notes while underlining the salient points the chairman had made, only to be interrupted by the first person to arrive.

'Good morning, Sir Julian,' said an out of breath junior.

'Good morning, Peter,' he replied. 'I will require you to make detailed notes of everything that is said at the meeting – a copy of which you will leave on my desk before you return home.'

'Of course, sir,' said Peter, as there was a knock on the door.

Lord Coe looked as if he hadn't slept for the past ten days, and now he was expected to deal with an emergency that could undermine seven years of dedicated work. Julian sympathized with the poor man. However, he accepted that, as the senior Olympic judge, he would be expected to offer impartial advice, and not be influenced by any personal feelings.

'I must apologize for asking you to take this meeting at such short notice,' said Coe after the two men had shaken hands, 'but time isn't exactly on my side if I'm to chair the daily press conference at ten o'clock, not to mention a medal ceremony that is scheduled to take place this afternoon.'

'Agreed,' said Sir Julian. 'May I suggest you sit on my right, and I'll put the professor on my left? Sir Keith can sit next to you, while Commander Warwick can sit beside the professor.'

No sooner had the head of chambers made this suggestion than Professor Cowan appeared, with Sir Keith Mills, the deputy chairman of the Games, following moments later. The Commander was the last to arrive, but then he'd had to come from the Olympic Park. Sir Julian couldn't remember when he'd last seen his son unshaven.

'Allow me to begin,' said Sir Julian, once introductions had been made and they'd all sat down, 'by thanking you for attending this meeting at such short notice. However, none of us can be in any doubt about the gravity of the situation and the consequences for all concerned were we to make the wrong decision.'

No one disagreed.

'I chair this meeting,' continued Sir Julian, 'in my capacity as an honorary Olympic judge. My duty is to listen carefully to what you all have to say before I pass judgement. To that end, perhaps it might be wise to ask Professor Cowan to make an opening statement.' He just avoided saying, on behalf of the Crown.

The professor sat bolt upright in his chair and placed a thick file on the table in front of him before he spoke. 'Good morning, gentlemen,' he said, and as it was eleven minutes past four, it was an accurate statement. 'My responsibilities, as you will know, are limited to testing any urine samples supplied by athletes who have progressed to the next round, or won medals in their event. It may interest the committee to know that, to date, only three competitors have been disqualified during the Games. Two Turkish athletes, following the semi-finals of the weightlifting, and one heavyweight boxer from Colombia. However, after the events that took place in the main stadium yesterday,' continued the professor, 'over a hundred urine samples were sent to my laboratory in Harlow for testing, and I can report that two contained banned substances.'

Still no one interrupted as they waited to hear the names of the two athletes involved.

'You won't be surprised to learn that my team of highly trained scientists checked and double-checked, in fact triple-checked at Lord Coe's insistence, both the A and B samples of the athletes concerned. Unfortunately, they confirmed that both samples contained Turinabol, a banned substance under the revised Olympic code.' Eight eyes were trained on him, waiting to hear the names. 'The athletes involved,' he said, 'were Usain Bolt and Mo Farah.'

'I don't believe it,' was Sir Keith's immediate reaction.

'I don't want to believe it,' said Seb Coe, 'but having led a crusade against drug cheats following Ben Johnson's disqualification in Seoul, I'm left with little choice but to announce at the morning press conference in a few hours' time that both athletes concerned have been disqualified and will take no further part in the Games.'

'But Bolt has just qualified for the final of the one hundred metres, and is the odds-on favourite to win,' said Sir Keith, 'and if Farah were to achieve the double, with victories in both the ten thousand metres and the five thousand later in the week, he would join an elite group, making him part of Olympic history.'

'Before we get ahead of ourselves,' said Sir Julian, 'perhaps I might be allowed to ask the professor some obvious questions, as I would of any client, in the hope of finding a weak link in the prosecution's argument.'

The professor nodded.

'If an athlete wins a medal, a gold as Mo Farah did yesterday evening in the ten thousand, or should an athlete progress to the next round, like Usain Bolt, they are then automatically tested to find out if they have taken a banned substance that would disqualify them from taking any further part in the Games. Is that correct?'

'Quite correct,' said the professor, as if dealing with one of his brighter pupils.

'But how is that test carried out?' asked Sir Julian.

'The athlete concerned is accompanied to a testing area, where they have to provide either a blood or urine sample,' said the professor. 'If they choose to provide a urine sample, it will be witnessed by a specially trained Sample Collection Officer, who then transfers the urine from the collection vessel into two sample bottles, labelled A and B. These are then sealed and labelled before being sent by a special courier van to the drug-testing centre in Harlow. Sample A is tested, while Sample B is stored in case further testing is required.'

'And how are these Sample Collection Officers chosen?' asked Sir Julian.

'They are independent officials from a neutral country assigned on a rota,' explained Coe. 'All of them have vast experience in the field and were vetted long before the Games opened.'

'Who were the two SCOs on this occasion, may I ask?' said Sir Julian.

Sir Keith began to tap away on his iPad, while everyone else waited. 'In the case of Usain Bolt, it was a Russian called Igor Semolov and, for Farah,' he continued tapping, 'Jin Chun Dhang, the official Chinese representative.'

'How very interesting,' said William, speaking for the first time.

Sir Julian looked across at his son. 'What are you suggesting, Commander?'

'We have already discovered to our cost,' said William, 'that the Russians have a vested interest in undermining the London Games.'

'Details, Commander,' demanded Sir Julian, as if cross-examining a hostile witness.

'Even before the opening ceremony, my team and I dealt with a variety of incidents unquestionably orchestrated by the Russians. It has become abundantly clear that they consider the Olympic Games is a misnomer and the word

Olympic should be replaced with *War*. If Bolt and Farah were to be disqualified, that would be the only thing the London Games would be remembered for. All our hard work and successes would be forgotten overnight. Ask any Canadian.'

'I assume you all read the story in the *Daily Mail* concerning a Russian high jumper, Natasha Korova, which only confirmed something we've suspected for years,' came in Sir Keith. 'Namely, that the Russians have a state-sponsored doping programme, with the single purpose of winning as many medals as possible, preferably gold.'

William suppressed a smile. He was proud of his daughter. She'd nailed the Russians far more convincingly than a thousand officials.

'We suspect the Russians may be working alongside the Chinese,' came back William. 'They've made no secret of wanting the Beijing Games to appear a triumph when compared to London.'

'None of this would be admissible as evidence in a court of law,' said Sir Julian, 'as you well know, Commander.'

'Possibly not,' said William, refusing to back down, 'but I'd be very interested to know if these Sample Collection Officers were the first choice?'

'That should be easy enough to establish,' said Sir Keith, who began tapping away again on his iPad. A few moments later, he frowned. 'The Commander may have a point, Sir Julian, because neither of them was originally listed on the daily rota.'

'Then who should have carried out the tests?' demanded Sir Julian.

'In the case of Mo Farah,' said Sir Keith, 'the designated observer was an Italian called Tony Cressi, who called in earlier in the afternoon to say he was unwell.'

'Why am I not surprised?' said William, loud enough for everyone to hear.

Sir Julian scowled. 'And Bolt?' he asked.

'His observer should have been a Brazilian official, who failed to turn up.'

'Doesn't it strike you as something of a coincidence that both the delegates observing the athletes who tested positive just happened to be last-minute substitutions?' said William, 'and surprise, surprise one of them turned out to be Russian and the other Chinese. I rest my case.'

'Not unless you have proof,' said Sir Julian, 'and I shouldn't have to remind you, Commander, coincidence isn't evidence, however much you might want it to be.'

William wanted to protest, but knew his father was right. He remained silent.

'However much we would all like to believe the two athletes concerned are innocent,' continued Sir Julian, 'I cannot easily dismiss the findings of Professor Cowan, one of the most eminent and respected authorities in his field, and my first responsibility as an Olympic judge is to be influenced only by the facts in this case. The fact is that both athletes, however celebrated, tested positive for Turinabol, a banned substance under the Olympic rules.'

A gloomy silence descended on those seated around the table as they waited for the judge to deliver his verdict.

'I therefore have no choice but to . . .' Sir Julian concluded when a hand was tentatively raised. 'You wanted to say something, Peter?'

'I have a question, sir.'

All eyes switched to the young man seated at the far end of the table, who until then had only been making notes.

Sir Julian nodded once again.

'Let us assume for a moment that both the athletes concerned are innocent,' said Peter. 'If they are, I think I may have found a way of proving it.'

The older men seated around the table were now hanging on the younger man's every word.

'Both athletes are due to compete again in the next couple of days,' said Peter, looking down at an events timetable in front of him. 'Bolt in the final of the hundred metres this afternoon, and Farah in the first round of the five thousand tomorrow. So, my question is' – Peter looked directly at the professor – 'if they are both guilty of taking Turinabol, would it show up again when they were next tested?'

'Without a doubt,' was the professor's immediate response. 'Turinabol would be detectable in the urine for at least another week, possibly a fortnight. However, the Olympic guidelines on the subject do not prevaricate.' He turned the pages of a small, black leather Rule Book in front of him, stopping only when he found the entry he needed. 'If any athlete is shown to have taken an illegal substance, they will automatically be suspended pending an enquiry,' he read out.

'Then it's back to square one,' said Coe.

'Possibly not,' suggested Sir Julian, 'because as an Olympic judge, I have the authority to hold up a suspension while an enquiry is taking place. There is nothing to prevent me carrying out that enquiry and reporting back to this committee in, say, forty-eight hours, after both athletes involved have competed in the next round.'

'But who will carry out the observation this time?' asked William.

'I will,' said the professor without hesitation, 'and if I find that either or both athletes test positive for Turinabol, or any other illegal substance, they must be disqualified without further discussion.'

'Agreed,' said Coe, 'but it won't stop me falling on my knees and praying for the next forty-eight hours.'

'In which case, you'll need a bishop and not a judge to advise you,' suggested Sir Julian.

Laughter broke out, where only moments before humour wouldn't have seemed possible.

'I must thank you, Sir Julian, for your wise counsel,' said Coe, 'for which this committee will be eternally grateful.'

'Let us hope,' said Sir Julian, 'that eternally is the right word. However, it's not me you should be thanking, but my junior.'

The rest of the committee turned to face Peter and began to applaud.

'Enough!' said Sir Julian, raising a hand. 'Mustn't allow it to go to my grandson's head.'

'I had no idea he was your grandson,' said Coe, giving Peter a warm smile.

'You don't know the half,' said Sir Julian, looking across at the Commander.

• • •

Artemisia wept when she saw the same photograph on the front page of almost every paper the next morning. On day one, her story had run exclusively in the *Daily Mail*, but now every other paper had followed it up.

She stared at the image of a young woman stepping off an Aeroflot flight that had just landed in Moscow. She was met by two thugs who didn't need the letters *GRU* printed on their backs to know which team they represented.

Her editor seemed chuffed that every other paper had been given no choice but to follow up his exclusive.

The *Evening Standard* carried the Russian Minister of Sport's statement on their front page:

'Ms Natasha Korova, one of Russia's most admired and respected athletes, had to leave the Olympics and return to Moscow when she learned her mother had suffered a stroke. Natasha is now at her mother's bedside with the rest of the family. She hopes the press will respect her privacy.'

'Will anyone believe that rubbish?' Artemisia asked Robert over breakfast, after she'd read the article a second time.

'It's been written for domestic consumption,' Robert replied, 'and as the *Daily Mail* won't have a huge circulation in Moscow, they can keep the truth well hidden from their own citizens.'

'They'll live to regret it,' said Artemisia.

'Ah,' said Robert, 'so now you're going to take on Putin?'

'He can't be any worse than my editor.' Artemisia put down her mug of tea. 'It's just so unfair.'

'I know,' said Robert, placing an arm gently around her shoulder. 'But the real world isn't fair, ask any politician.'

'But I feel I've failed them.'

'You did everything you possibly could,' said Robert, trying to comfort her, 'and Natasha made it clear that her father wanted her to expose them.'

'It hasn't been enough.' She sat up straight and brushed away a tear. 'But I'm not done yet. Alain and I have agreed to stay in touch, and if there's anything that can be done to help Natasha, we'll do it. I'll go on fighting on their behalf for as long as it takes. In fact,' she declared, 'I won't be satisfied until we finally attend their wedding.'

'Or they attend ours,' said Robert.

END GAME

Artemisia looked up at him in silence for a moment, which Robert took advantage of.

He fell on one knee, removed a small leather box from an inside pocket and said, 'Artemisia, I adore you, and I want to spend the rest of my life with you. I can only hope you'll agree to be my wife.'

Artemisia remained silent as Robert opened the leather box to reveal a small diamond ring. He didn't move as he waited for her reply.

'Of course I will,' replied Artemisia. 'I'm only surprised it's taken you so long.'

CHAPTER 25

Thursday, 9 August – day 14 of the Games

'Have you heard the news?' asked Christina, as she poured herself a cup of coffee.

'No,' said Wilbur, looking over the top of yesterday's copy of the *New York Times*. 'What have you been up to this time?' he asked. 'Finally killed off your ex-husband?'

'Good idea,' said Christina, 'but that may have to wait until after this evening's board meeting. No, it's Artemisia – and it's double good news, in fact. Firstly, Beth tells me that she and Robert are finally engaged, and secondly, Artemisia's landed her second front-page scoop.' Christina handed Wilbur her copy of the *Daily Mail*.

Wilbur took his time reading the article, his smile broadening with each paragraph. 'The *New York Times* has been reporting their suspicions about the Russians for the past year,' he said, 'and now Artemisia has trumped them.'

'Of course she has,' said Christina. 'She's the daughter of her mother.'

'I think you'll find,' said Wilbur, 'that William was somehow involved in her creation, but I agree Arte should be proud, because her piece is a first-class example of investigative journalism.'

'Although she'll be distressed by the final outcome,' said Christina. 'God knows where that brave young woman is while we're enjoying coffee and croissants in Chelsea.'

'That's hardly Artemisia's fault,' said Wilbur. 'She wasn't the one who made the decision to expose their rotten system, and Ms Korova will have been well aware of the risk she was taking.'

Christina sighed. 'Artemisia won't see it that way, but I'm glad she has Robert to comfort her. I think I'll give her a call.'

'And don't forget to offer my congratulations, too,' said Wilbur, as he poured his wife a cup of coffee. 'And dare I ask,' he continued, turning to a different subject, 'if you haven't already murdered your ex-husband, have you decided whether to back him in his desire to join the board of the Fitzmolean?'

'I can't make up my mind,' admitted Christina, as she cracked an egg. 'I have to ask myself, if I were to try and prevent him from taking a place on the board, would I be responsible for jeopardizing the museum's chances of inheriting a unique private collection?'

'My bet,' said Wilbur, 'is that offer is nothing more than a sprat to catch a mackerel, and you're about to discover just how many mackerels you have on your board.'

'But my term of office ends in December,' Christina reminded him, 'so do I have the right to try and prevent him joining the board? Even though I've no doubt Miles has an ulterior motive for wanting to be a board member.'

Wilbur finally abandoned his newspaper, drained his coffee, and said, 'Like what?'

'If I knew that, my darling,' said Christina, 'I'd know how to cast my vote.'

• • •

'I'm only sorry,' said Christina, 'that it has proved necessary to call this emergency board meeting at such short notice, but when you learn why, I think you'll agree that, as chair, I wasn't left with a great deal of choice.'

The eight board members sat in silence around the table, listening intently.

'I'll ask our director to brief you,' said Christina.

Beth was seated in her usual place at the far end of the table. She opened the file in front of her and began to read a well-prepared statement. 'You are all aware that as part of our Olympic exhibition, we currently have on loan a Vincent Van Gogh self-portrait. Since receiving that painting, we have been informed by the Russian Embassy that when the exhibition is over, this particular painting should not be sent back to St Petersburg with the rest of the Hermitage collection, but should be handed over to Mr Miles Faulkner, no less.'

Christina noticed that one or two of the board didn't seem surprised, while the others began to chat among themselves.

It was some time before they settled enough for Christina to take back control. 'As you all know,' she began, 'Miles Faulkner is my ex-husband, and I can assure you he is not a man to be dealt with lightly. He has been in prison for various crimes in the past, although – I must admit – not for some years.' She took a long pause before adding, 'He has also written a letter to the director concerning the Van Gogh that you should be made aware of.'

Members were now sitting on the edge of their seats.

Christina looked across at Beth, who replaced one letter with another. 'Mr Faulkner has written to let me know he will make arrangements to collect the Van Gogh at our convenience. He added that he wasn't in any hurry, should we wish to continue displaying it.'

'How very generous of him,' commented one board member, who was well aware of what was coming next.

'He went on to say,' continued Beth, reading directly from the letter, 'that he remained a great admirer of the Fitzmolean and, with that in mind, he has decided to rewrite his Will and leave his entire collection to the museum.'

'Bravo,' declared one board member, a little too loudly, while a couple of others began to applaud. It was some time before Beth could read the final paragraph of the letter.

'However, this offer comes with a caveat,' she said, which quickly brought the board members back to order. She looked back down at the letter. 'Mr Faulkner hopes that, given the circumstances, you might consider inviting him to join the board.'

This caused an even noisier outburst of chattering, which left Christina in no doubt that the board was divided.

'Of course, the offer is incredibly generous,' Christina conceded, once order had again been restored, 'but we should remember that Mr Faulkner has it in his power to rewrite his Will at any time in the future.' She didn't add:

as he has done to my knowledge on several occasions in the past.

'I, for one,' said Lady Morland, 'am willing to take Mr Faulkner at his word, and I'm bound to ask if there is any reason to believe he hasn't made the offer in good faith?'

'None that I'm aware of,' admitted Christina, 'but that's not something I personally would feel confident we can rely on in the future. However, as I am standing down as your chairman at the end of the year, I felt I should leave it to the board to make such a far-reaching decision.' She turned her attention to the company secretary. 'Given the circumstances, Mr Parker, perhaps you would guide us on the procedure we should take.'

'I feel I should point out from the outset, Chair,' said the company secretary, as he rose from his place, 'that this decision cannot be made with a single vote, but will require the board to vote twice. Firstly, to decide if we should accept Mr Faulkner's generous offer to donate his collection to the museum, and then, if the board felt able to agree on that, a second vote would be necessary to determine whether Mr Faulkner should be invited to join the board.'

'I fear one depends on the other,' said Christina quietly, 'but let's at least find out if this matter can be easily resolved.'

'I'll need a proposer for the first motion,' said the board secretary.

A hand shot up.

'Mrs McBride,' he said, writing down her name in the minutes book, 'and a seconder.'

Lady Morland didn't hesitate to raise her hand.

The secretary added her name before he looked up and

enquired, 'Those in favour of accepting Mr Faulkner's offer to donate his collection to the museum in his Will?'

Five hands were raised immediately.

'Those against?'

A single hand went up.

'I declare the motion carried by five votes to one, with three abstentions,' declared Parker.

Chattering broke out once again, but quickly ceased when Parker continued.

'The second motion,' said Mr Parker, 'is that we should invite Mr Faulkner to join the board. Those in favour?'

Only three hands were raised this time.

'Against?'

Three more hands went up.

'The second motion,' said the secretary, 'has resulted in a tie of three votes each, with once again three abstentions, which leaves you, Madam Chair, with the casting vote.'

Three board members looked pleased, as they were sure they knew which side Christina would come down on, while three others looked disappointed.

'Before I cast my vote, can I convince either of the other two abstainers to change their minds?' asked Christina, looking around hopefully. She waited, as one member appeared to hesitate but, to Christina's dismay, four hands remained resolutely below the table.

'The director,' continued Christina, 'had fully briefed me on the situation, so I have had some time to consider my position should the crucial vote end in a stalemate. As my term of office comes to an end in only a few months, it is with a heavy heart that I cast my vote in favour of Mr Faulkner being invited to join the board. I can only hope the rewards will outweigh my reservations.'

A small round of applause followed, while the rest of the board remained silent.

'Then the motion is carried by four votes to three, with two abstentions,' declared the company secretary.

Christina waited once again for the voices to be still, before she said, 'Is there any other business?'

'Yes, Madam Chair,' said Beth. 'In view of the board's decision, I have been left with no choice but to resign as your director.'

CHAPTER 26

Friday, 10 August – day 15 of the Games

SIR JULIAN WAS GOING OVER the finer details of a fraud case when his secretary rang to let him know that Professor Cowan was on the line.

'Please put him through, Miss Longstaff,' said Sir Julian. Over the years, whenever Julian had been kept waiting to hear a jury's verdict, he'd always managed to remain calm and detached. But he was neither when the professor came on the line.

'Good morning, Sir Julian.'

What are the results of the tests? Julian wanted to say, but satisfied himself with, 'Good morning, Professor.'

'I hope you are well,' said the professor.

'I am, thank you,' said Sir Julian, 'and hope you are too.'

'Just recovering from a slight cold,' said the professor, 'but nothing life-threatening.'

Julian didn't respond for fear it would only hold things up.

'On to the purpose of my call.' The professor coughed. 'I've now had the chance, along with two of my senior colleagues, to check and double-check the urine samples supplied by Usain Bolt following his victory in the semi-final of the one hundred metres.'

And, and, and, Sir Julian wanted to say, but somehow remained silent.

'I have to report,' said the professor, 'there is no sign of Turinabol or any other prohibited substance in his urine. So, as far as I'm concerned, he can progress to tomorrow's final without his reputation being tarnished in any way.'

'Good news indeed,' exclaimed Sir Julian. 'But what about Mo Farah?' he asked, now on the edge of his seat.

'That took a little longer,' admitted the professor, 'because we only received the five thousand metre samples late last night and, sadly,' he paused, 'I've had to disqualify one of the competitors.'

'Was it Mo Farah?' pressed Sir Julian, no longer able to contain himself.

'No, certainly not,' exclaimed the professor, 'it was one of the Russians. There was nothing to suggest that Farah had taken an illegal substance of any kind.'

Sir Julian breathed a sigh of relief. 'Thank God for that.'

'But he does have a problem,' said the professor.

'But you just said . . .'

'After winning the ten thousand metres on Tuesday and qualifying in the five thousand semi-final yesterday, which, following all that bumping and barging, must have been a pretty exhausting experience,' said the professor, 'I can only wonder how much energy the poor man will have left for the final tomorrow.'

'I suspect,' said Sir Julian, 'that a home crowd, adrenaline, and the thought of being the first Englishman in Olympic history to achieve the double may enter the equation. But if you'll forgive me, Professor, I ought to phone Lord Coe and Sir Keith to let them know the good news.'

'Of course,' said the professor. 'And before you go, Sir Julian, would you please pass on my regards to your grandson? After all, he's the one who saved the day.'

Saturday, 11 August – day 16 of the Games

'Sir Julian,' said the judge, adjusting his red robes as he looked down from the bench, 'I think this might be an opportune moment to break for the day.'

'As you wish, m'lud,' said Sir Julian.

The judge turned to the jury and said, 'I'm breaking a little early this afternoon. It's been a long trial, and I think you should all have a rest before I begin my summing up on Monday.'

The nods and looks of approval on the faces of the jury rather suggested they agreed with His Lordship's judgement.

Mr Justice Camoy adjusted his robes, rose and bowed to the court. Once he'd departed, the room emptied in record time.

Sir Julian headed straight for the barristers' room, with Peter in tow. No one was surprised to find the television was already on and surrounded by their colleagues.

Brendan Foster was offering his opinion as the finalists entered the stadium to prolonged applause. 'I spoke to Mo Farah earlier today and he told me, much as he'd like to perform the double, after winning the ten thousand metres earlier in the week and coming through the first round of the five thousand on Wednesday morning, he was emotionally drained and physically exhausted. He confessed that he doubted if he was in with a serious chance of winning a medal, and asked for his supporters to be understanding.'

• • •

William slipped out of the Gold Suite, telling Rebecca he'd be back in fifteen minutes. She didn't have to ask why. He joined Ross, who he found leaning over the railing at the top of the lower stand, waiting for the announcer to call out the names of each competitor and the countries they represented. If World War Three had been declared, no one would have moved.

The crowd fell silent as the fifteen finalists took their place on the starting line. As each name was called out, they were greeted with respectful applause, until the announcer said, 'Number three, representing Great Britain, Mo Farah,' when the whole stadium rose as one and erupted with a roar that would have impressed a lion.

'On your marks,' declared the starter, which created its own eerie silence. 'Set,' a second later, and when the gun went off, 160,000 eyes remained fixed on one athlete. He slipped into the back of the field and completed the first lap in seventy seconds, and William feared Brendan Foster might be right, he was spent. It wasn't until the third of the twelve laps that Farah eased up into the middle of the leading group, running slightly wide to avoid making contact with any other runner. He held this position for another three laps before moving into third place behind Dejen Gebremeskel and the leader Yenew Alamirew, both from Ethiopia. Both of them world-record holders.

By the time the runners strode past the three thousand metre mark, no one in the stadium was sitting.

• • •

END GAME

Mr Justice Camoy was banging on his desk, having abandoned his glass of whisky. His secretary rushed in, assuming he needed something urgently.

Seven men and five women had remained in the jury room, only wanting to deliver one verdict.

Sir Julian was applauding, while some of his younger colleagues were already on their feet, cheering, joining in the chant, 'Go Mo Go,' as Farah took the lead for the first time with seven hundred metres to go.

'Has he gone too early?' Brendan Foster asked the twenty-seven million people following the race on television. The streets of Britain were empty.

The roar that emanated from the crowd was such that no one in the stadium could hear the bell sounding for the final lap. Farah set off on a sprint with the fresh legs of a four-hundred metre runner, while the rest of the world chased after him.

He held them off until he entered the home straight, and with a hundred metres to go, he seemed to change gear. The roar of the crowd reached a crescendo, and could surely have been heard at Hyde Park Corner when Farah crossed the line, after running the last lap in 52.9 seconds.

He had secured his second Olympic gold medal in a week and could claim immortality.

No one left the stadium as the victor jogged slowly around the outside of the track, acknowledging the cheers of the spectators as they continued to chant in unison, 'Go Mo Go!'

The crowd didn't fall silent for the next thirty minutes, as no one was willing to leave before the medal ceremony took place.

Once the podium had been placed in the middle of the home straight, and the three medallists had taken their places behind it, the crowd finally fell silent as they waited for the official result to be announced.

'The five thousand metres final,' declared the announcer, 'the winner of the gold medal in a time of thirteen minutes, forty-one point six . . .'

The roar that erupted from the crowd was so loud that no one heard the name of the winner, but it was Mo Farah who jumped up onto the podium to be presented with the gold medal.

The three young women who were carrying the medals on plush cushions stepped forward for the presentation.

Mrs Dagmawit Girmay Berhane, General Secretary of the Ethiopian National Olympic Committee, bent down and gave Jojo a warm smile, before she picked up the gold medal from its cushion, walked across to the podium and placed it around the neck of the victor. She then presented his two closest rivals, and her fellow countrymen, with their silver and bronze medals.

Just as the crowd thought the moment had passed, a jester appeared on the track in the form of Usain Bolt. He leapt up onto the podium and joined Mo, striking the familiar 'Mo Bot' pose, to which Mo responded with Usain's 'To di World' stance, and for a brief moment in time, the world was united.

William quickly returned to the Gold Suite to keep his eye on the departing crowd, while Ross remained behind on the terrace and watched his daughter as she left her field of dreams.

The judge poured himself another whisky, while the jury hugged each other like old friends.

When the television was finally turned off, Sir Julian turned around and gave his junior a respectful bow.

• • •

END GAME

When the track and field events ended later that evening, with the Americans once again winning the four-by-four-hundred metres relay, William and his team didn't even stop to catch their breath as they began to prepare for the closing ceremony.

The Hawk was on the phone moments later to congratulate William on the professional role he and his team had played during the Games.

'I'm aware that, in Kipling's words, you have in the past month had to face both triumph and disaster, but I can assure you these Olympics will be remembered as a triumph.'

William thanked his boss, but didn't tell the Assistant Commissioner that he wouldn't be treating those two imposters just the same until after the closing ceremony.

Tonight, he was taking Beth out for dinner, in an attempt to make sure his marriage remained 'Happily ever after', to quote Artemisia. Meanwhile, all the team had their special assignments. Ross was to tail Faulkner and never let him out of his sight. Paul was allocated to the Russian Ambassador, while Rebecca was to keep an eye on the Chinese Ambassador. If any two of them were to meet up at the same time, William was to be informed immediately.

He didn't intend to relax until the Olympic flag had been passed on to the Mayor of Rio, the spectators had gone home, and the stadium was finally empty.

CHAPTER 27

Saturday, 11th August – day 16 of the Games

THE REST OF THE DAY ran smoothly enough, with no unscheduled meetings taking place. In fact, William began to wonder if he was becoming paranoid and the closing ceremony would be an anticlimax. He only hoped it would be. But he still didn't relax.

When he left the stadium, William hailed a taxi – a necessary expense if he wasn't going to be late for Beth. In fact, the first thing he said to the maître d' as he entered Le Caprice was, 'Tell me I got here before my wife.'

'You are the first to arrive,' the maitre d' confirmed, as he took William to his table, but only just, because William had just sat down when Beth appeared.

'Can I show you to your table, madam?' asked the maître d'.

'Thank you,' said Beth, who had never dined at Le Caprice before, and was amused to see how many familiar faces littered the room.

The maître d' guided her to a table in the corner, where her host was waiting. He stood up the moment he saw her.

'Good evening,' she said, offering her hand. 'My name is Beth Warwick and I have a feeling we've met before, but I can't remember where.'

'I deserved that,' said William, as he took his wife in his arms. 'But I promise to make it up to you. It's the closing ceremony tomorrow and after that I'll be handing over to DI Adaja for the Paralympics.'

'When perhaps we can share a few treasured memories together,' suggested Beth, 'like how we first met, somehow became engaged, married, and ended up with two wonderful children.'

'I do adore you,' said William, as he held back her seat.

'And I love you too,' admitted Beth, as she sat down. 'But I'm trying to remember why.'

William took her hand, and a concerned smile appeared, replacing the gentle rebuke.

'How are you all coping after losing Jackie?' she asked quietly.

'Not well,' admitted William. 'And it doesn't help that the murderer is still on the loose but, thanks to Arte, at least we have a photo of the suspect, and a piece of evidence that even she won't be able to hide.'

Beth was just about to ask what piece of evidence when the maître d' appeared by their side. Beth opened the menu and remained silent for a moment, before she said, 'That was easy enough. Smoked salmon and veal piccata, please.'

'And you, sir?'

'The Parma ham and melon followed by a rump steak, well done,' said William.

'So predictable,' sighed Beth, as she handed back her menu to the maître d'.

'And your choice of wine, sir?' asked the maître d'.

'Why don't you decide what will complement our selection?' said Beth sweetly.

'Well, that should take care of my wages for the next month,' said William, as the maître d' bowed and disappeared. 'How are the children?'

'I'm so glad you asked,' said Beth, 'and your starter for ten is, can you remember their names?'

'Let's begin with Artemisia,' said William, playing along.

'Her article has been picked up by every other paper and looks as if it will run and run, which you may have missed, stuck down in your dungeon.'

'I can assure you, I didn't miss it,' said William, 'But has the editor offered her a full-time job, as he promised, if she came up with a genuine exclusive?'

'Yes, he has,' replied Beth. 'She begins life as a junior staff reporter the day after the Paralympics have ended.'

'Well done, Arte,' said William, raising an empty glass.

'She's still struggling with guilt after what happened to Natasha,' said Beth, as a plate of thinly sliced smoked salmon was placed in front of her.

'I suspect,' said William, 'that's a common problem for journalists when faced with such a dilemma. How to remain detached so that it never becomes personal. You know Robert called me to ask for my permission to propose to Arte?'

'How wonderfully old-fashioned of him,' said Beth.

'And for her to agree,' said William. 'A lot of young people don't bother with marriage nowadays, and as for having children . . .'

He held Beth's hand again as if it were a first date.

• • •

Paul sat on his motorbike outside the Russian Embassy, but there was no sign of the Ambassador. He watched as a dozen guests, dressed in dinner jackets, went inside, only to reappear a couple of hours later and climb back into their cars, to go their separate ways.

He hung around for a couple more hours, and didn't leave until the last light in the embassy had gone out, when he returned home, hoping to grab a few hours' sleep before returning to the stadium well in time for the closing ceremony.

• • •

The maître d' reappeared by their side. 'I have chosen the Chablis 2001, madam, which I hope will meet with your approval.'

After taking a sip, Beth said, 'Quite superb, it couldn't be better, and you can give my would-be boyfriend half a glass. No more.'

'And dare I ask about Peter?' said William, as he sipped his wine. 'What has he been up to?'

'Funny you should ask that,' said Beth, 'because on Wednesday he left the house just after three in the morning and got back home just in time for breakfast. When I raised the subject with him, he behaved like a lawyer. I wondered if *you* could throw any light on it.'

'A young woman, perhaps,' said William.

'Good try, Commander, but I suspect you know only too well where you both were at that time in the morning, even if you're not going to let me in on the secret.'

'How are things at the Fitz?' William asked, changing the subject.

'Couldn't be much worse,' admitted Beth.

'Has Christina burnt down the museum on your day off?' he asked, as the maître d' poured them both a second glass of wine.

'Far worse,' said Beth. 'Miles Faulkner has been elected to the board, so I . . . well, I felt I had no choice but to resign.'

'I had no idea,' said William, once again taking her hand. 'I'm so sorry. But why didn't you tell me?'

Beth remained silent as their plates were whisked away. 'Because you have quite enough to worry about,' said Beth, 'and after Jackie, I just . . . I didn't want to add to your problems.'

'I'm so very sorry,' repeated William, squeezing her hand. 'But surely Christina put up a fight? The last thing she'd want is for her ex to be taking her place on the board.'

'The vote went against her after Faulkner promised to leave his private collection, including the Van Gogh self-portrait, to the Fitz. Once the board had voted five to one to accept the offer, Christina didn't feel she had the right to oppose his election, even though, as Wilbur pointed out, now that he's on the board, there's nothing to stop him rewriting his Will and not informing them.'

'I suspect he has his eyes on higher things,' said William, moving on.

Beth emptied her glass. 'Like what?'

• • •

Ross sat behind the wheel of his taxi at the end of Cadogan Square that evening and when Faulkner appeared, just after seven, dressed in his familiar long black coat with velvet collar, Collins leapt out of the Rolls and opened the back door to allow his master to climb in.

Collins drove him to the Savoy, where he disappeared inside, no doubt heading for his usual watering hole.

The only surprise was that Booth Watson arrived a few minutes later. Ross had never known him to be late before.

• • •

Rebecca's evening was proving equally uneventful. She had followed CN1 when it left the residence on Portland Place all the way to Chinatown, where it had parked outside his Excellency's favourite restaurant, and she had watched as the Ambassador and his wife disappeared inside. She sat alone, munching a ham sandwich, which she tried to make last as long as possible. She heard the news on the hour twice.

The Ambassador and his wife reappeared just before the ten o'clock news, climbed into the back of their limousine and were whisked away.

Rebecca brushed a crumb off her jacket before following them back to the residence. She didn't go home until she'd seen the driver park the car and disappear inside the back door of the embassy.

• • •

'If I remember correctly,' said William, as a succulent steak was placed in front of him, 'it can't be too long before Christina stands down as chairman.'

'At the end of the year,' said Beth. 'But if Faulkner were to become the next chairman, I think Christina will finally carry out her threat to kill him.'

'It will be quite hard for him to become chairman,' said William, 'if he's in jail.'

'That's the first piece of good news I've heard in weeks,' said Beth. 'I don't suppose you intend to tell me how you're going to pull that one off?'

William gave her a sphinx-like smile.

'I thought as much,' said Beth. 'And because Jojo was a member of the presentation party, she will be allowed to join the British team out on the track for tomorrow's closing ceremony.'

'Lucky girl. While you'll only be allowed to sit in a reserved box with Christina, Wilbur, the twins and Robert for company.'

Beth dropped her knife and fork, threw her arms around William and said, 'All is forgiven.'

'However, I must warn you,' said William, 'you'll be sharing the box with the two professors, a general and two REME sergeants – but at least you'll be in the front row.'

Beth raised an eyebrow in hope of an explanation.

'Don't even ask,' said William. 'It's a very long story.' He paused to take a sip of the wine, before he said, 'Well, several long stories.'

• • •

Ross watched as Faulkner, with Booth Watson in tow, pushed their way through the swing doors of the Savoy and emerged onto the pavement just after ten twenty. Faulkner climbed into the back of his Rolls, while the ever-reliable Collins held open the back door.

As the car drove off, Booth Watson began walking down the Strand in the direction of his flat in Middle Temple.

Ross followed the Rolls, and when Collins dropped his boss outside his home in Cadogan Square, he watched him enter the house before Collins drove off.

END GAME

Ross didn't depart until the light in Faulkner's bedroom had gone out. By the time he crept into bed, Alice was fast asleep.

• • •

'Are you taking me home this evening, Commander?' asked Beth, before she devoured her last morsel of veal, 'or do you feel we haven't known each other long enough?'

'We certainly haven't known each other long enough, my darling,' said William, 'but I'm still going to take you home, even though you're not a cheap date.'

'And don't expect me to go along with this modern habit of splitting the bill on a first date,' said Beth, 'because I don't have to remind you, I'm unemployed.'

'Would you care to see the dessert trolley, madam?' asked the maître d'.

'No, thank you,' said Beth. 'It was a wonderful meal and the wine was quite superb.'

'And you, sir?'

'Just the bill,' said William, as he took out his wallet, fearing the worst.

'It's on the house, sir,' said the maître d'. 'The restaurant has been packed night and day during the Olympics, and we're all well aware you are in charge of security for the Games, so we felt in the circumstances it was the least we could do.'

'Thank you,' said Beth, as the maître d' bowed and left them.

'I agree with you, my darling,' said William, as he placed his wallet back in his pocket. 'We should come here more often.'

• • •

They met at midnight on a yacht moored on the Thames, just off Putney. All the lights had been switched off, except those below deck in the captain's quarters. The motley crew seated around the table consisted of two ambassadors, one undersecretary, one state terrorist and one traitor.

Although Faulkner owned the yacht, it was Ambassador Mikailov who opened proceedings. 'My masters in Moscow are not best pleased,' he stated, which didn't come as a surprise to anyone present. 'The torch relay fiasco, the opening ceremony failure and our inability to have either Bolt or Farah disqualified, despite successfully spiking both their urine samples, have made us all look amateurs at best, and incompetent at worst.'

'Not helped by killing Sergeant Roycroft,' said Faulkner, staring across the table at Sun Anqi. 'If you'd satisfied yourself with stealing her mobile, they might have thought you were nothing more than a pickpocket, whereas now we've got Warwick and half the Met Police looking over our shoulders.'

'I didn't have a choice,' Sun Anqi replied sharply. 'If Roycroft had still been around to identify me, I would have had to call my whole operation off, and years of planning would have gone down the drain, to quote the British.'

'Resulting in the Games being a triumph for London and a disaster for us,' said the Ambassador, looking around the table. 'Remembering that Petrov has been seen by at least one of Warwick's team, I think it might be wise for him to lie low and certainly not attend the closing ceremony.'

'All of you should avoid the closing ceremony,' said Sun Anqi, closing down any further interruptions.

The focus of attention switched from one side of the table to the other.

Sun Anqi didn't need to open a file, as she knew every detail of her script, like an accomplished actor playing a leading role. She didn't require the assistance of politicians, mandarins, or an Englishman, who she had no doubt could be bought by the highest bidder. Sun Anqi addressed the team as if the amateurs had been given their chance, squandered it, and now the professionals would be taking over.

'Gentlemen,' she began, 'let me assure you that I have been fine-tuning my plan for several months and have left nothing to chance. However, I must warn you that the climax will not come until the eleventh hour, when Jacques Rogge will deliver his closing speech from the podium as President of the International Olympic Committee. I have a copy of his speech, which has already been circulated to the press, although it has been embargoed until after the closing ceremony, by which time it will be irrelevant.

'However, when Rogge taps the microphone – and he always taps the microphone before he begins a speech – I will already be by the front of the stage standing among the British team, waiting for his opening words: *Your Royal Highness, my lords, ladies and gentlemen, London has hosted a truly memorable Games . . .*

'The moment Rogge delivers these words, every eye in the stadium will be on him. I will wait until he reaches, *London will be remembered as one of the most successful Games of the modern era.* That will be my cue to release five ampoules of the nerve agent, Sarin, from my trainers which will kill all those standing around me within moments.'

'You included,' said Wei Ming quietly.

'That is the reason my plan is foolproof, Your Excellency,' Sun Anqi reminded him. 'However,' she continued, 'the death of several members of the British team will only be a small part of what I have planned for London's swansong.'

Faulkner tried to remain detached.

'Don't spare us the details,' said Wei Ming, enjoying every moment.

'Once the liquid has vaporized, it will quickly spread, either killing or debilitating almost everyone in its path. Those close to me will die within moments, while anyone nearby will suffer seizures and paralysis, which may not surface for weeks, but I can assure you will get them in the end. And for those who panic and flee from the stadium imagining they're safe, some will be carrying the gas on their clothes so we must hope they get onto a tube, an enclosed space, where they will unwittingly spread the gas. I'm only sorry I won't be around to witness it. However, given the circumstances, I recommend that none of you attend the closing ceremony, because nerve agents don't discriminate. If all goes to plan – and it will,' said Sun Anqi, 'Prince Harry, who will be representing the Queen, and the British Prime Minister, along with several other heads of state, leading politicians and so-called dignitaries, will be attending their last public function. And there will only be one country to blame, and one person in particular,' continued Sun Anqi, 'namely Commander Warwick, which should at least make you a happy man,' she added, staring directly at Faulkner.

'But if that were to happen,' came back Faulkner, 'many of your own countrymen will die.'

'A sacrifice we are willing to make,' said the Chinese Ambassador, 'as it will convince the rest of the world we couldn't possibly have been involved.'

Faulkner couldn't believe what he was hearing. He now knew just how right Booth Watson had been when he'd advised: *Walk away while you still can.*

'But won't you still have a problem getting into the stadium?' asked Mikailov.

'Not while there are three hundred other athletes to

accompany me,' said Sun Anqi. 'You see, I will be wearing two tracksuits – one in the Chinese team colours, to get me into the stadium with the rest of the team, and another one underneath to make sure I can join the British team unnoticed.'

'But what if you are searched on your way in?' asked Petrov.

'I will be wearing the official Chinese team kit, so there's no reason for anyone to be suspicious.'

Faulkner leant slightly forward in his seat. 'But what if someone recognizes you? We don't think your cover has been blown, but, if Roycroft managed to send any images to Warwick . . .'

'I have the photographs and, just in case you've forgotten, I removed the only witness who could have identified me.'

'But the place will be swarming with security guards . . .'

'I'm well aware of that, Mr Faulkner,' said Sun Anqi, contemptuously. 'But I have identified a weakness that you British suffer from – something they are taught in their public schools from an early age.'

'And what might that be?' asked Faulkner.

'That women are the weaker sex,' said Sun Anqi, 'and that weakness is something I intend to take advantage of.'

Faulkner didn't press her for details, not least because he had learnt over the past few weeks that Sun Anqi wouldn't share them with her own countrymen, let alone an Englishman she didn't trust.

'I am confident that not only will I succeed,' said Sun Anqi, 'but also that the London Games will only be remembered for its closing ceremony.'

'And not as a glorious triumph to be compared with Beijing,' said Wei Ming.

'Over my dead body,' said Sun Anqi.

• • •

The first appointment Mr Booth Watson had the following morning was with an out-of-work actor who'd played Faulkner at the Savoy the night before – an uncanny resemblance.

After he'd been paid a thousand pounds in cash for his night's work, he only had one question for his paymaster before he left, 'Can I keep the coat?'

Booth Watson agreed to his request, but only after he'd signed a non-disclosure agreement.

The Chinese extra was the next to appear and receive his equity fee. He told Booth Watson the meal had been excellent, and he'd enjoyed the company of the Chinese Ambassador's wife, who had clearly known the part she was expected to play in her husband's absence. 'Should you wish a repeat performance,' said the understudy, 'I'd be only too happy to oblige.'

'I'll keep that in mind,' said Booth Watson, who had no intention of ever seeing the man again.

The two Russian actors were paid in full, even though their services hadn't been required, and they left Booth Watson's chambers none the wiser.

After paying off the last of the thespians, Booth Watson took a taxi to the Savoy to have lunch with the real Miles Faulkner, where he reported on the successful outcome of his role in the deception. But then he listened intently to his client while he revealed what was going to happen at the closing ceremony.

Booth Watson didn't remind Miles that he had advised him on more than one occasion to walk away while he still could, because it was now too late.

THE CLOSING CEREMONY

The curtain falls

CHAPTER 28

Sunday, 12 August 2012

ARTEMISIA DECIDED TO VISIT the Olympic Village one more time so she could thank Kelly and find out if she'd achieved her aim of adding a gold medallist to her collection. Not that she'd be mentioning it in any of her articles.

When Artemisia arrived outside the entrance to the village, she was greeted by over a thousand fans who were waiting hopefully for a chance to see one of their heroes before they returned to distant lands. She would have liked to conduct a vox pop interview there and then, but didn't have the time if she still hoped to be on time for the closing ceremony.

Artemisia said *hi* to Jim and blew him a kiss, before she strolled into the village to meet up with scores of nostalgic athletes who were preparing for the closing ceremony, not all of them looking as if they would make it.

She had almost given up any hope of finding Kelly, when she spotted a Bulgarian basketball player bending down and kissing her gently on the cheek, before leaving to rejoin his team.

Artemisia rushed across to join her. 'I wanted to say goodbye,' she said, 'and tell you how much I've enjoyed your company during the past fortnight.'

'Me too,' said Kelly. 'But won't you be joining our team for the march past?'

Artemisia felt embarrassed and was about to admit . . . when Kelly said, 'Of course you won't,' accompanied by a huge grin. 'I was pleased you got your exclusive,' she added, 'and I can tell you the rest of the team were delighted you exposed the Russians for the cheats they are.' She paused, and said quietly, 'I was in tears when I read your article. Poor Natasha and Alain. They both paid a heavy price to let the world know the truth.'

'I agree,' said Artemisia, 'and I only wish I could have done more for them, but I haven't given up, even if my editor thinks it's old news.' She looked at her friend and said, 'When did you realize I wasn't really Annie Charnock?'

'About five minutes after meeting you,' said Kelly, laughing.

'I'm sorry I had to lie to you.'

'Don't be. It takes real courage to do what you did, and in the end you told a story that people needed to hear.'

They hugged each other like old friends, and as Artemisia turned to leave, Kelly said, 'If you're ever in Bristol, Artemisia, make sure you look me up, because I'd like you to meet my husband.'

• • •

'Final check,' said William over the radio as he looked up at the bank of CCTV screens above him. 'Where are you, Inspector Hogan?'

'I'm standing by the long jump pit opposite the Royal Box,' came back Ross, looking up at the moving camera. 'I've thirty officers spread all around the ground facing the stands. If any trouble breaks out, we can move in at a moment's notice.'

'But also be prepared for what might happen in the centre of the field,' said William, 'especially when Rogge is delivering his closing address. He'll be surrounded by thousands of athletes and officials from all around the globe enjoying themselves. Be on the lookout for one of them who isn't celebrating.'

William moved onto the next screen, 'Chief Inspector Adaja?'

'I've got a hundred officers at the West Entrance to the stadium, sir, where all the different teams are lining up for the parade. It's all a bit casual compared with the opening ceremony, but seems to be running smoothly enough. The teams are going to be led into the stadium by the Greeks, according to tradition, and they'll be followed by around eight thousand athletes and officials – each vetted and security cleared. The final team to enter the arena will be the British, as the host nation, led by our captain, Ben Ainslie. He's going to carry the Union Jack and will be followed by around five hundred members of the British team. Once they've circled the track, they'll take their places in the centre of the ground behind the stage, and then the celebrations will begin.'

'Inspector Pankhurst?'

'I'm on the roof of the stadium, sir, along with twenty-six officers who'll have their binoculars trained on the stands throughout the evening. If they spot anything suspicious, I'll brief Inspector Hogan immediately.'

'Don't relax, Inspector, even for a moment.'

'Sergeant Roycroft,' he said, but no reply was forthcoming. William felt a pang of grief for his fallen colleague, before he recovered and switched his attention to the Royal Box, where the Assistant Commissioner was awaiting the royal party. Sniffer dogs were going about their business, tails wagging, while two young constables with metal detectors were checking under every seat.

The Hawk came on the line, 'With a bit of luck, William, and we're due some, there will be no rogue cyclists or disgruntled taxi drivers to hold the royal party up this time, but we're still not leaving anything to chance. I'll be outside the VIP entrance when Lord Coe accompanies Prince Harry to the Royal Box. HRH will take the salute as each team marches past. In truth,' said the Hawk, 'my biggest problem is the seating plan.'

'I'm not sure I understand, sir,' said William.

'With five of the guests coming from three different royal families, as well as four heads of state in attendance, I'm not sure if our Prime Minister should sit in the front row, the middle row or even the back row.'

I wish that was my only problem, thought William, as another phone began to ring.

• • •

Long before the appointed hour when the West Gate was due to open, athletes from all around the world were beginning to take their places in the longest queue on earth, while they waited to enter a packed stadium. They had come to bid farewell before the Mayor of London passed the Olympic flag to the Mayor of Rio de Janeiro and the Games of the Thirtieth Olympiad were declared closed.

Inspector Adaja had already briefed his legion of officers, who would be responsible for security. Each of them had studied photographs of both Sergei Petrov and Sun Anqi and, in the case of Sun Anqi, were on the lookout for a scorpion tattoo on her neck.

Paul had instructed his officers to be vigilant at all times, but not obtrusive; after all, the closing ceremony was always a much more relaxed affair than the opening.

'It's a fine line, which you must tread carefully,' Paul had warned them. 'A bottle of champagne isn't an offensive weapon, especially when it's full, and if someone tries to steal your helmet, don't arrest them. Should anyone kiss you, say "thank you", whatever their nationality and whatever their sex, but don't return the compliment.'

No one laughed.

'While you'll be looking for two individuals in particular, you'll still have to remain alert for any other problems that might arise when you least expect it.'

The Hawk, meanwhile, had phoned the royal protocol officer at Buckingham Palace, who had drawn up a seating plan for him.

Paul couldn't wait for the gates to open at eight o'clock so he could get the show on the road – or, to be more accurate, on the track.

Ross's cadre of highly trained undercover officers were all wearing British tracksuits to make sure no one would give them a second look. They had already taken up their positions around the ground an hour before the gates were due to open.

Rebecca's unit continued to scan the empty stands as they waited for the crowd to enter the stadium, but all they saw were dogs sniffing under every seat.

William wasn't taking any chances.

• • •

A phone rang in the Gold Suite. William grabbed it while still looking up at the CCTV screens.

'Can I open the entrance gates, Commander?' asked the stadium manager. 'It's four minutes past eight, and a few of the punters are beginning to get restless.'

'Yes,' he said, and moments later he watched as a steady flow of spectators began to make their way into the stands, determined not to miss a moment of the final evening.

Most of them were smiling, boisterous, some even singing, although William spotted a few who'd already had a little too much to drink. His eyes went on searching for one man and one woman in particular, but all he spotted was a drunk who just about made it to his seat before falling asleep.

During the next forty minutes, the stands slowly began to fill. The atmosphere was buzzing with anticipation, while William tried to remain calm. He must have been the one person there who wished the curtain had already come down and the Mayor of Rio de Janeiro had left the stadium holding the Olympic flag and, with it, the problems of the next four years.

William's attention switched to another screen, where he spotted Beth, Wilbur, Christina, Peter, Artemisia and Robert sitting in a reserved box in the special emergency stand on the far side of the ground. He smiled for a moment as he watched them introduce themselves to his other guests, all of whom had played their part in making the Games a success.

His eyes moved on to the Royal Box to see Prince Harry arrive. He shook hands with William's father who, as the senior Olympic judge, had been invited to join the royal party, even if he would be sitting in the back row.

The stadium manager was back on the radio. 'Can I open the West Gate, Commander, and allow the athletes to enter the stadium so the parade can begin?'

END GAME

'One moment,' said William. 'Are you all ready?' he asked his team.

'More than ready,' said Paul, as he looked at the thousands of athletes who had been celebrating for the last hour.

'No problems on the ground,' said Ross over his radio.

'Or on the roof,' chipped in Rebecca.

The Hawk was chatting to Prince Harry, so William didn't interrupt him.

'Yes, you can open the West Gate,' said William.

• • •

The band of the Royal Marines struck up 'Land of Hope and Glory' as the West Gate opened to allow the first team to enter the stadium. Greece led the assembled athletes into the arena, their blue and white flag fluttering in the breeze. They were greeted with a warm welcome from the waiting crowd as they stepped out onto the track. When they passed the Royal Box, they lowered their flag, and Prince Harry, representing the Queen, took the royal salute.

As each new country entered the stadium, they were welcomed with cheers from different sections of the crowd, but the loudest roar erupted when the host nation finally appeared and eighty thousand people rose to their feet to acknowledge a team that had won sixty-five medals, twenty-nine of them gold. The largest haul since 1948, when the Games were last held in London.

Ben Ainslie led his compatriots onto the track holding the Union Jack aloft for all to see.

• • •

As the Chinese team progressed slowly towards the entrance to the stadium, a dozen security guards scoured the rows of assembled athletes in search of a man or woman who matched the photographs they had been issued. An almost impossible task, as they were all dressed identically in red and white tracksuits.

Without warning, one of the Chinese team collapsed onto the ground and several athletes surrounded her. The nearest police officer was quickly by her side.

'I think she's fainted,' said a teammate, anxiously. 'We were kept waiting for over an hour before they unlocked the gates.'

The young officer looked embarrassed. 'Perhaps it might be wise for her to return to the Olympic Village?' he suggested, aware that the procession was being held up.

'We'll take your advice, officer,' said another woman, coming in bang on cue, as she helped her teammate back on her feet.

Paul and several of his security team were now taking a closer interest, carefully checking not just their faces but their necks. No scorpion to be seen. Paul turned his attention back to the rest of the Chinese team, who were continuing to move slowly towards the entrance to the stadium.

The three athletes concerned turned around and began to walk in the opposite direction, having played their part in the charade.

Sun Anqi, an Olympic scarf around her neck, progressed slowly forward with her team as they entered the stadium.

• • •

The phone was ringing. William grabbed it. 'Warwick,' he said.

'Alan Mitchell, Commander,' said a voice he didn't recognize. 'Air traffic control.'

'What can I do for you?' asked William, fearing the worst.

'A small twin-engine aircraft has just appeared on my screen. The plane took off from a private airfield near Bournemouth, but despite being instructed to change course, it continued heading towards the stadium. Do you want me to contact RAF Northolt?'

RAF Northolt meant only one thing to William. Two fighter jets would be scrambled immediately and would intercept the aircraft. If they thought it might cause any real danger to the public, they would blow it out of the sky. The events of 9/11 immediately sprang to William's mind, reminding him that even a light aircraft could cause mayhem in such a confined space.

'Yes, call Northolt,' said William. 'But tell them to use their common sense.'

'I don't have the authority to do that,' said Mitchell. 'Way above my pay grade.'

'Right, leave it to me,' said William. He put down one phone and picked up another. 'Get Air Marshal Lowery on the phone, urgently.'

'He's sitting in a Grand Tier box on the far side of the ground, sir.'

'Ask him if he could join me in the Gold Suite immediately. Tell him it's an emergency.'

• • •

Miles Faulkner sat alone in his flat, watching the scene unfold on television, with the crowd cheering and applauding each team as they entered the stadium. There was nothing left for him to do except watch the drama unfold – at a distance.

His mind drifted back to his meeting on the yacht the previous night, and for a moment he hoped that Sun Anqi had been apprehended before she entered the stadium – but knowing that woman, he doubted it.

Miles had never believed he was capable of having second thoughts, but when the camera zoomed in on the British team, who were uninhibitedly celebrating the part they had played in a triumphant Games, several of them wearing medals around their necks, he felt something most unusual – guilt.

The camera zoomed back to reveal so many young participants coming to the end of their Olympic dream, but at the beginning of their lives.

He looked up at an empty space on the wall where the Van Gogh would hang that would unquestionably be the pride of his collection.

And then his thoughts turned to other people's lives. Innocent bystanders who Sun Anqi had dismissed without feeling, for what she described as 'the greater cause'.

Was possessing a Van Gogh a 'greater cause' or was he no better than Sun Anqi?

Once again, he turned his attention to the blank space on the wall.

• • •

Three phones were ringing at the same time. William grabbed the red one and listened carefully.

'RAF Northolt, Flight Lieutenant Penrose reporting in, sir. We are in pursuit of the light aircraft. Feeding through visual now.'

END GAME

William and Air Marshal Lowery stood alongside the bank of CCTV screens watching the aircraft heading towards them. It looked harmless enough, but what if it was full of explosives?

'I don't think it's explosives he's carrying, sir,' said the Flight Lieutenant, 'but a message that's clear for all to see.'

They both looked up at the little plane to see a banner fluttering from its tail declaring, FATHERS 4 JUSTICE.

The Air Marshal burst out laughing, before he said firmly, 'Buzz him, lads, and then escort him back to Bournemouth, and don't let the pilot out of your sight until you see the plane taxi to a halt.'

'Roger that, sir,' said the Flight Lieutenant, as the two planes eased into place.

'Thank you, Flight Lieutenant,' said William, before putting down the phone.

'As he didn't enter restricted air space,' said William, putting down the phone, 'as far as I'm concerned, it never happened.'

'Roger that,' said the Air Marshal, with a grin, 'and, if it's okay with you, Commander, I'll return to my seat before the balloon goes up.'

'Yes, of course, sir, and thank you. I hope you enjoy the rest of the evening.' William hadn't even finished speaking before another phone began to ring.

'You too, Commander,' said the Air Marshal as he left the Gold Suite.

William picked up the second phone, to hear Rebecca's familiar voice. 'Commander?'

'Any sign of Sun Anqi or Petrov?' was William's first question.

'Negative, sir. No one has reported seeing anyone answering their descriptions. But one of my officers has spotted something he thought you ought to know about immediately. If you look at your end screen' – William followed her instructions – 'you'll see two empty boxes in the Grand Tier section near the Royal Box, which is strange to say the least, as the event's been sold out for the past six months.'

'They could be held up in traffic,' said William, 'or even ill.'

'The Grand Tier boxes hold twelve,' said Rebecca. 'That's an awful lot of people to be held up or suddenly taken ill.'

'I'll check who's meant to be in those boxes,' said William. 'Stay on the line.' He picked up another phone, and while he waited for the stadium manager to answer, his eyes remained fixed on the two empty boxes.

He glanced up at another screen to see the Russian team passing the Royal Box and lowering their flag. Was it his imagination, or were there far fewer competitors taking part than in the opening ceremony? A quick check among the older officials and there was certainly no sign of Petrov.

'How can I help you, Commander?' asked the stadium manager.

'There are two empty boxes in the Grand Tier section – can you find out who is meant to be occupying them?'

He heard the noise of tapping coming down the phone before the stadium manager came back on the line. 'One of the boxes is reserved for the Chinese Ambassador and his party, and the other' – more tapping – 'is allocated to the Russian Ambassador and his guests.'

William felt his heart rate quicken. Now he understood why Petrov was nowhere to be seen, but it still didn't explain the absence of both ambassadors. His eyes moved on to a smaller box, also empty – the same box Faulkner and Booth Watson had occupied during the opening ceremony.

And William accepted that wouldn't be a coincidence.

• • •

'Sir Julian,' said the Prime Minister, leaning back, 'in your capacity as an Olympic judge, have you been faced with any problems during the past couple of weeks that required you to make a delicate decision?'

'None that I can think of, Prime Minister,' said Sir Julian. 'One of the Turkish weightlifters was caught shoplifting in Harrods, but I was able to convince the manager to drop the charges.'

Cameron smiled. He'd been Prime Minister long enough to know when he wasn't being told the whole story. 'How interesting,' he said.

• • •

A third phone was ringing, but William was already on two other lines. He cut off the stadium manager and picked up the second phone.

'Sergeant Davidson, sir. Bournemouth airport.'

'How can I help, Sergeant?'

'I've arrested the pilot of the light aircraft that was heading for the stadium, but I'm not quite sure what offence to charge him with.'

'Shoot him, for all I care,' said William, as another phone began to ring.

'The man has a genuine grievance, sir,' said the sergeant. 'He hasn't been allowed to see his two teenage daughters for the past four years.'

'Then lock him up for the night, but don't feed him.'

'I just wondered, sir, how I would feel if I hadn't been allowed to see my two sons for the past four years.'

William sighed. 'I apologize, Sergeant. My mind was elsewhere.' He was still staring at the empty boxes where the

Russian and Chinese ambassadors were meant to be sitting and had allowed himself to become preoccupied. 'Don't charge him, but don't release him until the stadium has been cleared this evening.'

'Understood, sir. I'm sorry to have bothered you.'

William felt even more guilty.

Boom!

William's heart missed a beat when he looked up at the screens to see a cannon go off, and moments later a pathetic figure crawled out of the barrel and fell onto the stage in a heap. The audience screamed with delight when Eric Idle lifted himself slowly off the ground, grabbed a microphone and began to sing 'Always Look on the Bright Side of Life', accompanied by a choir of eighty thousand out-of-tune voices.

William was humming along with the rest of the crowd when the door of the Gold Suite burst open to reveal two burly security guards firmly holding onto the last person on earth he'd expected to see.

'He demanded to see you personally, sir,' said the senior officer. 'Claimed it was a matter of life or death.'

The two men faced each other like ancient warriors on a battlefield.

'What do *you* want?' demanded William.

'To save the lives of countless innocent people,' said Faulkner, with an urgency that didn't suggest levity.

William stared at him for a moment, unable to believe what he was hearing. Was this yet another distraction, meant to take his eye off the real danger about to take place in the stadium?

His immediate reaction was to ask the two officers to throw him out of the stadium, which would have given him a great deal of pleasure. But William had to accept that he might later regret it.

He dismissed the two officers with a nod and waited for them to leave the room before he said, 'Since when have you given a damn about the lives of innocent people? And whatever you have to say, why should I believe a word of it?'

'Because I was responsible for having Bolt's and Farah's urine samples spiked,' said Faulkner, 'with the aim of getting them disqualified.'

Such a blatant admission took William by surprise. He found it hard to believe that a career-hardened criminal could suddenly be wanting to cooperate with him of all people. But there was something about his demeanour and the tone of his voice that caused William to continue to listen as he pressed the radio button that connected him to his inner team.

'I also know why two of the Grand Tier boxes are empty,' said Faulkner. 'But more importantly, I know what was in the shoebox you never got your hands on.'

William carried on listening, and couldn't help wondering if this was nothing more than a ploy to keep him fully occupied while others carried out Faulkner's bidding. He made no attempt to interrupt the witness while he was still confessing.

'But even I can't stomach what they have planned for the climax of tonight's closing ceremony,' admitted Faulkner.

William looked more carefully at a man he thought he knew. Could it be possible that at this late stage in his criminal career, Faulkner was feeling guilty about a crime not yet committed?

'If you move quickly, Commander,' said Faulkner, with an

urgency William had not experienced before, 'you might still have enough time to prevent the worst from happening.'

'The worst?' William repeated, unable to hide the suspicion in his voice.

'There could be a terrorist out there among the Chinese athletes,' said Faulkner. 'She's wearing two tracksuits and a pair of Olympic shoes that aren't exactly regulation.'

'What's her purpose?' demanded William, now almost convinced Faulkner was telling the truth.

'Just before the firework display begins, she's going to take off her national tracksuit, while everyone else will be looking up into the sky. Beneath the Chinese tracksuit, she's wearing the official Great Britain Olympic team kit.' He paused. 'She's then going to head towards the British team and when she reaches them, while everyone is still distracted by the firework display, she'll bend down and untie her shoelaces. She's got several ampoules of the nerve agent, Sarin, hidden in her trainers and when she removes them to break the ampoules, the liquid will vaporize and release enough gas to obliterate most of the British team.'

William didn't need to be told about the dangers of Sarin and the chaos it had caused on an underground station in Tokyo. Every officer in the Met had been fully briefed by Interpol and William could still remember being horrified and not just by a senseless, evil act that had caused so many deaths, but the realization that one person could hold in their hands a weapon of mass destruction that could, at any given moment, destroy a dream and replace it with a nightmare from which you would never wake.

His first thought was of his family seated in their box, but they were only part of a much bigger family he was responsible for.

Above them, the crowd continued to cheer long after 'Always Look on the Bright Side of Life' had finally come to an end.

'If what you're suggesting is true,' said William, 'she would be the first to die.'

Faulkner nodded. 'But you have to remember, she's a zealot who will happily sacrifice her own life – even those of her countrymen – to achieve her aim.'

William tried to remain calm, aware he was now in the hands of someone he'd never been able to trust in the past. But what choice had he been left with while so many lives were at stake?

'How on earth can we identify her?' asked William, as he stared up at the vast Chinese team bunched together, row upon row.

'Her tracksuit,' said Faulkner. 'The moment she takes her top off and begins to walk towards the British team, she will be one blue and white tracksuit amongst a sea of red.'

'Rebecca!' shouted William, looking up at the screen.

'Heard every word, sir,' confirmed Rebecca, 'and my entire team is now focused on the Chinese squad in search of a British tracksuit.'

The silence that followed seemed an eternity to William.

He considered his options once again. They were, to say the least, limited. A tannoy announcement to warn the crowd what was about to happen, followed by an emergency evacuation? A drill that had been practised several times during the past year, but this time would be for real, not a rehearsal. Out of the question, William decided. If he were to make such an announcement, Sun Anqi could release the gas before he had completed his second sentence.

And then a clear voice interrupted his thoughts. 'Clocked her.'

'Are you certain?' asked William, no longer attempting to mask the anxiety in his voice.

'She's taking off her tracksuit, sir,' said the officer, 'and, yes, she's wearing a British tracksuit underneath.'

'Whatever you do, don't lose sight of her,' said William, painfully aware what might happen should any member of his team make one false move.

Twenty-six binoculars stared down from the roof, all of them focused on one person.

'Count down,' declared the announcer over the loudspeaker.

'Is your team in place, Ross?' asked William over the phone as the crowd began to chant in unison: *ten, nine, eight* . . .

'And ready to strike,' said Ross, not wasting a word.

'And have you got her in your sights?'

'She's just left her own team and is now heading towards the British contingent.'

'Sniper team, do you have a clear shot?' asked William, his calm voice belying his pounding heart.

'Negative, sir, and I must warn you the bullet could hit an innocent athlete, in front of eighty thousand witnesses.'

Several of the screens now showed a woman moving slowly across the centre of the stadium towards the British team. William hesitated, aware that eighty thousand lives were now in his hands.

'Sir, can I give the authorization to fire?' asked Rebecca.

The screens continued to show a joyous crowd of young athletes around Sun Anqi, who she ignored while she kept advancing towards her target.

William made a decision.

'Negative,' he said, before repeating, 'Negative. Ross, how close is the target to you?'

'About ten yards away,' said Ross.

Seven, six, five . . .

'Don't make a sudden move,' said William, 'because she won't hesitate if she thinks . . . Oh my God.'

'What's the problem?' asked Ross.

William was staring directly at Jojo, who was standing just a few yards away from the British team captain, while Sun Anqi continued to move slowly but surely towards Ben Ainslie. William made another decision – not to tell her father. 'Nothing important, Ross,' he said. 'How far are you from the target now?'

'She's just passing me,' whispered Ross, 'but as I'm wearing a British tracksuit, she didn't give me a second look.'

Four, three . . .

'And are the rest of your team in place and ready to move?'

'On your command,' said Ross.

Sun Anqi's image now filled several CCTV screens. Ross followed the lone woman as she continued on towards the British team, while the crowd joined in the countdown.

'How close are you now?' asked William.

'Just a few yards, no more,' he whispered.

'You're not close enough,' said William firmly. 'Get closer.'

Ross weaved his way through the noisy, boisterous crowd until he was only a pace behind her.

Two, one . . . the crowd shouted, and suddenly all the lights in the stadium went out, leaving the eighty thousand spectators in darkness.

'Permission to engage, sir,' whispered Ross.

In that split second, two thoughts flashed through William's mind. Am I giving the order to kill an innocent person, as had happened to a colleague when he'd shot Jean Charles de Menezes at Stockwell underground station, or am I saving the lives of countless innocent victims?

'Granted,' said William.

'Repeat the order,' said Ross, keeping strictly to Queen's regulations.

William hesitated, but only for a moment. He thought of the eighty thousand people in the crowd whose lives depended on his decision. He thought of his own family, sitting amongst that crowd. He thought about Jackie, whom this woman had murdered without a thought.

Sun Anqi began to crouch down.

'Granted,' repeated William without emotion.

Ross took a deep breath and stepped forward. He hesitated, just for a moment – and then he saw the scorpion tattoo on her neck.

He tapped her firmly on the shoulder and Sun Anqi instinctively turned around, a startled look on her face as she immediately recognized Ross. Ross took her in his arms like a long-lost lover, but that's where the love affair ended. Sun Anqi tried desperately to bend down and reach her shoelaces, but a firm arm encircled her slender neck and with a well-practised movement, Ross snapped her spinal cord. Sun Anqi's limp body fell forward and she collapsed onto the ground in front of him. She never saw the blanket of fireworks that lit up the sky.

Four of Ross's team were by his side within seconds, stretcher in hand. Six more surrounded him as he picked up the dead body and lowered it onto the stretcher.

When Ross looked down at the prostrate body, his only thought was of Jackie and the eighty thousand people she had sacrificed her life for.

• • •

Jojo turned around to see a stretcher being carried away. She could have sworn one of the bearers was her father. Poor woman must have fainted, she thought. But once they were out of sight, she was distracted by the final burst of fireworks that lit up the sky, with the five Olympic rings in the colours of the five continents to herald the end of the display.

William's eyes never left the screen as the body was whisked away. He continued to follow Ross's progress until the stretcher bearers reached a waiting ambulance parked by the stadium entrance, back doors already open. The stretcher was eased gently and slowly into the back of the ambulance, supervised by a man dressed in a full HazMat suit.

William listened to the doctor's firm instructions coming over Ross's radio: 'All four of you will have to accompany me to the hospital,' he told Ross, 'where you'll remain in isolation until we can be certain none of you is contaminated.'

Ross climbed into the ambulance, followed by the other stretcher bearers. The doors slammed and the ambulance took off. No sirens, no flashing lights. Never happened.

'We have a lot to thank you for, Mr Faulkner,' said William, as he swung around to face his old adversary, but he was nowhere to be seen.

'Can I ask you a question, sir?' asked Rebecca over the phone, as the crowd continued to show their rapturous appreciation of the firework display.

William didn't respond as Jacques Rogge, President of the International Olympic Committee and Lord Coe, the Games chairman, left the Royal Box and stepped out onto the track. They were welcomed by a fanfare of trumpets and a standing ovation as they made their way up onto the stage.

William knew only too well what Rebecca's question would

be, but it didn't stop her asking: 'Was that voice I heard in the background who I thought it was?'

William put down the radio without responding as Rogge placed his speech on the lectern and tapped the microphone.

'London,' he said to a silent, attentive audience, 'will be remembered as one of the most successful Games of the modern Olympic era . . .'

BOOK FOUR

CHAPTER 29

Monday, 13 August

WILLIAM DIDN'T LEAVE THE STADIUM until the sweepers had made sure there was no sign of what had taken place at the closing ceremony only a few hours before. He told the rest of the team before they left that he would allow the eight o'clock debriefing meeting to be moved to twelve noon. After all, the stadium would be all but deserted for two weeks until the Paralympics began.

William didn't open his front door until just after four a.m., and he fell asleep within moments of climbing into bed.

When a sleepy Commander joined his wife and son in the kitchen for breakfast a few hours later, they were all discussing the triumph of the previous night. He wouldn't be telling them how close it had been to a disaster. Beth placed a plate of eggs and bacon in front of the stranger sitting opposite her. He picked up his knife and fork and was about to join in the conversation when the phone rang.

Despite the look on Beth's face, he reluctantly answered it.

Beth gave in and picked up her copy of the *Guardian*.

'Good morning, William,' said his father. 'I wanted to let you know that, as you requested, the CPS . . .'

By the time he'd completed the call, Peter had left for work and his curled-up fried egg didn't look quite so appetizing.

Before he could start eating, however, Beth slid the newspaper under his nose and pointed out an article, which he would have missed as he rarely bothered with the *Guardian*. The article, written by a staff reporter, was on page seventeen below the fold.

The French national high jump champion and three times Olympian, Alain Mesnil, was found dead at his home in Lyon last night. The police have let it be known that there are no suspicious circumstances involved and they will not be interviewing anyone concerning the untimely death.

Mr Mesnil left a suicide note addressed to Ms Natasha Korova, Russia.

'How tragic,' said William. 'Arte will be devastated. Under that cynical exterior is someone who will blame herself.'

'Perhaps you could call her,' said Beth, 'as I have to go to the Fitz. It's my last week at the gallery and, as the Hermitage exhibition closes today, I can't afford to be late.' She kissed him on the forehead and left before he could respond.

William immediately called Arte and tried helplessly to comfort her between the tears, and failed.

'Don't worry, Dad, I'll be all right,' she said, before she finally put down the phone.

END GAME

He knew she wouldn't be all right, and was pleased to hear Robert was with her.

After considerable reflection, William turned his attention to the rest of the morning papers.

Dream GB – declared the headline in the *Sun*.

Goodbye to the Glorious Games – *Guardian*.

Out with a Bang – *Mail on Sunday*.

Farmer in the Shetland Islands didn't realize the Olympics was taking place – *The Scotsman*.

He looked down at the dog snoozing by the back door and said, 'Can you keep a secret, Peel, because I'm going to tell you what the headline might have been: Chinese Terrorist Killed at Closing Ceremony by Decorated Police Officer. Hundreds of Lives Saved.'

The dog wagged its tail.

The phone rang a second time, and he picked it up to hear Ross's wife, Alice, asking if she knew why her husband hadn't come home last night.

• • •

Miles joined Booth Watson at the Savoy for a late breakfast. A stack of the morning papers was piled on a chair by Booth Watson's side. He had been pleased to find his client's name didn't get a mention from the first page to the last.

'So you finally took my advice,' he said, once his client had unfolded his napkin and tucked it under his chin.

'Reluctantly,' admitted Miles.

The maître d' poured him a steaming cup of black coffee. 'Your usual, Mr Faulkner?'

'The full English,' confirmed Miles.

'I'm glad to hear you finally saw sense,' said Booth Watson, once the maître d' had departed, 'because I've scoured all the morning papers, and there's nothing to suggest that the closing ceremony was anything but a resounding success.'

The look on Faulkner's face didn't suggest he was in agreement.

Booth Watson's mobile began to purr. He was about to reject the call when he saw the three letters that had appeared on his screen. 'I have to take this,' he said. 'It concerns you.'

Miles watched as the suggestion of a smile appeared on his lawyer's face. The smile became broader by the second, until it was positively beaming by the time he ended the call.

'That was the CPS,' said Booth Watson, 'phoning to let me know they'll be dropping all the charges against you.'

Miles didn't look surprised. Much as he detested the man, he had to admit Commander Warwick kept his word.

'That's cause for celebration, don't you think?' said Booth Watson, raising his coffee cup.

'Try not to forget, BW, what I've had to sacrifice in exchange for—'

'I'm not so sure about that,' said Booth Watson. 'Everyone involved in yesterday's failed attack will now be running for cover. Don't forget that the Hermitage exhibition ends this evening, and I've already arranged for the painting to be collected from the Fitzmolean first thing in the morning. When I called the director to confirm, there wasn't any suggestion she'd been instructed otherwise.'

A smile finally appeared on Faulkner's face, only to disappear when he recalled Petrov's threat of what would happen to him should he ever betray them. However, now that Sun Anqi was no longer in the picture, and the rest of the team, to quote Booth Watson, would be running for cover, perhaps he'd got the best of both worlds. 'And equally important,' said Booth Watson, interrupting his thoughts, 'it will no longer be necessary for you to pack your bags and leave for the States.'

'Which also means,' said Miles, 'that I can take my place on the board of the Fitzmolean and start working on my next coup.'

BOOTH WATSON COULD ONLY ADMIRE how deftly Miles somehow managed to move on to his next venture, without appearing to draw breath. 'And your Will?' he asked.

'Can remain in favour of the Fitzmolean until I'm safely ensconced in the chair, when . . .'

Booth Watson's mobile began to vibrate once again. 'It's Bernie Longe,' he said, when he saw the name appear on the screen.

'He obviously hasn't been able to raise the rest of the money required to purchase the stadium before the deadline runs out, so that's two birds that can be killed with one stone.' Miles put down his coffee, looked across at Booth Watson and said, 'Don't answer the phone. Let him sweat for a little longer.'

Booth Watson switched off his mobile.

• • •

Twelve chimes struck out across Westminster as the team took their places around the large, circular table in the Assistant Commissioner's office. There were two vacant places: Ross's and Jackie's. All eyes lingered on Jackie's empty seat when the Hawk called the meeting to order.

'Welcome back to the real world,' he said. 'Let me begin by telling you that earlier this morning I received a call from the Home Secretary to congratulate all those concerned with the security of the Games, which, in her words "went off without a hitch". I sometimes wonder,' he added, 'if our masters in Whitehall have any idea what goes on behind closed doors without their knowledge?'

A wry smile appeared on William's face, but he didn't offer an opinion.

The Hawk listened intently as each of his officers presented their reports. None of them mentioned why Ross Hogan was not at the meeting.

'I also wonder,' said the Hawk, once William had finished his summing up, 'if I'm every bit as much in the dark as the Home Secretary.'

William should have seen that coming.

'I am, of course, aware,' he continued, 'that a lone pilot in a light aircraft was arrested for violating air space and, after spending the night in jail, was later released without charge. I've even been told about the drunk who slept throughout the entire ceremony, and only woke when the Grenadier Guards—'

'The Royal Marines, sir,' said Paul, immediately regretting the intervention.

'When the Royal Marines played "Jerusalem".' The Hawk paused and looked slowly around the table. 'What I can't be sure about, but perhaps one of you could enlighten me, is why the lady who collapsed during the firework display and was driven off in an ambulance doesn't appear on any hospital records and, what's more, hasn't been seen or heard of since?'

'She died before she reached the hospital,' said William, without further explanation.

'A sentence that covers a multitude of sins, Commander, but it doesn't answer my question.'

'What I can tell you, sir,' said William, 'is that no one has claimed the body.'

'How convenient,' said the Hawk.

William didn't offer an opinion.

'I also found it rather strange,' continued the Hawk, 'that last night there were two empty boxes near the Royal Box – one that should have been occupied by the Russian Ambassador and his guests, and the other by the Chinese Ambassador.' The Hawk looked around the table, to be greeted with 'not me guv' looks. 'It wasn't until this morning, when I received a phone call from no less a figure than Sir Julian Warwick QC,' continued the Hawk, 'that one half of the mystery was resolved. He informed me that the CPS will be dropping all charges against Miles Faulkner for his ticket scam, even though he managed to pocket a small fortune, and was as guilty as sin.'

Silence prevailed.

'There has to be a simple explanation,' continued the Hawk, looking directly at William, who – like a practised criminal – had taken counsel's advice and remained silent.

'And finally, I'm bound to ask, why is Inspector Hogan not among us today?'

'Inspector Hogan is in hospital,' said William, 'although he's due to be discharged later this afternoon. I've told him to take the rest of the week off.'

'By which time, I suspect, you are hoping I will have forgotten what my next question was going to be.'

'It might also be wise,' William said, glancing at Rebecca and Paul and then back at the Hawk, 'to let Sinclair know he can now close his investigation into Jackie's death, as the killer is no longer at large.'

'A very clever non sequitur, Commander. May I suggest

you all now return to your duties,' he paused, 'with the exception of Commander Warwick.'

While Paul and Rebecca left, William remained seated and thought about the events of the past few hours and how much he could tell the Hawk. When he'd arrived back in his old office earlier that morning, his first call had been to the Chinese Embassy to inform them of the death of Sun Anqi. The Deputy Ambassador claimed he'd never heard the name, and whoever this Sun Anqi might be, she certainly wasn't a member of the Chinese Olympic squad who, incidentally, would be flying home later that morning.

When William had then asked to be put through to the Ambassador, he was informed that Mr Wei Ming had been called back to Beijing at short notice, and his replacement had not yet been announced.

William's next call was to the unregistered hospital, and was told they had no record of a Ms Sun Anqi on their files. William didn't press the senior staff member for further information, aware none would be forthcoming. Only a handful of people knew as much as William did, and for their own reasons would be taking the secret to their graves. One of them quite literally.

But in his opinion, there was no need for the Hawk to be among them.

'What exactly happened last night?' the Assistant Commissioner asked once they were alone.

William paused. 'Do you know, I read Queen's regulations before I came to work this morning, sir.'

'Unputdownable,' said the Hawk. 'But what has that got to do with last night, Commander, dare I ask?'

'My attention was caught by regulation 1062,' said William.

'Enlighten me.'

'If the Assistant Commissioner learns of anything that might endanger public safety, it is his duty to inform the Commissioner immediately.'

'Rightly so,' said the Hawk.

'The regulation goes on to say that the Commissioner must then inform the Home Secretary of said danger, who should in turn brief the Prime Minister.'

'And?'

'And,' said William, 'the Prime Minister would undoubtedly feel it necessary to alert his most trusted colleagues in the Cabinet, not least the Defence Secretary and the Foreign Secretary, which would surely result in it finding its way into the press within days.'

The Hawk stared at a man he both admired and trusted. A man willing to take responsibility for his actions and not simply pass the buck.

The Assistant Commissioner remained silent for some time before he said, 'I accept your judgement, Commander.'

• • •

'You and your men, Inspector, have all been cleared of any contamination and are free to leave,' said the doctor, no longer in a protective suit, but in a long white coat, with a stethoscope around his neck.

For the past twelve hours, Ross had been at a hospital that wasn't listed on the NHS, being probed, poked and scanned by various men and women in white suits. He was now wearing a hospital gown, pyjamas, slippers and a pair of ill-fitting paper pants. His clothes, including his watch and wedding ring, had apparently been placed in an incinerator, along with several other unrecorded objects.

'Can I ask you a question, doctor?' asked Ross innocently.

'Please do, Inspector.'

'What happened to the dead woman we brought in last night?'

'She joined your clothes in the incinerator,' said the doctor, without emotion. He paused, 'You look disappointed, Inspector.'

'Yes, I am,' admitted Ross.

'May I ask why?' enquired the doctor.

'I only wish she'd been alive at the time,' said Ross.

CHAPTER 30

Sunday, 19 August

REBECCA LOOKED AT HER WATCH: seven o'clock. 'Doesn't it feel strange,' she said to Ross, as they sat together in the Gold Suite, enjoying a cup of tea and what was left of last week's biscuits.

'Strange?' repeated Ross.

'Only a week ago, there were eighty thousand spectators sitting out there watching a spectacular firework display, clapping, singing, cheering, and now there's just the two of us . . .'

'And the nightwatchman,' Ross reminded her, as he looked up at the CCTV screens revealing a deserted stadium.

'And in ten days' time, it will, once again, be full for the Paralympics,' said Rebecca, looking at her watch.

'Let's hope they're not quite as eventful as the Olympics.'

'Especially as William will be away on holiday from tomorrow and Paul will be in charge.'

'Chief Inspector Adaja is well up to the challenge,' responded Ross, with a smile. 'And once the Paralympics have run their course, we'll all be looking for another job. Perhaps you already know what you'll be doing?'

'I'm being transferred to the drugs squad,' said Rebecca. 'And you?'

'I'll be staying with the boss,' said Ross. 'No one else will have me.'

Rebecca laughed. 'Which boss?'

'William, of course,' revealed Ross. 'Don't forget, the Hawk will finally be retiring at the end of the year.'

'And I hear Paul is going to be promoted to Superintendent in charge of the fraud squad.' Rebecca glanced at her watch once again.

'Continually looking at your watch won't make the time go any faster,' said Ross. 'So, where do you have to be, and when?'

'It's Maureen's birthday,' admitted Rebecca, 'and I'm meant to be taking her for dinner to make up for—'

'What time?' asked Ross.

'I could only book a table for seven o'clock,' said Rebecca, 'before going on to a late-night show.'

'Then you'd better get going.'

'But I don't come off duty until Paul takes over for the night shift . . .'

'The boss goes on holiday tomorrow,' said Ross, 'and by now, the Hawk will have left for the night, so I think just this once . . .'

'You wouldn't have said that a week ago – but thank you,' said Rebecca. She grabbed her bag and beat a hasty retreat before Ross could change his mind.

Ross glanced up at the bank of CCTV screens, to be greeted with row upon row of empty seats. Then one of the screens flickered and went blank. He smiled. William, being a belt and braces man, had since the opening ceremony problem installed a back-up system in the Gold Suite that only the inner team was aware of.

Ross flicked a switch below his desk, and the blank screen lit up again.

He took another look at the screens, each displaying an empty stadium, and then decided to make himself a cup of tea.

• • •

The nightwatchman was standing by the front gate, waiting for them to arrive. Longe and his two bodyguards turned up on time, with another man in tow he didn't recognize. He assumed he must be another bodyguard, although he couldn't understand why he was dragging two heavy suitcases behind him.

A thick wad of notes changed hands as Longe entered the stadium. He looked up anxiously at a camera and said, 'Is it safe?'

'Yes,' replied the groundsman. 'The three CCTV cameras looking out onto the track are *kaput*, and won't,' he said confidently, 'be working again before the electrician arrives in the morning to fix them.'

'You've done well,' said Longe, 'and if we all get out without being sussed, you'll be paid double.'

The nightwatchman closed the gate, locked it, and led them down the steps into a long dark corridor. 'I've worked out a secure route from the gate and back,' he said, 'so you won't be seen coming or going.'

'How many coppers on duty?' asked Longe, as he followed the nightwatchman along the corridor.

'Just the one, Bernie. The other one left early, and the night shift isn't due on until eight.'

'We'll be long gone by then,' said Longe.

They emerged from the tunnel and walked out onto the track, where Longe sat down in the front row of the stand. The two thugs took a seat either side of him, while the man with the suitcases tucked himself behind a pillar out of sight.

Longe surveyed the empty stadium before him, then instructed the nightwatchman, 'Make sure you're waiting for our two guests, who should be arriving any moment, then bring them straight to me.'

The nightwatchman quickly retraced his steps to the front gate, to find two strangers waiting for him.

• • •

Ross had his back to the CCTV cameras as he waited for his tea to brew. He took his time – a rare luxury after the last few weeks of endless, dawn-to-dusk activity. He raided the biscuit tin of its last inhabitants before pouring himself a cup of tea and taking a sip.

Mug in hand, he turned around, spilling some tea on the floor.

He stared at the CCTV screens, put the mug down and made a phone call.

• • •

The nightwatchman unlocked the gate to welcome Mr Longe's guests. He gave them a cursory nod, but only after another, smaller wad of notes had changed hands. He took them on the same route into the stadium and out onto the track, where Mr Longe was waiting for them.

'Welcome, Mr Faulkner,' said Longe, as they entered the arena. He stood up, his two heavies just a yard behind, their eyes never leaving Faulkner.

Longe offered an outstretched hand, but Miles ignored it.

'I'm glad you brought your lawyer with you,' said Longe, ignoring the slight, 'because we're going to need his expertise once we've agreed terms.'

The nightwatchman slipped away, but couldn't miss the man with his suitcases hidden discreetly behind a pillar, listening to every word.

Longe looked slowly around the stadium before he said, '"All these things I will give you", to quote a friend of mine.'

'But you seem to have forgotten,' replied Faulkner, 'our Lord turned him down.'

'And look where that got him,' said Longe.

'And you need to remember, they're not yours to give until the contract is signed,' said Faulkner. 'Try not to forget that nine million pounds is a very large sum of money, with no guarantee of success.'

'No more than we agreed,' said Longe, his tone becoming sharper, 'and just think about the return you'll be getting on your investment, Mr Faulkner.'

'Only if West Ham sign the contract,' responded Miles. 'Otherwise, I stand to lose the nine million I'll have paid you, and perhaps that's a risk I'm not willing to take.'

Behind him, Booth Watson stood watching the two sparring partners warily, and was already wishing he hadn't agreed to accompany Miles.

'But there's no risk involved, Mr Faulkner,' said Longe. 'West Ham have all but agreed to cough up the two and a half mil a year to rent the stadium for their home matches. So, in four years' time, you will have your capital back, and from then on, every penny we make will be profit.'

'*We*,' repeated Faulkner. 'How much do you imagine your split will be?'

'Fifty-fifty,' said Longe confidently, 'just like we agreed.'

Faulkner's eyes remained fixed on his would-be partner. 'So, I have to put up the rest of the money to make sure you can close the deal, in the hope that West Ham will end up renting the ground. And for that, you're expecting me to be satisfied with only fifty per cent of the profits?'

'Yeah,' said Longe. 'That seems fair, because without me there *is* no deal.'

'And without my money,' came back Miles, 'there's *certainly* no deal.'

'Well, given the circumstances,' said Longe, 'why don't we say sixty-forty in your favour?'

'Well, given the circumstances, why don't I just tell you to bugger off?' retorted Faulkner, a note of defiance creeping into his voice.

The two heavies jumped out of their seats, making Booth Watson wish he had another appointment, but Longe raised an arm and said, 'Not yet, boys.'

They both retreated like lapdogs, but the words *not yet* sent a shiver down Booth Watson's spine.

'You see,' said Faulkner, still looking directly at Longe, 'there's something you haven't fully appreciated. Cash is king.' He gave the jumped-up mafia boss a condescending smile. 'However, I'll tell you what I'm willing to do. I'll loan you the further eight million so you can close the deal, but on one condition.'

'Seventy-thirty?' suggested Longe, appearing to give way once again.

'Not a hope,' said Faulkner. 'Once the capital and the interest have been fully repaid, you'll be lucky to end up getting ten per cent of the profits, which will still net you around a quarter of a million a year. Not a bad return for buying a bent councillor a villa on the Costa del Sol.'

'And if I agree to those terms,' said Longe, 'you'd be willing to cough up the eight million,' he paused, 'before the end of the week?'

'You can have it right now,' said Faulkner, turning to face his lawyer.

Booth Watson bent down, opened his Gladstone bag, and extracted a signed cheque for eight million pounds, which he handed over to Longe.

After checking the noughts, Longe smiled for the first time. 'That's all I need, Mr Faulkner,' he said, 'because once I've cashed your cheque, you'll become surplus to requirements.'

'Thanks for the warning,' Faulkner responded, not attempting to hide any sarcasm. 'But if that's your attitude, it will only take one call to my bank and the cheque will bounce all the way back to Stratford, while I suspect Councillor Dawson won't be too fussy about who pays him, as long as he gets his retirement home on the Costa del Sol.'

'But there's something else you haven't considered,' said Longe, the confidence returning to his voice.

'And what might that be?' asked Faulkner.

Longe ignored the question. He simply nodded, and his two heavies stepped forward and began to walk slowly towards the long jump pit. Booth Watson watched in disbelief as they picked up two spades and began to dig.

'You don't frighten me,' said Faulkner, standing his ground, 'because without my money, you don't have a deal.'

'Funny you should mention that, Mr Faulkner,' said Longe, as the two men went on digging, his voice now revealing a harder edge. 'Somethin' I forgot to mention. Just a couple of days ago, I had a visit from a Russian gentleman who used to be an associate of yours.'

Faulkner looked worried, while Booth Watson was sick in his mouth, but swallowed it.

• • •

Ross's gaze hadn't left the CCTV screens for a moment, and although he couldn't hear a word passing between them, he didn't need to be told it wasn't a friendly conversation. He now regretted allowing Rebecca to leave early. As the two men continued to throw shovel upon shovel of sand out of the long jump pit, Ross's eyes fell on a figure sitting in the shadows in the corner of one screen. He was secreted behind a pillar, with what looked like two large suitcases next to him. Although he couldn't see the man clearly, there was something familiar about him.

Ross made a second call.

• • •

Paul yawned as he came to a halt at a roundabout just about a mile from the stadium. He didn't much care for being a glorified nightwatchman. It was soul-destroying work. He was looking forward to the Paralympics in ten days' time, when he would be taking over William's role as Gold Commander and calling the shots. Then, after a well-earned holiday, he'd be joining the fraud squad as a Superintendent. He couldn't wait to get back to banging up some real criminals.

As he came off the roundabout back onto Olympic Way, his phone rang. Once he heard what Ross had to say, he switched on his siren and broke the speed limit.

• • •

'I thought that might surprise you,' said Longe, with an exaggerated sigh. 'And what else do you think your Russian friend told me?'

Faulkner made no attempt to respond.

'That you made a deal with him but welched on it at the last minute. I told him that was par for the course. And would you believe it,' said Longe, 'my new friend was willing to come up with the eight million I still need, and even agreed on a fifty-fifty split . . .' He paused. 'But on one condition.'

'But you've got my money now,' said Miles, sounding unsure of himself for the first time.

'You're right about that, Mr Faulkner, and I'll be cashing your cheque first thing in the morning.'

Miles glanced over his shoulder at Booth Watson, who didn't seem to have any considered advice to hand. Faulkner hesitated for a moment before he gave a little ground. 'Okay. I'll also agree to fifty-fifty.'

'But I've already got that,' said Longe.

The two heavies had finished digging and were climbing back out of the pit.

• • •

Ross made a third call.

Rebecca put down her knife and fork and reluctantly answered her phone. Although Ross whispered, he didn't leave her in any doubt she wouldn't be seeing the late-night film. Rebecca got up, said 'Happy Birthday, Maureen,' and left her credit card on the table before rushing out of the restaurant.

• • •

Faulkner stared down into the hole and swallowed hard. 'I'm willing to agree on sixty-forty in your favour,' he said, spitting out the words.

'No, thank you, Mr Faulkner,' said Longe. 'Now I've got your cheque, as well as the Russian gentleman's eight million, as far as I'm concerned, it's double or quits.'

'Double or quits?' repeated Faulkner.

'Yeah, I get double, while you quit.'

Booth Watson gasped, but could only watch as one of the heavies picked up a spade and strolled menacingly towards Faulkner.

'You can't be serious,' Miles stammered, as the thug raised his spade.

'Never been more serious, Mr Faulkner,' said Longe.

'I'll pay you seventy-thirty,' said Faulkner.

But the heavy kept advancing.

Suddenly, with a swing that would have impressed a seasoned baseball player, the heavy struck Faulkner in the back of his legs. He collapsed on the ground with a scream that echoed around the ground.

'Nice one,' said Longe.

'Take the eight million,' said Faulkner, now on his knees.

'You seem to have forgotten, Mr Faulkner, that I've already got it,' said Longe, holding up the cheque.

The other heavy stepped forward, picked Faulkner up

off the ground and threw him over his shoulder as if he were a sack of potatoes. He carried him across to the long jump pit and dropped him unceremoniously into the gaping hole.

Booth Watson, now frozen to the spot, looked on in horror.

Faulkner tried to clamber back out, but the man with the spade struck him on the head – not hard enough to knock him out, but just hard enough to make sure he didn't try to climb back out a second time. A different scream rang out across the empty stadium, pain mingled with fear.

'Ah,' said Longe. 'Something I forgot to mention, Mr Faulkner – your Russian friend's one condition.' He paused. 'I had to make sure you could never do another deal. I happily agreed to his terms.'

Longe didn't need to give an order, because the two men had already begun to shovel the large mound of sand back into the hole. It was covering Faulkner's shoulders within moments, but they still continued to ignore his pleas, followed by cries as they piled more and more sand on top of him.

Faulkner screamed out to Booth Watson, but his lawyer, head bowed, was being violently sick, as the sand continued to be deposited relentlessly, shovel after shovel, on top of his client.

Faulkner's body was now almost covered, but his eyes were still staring up at Longe, his lips barely moving.

Longe bent down, as only one ear was still visible, and gave his former partner a warm smile.

For a moment – just a moment – Faulkner thought he might still survive.

'Name your price,' he moaned, spitting out some more sand.

Longe merely smiled. 'I thought you'd like to know that

an old friend has dropped by to wish you better luck in the next world.'

• • •

Ross put down the phone, praying the cavalry would be appearing at any moment.

He continued watching the CCTV screens, to be taken by surprise once again as he saw the man who'd been hidden behind the pillar step out and walk slowly across to join Longe by the long jump pit.

A Russian spy and a London gangster.

Two men who only had one thing in common: self-interest. Their own.

Ross was well aware of his responsibility as an officer of the law, but didn't find it easy put aside his personal feelings.

Faulkner had been responsible for the death of his first wife, Josephine, and he was the reason Jojo had grown up without a mother. He'd also been responsible for the death of Avril Dubois, whose evidence – had she made it to the witness box – would have sent Faulkner to prison for the rest of his life. And would Ross ever come to terms with the terrible death of Jackie, his colleague and close friend, who had died because Faulkner turned a blind eye?

Ross then thought about the blindfolded lady, perched on the roof of the Old Bailey weighing up the balance of justice, and became painfully aware that whatever decision he made, he would have to live with it for the rest of his life.

He'd spent the whole of his professional career protecting the public from the kind of two-bit gangsters who were now surrounding the long jump pit. But did that make *Faulkner's* life worth saving?

END GAME

But he finally realized there was one overriding factor to consider: common sense. If he did decide it was his duty to attempt to arrest the four men, and save Faulkner's life, what were the odds of him ending up in the long jump pit sharing the same grave as his old adversary?

Ross compromised, not something he often did, and continued hoping that the Light Brigade would arrive in time to arrest the four villains and save the fifth.

• • •

Faulkner stared up at the Russian undersecretary, who didn't favour him with a smile. He pleaded for the last time, as Petrov picked up a spade, filled it with sand and allowed it to fall slowly onto Faulkner's face.

The pleading turned to a whine, followed by total silence, as Petrov continued shovelling until Faulkner was out of sight.

Having completed his task as a grave digger, Petrov stood back and watched as the two thugs raked over the grave. He retrieved the two heavy suitcases from behind the pillar and handed them over to Mr Longe. 'I should have dealt with you in the first place,' said Petrov, before making his way out of the stadium. When he reached the entrance and the night watchman opened the gate, he didn't leave a tip.

• • •

'I'd quite forgotten about you, Mr Booth Watson,' admitted Longe, once Petrov had departed, 'but then, to be fair, you weren't part of the Russian gentleman's agreement. So, I'll tell you what I expect you to do . . .'

'Anything, anything,' spluttered Booth Watson, as he fell on his knees, his hands cupped in prayer.

'I'm going to bank this cheque for eight million first thing in the morning and, should it bounce, I think it only fair to warn you there's a triple jump pit on the other side of the track and, although in your case it may require a lot more digging, I have a feeling my men are up to the task.'

Booth Watson swallowed hard. He didn't doubt it.

'So, Mr Booth Watson, should anyone ask after Mr Faulkner, you will simply say he's abroad on business and not expected back in the near future. And while he's away,' continued Longe, looking down at the freshly raked sand, 'you'll draw up a contract to work exclusively for me. No doubt, you'll charge an outrageous fee, while at the same time you'll still be collecting a thousand pounds a day from your late client.' Longe grinned, before once again glancing over his shoulder at the long jump pit. 'So, I think you'll agree, on balance you've come out of this deal rather well.'

Booth Watson nodded, before making an even more hasty retreat than Petrov. As he left the stadium, he spotted flashing lights in the distance and for the first time in years, he began to run.

• • •

Longe looked up to see the nightwatchman charging down the steps towards him, screaming, 'Police, police!'

A word that had Longe and his two henchmen running for the nearest exit, but when they reached the gate the night watchman was nowhere to be seen.

Longe knew he was trapped. He turned back and began to run towards the track, only to see half a dozen armed police officers heading towards him. He quickly swung around to face an even larger group of coppers coming from the opposite direction.

Moments later, the three of them were surrounded, handcuffed and led away.

Paul ran down the steps and out onto the track to find Ross frantically digging. He quickly joined him, grabbed the other spade and they both carried on digging until a body appeared. Ross had seen enough bodies to know this one was dead.

• • •

William skidded to a halt just as Longe was about to be bundled into the back of a police van.

Many things had given William pleasure over his years with the Met, but few as much satisfaction as seeing Longe and his two cronies arrested for attempted murder.

As the police van drove away, William turned to see Ross and Paul coming out of the entrance to the stadium tugging two suitcases.

'Going anywhere?' asked William.

'I wish,' said Ross, as he stopped and unzipped one of the suitcases to reveal row upon row of neatly stacked fifty-pound notes filling every inch of available space.

One of the young constables couldn't stop gawping.

'So where's the omnipresent Mr Booth Watson?' demanded William.

'Got clean away,' admitted Ross, 'but what he doesn't realize is that we have him on camera starring in his own home movie.'

Ross looked across to see Rebecca jumping out of her car and running towards them.

'Sorry you missed the main feature,' said Ross, as William

zipped up the suitcase and instructed Paul to take them both back to the Yard. But no one moved as two paramedics carrying a stretcher walked slowly towards them.

William stepped forward and pulled back the sheet, as if he needed to be certain Faulkner hadn't escaped his clutches once again. He stared down at his old nemesis, well aware his final act had been one of courage and ultimately self-sacrifice.

He touched his forehead in respect, a gesture he wouldn't have thought possible a week ago.

But then real life is so often stranger than fiction.

'Change the charge to murder,' said William, as he replaced the sheet over Faulkner's head, allowing the stretcher bearers to continue on their way to a waiting ambulance.

CHAPTER 31

Monday, 20 August

BY THE TIME DANNY PULLED UP outside number 37 Cadogan Place early the next morning, William had rehearsed his unwritten script more than a dozen times.

He got out of the car and made his way quickly up the steps to the front door. He knocked once and stood back. He was just about to knock a second time when the door opened.

'Good morning, Mr Collins. My name is—'

'I know who you are,' snarled Collins, 'and you're wasting your time. Mr Faulkner is away and I'm not expecting him back for some time.'

Collins was about to slam the door when William said quietly, 'Mr Faulkner won't be coming back.'

Collins hesitated, a look of disbelief crossing his face, and it was some time before he recovered enough to say, 'What do you mean, won't be coming back?'

'I'm sorry to be the bearer of bad news, Mr Collins,' said William quietly, 'but your employer is dead.'

'That's not possible,' said Collins, 'he had a business meeting yesterday evening with Mr Booth Watson and—'

'Bernie Longe,' said William.

Collins turned white and began to shake uncontrollably.

When he spoke again, he took William by surprise. 'Won't you come in, Commander?' he said, his tone changing. He led William into the front room and offered him a seat, while he remained standing.

'I'm afraid,' said William, 'that what I'm about to tell you will make you very angry.'

Collins stiffened, but the shaking had stopped.

'Mr Faulkner has been murdered,' he said quietly.

'Murdered?' repeated Collins. 'By who?'

'Bernie Longe and two of his thugs,' replied William.

The shaking began again, but this time caused by rage. 'I warned the boss Longe wasn't to be trusted and he shouldn't go to the stadium without me, but . . .' He suddenly stopped in mid-sentence, before he added, 'But Mr Booth Watson was with him, so he must have witnessed the murder?' said Collins.

'Yes, he did,' said William, 'but he quickly switched sides to save his own skin.'

It was some time before Collins delivered his next sentence, very quietly, 'Well, I don't switch sides quite that easily, Commander Warwick, so you can count on me to do anything I can to put those bastards behind bars, Booth Watson included.'

'Anything?' said William.

'Anything,' repeated Collins firmly.

'When the case comes to court, will you—'

'Give evidence on behalf of the Crown?' said Collins.

William waited for his response.

'When I said anything, I meant anything.'

William changed tack. 'I believe Mr Faulkner made a Will quite recently,' said William. 'I'd like to get my hands on it before Mr Booth Watson can rewrite it.'

'The original is in the safe, Mr Warwick, but I'm not allowed to open it without Mr Faulkner's permission . . .' Collins stopped in mid-sentence and then left the room without another word.

While William waited for him to return, his thoughts turned to Beth, who'd looked incredulous when he'd explained over breakfast why he'd run out of the room the night before while she was still packing for their holiday. He'd promised to make it up to her. His thoughts moved on to the only question Beth had asked: why was Ross alone when the murder took place, because Sinclair would be certain to ask the same question.

His thoughts were interrupted when Collins reappeared, carrying a thick cream parchment tied with red ribbon, which he handed to William.

William thanked him, but before he rose to leave, he warned Collins not to be surprised if Booth Watson was his next visitor.

'Don't worry, I'll be waiting for him,' said Collins, as he accompanied the Commander back to the front door.

William thanked him once again, before he jogged down the steps and got back into his car. He was just about to call the Hawk, when a taxi drew up outside number 37.

He watched as Booth Watson climbed out and paid the cabbie before making his way up the steps to the front door.

He knocked firmly and waited, but it was some time before the door was opened.

Booth Watson gave Collins a warm smile and was about to step inside when it was slammed in his face.

• • •

Rebecca waited at the Departure Terminal for the passenger to appear.

When he arrived, he made his way straight to security, where he showed his boarding pass before passing through the barrier.

Once he was out of sight, Rebecca joined the queue. She produced her warrant card, skipped security, and followed him through duty-free, while keeping her distance.

The passenger checked the departures board before proceeding to Gate 43, where he took a seat and waited for his flight to be called. Rebecca took a place three rows behind him.

A few minutes later, the attendant on the departures desk announced, 'Aeroflot Flight 025 to Moscow is now ready for boarding. Will all first-class ticket holders and priority boarding please come forward?'

He didn't move and neither did Rebecca.

The next call was for business class, but he remained in his seat, which surprised Rebecca. In fact, he didn't join the queue for boarding until economy class was called, when he finally joined the back of the queue.

Rebecca watched as he made his way over to the departure desk, where once again he presented his boarding pass and passport for inspection, before proceeding down a long corridor and disappearing out of sight.

Rebecca didn't follow him this time, but then she was no more than an observer, who had been ordered to report back what she'd witnessed, but not quite yet.

She got up and strolled across to a nearby window, which gave her a clear sighting of the waiting plane. Rebecca watched as the few remaining first-class passengers began to board, and didn't stray while she waited for him to reappear. She didn't have long to wait before he walked out onto the tarmac, climbed the steps and boarded the aircraft. Rebecca hung around until she saw the heavy aircraft door slam shut, and still didn't move when the aircraft taxied out onto the runway and took its place in the long queue for take-off.

She watched as the Aeroflot jet accelerated down the runway, took off and finally disappeared through a bank of clouds. Then she dialled a number on her mobile, which was answered immediately.

'His plane took off a few moments ago,' said Rebecca, 'but I still don't understand why you didn't allow me to arrest him, charge him and bring him back to stand trial.'

'That wasn't my decision,' said William, 'and while I might agree with you, the mandarins in Whitehall clearly have their own agenda. However, I can tell you that on arrival in Moscow, Mr Petrov will not be going home, but will be accompanied onto a domestic flight that's destined for Irkutsk in Siberia, which I can assure you is not a tourist hotspot.'

• • •

'Do you usually come dressed in such a casual manner, Hogan, when being interviewed by a senior officer?' asked Sinclair.

'I was about to set off for the airport when you called, sir,' retorted Ross. 'I'm meant to be catching a plane to Dublin.' He sat down in the chair opposite the head of the murder squad, without being invited to do so. Ross had memorized and rehearsed his story, but he knew he had to tread carefully to ensure Rebecca's unblemished record remained uncompromised. 'I hope this won't take too long,' said Ross, 'as my mother was taken into hospital last night.'

Sinclair was momentarily taken aback, but quickly recovered. 'May I ask what your mother is suffering from?'

'She had a stroke during the night,' replied Ross.

'And of course,' said Sinclair, returning to the attack, 'I will be able to confirm that with the hospital?'

'In my experience, Commander,' said Ross, 'hospitals have strict rules about patient confidentiality, and will only speak to relatives or close family members. But you're welcome to give St Vincent's a call.'

A flicker of embarrassment crossed Sinclair's face, but not for long.

'You'll be well aware, Hogan, that I'm investigating a very sensitive matter, and it is my responsibility, however unpalatable, to make sure that a senior officer – in this case you – was not involved in a serious crime. A man was murdered last night at the Olympic Stadium, while you were on duty.'

Ross remained silent.

'The suspect and his two associates have already been charged, but the question remains: how was it possible for this crime to be carried out right under your nose? With that in mind, I need to ask you a few questions, so I fear you'll have to take a later flight.'

As pompous as ever, thought Ross, but simply said, 'If you say so, sir.'

'Can I begin by asking you to confirm you were on duty at the Olympic Stadium yesterday evening?'

'As I have been for the past six weeks, sir,' replied Ross.

'And you allowed a fellow officer to leave her post early. Is that also correct?'

'Yes, it is, sir. Inspector Pankhurst hadn't had an evening off during the Olympics, and as it was her partner's birthday yesterday and she'd booked a restaurant and tickets for the cinema, I allowed her to leave a little earlier than usual. As the senior officer, I take full responsibility for my decision.'

'And you expect me to believe that it's no more than a coincidence that during that period of time, just after Inspector Pankhurst left and before Chief Inspector Adaja came on duty, the murder took place?'

'What are you suggesting, Commander?' asked Ross, his voice rising with every word.

'I wasn't suggesting anything, Inspector,' said Sinclair calmly. 'I was simply asking you a question.'

'That isn't worthy of an answer,' said Ross, barely able to control his temper.

'Then let's move on, shall we, to an equally unexplainable mystery, Inspector, namely that during the period of time when you were alone in the Gold Suite watching a murder take place on CCTV, you made no attempt to go to the victim's rescue.'

'There were five of them,' said Ross, 'while I was on my own.'

'Only because you'd released Inspector Pankhurst early,' Sinclair reminded him.

'I immediately called my senior officer, Commander Warwick, as the phone records will show. He then called in the firearms unit, who arrived in time to arrest Longe and his associates before they could escape.'

'Not all of his associates,' Sinclair pointed out. 'The mystery man, the one who turned up with two suitcases full of cash, somehow managed to escape.' Sinclair paused, but Ross didn't offer an opinion. 'Perhaps you were expecting to get part of the proceeds for staying out of harm's way,' suggested Sinclair.

'If I had,' said Ross, 'I wouldn't have turned up for this interview, but got on the plane, never to be seen again.'

'Let us, for the moment,' said Sinclair, 'give you the benefit of the doubt and assume you didn't know a murder was about to take place, and despite having won the Queen's Gallantry Medal for bravery, you thought it was no more than Faulkner deserved?'

Sinclair had a point. True, he was outnumbered, but would he ever be able to say, hand on heart, that his attitude might have been different had it been someone other than Faulkner?

Ross looked the commander in the eye but didn't answer.

'Given the circumstances, Inspector, it might be wise for you to leave now and catch your flight to Dublin, but we will, of course, reconvene as soon as you return,' continued Sinclair, turning a page in his diary. 'Shall we say next Thursday at ten o'clock, and perhaps this time you could come appropriately dressed?'

'I'm afraid that won't be possible, sir.'

'And why might that be?' asked Sinclair. 'Another relation at death's door, perhaps?'

'No, sir. But I do have an appointment next Thursday at ten o'clock with someone who outranks you.'

'I would point out, Hogan,' said Sinclair, 'that Commander Warwick doesn't outrank me.'

'I wasn't referring to Commander Warwick,' said Ross.

'Then dare I ask who?' said Sinclair, not attempting to hide any sarcasm.

'Her Majesty the Queen, at Buckingham Palace, sir, and you can be assured I will be appropriately dressed to receive Sergeant Roycroft's posthumous award of the Queen's

Gallantry Medal on her behalf.' He took the invitation out of his pocket and placed it on the Commander's desk.

'Then I'll have to change the date,' said Sinclair, trying to sound as if he was still in control.

Ross paused, before playing his trump card. 'Perhaps it might be wise, sir, to postpone our meeting until after the Home Secretary has made her decision as to who she'll be appointing as the next Commissioner of the Metropolitan Police. I only mention this, sir, because I think if you were to suspend your rival's second in command, it might look personal.'

Sinclair made no attempt to hide his anger when Ross stood up, gave him a warm smile, and said, 'However, Commander, should *you* be appointed as our next Commissioner, you needn't bother to try and suspend me, because I'll resign the same day.'

CHAPTER 32

THE ASSISTANT COMMISSIONER and Commander Warwick sat on the back seat of the Hawk's car and went over their script once again.

'Before we go in,' said the Hawk, 'my first question is, do you want to play the good cop or the bad cop?'

'The bad cop,' said William without hesitation.

'Then you'll be playing out of character for a change.'

'And so will you, sir,' replied William.

The Hawk gave William a slight bow before he climbed out of the car and they headed for the Porter's Lodge.

'Let's just hope Booth Watson doesn't realize we've already seen his Oscar-winning performance,' said the Hawk, 'thanks to you installing a back-up recording system in the Gold Suite.'

'I only give it a fifty-fifty chance,' said William, as they approached the Porter's Lodge. 'Not a lot gets past that man.'

The porter only needed to glance at the two warrant cards

before he said, 'Shall I let Mr Booth Watson know you're on your way?'

'No, please don't,' said the Hawk.

Not a word passed between them before they entered Booth Watson's private domain uninvited. They were surprised to find his secretary standing on the top step waiting to greet them. Not a good sign.

'Mr Booth Watson will only keep you a few moments, Assistant Commissioner,' she said. 'He's on a call to a client.'

'We're happy to wait,' said the Hawk, as she ushered them towards the two chairs outside his office.

'Sorry about you having to cancel your holiday at the last minute,' said the Hawk after he'd sat down.

'It's Beth you should be apologizing to, not me,' responded William, 'although I'm about to give her a present that will guarantee all is forgiven.'

'Diamonds, caviar, champagne?'

'Something she covets far more than all three of those put together,' said William.

'What could that possibly be?' asked the Hawk.

'One hundred and forty-two priceless oil paintings, along with twenty-seven rare sculptures.'

'How did you pull off that coup?' demanded the Hawk.

William would have told him if the door to Mr Booth Watson's office hadn't opened to reveal a portly figure filling the doorway.

'I'm sorry to have kept you waiting,' he said, sounding not at all apologetic, 'but I'm expecting a call from an important client.'

William wanted to say *Bernie Longe, by any chance*, but it wasn't part of his 'bad cop' routine.

'Won't you sit down, gentlemen,' Booth Watson suggested,

as he pointed to two comfortable chairs on the other side of his desk.

'No, thank you, sir,' said the Hawk. 'We'd prefer to stand while we ask you a few questions.'

'Only too happy to oblige,' said Booth Watson, not sounding quite so assured.

'Can I confirm,' opened the Hawk, 'that you were present at the Olympic Stadium last night, where you witnessed your client, Miles Faulkner, being murdered by Bernie Longe and two of his associates?'

William's eyes remained fixed on Booth Watson, but the wily old lawyer gave nothing away. However, the amount of time he took to answer the question rather suggested he was weighing up the options.

'The important call I was waiting for,' Booth Watson eventually said, 'was a return call from the director of the CPS,' a smile returning to his face.

'But if I remember correctly, Mr Booth Watson,' said William, 'you told us the call you were waiting for was from an important client.' He paused, 'Unless, of course, the director of the CPS is one of your important clients, which shouldn't be too difficult to establish.'

'Perhaps you could ask your secretary to join us,' said the Hawk, before he could reply, 'as presumably she put the call through.'

'I made the call direct,' said Booth Watson, a little too quickly, 'but he wasn't available, so I left a message asking him to call me urgently.'

'Which, once again, shouldn't be difficult to confirm,' said the Hawk.

This finally silenced Booth Watson, but not William.

'I feel sure I don't have to remind you, Mr Booth Watson,'

he said, 'that it is an offence for an officer of the law not to report a crime they have witnessed – to the proper authorities and at the first possible opportunity.'

An even longer silence followed, before Booth Watson eventually murmured, 'But you have to understand that Longe was threatening me with the same fate as Faulkner if I opened my mouth.'

'Which, no doubt, is why you went round to Mr Faulkner's home earlier this morning to warn Collins what had happened.'

'That's correct,' said Booth Watson, 'but he slammed the door in my face. However, as soon as I got to my office, I called the director of the CPS and told him exactly what had taken place.'

'So it wouldn't be true to suggest that you now represent Mr Longe?' suggested William, removing the pin from his own hand grenade.

'Of course it isn't,' said Booth Watson, an appalled look appearing on his face. 'Let me assure you, gentlemen, there are no circumstances that would allow me to represent someone who'd murdered my oldest and dearest friend.' He paused before adding, 'What sort of man do you take me for?'

If the phone on Booth Watson's desk hadn't begun to ring, William might have told him.

Booth Watson ignored the insistent ring, but the Hawk quickly stepped forward and jabbed the answer button. If it was the director of the CPS on the other end of the line, they had no case.

A desperate voice came over the speakerphone. 'It's Bernie Longe, Mr Booth Watson. I've been arrested for Faulkner's murder,' he bleated, 'and am only allowed one call, so now you're going to get a chance to earn your thousand pounds a day.'

'Shut up, you fool. The police are with me,' he shouted, as he took a pace forward, but William stepped in between them, preventing Booth Watson from grabbing the phone and ending the call. He was enjoying his role as bad cop.

'Mr Booth Watson will call you back,' said the Hawk, in a soothing tone.

'But when?' said Longe, still sounding desperate.

'I can't be sure,' admitted the Hawk, 'but if I had to guess, I would say anywhere between six and ten years' time.'

'And that's the man,' said William, as the Hawk bent down and ended the call, 'who you've just said you wouldn't be willing to represent at any cost, because he'd killed your oldest and dearest friend?'

'Yet it would appear,' added the Hawk, before Booth Watson could respond, 'that Longe, by his own admission, is already paying you a retainer of a thousand pounds a day.'

'You have both exceeded your authority,' said Booth Watson, pushing William to one side and heading towards the door, 'so I suggest you leave before I call the—'

'Call who, Mr Booth Watson?' asked the Hawk, 'the director of the CPS?'

'. . . and don't come back until you have a warrant for my arrest,' he said, not lowering his voice.

The Hawk allowed the suggestion of a smile to cross his face, as he extracted a document from an inside pocket. 'Funny you should mention that,' he said, 'because, Mr Booth Watson, QC, I'm placing you under arrest. I'm sure I don't have to remind you that it's an offence to aid or abet an offender when you know, or have reason to believe, that said person has committed an offence.'

The Hawk stepped forward, pulled Booth Watson's arms

behind his back and handcuffed him. 'I haven't done that for years,' said the Hawk, sounding rather pleased with himself.

'You do not have to say anything,' William instructed Booth Watson, who was now trembling from head to toe. 'But it may harm your defence if you do not mention when questioned something which you later rely on in court. Anything you do say may be given in evidence.'

William must have delivered those words over a hundred times during the past thirty years, but they had never given him the same satisfaction.

• • •

Councillor Dawson looked around the packed room, a smile of satisfaction rarely leaving his face, as he greeted fellow councillors, friends, staff members, the borough mayor, and even the local MP.

Maurice Dawson had spent some considerable time preparing his farewell speech, and had delivered it once again in the bath earlier that morning, with his wife as a Pope-like audience.

'Fitting and appropriate for the occasion,' she had assured him, as he climbed out of the bath and dried himself, before donning a dark blue, double-breasted suit, white shirt and West Ham tie.

A passing waiter refilled his champagne glass as he continued chatting to the mayor about his twenty-seven years on the council, ending his days as chairman of the Development and New Projects Committee.

'And how will you be spending your well-earned retirement, Maurice?' asked the mayor.

'I've purchased a small residence in Marbella, so should

you ever find yourself in that part of the world, I do hope you will visit us,' he replied, as he looked over the mayor's shoulder to see a smartly dressed couple entering the room, who he didn't recognize.

They glanced around the gathering and, once they spotted the guest of honour, they began to walk in his direction, no doubt, Maurice assumed, to offer their congratulations, and best wishes for the future.

As the two of them approached him, he gave them a warm smile.

'Councillor Maurice Dawson?' asked one of them, not returning his smile.

'Yes, indeed,' replied Maurice.

'I'm Chief Inspector Paul Adaja, and this is my colleague, Inspector Rebecca Pankhurst, and I have a warrant for your arrest.'

The blood drained from Councillor Dawson's face, as the mayor backed off.

'On what charge, may I ask?' Dawson stammered as the guests fell silent.

'Fraud and misappropriation of public funds,' said Rebecca, before Paul added, 'You have two choices, sir. We can charge you here and now, or you can leave quietly and we can carry out the formal procedure back at the station. The choice is yours.'

'Please don't handcuff me,' said Dawson, which hadn't been the opening line of his speech.

'I don't think that will be necessary,' said Paul. After arresting and cautioning the suspect, he took one arm while Rebecca held onto the other.

They led the prisoner out of the room, and not up onto the stage.

EPILOGUE

Four months later

EPILOGUE

December 2012

BETH HAD TO TAP THE MICROPHONE several times before all the guests fell silent. Once she had gained their attention, she looked down at the packed audience and gave them a warm smile before delivering the opening words of her speech.

'Who would have thought it possible,' began Beth, 'that the day would come when I'd be standing on this stage singing the praises of Miles Faulkner?'

A smattering of laughter broke out.

'But that day has surely arrived, because this sell-out exhibition would not have been possible without his truly generous bequest, which is why we have named this room the Miles Faulkner Gallery, as a lasting tribute to his memory.'

A warm round of applause followed, and even Sir Julian and the Hawk managed to join in.

'This extraordinary endowment has raised the reputation

of the Fitzmolean overnight,' said Beth. 'When I first became director in 1996, the *Guardian* described the Fitz as top of the second division in the museum league. But now, thanks to this munificent endowment, we have surely been promoted to the premier division,' she paused, 'where we intend to stay.'

The burst of applause that followed lasted for some time, and allowed Beth to turn the page.

'How appropriate it is,' Beth continued, once the applause had died down, 'that those of you who join us tonight to celebrate this special occasion are the gallery's closest friends and supporters, along with our respected in-house team, led by Christina, who chaired her last board meeting this afternoon, having served the museum for over a decade.'

The outburst of applause caused Beth to pause before she could complete the sentence. 'However, I know you will be delighted to learn that the board voted unanimously to invite her husband, Wilbur, to take her place as chairman.'

No one looked more surprised than Wilbur, but the prolonged applause left him in no doubt how the guests felt about the appointment.

'As you all know, Wilbur has been a generous supporter and benefactor of the museum over many years. He once told me: "I never needed to make a pre-nup with Christina, but I sure should have made one with the Fitzmolean".'

Laughter and applause followed.

When Beth turned to the last page of her speech, her voice became quiet and thoughtful. 'I read in the press quite recently,' she said, 'that I'm being tipped to become the next director of the Victoria and Albert Museum.' A sudden hush fell over the room. 'So, it's only fair to let you know,' she paused, 'I ain't goin' nowhere.'

Beth quietly stepped off the stage to join her guests, accompanied by the loudest cheer of the evening ringing in her ears.

'Thanks for the warning,' said Wilbur, as he gave Beth a hug. 'It doesn't bear thinking about, you during the day and Christina at night. How long can I hope to survive?'

'You have to survive for at least a decade,' said Beth. 'That's what's recorded in the minutes.'

'Great speech,' said Christina, as she walked across to join them. She lowered her voice and asked, 'But how much do we owe to William for getting his hands on Miles's Will before . . .'

'When I showed William an early draft of my speech, he crossed out that particular paragraph, suggesting that perhaps it was better they weren't told the whole story.'

Beth smiled as she looked across the room to see William chatting to his father and the Hawk.

• • •

'I'm reliably informed,' said Sir Julian, 'that the Home Secretary, after consulting the Mayor of London, has made her recommendation to the Prime Minister as to who should be the next Police Commissioner. As tradition demands with any public appointment, the PM was presented with two names, leaving him to make the final decision.'

'No prizes for guessing the other name,' said the Hawk.

'It won't have done Sinclair any harm,' suggested Julian, 'that Bernie Longe ended up with a life sentence, and Booth Watson was sent down for seven years.'

'I think Booth Watson got off lightly,' said the Hawk.

'So how long should he have been sentenced for?' asked Julian.

'He should have been deported.'

'Dare I ask where?'

'Australia, of course,' said the Hawk.

'Which reminds me,' said Julian. 'I've got a couple of tickets for the opening day of the Test match at Lord's against the Aussies, and wondered if you'd care to join me, Jack.'

William suppressed a smile. He wondered if the day would ever come when he felt able to address the Hawk as Jack.

Laughter broke out nearby, and William turned to see Jojo chatting to Ross and Alice.

• • •

'Will you be leaving the force when the Hawk retires?' Jojo asked her father.

'That rather depends on who our next Commissioner is,' said Ross. 'I've already given my word to one of the candidates that I'll be happy to stay on if he gets the job, while making it clear to the other that, if he's appointed Commissioner, I'll resign the same day. Frankly, the decision is in the Home Secretary's hands, not mine.'

'Then we must all pray that William gets the job,' said Alice, 'because I don't need your father under my feet all day.'

'But why would you have to resign if Sinclair gets the job?' pressed Jojo.

'He might ask me how your grandmother is,' said Ross, 'and I'd have to admit she's in perfect health. So, Jojo, if I do have to resign, will you take pity on your dad and join him for lunch from time to time?'

'Not a hope,' said Jojo, 'unless you can join me at the Algonquin, because I'm off to New York next week to do a photoshoot for *Vogue*.' Jojo stood on her toes and kissed her father on the cheek before leaving him and Alice to admire a Van Gogh.

'I could have sworn,' said Alice, taking a closer look at the masterpiece, 'that I saw this particular painting at the Russian Embassy only a few months ago.'

'Do you think Jojo will make the cover of *Vogue*?' asked Ross, as he looked across at his daughter, who was chatting to Artemisia and Peter.

• • •

'I'm surprised you had the nerve to turn up this evening,' suggested Peter, 'after reading your article about tonight's opening in the *Mail*. The headline alone—'

'I don't decide the headline,' said Artemisia. 'That's a sub-editor's job.'

'What was the headline?' asked Jojo innocently.

'Buried-Alive Gangster Leaves His Spoils to the Fitzmolean,' said Robert, unable to suppress a grin.

Artemisia smiled. 'Which I feel I should point out is the reason this show's a complete sell-out.'

'That wasn't how Mum saw it when she read your piece over breakfast this morning,' Peter warned her.

'Then she isn't going to like my follow-up story tomorrow,' admitted Artemisia, 'although it will guarantee that Mum will have to extend the show for months. The headline is' – she paused, and made them wait for a moment before she announced, 'Why Did the Russians Hand Over One of Their Masterpieces to a Second-Rate Crook?'

'And the answer?' asked Jojo.

'You'll have to buy tomorrow's paper,' said Artemisia, 'and read my latest exclusive.'

'Faulkner would sue if he was still alive,' said Peter.

'But he isn't,' came back Artemisia, 'and the Russian Ambassador's been called back to Moscow, so he's hardly going to object. Shame, though, because I would have liked to have interviewed both of them and heard their side of the story.'

'And on behalf of the defence, m'lud,' said Peter, clinging onto the lapels of his jacket, imitating his grandfather, 'I would suggest to the jury that after viewing this magnificent exhibition, you can only conclude that my client, Mr Miles Faulkner, was not a second-rate crook, but in fact a master criminal.'

'Not bad,' said Artemisia, jotting down her brother's words, as she glanced across to the other side of the room to see her father breaking one of Beth's golden gallery rules. His phone was ringing, and he was checking the name of the caller.

'You answer that at your peril,' said Beth, 'because the last time you did, we didn't get a holiday.'

William looked at the screen. 'It's the Home Secretary,' he whispered.

Beth was unable to hide her excitement. 'Then you must have got the job.'

'Not necessarily,' said William calmly. 'Mrs May is a courteous woman, who will call the loser first to let them know it was a close-run thing.'

William left the packed, noisy room and almost ran out into the corridor, before he pressed the green button on his mobile and said, 'Good evening, Home Secretary.'

18 January 2013

WILLIAM PUT A PHOTOGRAPH of his wife on one side of the desk and another of the twins as teenagers on the other. He then placed a small silver carriage clock between them, which Beth had given him to celebrate their twenty-fifth wedding anniversary. But pride of place went to a truncheon he'd carried as a young constable when he was first on the beat in Lambeth. The Field Marshal's baton.

The phone on his desk began to ring. He wondered who his first caller would be. 'It's the Home Secretary on line one, sir,' said his staff officer.

'Good morning, Home Secretary,' said William.

'Good morning, Commissioner,' replied Mrs May. 'I'm sorry to throw you in at the deep end on your first day, but the Prime Minister wants to see us both at ten o'clock this morning.'

'To discuss anything in particular?' asked William.

'London Bridge,' said the Home Secretary.

'I didn't know the Queen was ill,' said William, sounding concerned.

'She isn't,' said the Home Secretary. 'But we carry out an annual briefing at Buckingham Palace, so you'll need to be brought up to speed. You could do worse than have a word with Jack Hawksby, as he was in charge of the Queen Mother's funeral.'

No sooner had William put the phone down, than his staff officer appeared, carrying an armful of files marked urgent, which he placed on the desk in front of him.

'I need to see the Assistant Commissioner as soon as it's convenient,' said William, as his phone began to ring again. His staff officer picked it up. 'It's your wife,' she said, passing over the phone.

'I was only calling to wish you luck on your first day in the job,' said Beth. 'Any problems so far?'

'Nothing that can't wait,' said William, as he looked at the pile of thick files that occupied his in-tray.

'Will you be home in time for dinner?'

'I wouldn't count on it,' he said, now staring at the mounting number of emails in his inbox.

'How long are you likely to be Commissioner?' asked Beth, suppressing a laugh.

'Five years is about the normal term,' said William. 'But why do you ask?'

'Because Wilbur is asking me how much longer I'm willing to continue as the director of the Fitzmolean, and now I know the answer. Goodbye, my darling,' she said, when she heard a knock on William's door.

William looked up to see the Assistant Commissioner entering the room.

END GAME

'Good morning, Jack,' said William, as the Hawk walked across to join him.

'Good morning, sir,' said the Hawk. 'I understand you wanted to see me.'

Twenty-two incidents are included in *End Game* that might have taken place during the 2012 London Olympics.

Thirteen did. Nine did not.
How many can you get correct?

1. Attempt by Critical Mass, a group of cyclists, to prevent the Queen from reaching the Olympic Stadium in time for the Opening Ceremony. ☐
2. Attempted cyberattack on the National Grid by the Chinese during the Opening Ceremony. ☐
3. An illegal drug added to Usain Bolt's and Mo Farah's urine samples in an attempt to have them disqualified. ☐
4. Suspected IRA van with a bomb on board reported heading towards London on the day of the Opening Ceremony. ☐
5. Attempt by the Russians to interfere with the stadium generator and broadcasting facilities during the Opening Ceremony. ☐
6. Attempt by the Chinese to release a nerve gas during the Closing Ceremony. ☐

7. A female Russian athlete was abducted and flown back to Moscow during the Games. ☐
8. A London taxi driver abandoned his taxi on Tower Bridge and jumped into the Thames an hour before the Opening Ceremony and was rescued by the river police. ☐
9. South Korean national flag displayed on a screen before the start of a football match between North Korea and Colombia. ☐
10. A report by the Russian volleyball team of a shot fired on their coach while driving to Earl's Court. ☐
11. Fathers 4 Justice light aircraft headed towards the stadium during the Closing Ceremony and intercepted by a fighter jet. ☐
12. An additional 3,500 army personnel had to be drafted in just days before the Games began due to a lack of trained security staff. ☐
13. A French athlete committed suicide after his Russian fiancée was abducted and flown to Moscow. ☐
14. Brad Pitt and Angelina Jolie applied to run in the torch relay, but were turned down. ☐
15. Taxi drivers staged a protest because they were not permitted to pick up passengers within three miles of the Olympic Park. ☐
16. Terrorist attacks on London public transport the day after the successful vote took place in Singapore. ☐
17. Man arrested for attempting to put out the torch relay flame while on its way to the Olympic Park. ☐
18. Man murdered and buried in the long jump pit after the Games had ended. ☐
19. West Ham football club obtained a lease on the Olympic Stadium for £2.5m per annum. ☐

END GAME

20. A police officer was pushed under a tube train during the second week of the Games. ☐
21. A reserved stand was put aside for holders of counterfeit tickets. ☐
22. Three people fainted when the Queen jumped out of the helicopter during the Opening Ceremony. ☐